"Geralyn Dawson de[...] the romance ge[...] tenderness, passion[...] suspense. With her [...] rip-roaring plots, Dawson always delivers."
—Lisa Kleypas, *New York Times* bestselling author

Praise for Geralyn Dawson

Never Say Never

"Dangerous, romantic, always well-written . . . the narration remains smooth, the dialogue compelling, and the attraction between the leads palpable."
—*Romantic Times*

"Outstanding! An author after my own heart. . . . Witty, creative . . . a perfect read for adrenaline junkies or addicted romance readers . . . a top pick."
—Romance Readers at Heart

"Dawson continues to weave superb storytelling with sexy characters . . . excellent! I'm anxiously awaiting the third book in the series."
—The Romance Readers Connection

"Combines romance, humor, and adventure to create a light, entertaining read."
—*Affaire de Coeur*

"Dawson takes two very appealing leads and shakes and stirs them up to create another winner. . . . Matt and Torie's chemistry sizzles from the moment they meet. . . . Dynamic characterizations, crackling and often-funny dialogue, a hot romance, and a nice touch of suspense make *Never Say Never* a top contender for your October reading list."
—BookLoons

continued . . .

Also by Geralyn Dawson

Give Him the Slip
Never Say Never

GERALYN DAWSON

ALWAYS LOOK TWICE

A SIGNET ECLIPSE BOOK

SIGNET ECLIPSE
Published by New American Library, a division of
Penguin Group (USA) Inc., 375 Hudson Street,
New York, New York 10014, USA
Penguin Group (Canada), 90 Eglinton Avenue East, Suite 700, Toronto,
Ontario M4P 2Y3, Canada (a division of Pearson Penguin Canada Inc.)
Penguin Books Ltd., 80 Strand, London WC2R 0RL, England
Penguin Ireland, 25 St. Stephen's Green, Dublin 2,
Ireland (a division of Penguin Books Ltd.)
Penguin Group (Australia), 250 Camberwell Road, Camberwell, Victoria 3124,
Australia (a division of Pearson Australia Group Pty. Ltd.)
Penguin Books India Pvt. Ltd., 11 Community Centre, Panchsheel Park,
New Delhi - 110 017, India
Penguin Group (NZ), 67 Apollo Drive, Rosedale, North Shore 0632,
New Zealand (a division of Pearson New Zealand Ltd.)
Penguin Books (South Africa) (Pty.) Ltd., 24 Sturdee Avenue,
Rosebank, Johannesburg 2196, South Africa

Penguin Books Ltd., Registered Offices:
80 Strand, London WC2R 0RL, England

First published by Signet Eclipse, an imprint of New American Library,
a division of Penguin Group (USA) Inc.

First Printing, September 2008
10 9 8 7 6 5 4 3 2 1

Fifteen years ago, I dedicated
my first book this way:

For Steve

*Thanks for the time, the understanding,
and the support.
You've shown me what a true
Texan hero is all about.*

Twenty-one books and a few novellas later, I am
blessed to know that some things never change.

Acknowledgments

I want to thank Sally Sorenson and Will Sankey for their help with things Hawaiian. Colorado girl Nicole Burnham helped get me to Telluride. Christina Dodd showed me Seattle, Mary Lou Jarrell took me to Kansas, and Mary Dickerson put her Philly Girl experience at my disposal. Thank you, my friends!

Thanks, also, to my editor, the *wonderful* Laura Cifelli, for loving the Callahan men and being such a joy to work with.

Chapter One

Late summer
Lanai, Hawaii

The things we do for family.

Mark Callahan sucked a peppermint while his bloody hands clutched the coarse holds of the blue-black rock face. Halfway up the two-hundred-foot cliff, he searched for the next foothold. Below him, ocean swells crashed violently against the rocks. Above him, a three-quarter moon and a sky full of stars cast a silvered light across the land. When the wind blew just right, he could hear soft music and occasional laughter drifting from the grounds of the estate called Hau'oli.

From the Zodiac anchored at the base of the cliff, his brother Matt's voice sounded in his earpiece. "You doing okay, bro?"

"Nice of you to ask," he drawled in reply, the sarcasm in his voice unmistakable as he rolled the hard candy around his mouth.

"You scared the shit out of me during that slide. I dropped my mike. Took me a couple minutes to find it. What happened?"

"I damn near fell—that's what happened. The wall pancakes from ten feet of solid basalt to ten feet of fractured, crumbly rock. Lost my footing. Sliced my hands to hell."

"Well, be careful. We don't have time for you to climb the cliff twice."

His brother's sympathy overwhelmed him, so Mark responded, "Bite me."

His foot found purchase on a narrow ledge and he ascended another step. Filling his lungs with salt-scented air, he looked up. Fifteen minutes more, he figured as the last of his peppermint melted away. Maybe twenty. He had plenty of time.

Mark knew what he was doing. He'd climbed more-dangerous cliffs in his life under far worse conditions. One instance in the mountains of Afghanistan stuck out particularly vividly in his mind. Wind blowing like a sonofabitch. Gunfire from down below pinging off the rocks all around him. Tonight's climb was a walk along the Brazos compared to that.

Besides, he'd prefer the challenge of a cliff to what awaited him above. He was crashing a party, the kind with expensive food and liquor and women—women whose smiles were as plastic as the boobs on their chests. Not at all his idea of fun.

He adjusted his night-vision goggles, then spied another foothold. He worked steadily, capably, and quietly until he reached the top of the cliff. "I'm here. Signal Luke."

"Roger."

"No, not Roger. Luke," he murmured back, easing the tension with the old, bad joke.

Mark cautiously lifted his head and studied the area in front of him. Solar lamps and spotlights illuminated the area. Beyond a short hedge of flowering bushes, lush green grass stretched toward the house some thirty yards away. To his left he spied a resort-style pool and tropical waterfall and spa. A tennis court lay off to his right. This stretch of land along the cliff was the only section of the estate's border not fenced, though his research had indicated the existence of a buried cable perimeter-intrusion-detection system. Judging by the presence of guests milling on the lawn, the protective alarms were disabled for the evening, just as he'd anticipated.

Excellent. His gaze swept the area, then snagged on a woman dressed in red facing away from him. *Whoa.* He popped another peppermint into his mouth and savored.

The gown exposed most of her back and clung like a second skin to a shapely, world-class ass. She was tall and lean, and she wore her auburn hair piled high on her head. The long slit in the back of her dress revealed shapely legs that stretched on forever. From this angle, anyway, she was one fine example of womanhood. He wished she would turn around. Wished he was closer so he could see her more clearly. Something about her called to him.

Hold on, Callahan. Remember where you are. What she's liable to be.

He'd outgrown porn queens years ago.

Seconds later, the first explosion sounded, followed quickly by another, then a third. Luke's distraction successfully alarmed the guests strolling on the lawn and sent them scurrying for the protection of the house.

The woman in red took off in the opposite direction, toward the pool area. Hmm. Curious.

A guard rushed past Mark's position, pulling his sidearm as he ran toward the booms. Luke's string of high-explosive, not-legal-in-the-good-old-USA firecrackers was doing its job.

Mark pulled himself up over the crest of the cliff onto level surface. He ducked behind a flowering bush,

stripped off his black jumpsuit, and used it to wipe
the blood from his hands. After stashing the suit and
his climbing shoes in the shrubs, he removed his dress
shoes from his pack and slipped them on. A quick
glance confirmed that no one was looking his way, so
he shot the cuffs of his tuxedo, stepped out onto the
lawn, and strolled toward the house.

Glass doors led into a sumptuous formal living and
dining suite with a wall of floor-to-twelve-foot-ceiling
windows that provided a panoramic view of the Pacific. *Bet the daylight view takes a man's breath away.
Kinda like the woman in red.*

The guests stirred in concern over the commotion
outdoors until security personnel began circulating word
of firecrackers and troublemaking teenagers at the neigh-
boring estate. Mark accepted a glass of champagne from
a passing waiter and returned his attention to his surroundings, idly noting the opulence of the furnishings
and design of the luxurious estate. The style was classic
Louis XV, with magnificent marble and murals, crystal
chandeliers, and embroidered silk draperies that framed
Technicolor views of the Pacific Ocean.

Obviously, porn paid exceptionally well.

The estate's owner, Harvey P. Selcer, was a second-
generation pornographer who used his father's string
of adult bookstores to launch Selcer Films back in the
1980s. A B-school graduate, Harvey brought modern
marketing techniques to the industry, and today Selcer
Entertainment Group was sometimes referred to as
the Microsoft of the porn world. Now in his fifties,
Harvey had billions in the bank, a Hugh Hefner reputation, and Howard Hughes paranoia.

And a porn-queen girlfriend born and raised in
Brazos Bend, Texas.

Hence, the Callahans' presence at this party. Sophia
Garza had called home for help, claiming that Selcer
wouldn't allow her to leave the estate. Her great-

aunts, Maria and Juanita Garza, had asked the Callahan brothers to solve the problem. Mark didn't care a flying fig about Sophia—she was a pitiful, pitiable figure in his opinion—but he loved the Garza sisters. They had worked for his family for years and become family in the process. He and his brothers had made this trip for them.

A woman dressed in blue sidled up next to him. Not Sophia—her pretentious habit was to always wear pink. "Hello, handsome. I don't believe we've met before. My name is Eloisa. What's yours?"

Mark arched a brow and gave her a swift once-over. Bleached, Botoxed, lifted, and implanted. He didn't bother to smile as he replied, "Not interested."

She huffed off as Matt spoke into his ear. "Don't be such an ass. Socialize. Remember, you need to blend in."

What he needed was to find Sophia and get the hell out of here. With that objective in mind, he made his way toward one side of the bronze, wrought-iron twin staircase, thinking he could more easily observe the crowd from the upper mezzanine.

Halfway up the staircase, Mark hesitated. The hair on the back of his neck rose. In his peripheral vision, he caught sight of the woman in red. *There is something about her. . . .* But as he turned his head to look at her fully, the sight of another person stopped him in his tracks.

Dark hair worn long and tied in a ponytail. Thin, harsh features. Narrow black eyes. Mark swallowed what was left of his peppermint. "Holy shit."

"What is it?" Matt asked.

"Not what. Who. Radovanovic is here."

There was a long pause on the other end of the wire before Matt said, "You're kidding."

"Christ, no." Mark almost, *almost* pulled his 9mm from his shoulder holster and shot the bastard dead.

Rad might not be the one who actually kidnapped and murdered Mark's brother John, but as Ivars Ćurković's first lieutenant, he'd damned sure protected the man who had.

In that moment, Radovanovic lifted his head and caught sight of Mark. The shock in the Eastern European's eyes quickly morphed into fury. He and Mark had gone a few rounds more than once in the past.

"You need to get out of there," Matt said.

"No shit. He's seen me." Mark knew he was in a vulnerable position and should move, but he'd be damned if he'd break eye contact first.

Matt let out a long string of curses.

"No sign of Sophia yet, either," Mark murmured when Matt paused to catch a breath. "Maybe I should just kill him."

Matt hesitated a moment before saying, "No. We don't have the necessary connections in Hawaii, and the red tape would be hell. What the hell is Radovanovic doing there? He's on the wrong damned side of the world!"

Finally, Rad caved and shifted his gaze away. Mark continued up the staircase, his mind considering and discarding various scenarios of how to deal with this unexpected complication. What would the Croat gangster do now? Send his minions after Mark? Probably. He would want to know the reason why they'd both ended up in the same place at the same time.

Or maybe he'd run. He wouldn't know that Mark didn't have an army backing him up. Of course, Mark did have his brothers, who were better than most armies in the world.

Upon reaching the mezzanine, he turned to survey the scene below him once again. Rad stood beside the door leading to the pool area, and there, a flash of pink. Sophia, on Harvey Selcer's arm.

Hmm . . . That gave Mark an idea. Maybe he could pull this off, after all. He'd use Selcer to—

The familiar sensation of a gun barrel poking into his back stopped him cold.

"Of all the ops in all the mansions in all the world, he has to walk into mine," came a hauntingly familiar feminine voice. "Do exactly as I say, Callahan, and you might get out of here alive."

Mark's jaw had slackened in shock. "Annabelle?"

"Hush. Don't turn around, and for once in your stubborn, granite-headed life, listen to me."

Annabelle. It had been *Annabelle* in that red dress, not a porn queen. Although had she chosen that particular career path, she would have been a star.

"Give me your Glock."

Mark snorted. The last time he'd seen Annabelle, she had stolen not only his gun, but also his wallet and his clothes in a childish fit of pique. "Yeah, right. I know all about how you like to leave me naked."

"They're watching, Callahan. Don't be an ass."

Keeping her gun against his skin, Annabelle shifted around to his front, rubbing up against him in such a way that it appeared to casual observers that she was coming on to him. Her beautiful brown eyes snapped and flashed. He dropped his gaze to the full, creamy cleavage displayed by her plunging neckline.

"Shooting you might be one of my favorite dreams, but I'd prefer to do it on my own terms, not Rado-vanovic's. However . . ." She poked him hard with her gun.

He saw it wasn't the 9mm SIG she'd always favored, but a red Glock that reminded him of the pistol Matt's wife, Torie, owned. "A girly gun? You're using a girly gun now?"

"It was a gift to match my dress." She slipped her hand into his jacket and lifted his weapon. "From Rad."

Mark stiffened and everything inside him turned cold. "For God's sake, Belle. What are you involved in?"

Through the miniature speaker in Mark's ear, Matt said, "Mark? Care to share what's going on? Is a woman holding a gun on you?"

"She's not a woman. She's my wife."

Following a long pause, Matt said, "*Another* secret wife?"

"Yeah." Mark sighed. "Unfortunately, this one is still alive."

Annabelle Monroe wondered if she'd brought this disaster on herself. When Paulo Giambelli hired her for this job and handed over his dossier on Radovanovic, she'd been dismayed to read of his connection to the Callahan family. Apparently, Mark had crossed paths with Rad a time or two since his brother's death, with violent results. Consequently, after reading the file, Annabelle had spent way too much time thinking about Mark.

Earlier when she first spied that tall, broad-shouldered figure with his thick brown hair and jade green eyes, she had thought she must have conjured him up out of her imagination. Now, faced with the flesh-and-blood man, she decided that all that thinking about him must have kick-started some bad karma and summoned Mark Callahan to Hawaii. "I'm alive and I plan to stay that way. You're wired?"

He nodded. "My brothers."

"They're on the grounds?"

"They're close."

"Good. We might need reinforcements. Now move your buns, Callahan. I told Rad I'd bring you to the pool house."

He planted his feet and hardened his jaw. "I'm not letting you serve me up like borscht for ol' Boris."

"I wasn't planning to. Once we're outside, I'll let you overpower me."

He did a double take. "You? Miss No-Man-Will-Ever-Get-the-Better-of-Me Monroe?"

"It's the opportunity you've dreamed of for years." Annabelle turned her head and flashed Rad a confident smile. With a quick, deft move that no casual observer would have noted, she showed the Croat that she held both her own gun and Mark's. Softly, she said, "He'll expect us to go downstairs and out through the French doors. He might send backup. We'll go out through the kitchen on the opposite side of the house."

"Are you sure—?"

"Don't argue. Move. Look angry."

Mark shot a killing glare toward his old enemy. "Not a problem."

Annabelle's thoughts spun as they descended the staircase, and she analyzed this new development's effect on her plans. She couldn't abort the operation. Somewhere on this island, a woman was scheduled to die unless she and her team found a way to prevent it. But neither could she abandon Mark to Radovanovic.

I'm the only person allowed to kill Mark Callahan.

She threaded the way through the downstairs crowd, wishing she wore something less eye-catching than fire-engine red. They caught a bit of good luck when the latest female porn superstar entered the room near them, and the crowd surged forward to pay her tribute. Mark and Annabelle took advantage of the opportunity and ducked into the hallway that led to the kitchen.

As part of her preparations for the evening, Annabelle had obtained and studied blueprints of the house. She knew that Mark would have done the same, so when he moved in front of her, she allowed him to lead the way. He'd served as point man for the unit on most missions, so it was a natural response.

One that she regretted when instead of continuing toward the door that led outside, he opened the linen-closet door, flipped the light switch, and yanked her in with him.

Though the closet itself was oversized, shelving filled the majority of the space, leaving them uncomfortably close. "What are you doing?" she hissed.

"I'm not going any farther until I've heard a Sitrep."

Her gaze narrowed. "Did we have to do that here?"

He held up his hands, palms out. "Hey, I'm no more anxious to occupy a closet with you than you are with me. Last time we did this, we ended up married."

Annabelle closed her eyes, the memory of that incident alive in her mind as if it were yesterday. It had been a year after she'd officially separated from the army when their special military-intelligence unit reunited for the wedding of their explosives specialist, Jeremy Russo. To this day she couldn't explain exactly how it had happened. One minute she and Mark had been arguing about NCAA baseball over the groom's cake, and the next they'd been making out like teenagers on prom night in the coat closet.

She flushed at the memory. It had been hot in that closet that night, and it was hot in this one now. Callahan always did throw off a huge amount of heat. She smelled the ocean and his usual Armani aftershave on his skin, along with the scent of peppermint on his breath, and the familiar yearning washed through her. Damn the green-eyed devil. Devil Callahan—that's what people called him in his hometown. When he had confessed that one night in Cozumel after too many margaritas, she had responded that his hometown knew him well. Mark tempted her to sin like no other man she'd ever met—then and now.

Feeling herself starting to sway toward him, she yanked back and placed her hand against his chest. "All right, then. You talk first. What brings you to this porn party, Callahan? Looking to start a new career?"

He waited a beat, then answered, "Start? Honey, don't you know about that video of you and me that's up on YouTube?"

She sucked in a sharp breath before she realized that he had to be jerking her chain. No video of the two of them existed. She set her teeth and waited.

He sighed. "Did you notice the woman with Selcer earlier? The beautiful girl in her early twenties with long dark hair, dressed in pink?"

"Yes." The spurt of jealousy that she felt caught Annabelle by surprise. She did her best to ignore it. "Who is she?"

"Sophia Garza." His hands settled around Annabelle's waist. "She's our host's current girlfriend, and she's the reason I'm here. She's from my hometown, kin to some people I care about. She got in over her head in this business and now she'd like to leave and start over. Selcer has prevented it. We're here to get her out."

"You and your brothers and anyone else?"

"We don't need anyone else." The familiar arrogance had Annabelle rolling her eyes. "Hell, I could have done it on my own, but Maddie and Torie—my brothers' wives—insisted Luke and Matt tag along. I think they had plans to redecorate Matt's lake house and didn't want him around." He reached up and brushed a strand of hair away from her face. "That's my Sitrep. What about you, Belle? What the hell are you doing with Radovanovic?"

She didn't like explaining herself, but she knew this man well enough to realize that doing so would save time in the long run. "Do you remember Paulo Giambelli?"

"That Italian *poliziotto* who had the hots for you?"

She ignored the dig. "I'm working for him. He's private now, and he's been hired by a couple from Florence to find their daughter's killer. She disappeared from a Black Sea resort and her body turned up in a Sarajevo brothel three months later. A month after that, police in Paris discovered a film of her rape and murder during a raid on a warehouse whose owner had ties to the Russian Mafia."

He exhaled a harsh breath and his hand tightened its grip on her waist. The light in his eyes went agate hard and she could tell he didn't like her news one little bit. Half a minute ticked away before he spoke in a tone that was low and slow and deadly. "So, Rad is making snuff films now?"

The steady beat of Mark's heart beneath her palm reassured Annabelle. During their days as members of the unit, he'd been cool as ice during an operation. Under these circumstances, she found it comforting to know that hadn't changed during the past seven years.

She licked her lips, then said, "It's no surprise that he's heavily invested in human trafficking. Snuff films are a natural diversification for him. From what I've been able to piece together, he's here to fill a need for technical expertise and to expand distribution."

"Have you connected him to the dead Italian girl?"

"Not yet, but I expect it's only a matter of time. I was able to access his private computer and copy files. Paulo is working on the decryption now."

"I'm tempted to take Radovanovic out tonight," Mark mused.

"Bad idea, Callahan. We need to bring down the entire operation, not just the leader. Before you showed up, I was close to working my way onto his team."

He narrowed his gaze for a long five seconds, then spit out, "How?"

Whoa. Why the venom? Annabelle blinked as the

likely answer flashed like lightning. *He thinks I'm sleeping with Rad.*

Anger rolled through her. She had never whored herself for the job. Why would he believe her line in that particular sand had changed? "I'm his bodyguard," she fired back.

He snorted.

She wanted to hit him. "Rad wanted extra security while in Hawaii," she reluctantly explained, knowing that doing so would speed things along. "I opened my own agency in Honolulu a year ago. A big part of our business is providing private security for visitors to the islands. When Paulo learned that Rad had scheduled a trip here, he asked for my help. I contacted Rad and convinced him that my talents could be of use to him while he was in Hawaii."

"I'll bet," Mark muttered.

Annabelle sighed. Mark hadn't sniped this way on past operations, but then, they hadn't been on an operation together since the team disbanded. A lot had happened in the intervening years. Like their wedding. Maybe marriage changed even more things than she'd realized. "Rad is paranoid about security. He liked the idea of having me as the final line of defense."

"That's not all he liked."

"Jealous, Callahan?"

"Don't be ridiculous."

Yet the tightness in his voice sent a little wave of satisfaction rolling through her. "You are too jealous."

Seconds ticked by. Then he confessed, "It pisses me off, Belle. I don't like you being around Radovanovic at all."

He pulled her against him and nuzzled her neck. "You smell good. Jasmine, like the pikake bushes outside. Why aren't you living in that little Kansas hometown of yours selling cupcakes like your sisters?"

"Not cupcakes—kolaches. They're a Czech pastry."

"I know that." He nipped at the base of her neck. "They're a sweet treat. Just like you."

Annabelle's brain switched off as electric shivers raced up and down her skin. Instinctively, she arched her neck, allowing him better access to kiss and nibble and lick. Oh, God, she had missed this. Missed him. His right hand released her hip and trailed up to cover her breast at the same time his left hand shifted around behind her and pressed her into his prominent erection. She sucked in a breath as he let out a low groan that ended when he captured her mouth with his.

Mark. Ah, my Mark.

Abruptly, he broke off the kiss. "I need to turn this thing off."

She emerged slowly from a sensual haze. "From what I remember, that takes at least two days."

"Asshole," he murmured.

That wiped away the rest of the fog. "Excuse me?"

"Not you. Matt. My eavesdropping brother is talking in my ear."

"Oh." The wire. Her cheeks warmed with embarrassment.

"Dammit, though, he's right. This isn't the time for distractions. Why the hell do you always do that?"

"Me!" She shoved him hard enough to rock him backward and he bumped against the shelf.

"Ow! Hell, Annabelle, you're gonna give our position away."

"I'd like to give *you* away. Maybe I *will* take you to the pool house. I look exceptionally good in widow's black."

He flashed a wide grin, leaned over, and kissed her hard. "We'd better quit wasting time. Why don't you—"

"Wait," she interrupted. "You need to know something else. I'm trying to do more here than infiltrate

Rad's organization. There's a girl somewhere on this island who will die tonight if I don't find a way to stop it."

All sign of amusement was wiped from his face. "Tell me."

"He's picked out three men in the industry who he wants to own. I think he's setting them up to star in their own snuff film tonight so he can blackmail them tomorrow."

"How do you know this?"

"I put bits and pieces together. I could be wrong, but I doubt it. Mark, I can't walk away from this. From her."

"Of course not." He briefly touched her cheek. "What can I do to help?"

"Other than disappear, I honestly don't know. I can't take you to the pool house because Rad *will* kill you. I'll have to show up, though, and tell him you got away from me."

"He won't be happy about that."

"No. He's liable to fire me, and I'll lose my chance to find out where he is planning to film. Great. Just great." She scowled up at him. "Thanks for screwing this up, Callahan."

"Look, maybe it's best to forget about the entire organization in this instance," Mark suggested. "Boris Radovanovic needs to be dead. I *will* go to the pool house, only I'll be the one doing the killing."

She shook her head. "You won't get near him. He has a small army with him. Between his men and Selcer's, I'm amazed you made it into the house at all."

"I'm good."

Yes, that he was. Except for the one major way that had torn them apart, Mark Callahan was good at just about everything. "Then be good some more and come up with a plan that keeps the good guys alive and breathing."

Mark took hold of her hand and absently stroked his thumb across her knuckles. "How much does Selcer know about this meeting between Rad and his patsies?"

"Very little. Rad plays this all very close to his chest. I wouldn't have put the clues together if not for the information Paulo provided going into it."

"Any chance the girl is stashed on this estate?"

She shook her head. "No, I honestly don't think so. Rad couldn't set it up without Selcer's security people knowing something about it. All that concerns them is the party. Their instructions call for them to clear the estate at two a.m., which is business as usual."

She tried to pull her hand away, but he held her tight, his brow knit in thought. After a moment, he sighed. "All right. Here's the plan. Matt, you listening? I'll valiantly escape from Annabelle, then duck back inside and grab Sophia. I'll get her out on my own. In the meantime, I'm giving the wire to my wife. Y'all are now her assets to control." To Annabelle, he added, "Does that work for you?"

Annabelle concluded that he had made a good choice. She would be glad to have the extra backup. "Yes."

Mark yanked at the studs on his shirt and frowned at something his brother must have said. "That blows. All right, you stay in position." To Annabelle, he said, "The fireworks made the gate guards nervous. They've added more bodies. Matt thinks it is best I hand Sophia over to him, but Luke is free as of now." He detailed his twin's location, then added, "He'll be happy to explode something if that'll help."

"I'll keep that in mind," she said to Mark. Addressing his brother, she added, "Here's a number to call to coordinate with my team. Tell the man who answers the word is 'pistachio.'" She recited the phone number as she unfastened the buttons around her neck, then tugged the side zipper of her dress. The red silk spilled to her waist and she heard Mark suck in a breath. Her nipples went hard—she wasn't wearing a bra.

"Damn, Belle," Mark breathed.

"Give me the wire, Callahan."

His clothing rustled. "You'll need to get it. Be careful with the tape—we need it to stick to your skin, too."

Mindful of the minutes ticking by, Annabelle attempted to be all business as she slipped her hands into the gap of his shirtfront and snaked them around his torso, but she couldn't help but note the heat of his skin and the firm rip of muscle beneath it. His scent surrounded her and she wanted to fold against him, to press her bare breasts against his naked chest, to rub herself against him like a kitten and purr.

Good Lord. She blinked in shock at the direction of her thoughts. She had believed she was over this. Over him. "What's wrong with me?" she muttered beneath her breath.

"Don't ask me," he replied, his tone knowing. "Same affliction has a hold on me. It's all I can do to keep my hands off of you."

"Maybe once this is over, we should see a doctor." She grabbed hold of the small transmitter and tugged it from inside his shirt, pulling the tape away with it.

"A sex therapist?"

She handed him the transmitter. "I don't think couples with our particular problem qualify for their expertise."

Always observant, Mark positioned the device in the one spot at her waist just above her right hip where the drape of her dress would conceal its presence. But when he went to withdraw his hand, he took a northward, leisurely route. His thumb flicked her nipple, and Annabelle's nerves zinged straight to her core. She sensed the dampness gather between her legs. "Dammit, Callahan!"

"Sorry." He dragged her dress bodice up. "I lost my self-control."

"Well, you'd better find it." She zipped, buttoned, and glared, as angry with herself as she was frustrated with him. "We need to go *now*."

Mark nodded and slipped the miniature earbud from his ear and fitted it into hers. "Matt, I'm handing her over. Annabelle, meet my brother Matt."

Rather than the hello she expected, Annabelle heard him say, "Annabelle, abort this mission. I'll pay you one hundred thousand dollars. Hell, I'll pay you a million dollars. Short of killing him, do whatever you need to do—use any weapon at your disposal— but don't let my brother out of that closet."

Chapter Two

Mark watched Annabelle's eyes widen. "Excuse me?"

She listened a moment. Then her lips lifted in a smile. "I don't know whether to feel flattered or offended or embarrassed, Matt. That's some proposition on your part."

"What's going on?" Mark demanded.

She flashed him a sassy, self-confident grin. "Unless I completely misunderstood, your brother just offered me a million dollars to have sex with you. You must have really missed me bad, Callahan." She cracked open the door and peered out into the kitchen. "Wait a minute. . . ."

"A million . . ." *Dammit, Matthew.* "He's worried that I can't handle Rad."

She didn't look away from the door. "You're not handling Rad. I am."

Mark wanted her to understand why his brother would make such a lamebrain suggestion. "He thinks I'm going rogue. He doesn't believe I'll leave Rad to you."

"He doesn't know me, doesn't know my capabilities. But"—now she did glance away from the door and leveled serious brown eyes upon him—"he does know you. Are you thinking about changing the plan, Callahan?"

"Nope." Mark gave his head a definitive shake. "You are in charge of Rad. He's not even on my radar until Sophia is safe."

She studied him for a moment, judging his truthfulness. "I'll hold you to that. Now we're good to go. It's clear."

She opened the door wide and stepped out into the hallway, Mark close on her heels. As they crossed through the kitchen, he snagged a bacon-wrapped scallop and popped it into his mouth. If he couldn't satisfy one hunger, he'd settle for another. Seconds later, they exited the house and veered away from the lighting and into the shadows, where the heady scent of plumeria floated on the air.

Annabelle glanced around. "Okay, this is good. Do it."

Mark didn't need to say "Do what?" They had worked together on too many operations. They both knew what this one required. Nevertheless, he gritted his teeth and flexed his fingers before asking, "You ready?"

"Yes."

She lifted her chin. He made a fist, then hesitated. "I should take your gun. It'll be suspicious if I don't. Do you have a backup piece, Annabelle?"

"Yes." She handed him the little red gun, then resumed her lifted-chin stance. "Go ahead."

"Okay. Here goes." He drew back his fist. His stomach rolled. "Hell, I can't."

She scowled up at him. "Why not? You have before. We've done this at least three times that I can remember."

"But I hadn't slept with you then!"

"Oh, for God's sake." She rolled her eyes, then

grabbed her dress where it covered her breast and ripped it. "Just do it."

"What are you doing?"

"Giving Rad's men something to look at other than the transmitter."

The mental image that painted was enough to override his hesitation. He swung his fist, popping her on the jaw hard enough to bruise, and tried to ignore her wince. He mussed her hair, rubbed dirt and grass onto her gown, then paused. "I know you're a professional. I know you're better at this than ninety percent of the people out there, and I know we've done this more than once before. But this is the first time I've ever left my wife to face killers. You be careful, Annabelle. You be damned careful." He gave her a brief, hard kiss, then said, "Now."

In a well-practiced dance, they engaged in a struggle that took them out of the shadows of the Australian pines and into the moonlit lawn. He threw her down and pretended to spit on her for the benefit of anyone watching. She stayed down and he marched back into the shadows.

It was tempting to wait until the goons arrived, but now that he wasn't inhaling Annabelle's jasmine-scented perfume with every breath, he was able to think clearly and professionally. He needed to trust her to do her job while he did his.

Of course, what would it hurt if he did his job faster than expected?

Giving her one last look, reminding himself that Rad had no reason to move against her, he returned to the house. At least Radovanovic would be headed for the pool house by now. Rescuing Sophia meant getting past Selcer and his security—not an easy feat, but doable since Annabelle would keep Rad's men distracted.

Adopting a casual air, he sauntered back into the

mansion and resumed his search for Sophia. When he had no luck downstairs, he headed upstairs. He found Harvey Selcer giving a tour of the theater room with Sophia Garza on his arm.

All the time his thoughts were on Annabelle and what could be happening on the back lawn.

Uncertain about Selcer's familiarity with his guest list, Mark needed to keep his exposure to the man to a minimum. He ducked into the office across the hall-way and quickly formulated a plan. He paused at the desk to jot a note, which he then folded and concealed in his left hand before leaving the office.

Joining a couple who stood studying the oil painting hanging at the end of the hallway, he struck up a conversation and kept a watch on the theater room doorway. When Selcer and his group exited the room, Mark excused himself and headed toward them, keep-ing his head down as if he wasn't paying attention to where he was going.

His stance made it appear natural when he "acci-dentally" bumped into Sophia, made eye contact with her, and slipped the note into her bodice. These low-cut dresses were coming in handy tonight. "Sorry, sorry. Excuse me." Then he was striding away before ol' Harvey even noticed him.

Ten minutes later, he waited in place when Sophia opened the door to the master bedroom closet, a room as big as some houses. Her pink dress now sported a red wine stain all down the front. Good. The girl could take directions.

"Luke!" She rushed toward him and threw herself into his arms. "I can't believe you're here."

"He's not. I'm Mark." His twin was out there in the dark somewhere helping Annabelle. Untangling himself from Sophia, Mark added, "Your aunts sent me to help. Do you still want to leave?"

"Yes. Oh, yes. Please!"

"All right, then. You'll need to do exactly what I say. Do you have a pair of pants that aren't pink? I looked around in here, but I couldn't find any."

She shook her head. "I don't . . . wait. A friend left a duffel." She crossed to a section of the closet that held purses and totes and withdrew a green paisley bag. From inside, she pulled out a pair of dark indigo jeans.

"Excellent," Mark said. "Is there a shirt, too? Something that's not pink?" He shook his head when she held up a bright yellow T-shirt. "Nope. We need dark. Black, preferably."

"I don't have dark. I only wear pink."

He set his mouth in a grim line. He had no patience for affectations like that. Glancing around the closet, he grabbed a dark-hued man's shirt that he assumed was Selcer's off a hanger and tossed it to her.

"It'll swallow me," she protested as she held it up.

"Belt it. And I want your hair up and underneath this." He handed her a ball cap. "Wash off your makeup."

At that, Sophia Garza's mouth rounded in horror. "No makeup? But I never—"

"Exactly. No one will recognize you. Now, hurry and change."

She started stripping right in front of him, which reminded Mark of her recent employment. It made him sad. He remembered Sophia as a bright-eyed six-year-old who loved to ride the merry-go-round at the Brazos Bend Elementary School playground.

He turned away and busied himself testing the rope he'd fashioned from a collection of leather belts. They would work just fine to provide access to the ground from the bedroom balcony.

"Will this do?" she asked a few moments later.

Mark turned to look and saw not the tarted-up porn star but a fresh-faced girl who belonged in Brazos Bend. "Perfect. Let's go."

"Downstairs? Through the crowd?" Her teeth tugged worriedly at her lower lip.

"Nope." He hauled the loop of belts over his shoulder. "We're taking an alternate route."

They exited the closet and he was pleased to see that she had locked the bedroom door. He was less happy to see that she had left the lights blazing. They were visible to anyone outside. He quickly crossed the room and flipped the switches.

Moments later, they slipped through the French doors that led onto the master bedroom balcony. Mark surveyed the grounds below, waited for a pair of strolling guests to move beyond sight, then quickly fixed the belt rope to the balcony railing. This was the point at which they would be their most vulnerable, so they needed to get to the cliff's edge fast. "I'll go first," he told an uncertain Sophia. "When I signal, you follow."

"I'll fall!"

"I'll catch you."

As it turned out, he had to do exactly that. The woman was as clumsy as she was pretty, and she squealed and made way too much noise as she crashed toward the ground. Mark winced and worried. The next stage of the plan required absolute quiet. Was she up to it?

When a security guard rounded the corner at a run, he mentally added, *If we even get to the next stage of the plan.*

"Hold it right there," the guard said, his suspicious gaze shifting from the belt rope to Sophia to Mark. He carried a 9mm in his right hand.

Mark made a lightning-fast survey. Thirties. Military bearing gone a bit soft. Reflexes probably not what they should be. Surely part of Selcer's security rather than Radovanovic's?

"Is there a problem?" Mark asked, stepping toward the man, his palms up and out. The trick here was to move fast and give the man no time for thought.

It took only seconds. Mark rotated to the left, and at the same time his left hand came up and across and pushed the gun away. He gripped the wrist of the guard's gun hand, stepped forward with his left foot, and locked it behind his opponent's right leg and put him on his back. Then he kicked with his right foot and knocked the guard unconscious.

"Oh my God," Sophia breathed as Mark used the belts to secure the man before hoisting him onto his shoulder and dumping him into a stand of shrubbery that hid him from view. "You're a real-life James Bond."

Mark's lips quirked in a grin as he thought about how his sister-in-law Torie teased the Callahan brothers by referring to them as fictional heroes. "No, he's manning the Zodiac. I'm Jack Bauer and our twenty-four hours are ticking down. Let's go."

He grabbed her arm and ran for the bank of shadows where he'd stored his bag. There, he knelt and surveyed the area behind them. No guards. No Selcer. Good.

His gaze settled on the pool house. No Rad or Annabelle, either.

He tried to tell himself that was good, too.

Keep your focus, Callahan, he scolded himself as he fished in his bag for the harness and line and his flashlight. "Wait here," he told Sophia. Bending low to the ground, he covered the short distance to the edge of the cliff, where he lay on his belly and scooted forward at an angle. Dangling his arm, shoulder, and head over the ledge, he thumbed the flashlight's switch and signaled Matt with two quick flashes.

He blew out a breath of satisfaction when two quick bursts of light and a single long one answered back. He anchored the line, then tested it. Returning to Sophia, he said, "Lift your arms so I can get this around you."

She shook her head. "No . . . you're not . . . I can't . . ."

"It's the only way out, Sophia," he said simply. He shifted her trembling, wet-noodle limbs in order to fasten the harness around her.

"Maybe I should just stay."

Frustration rolled through him. "Is that what you want?"

"No." She whimpered a little. "Just promise me the rope won't break."

"The rope won't break and Matt is waiting below and in twenty-four hours you'll be home eating Maria's Snickerdoodles."

"I love Maria's Snickerdoodles."

"Then crouch down and follow me. *Quietly*." At the edge of the bluff Mark attached the harness to the line, tested his knots one more time, then said, "Here you go. Brace your feet against the wall. After the first twenty feet, it's a slope. We need to do this quickly, so pay attention. And Sophia? Once you're in the boat? Tell Matthew to head on out, that he was right. I'm staying to help Annabelle get that sonofabitch."

"Who's Annabelle?"

His muscles bulging, he lowered Sophia Garza over the side of the cliff and said, "She's the most hard-headed woman on the face of the earth."

Minutes later, he added softly and to himself, "And if she lets that damned Croat hurt her, I'll kill her."

Seated in the pool house, where the acrid scent of chlorine clung to the air, Annabelle wanted to throw every man on the estate over the cliff—Matt Callahan included. Except he was already at the bottom of the cliff, so that wouldn't quite work. Nevertheless, every man she dealt with tonight had caused her nothing but grief and she was tired of it.

While she waited for Rad's man to finish his tale of how he'd discovered her unconscious on the back lawn, she fretted about Mark. Had he evaded Selcer's security and located the woman? Was he even now lowering the porn princess down the cliff to his brother, or was one of Rad's goons holding him at gunpoint?

Would he be marched inside this pool house to die in front of her?

Why couldn't she get that picture out of her mind? He'd been in much more danger dozens of times during operations, and she'd never worried about him like this before. It made her crazy!

But then, so did the voice in her ear where Matt Callahan demanded, "What's going on? Are you all right? You haven't spoken in a full minute. All I can hear are Rad's people. Answer me, Annabelle. Give me a sign."

She couldn't give him a sign because Boris Radovanovic loomed in front of her. He was a darkly handsome man with Eastern European features—high cheekbones and a blade of a nose. At the moment he scowled down at her, the angles of his face harder and more prominent than ever. "I thought you said you could handle Mark Callahan. I am displeased with your failure."

Okay, Monroe, you're on. "I'm not real happy, either, Boris," she replied, wishing him an especially spectacular dive off the cliff. "I can't stand that misogynist jerk. He and I crossed paths one time during my career, and that was one time too many." She gingerly touched her eye. "I think the bastard gave me a black eye. The last time a man did that, I killed him."

Rad's expression softened just a little bit, which

eased some of her tension. "You are a most intriguing woman, Annabelle."

She allowed a smile to flirt about her lips. Ol' Boris had liked her from the beginning, which she credited to the fact that she was different from the women he ordinarily encountered. She didn't cower in fear before him. She didn't kiss his butt. She showed respect for his authority without groveling at his feet.

He'd made it clear from the moment she'd met him four days ago that he wanted to bed her, but that he also enjoyed the chase. Apparently, women who told Boris Radovanovic no were few and far between, and he liked the challenge.

"I'm an angry woman, Rad. I tripped over a sprinkler head and gave the SOB the opportunity to get the jump on me. Never mind that it was extra dark in that part of the yard because the moon was behind a cloud and I couldn't see. That's no excuse. And the fact that I allowed him to overpower me . . . well . . . it gets my back up. I am better trained than that."

"By the American military," Boris restated. "The army."

Annabelle recognized that he loved the fact that his enemies had provided the skills that now protected him, so she played it up whenever possible. "The marines, too. I did some specialized training with them."

Then, because she judged it time to up the ante, she added, "Of course, Callahan had some specialized training himself. He was good, Rad. Very good."

"He won't get off this rock alive," Radovanovic declared in an ugly tone.

Annabelle sat up straight and hid the shiver his words had sent skittering down her spine. "Wait a minute. I may not like the guy, but I didn't sign on to kill him."

"You signed on to be my bodyguard," Rad fired back. "He is a threat to my safety."

"Oh, I believe that." *Come on, Monroe. Make this good.* "He tried to convince me to abandon my job, babbling on and on about vengeance and some personal debt you owed him. I don't know what you did to him, Rad, but he acted a little crazy. Even worse, he isn't here alone."

The European's brows shot up. "What do you mean?"

"He said to tell you he has men waiting for you to leave Hau'oli. Lots of men. They have guns and equipment and who knows what else. Those firecrackers that went off earlier? He said that was all part of the plan."

Radovanovic spit out a stream of Croatian, then addressed his own men. Annabelle didn't let on that she understood the language and could follow the conversation.

"Is she telling the truth?" Rad asked his right-hand man, Petar Margetic.

"She's a woman." Margetic shrugged. "When do they ever tell the truth?"

"That's not helpful," Rad said with a dismissive wave of his hand.

"Who is this person?" one of the bodyguards asked, his heavy brow sinking even lower.

"Mark Callahan." Rad's lip literally curled. "He held a grudge against Ćurković that bled onto me after Ćurković died."

"Callahan," Margetic repeated. "He's related to . . . ?"

"Yes."

Margetic traced a scar on his face with his index finger. "If he knows your part in that, it's no wonder he has come after you."

Annabelle couldn't stop the slight widening of her eyes as Matt Callahan sent a string of downright filthy curses ringing in her ear. She decided the time had come to float her solution to the problem. "Excuse me, but I don't think we have time to waste here. I think you need to forget about killing Callahan and direct your attention to getting off this part of the island ASAP."

"How?" Margetic demanded. "This estate has only one road out. If Callahan is armed like you claim—"

"I have another way," she interrupted. "I am Rad's bodyguard, after all. I do what all good bodyguards do—I made a contingency plan."

One that would tee Mark off, she knew. She hadn't missed what he'd said about leaving Rad to her—*until after Sophia was safe*. He might as well have said right out that he intended to come after the man he held partially responsible for his brother's death. Never mind that now wasn't the time. The mansion burst at the seams with innocent people.

But Mark couldn't be objective when it came to John Callahan's killers. He would see this as an opportunity for vengeance, and emotions rather than intellect would direct his actions. A Mark Callahan guided by his emotions might not be the best champion for the woman set to star in a snuff film later that night.

Matt knew it, too, which was why he'd had a plan ready to put into place by the time Rad's man found her "unconscious" on the lawn.

Sorry, Mark. Annabelle finger-combed her hair and said, "I have a helicopter on standby. Let's get you out of here ASAP. I can take you straight to Honolulu and you can be out of the Islands by dawn. You and Callahan can face off another time when the odds are more in your favor."

Margetic frowned and looked at Rad. "What about the film?"

Everything hinged on this moment and Annabelle tensed as she waited for Rad to respond. Finally, he said, "Call for the helicopter, Annabelle. Petar, call your cousin. Tell him to . . . cancel . . . the film and get to Honolulu."

Cancel the film or kill the girl? When Margetic reached for his cell phone, Annabelle gripped his arm. "Wait. It would be a huge mistake to make an unsecured call right now. Callahan is an electronic spook. He has access to all sorts of secret government gadgets, and he'll be intercepting every call. You place that call and you're inviting trouble. I have a better way."

She lifted the hem of her gown all the way to her thigh, where she removed a pen from her garter. While the men stared at her leg, she clicked the pen, then said, "There. I have gadgets, too. The helicopter is on its way. Where is this person you want to contact? If he's close, we'll just stop by and pick him up on our way."

Rad and Margetic shared a significant look. Then Rad said, "We'll call him once we're away from here."

Damn. Annabelle made a show of shrugging. "If that's what you want, fine. But I don't know how he'll be able to hear you. It's loud in a copter."

Petar Margetic said, "She's right. Besides, it might be best if I assist my cousin in canceling the film. I'll make sure it's done right."

Rad pursed his lips, considering the idea, and when he nodded, Annabelle jumped in. "Where should I tell my pilot to drop him off?"

Rad gave an address, and in her ear, Matt Callahan said, "Bingo. Good job, Annabelle."

Minutes later, she heard the *whop whop whop* of a helicopter. "That's it. Be ready. We want to do this as fast as we can."

Matt said, "Sophia has almost reached my boat. I imagine Mark will be headed your way in minutes. You will be between his position and the landing area, so you should be able to get out of there before he reaches you. The pilot's name is Russell. Just keep a close watch. Don't let one of those goons shoot my brother."

"All right," she said to both men. "Let's go!"

With her skirt hiked above her knees to make it easier to run, she led the way toward the copter, well aware that they were attracting a crowd—especially since Rad's men ran with their guns out. The entire way she braced herself to see Rad go down. While it wouldn't be a total disaster if Mark shot him at this point—they did know now where to find the girl—it was better for everyone if Rad escaped and her cover remained intact until Paulo was able to act on the information she'd pilfered. That way they stood a better chance of bringing down Radovanovic's sexual-slavery operation and Mark wouldn't be facing a murder charge in Hawaii.

But when they bounded into the helicopter, she could see her husband running toward them, his arms and legs pumping like an Olympic sprinter's. Then when it became obvious he couldn't catch them, he stopped and took aim at Rad—until Annabelle put herself between the two men.

As the helicopter lifted off the ground, she elbowed Rad's bodyguard to keep him from taking a shot, then finger-waved to her husband. Moonlight illuminated the impotent fury that exploded in his expression as he stared up at the helicopter.

She sucked in a breath. *Whoa.* Ordinarily, she would not feel safer inside a helicopter filled with murdering Eastern European gangsters than she would down on the ground with her husband. But then, nothing about tonight had been ordinary, had it?

Annabelle grinned.

Chapter Three

Mark held his peace for a good eighteen hours. He popped peppermints rather than speak after he rendezvoused with Luke and they made their way to the rocky beach where Matt had grounded the Zodiac. He maintained his cool when Annabelle's local team informed him that they had rescued the hostage, a seventeen-year-old Russian girl found naked and bound in a vacation home rented by Radovanovic for a month. Mark even kept the lid on his temper as he and his brothers escorted Sophia back to their beachfront suite at the Kahala Hotel on Oahu, where they all caught a nap before they put Sophia on the red-eye for the overnight trip back to Dallas.

Only after the Callahans returned to the Kahala, with the intention to order dinner and enjoy a real night's sleep before heading home the following day, did Mark judge that the time had come to have a . . . discussion . . . with his brothers. He followed Matt and Luke into their suite, tossed his wallet, his Oakleys, and the rental-car keys on the Queen Anne coffee table, then declared, "You assholes."

His brothers shared a look that signaled they each

had something they wanted to say, too. As the eldest, Matt took the lead. He rolled up the sleeves of his light blue sport shirt. "Excuse me? Did the numb-nuts who kept secret from his family the fact that he's been married for four years make a comment?"

Luke's tone dripped sarcasm and radiated anger as he braced his hands on his hips and sneered. "Yes, Matt. The very same numb-nuts who also neglected to tell us for years that he'd had a wife and baby who died just called *us* assholes. Nervy bastard, don't you think?"

"Don't try to divert my attention," Mark snapped. "You let Radovanovic escape."

Luke lifted his chin belligerently. "Damned right we did. You weren't thinking clearly."

"You'd have done the same goddamned thing if you had a chance to kill that bastard."

"Not at the risk of the operation," Matt fired back.

"And you let him take Annabelle with him!" Fury surged through Mark's veins and his chest went tight. "He could have killed her."

Matt folded his arms. "It was the right thing to do and if you would think instead of just react, you'd know it. Once she told me she had been part of your unit, I knew to listen to her, and I'm glad I did. Her strategic planning on the fly was brilliant. You didn't see it because you were thinking with your dick instead of your head."

"That's bullshit."

"Oh? Then why were you copping a feel in a closet?"

Mark's fist caught him on the jaw and sent him sprawling. Luke wasted no time to defend his older brother and his fist plowed into Mark's face. A moment later, all three men were tumbling across the floor of the luxuriously appointed suite.

Grunts. Groans. An elbow to the gut. A fist to the

belly. They rumbled and rolled just like in the old days, bumping into furniture, knocking over a flower vase, and sending a porcelain figurine crashing to the floor. Somewhere deep inside himself Mark realized he needed the physical outlet, and he wallowed in the pleasure of the pain.

Then the suite's door opened and a pair of drop-dead-gorgeous women stepped into the room. Wearing a Hawaiian-print halter dress, redheaded Maddie Callahan shifted her toddler daughter Catherine from her right hip to her left and said, "Oh, for crying out loud. Thank God I gave birth to girls."

Luke's head came up at the unexpected sound of his wife's voice, and Mark's fist caught the distracted man right in the eye. Matt paused in midpunch to stare stupidly at his wife.

"I didn't know fighting-about-football season had arrived already," Torie Callahan wryly observed, her hand gently patting the back of Catherine's sleeping twin, Samantha, who had a handful of Torie's blond hair in her fist.

"Larry, Curly, and Moe," Maddie said, her tone partially amused, partially disgusted.

Matt dragged his hand beneath his bloody nose. "Sweetheart, what are you doing here?"

Torie settled the toddler onto her stomach on the sofa, gently untangling the girl's hand from her hair. She tugged at the bodice of her sleeveless green sundress, then slanted a look at Maddie. "Sounds just like a boy with his hand caught in the cookie jar."

Luke's green eyes widened with worry. "Is something wrong? Is there a problem at home?"

"Everything's fine at home," Maddie replied.

Torie flashed Mark a cat-in-cream smile that he recognized as a warning. "We decided to come meet our sister-in-law."

Mark groaned aloud, dropped flat on his back, and

banged his head against the lush carpet. "Christ. It hasn't been twenty-four hours. What did you do, Matthew, call her from the boat?"

"Hey, I had some downtime. I missed her." Matt held out his arms to Torie, winked, and said, "Aloha, Shutterbug."

Luckily for Mark, at that point Samantha woke up and started crying just as Catherine took note of the huge orange flower that had fallen from the spilled vase and decided to eat it. Maddie went into a minor is-it-poisonous panic as she snatched the flower from her daughter while Luke and Matt attempted to soothe the crying Samantha. Mark used the distraction to grab his shades and sneak out the door.

He wandered aimlessly around the resort, his thoughts scattered, his emotions in turmoil. *You stupid ass.* He should have realized he'd have to answer to the girls. It was bad enough that his brothers knew about Annabelle. Maddie and Torie wouldn't let him hear the end of it.

Dammit to hell and back. Maybe he shouldn't stop with escaping the hotel suite. Maybe he should escape the island. The state. The United States.

Wonder if I could buy a bunk on the space station.

The idea did have some merit. Watching his brothers with their wives, witnessing Luke cooing over his kids, was more than he needed to see right now. Not with Annabelle on his mind. Thoughts of his wife invariably gave rise to thoughts of his child—his own sweet baby girl, Margaret Mary, who had died before he'd ever had the chance to meet her.

Mark slumped into a wrought-iron bench in the garden area of the hotel grounds and stared out at the blue Pacific. She would be eighteen years old now, probably headed off to college. She would have been beautiful like Carrie, her mother, smart as a whip, and full of dreams and aspirations.

Instead, little Maggie was dead, killed in a car wreck along with her mother before she'd turned a month old. Because of Branch Callahan. Because Mark's interfering, thinks-he's-God father decided to take the baby away from Carrie while Mark was deployed during Desert Storm.

And Mark had spent the past eighteen years hating his father and running from relationships because of it. It hurt too much.

"Hey, handsome." Torie took a seat beside him, and clasped his hand. "Fancy meeting you here."

Mark slipped his sunglasses over his eyes. "Are you the designated interrogator?"

"Yes, but don't worry. I left my thumbscrews in Maddie's diaper bag." She pulled his glasses off and looked him straight in the eyes. "We love you, Mark, and we're worried about you. What's going on?"

He stared out at the ocean where the sunset painted the sky in hues of orange, crimson, and gold. Then he shrugged. "It's no big deal. Really."

Torie hooked one arm of his sunglasses over the neck of his T-shirt and said, "Marriage is a big deal. Really."

"Well, this is no real marriage."

"Tell me about it."

He closed his eyes and surrendered, giving her a brief, censored account of the events in Las Vegas. When he finished, she stared at him, her eyes glittering with shock. "Let me get this straight. Did you get married because you were drunk?"

"I wasn't drinking that night."

"Okay, then. Had you been secretly been in love with her for years?"

"No!" The very idea of that made him shift nervously in his seat. "It was just a spur-of-the-moment deal for both of us."

No way would he tell Torie that Annabelle had a

thing against premarital sex, and that, in combination with the make-out session in the closet and close proximity to a wedding chapel, had led to a marriage license signed with both their names.

"So, what . . . you just left Vegas and went about your separate lives pretending it didn't happen?"

"Not exactly. We got together every so often for a while. It worked for us." He closed his eyes and recalled those stolen days. The thrill of anticipation. The excitement of watching her arrive—he'd always made a point to get there first. The laughter they'd shared. The sex. God, the sex.

For a little while with Annabelle, he'd let down his guard. He'd begun to think that maybe, just maybe . . .

Of course, that sort of thinking bit him in the ass. "Until it stopped working."

"Why did it stop working?"

He shoved to his feet and stuck his hands in the pockets of his cargo shorts. "I need to walk. You want to walk?"

"Sure." Torie rose and strolled beside him on the path that wound through the hotel gardens.

She remained quiet, her question hanging on the air between them, while Mark attempted to put his thoughts into words. He liked that about Torie. He loved both his sisters-in-law deeply, but he and Torie clicked. Maybe her photographer's eye allowed her to see him, to understand him, in a way that even his twin didn't. Because he honored that connection, he chose to answer her honestly. "Annabelle decided she had that clock thing going on."

"Clock thing?"

"Kids. She wanted kids."

"Ah. The biological-clock thing."

Mark nodded, knowing he wouldn't need to say more. Torie would get it. She knew about Carrie and the baby and the car wreck. Though Matt and Luke had established a relationship of sorts with their father, he had not. He would not. Torie understood and didn't pester him to forgive Branch for his culpability. Without his saying another word, he knew that Torie would also understand that fatherhood wasn't for him. Not again.

She slipped her hand in his and they walked a few moments without speaking. "How long ago was that, Mark?"

"A couple years."

"Has there been a problem with the divorce going through?"

"We never actually talked about divorce," he said with a shrug. They hadn't talked at all since he'd shut their hotel door in New York and walked out of the Waldorf feeling angry, empty, and alone.

"Out of sight, out of mind?"

Not hardly. But he didn't intend to give Torie that ammunition. She sighed and they continued their walk along the flagstone path, where a groundsman lit tiki torches and the exotic fragrances of tropical flowers perfumed the air. She waited until they'd passed another strolling couple to ask, "What are you going to do now?"

"Go home. I have a bunch of work piling up on my desk. This thing with Sophia put me behind."

"Nope." She tugged her hand away, then slipped her arm through his. "What you are going to do is hang with your family while we're here on vacation. We're all due some time together. What I meant is, what are you going to say to your Annabelle when you see her?"

Mark's muscles tensed. "I'm not going to see her."

"Luke says her office isn't far from here."

"So?"

"So you need to settle things between the two of you."

"*Things* are fine between us. *Things* don't exist."

"But what about what she wants?"

"Hell, Torie, if she wanted anything from me . . . believe me, Annabelle isn't shy about asking. She's fine with *things*."

"I doubt that, Mark Callahan. Look, you can't stay married to someone you don't speak to for two years. It's wrong for you to leave her hanging, especially if her clock is ticking. Believe me, I know."

He heard something in her voice. "Is your clock ticking, Torie?"

Her mouth slid into a satisfied smile. "Not anymore. I'm pregnant. I'm due in May."

He stopped, grinned down at her, and gave her a big hug as she grinned back and continued, "But don't say anything. Matt wants to make a big announcement when we're all together. Now, back to your Annabelle. You need to do right by her, Mark. If you're not going to keep her, then let her go."

"Torie, honey, it's not like that. You don't know Annabelle. She's the most direct woman I've ever met. If she wanted a divorce, she would have asked for one by now."

"Maybe she doesn't know what she wants. Maybe she's been holding out hope that you'll change your mind."

Mark stared out at the gently rolling surf. "That is not gonna happen."

"I won't comment on how sad that is," Torie replied. "Does she understand how you feel? You're not exactly the most open person when it comes to emotions. Did you make it clear to her?"

He thought back to that last time in New York, her hurt silence, his defensive panic, right before she stole his clothes and decamped. "Yes."

Okay, even he heard the defensiveness in the word. "Maybe we ought to head back. Your husband's prob-

ably worrying that you finally wised up and ran off
with me."

"Ha. What he's worrying about is that I'll overtax
myself while taking a simple walk. The man has always
been overprotective, but since the minute that test
stick turned blue, he's been a bear."

Mark recalled the moment Carrie's test turned up
positive. The timing couldn't have been worse what
with him about to deploy overseas, but still, they'd
been giddy with happiness. The memory was bitter-
sweet.

The memory of Annabelle's announcement that day
at the Waldorf was a nightmare.

But that was a thought for another time, he told
himself, shaking the memory off. This time belonged
to Matt and Torie, and Mark truly was thrilled for
them, so he chatted with his sister-in-law about silly,
baby-related things until they stood outside the door
to the suite. There, Torie lifted her hand to touch his
cheek. "You'll talk to her?"

"Torie . . ."

"I'll keep the others off your back if you'll promise
to talk to her."

"You keep the others off my back, and I promise
I'll think about it."

For the next two days while playing tourist with his
family, he did little else. The time he spent entertaining his nieces made a particular impression. Finally,
on the morning of the day they were to leave, while
the women were in the hotel spa getting girly and
Matt had taken the twins to the beach to dig in the
sand, he rousted Luke from a lounge chair beside the
pool and said, "Put some clothes on and come with
me, would you?"

"Where you wanting to go?"

"To see Annabelle."

At that, Luke moved like lightning and twenty minutes later, the two men loaded into the rental SUV and headed for Kaimuki, where Annabelle lived in a two-story walk-up with an office downstairs. While Mark drove, he sensed his twin's curious gaze upon him. "What?"

"Nothing." After Mark snorted, Luke added, "All right. I'm just thinking about what a good brother I am. Do you have any clue about how much Maddie's gonna make me pay for this?"

"You mean for leaving the kids with Matt?"

"Nah, he volunteered to babysit this morning. Said he needs the practice. The guy is over the moon about the baby. He'll be fun to watch over the next eight months. No, what's gonna piss Maddie off is that I'm gonna get to meet Annabelle and she's not."

"You don't have to meet her. In fact, I'd rather you just wait in the car while I talk to her."

"The hell you say." Luke snorted. "I'm not gonna wait in the car. Why did you ask me to tag along if you wanted me to wait in the car?"

"You're my protection," Mark answered truthfully.

"You think she'll hurt you?" Luke pursed his lips and considered. "Yeah, I could see it happening. She's not exactly girly."

"I think she might do me."

"*Do* you?"

"Yeah."

Luke's mouth gaped. For a long minute, he stared at Mark, obviously at a loss for words at the idea that his brother wanted to avoid having sex with his wife. "You have something against sex, brother?"

"No, but if I'm alone with her, I'll have sex against something. Anything. It happens every damned time."

"No shit?" Luke's eyes widened with admiration.

Mark nodded grimly. "That's how this whole marriage began and I'm afraid it could keep it from ending."

"Why would you—?" Luke broke off abruptly. "Ending?"

Mark gritted his teeth as he spied the address he wanted on the left. A brass nameplate read MONROE INVESTIGATIONS and pots of blooming hibiscus sat on either side of the entry. He pulled his car into the parking spot marked RESERVED FOR MONROE CLIENTS and shifted into park. Then he sucked in a breath when the office door opened and Annabelle stepped outside. She wore a yellow polka-dot spaghetti-strap sundress and carried a watering pot in her hand.

He removed his aviator sunglasses and their gazes met and held. Beside him, Luke whistled softly. "Hell, Mark."

"Yeah. I know."

Annabelle let out the breath she'd been holding for three days. *He's here.* Finally. He'd come, just when she'd given up waiting for him.

It seemed as if she'd been waiting for him forever.

She concentrated on stopping the tremble in her hand that caused the stream of water to miss her hibiscus. The door to his SUV opened and he unfolded his tall legs from inside. He wore cargo shorts, flip-flops, and a Jimmy Buffett T-shirt—a far cry from his tux of the other night, but just as sexy. More sexy, even.

She turned to tend the other flowerpot, outwardly calm, inwardly a mess.

Someone sat in the passenger seat. Who? She darted a quick glance toward the passenger seat and saw . . . Mark. No, not Mark. His twin, his brother Luke. The DEA agent. Former DEA agent. Was he the one married to the photographer or the rock princess? The princess, she thought. Baby Dagger was married to Luke aka Sin Callahan. Mark was Devil. The dark-haired, green-eyed, silver-tongued Devil. Devil and Sin. My God, two of them. And Matt—

he'd sounded sexy on the radio the other night. Three. Hadn't Mark once said that John had been the good-looking Callahan? Four.

Bet the girls in the town where they grew up were all still wandering around in a daze. Four of them.

But she cared about only one. Hers. At least, he'd been hers for a while. Sort of. As much as Mark Callahan could belong to anyone.

The car door shut with a solid *whop*. Annabelle's mouth went so dry that she considered bringing the water spout up to her mouth. Pure grit enabled her to paste a smile on her face and say, "Hello, Mark."

"Annabelle."

"I thought you'd be long gone from Hawaii by now."

"We're leaving today."

"I see." She emptied the last of the water into the flowerpot, summoned up her nerve, and said, "So you came to tell me good-bye?"

He shoved his hands into his shorts back pockets. "Can we go inside?"

"Sure." She nodded toward the car. "What about your brother?"

"He'll wait. He's waiting."

"He doesn't want to come in?"

"Only if it's necessary." Lowering his voice, he muttered, "If the situation becomes dangerous."

Dangerous? She considered it for a moment, then said, "I'm not going to kill you, Callahan. And I rather like this dress and I don't want to ruin it, so maiming and torture are out, too."

"That's not what I'm talking about."

"What . . . ?" He gave her that familiar smoldering look. Oh. "We are not having sex!"

He winced with regret. "I know. I know." He gestured toward the door and Annabelle led him inside.

Mark glanced around her office and approval gleamed in his eyes. "Nice place. It fits you, Annabelle."

"Yes, it does." Her office furniture was solid wood with clean lines and utilitarian function. She had comfortable seating for her clients and fresh flowers for herself. Under other circumstances she would have invited him to check out her electronics in the back office because inside his athlete's body lurked the quintessential computer geek. He would appreciate her setup. But she would no sooner invite Mark Callahan into her back office than she would invite him back into her bed.

Which she wouldn't do. Really.

Not on a bet.

Never again.

Damn.

Dear God, I've missed him.

She forced a smile. "So, what brings you here, Callahan? Did you come to bust my butt about Rad?"

"I wanted to, but I beat up on my brothers instead. Can't say I'm happy with the decisions you-all made."

"They were the right decisions." Annabelle's chin came up. Be hanged if she'd apologize.

"Not for me. Rad walked away."

"Actually, he flew away and you are letting your desire for vengeance get in the way of your good sense, Callahan."

"Doesn't much matter now, does it?" he said with a shrug. "Mark my words, though. He's a bad penny who will turn up again. You'd better be ready for him."

"Paulo will take care of Rad and his organization."

Mark shook his head. "Don't count on it. Your Italian doesn't know what he's getting into with those boys."

"He's not *my* Italian." Anger flared within her. He didn't want her, but he didn't want anyone else to want her, either? Damn him.

"Bet he still wants to be," he murmured as he wandered over toward the bookcase and picked up a framed picture of Doc, her first foster rescue dog. "Good-looking boxer. I'm partial to brindles. He's yours?"

Apparently, he'd finished talking about Radovanovic. That was fine with Annabelle, but she didn't care to follow him down that particular small-talk path. She was well aware that she was funneling her maternal feelings into the rescue program, and she had too much pride to let Mark know that. "He belongs to a friend. Let me ask again. Why are you here?"

He returned the frame to the bookcase, drew a deep breath, then faced her. His jade eyes remained expressionless as he said, "I came to talk about a divorce. I think it's time we did it."

Oh. Well. With that, he extinguished the last flicker of hope burning in her heart.

I really do want to kill him. Instead of reaching for her weapon, she summoned the professional inside her and used every ounce of acting skills she possessed to calmly state, "Okay."

That surprised him, she could tell. Had he expected her to protest? Burst into sobs? Fall down on her knees and plead? Not in this lifetime. She folded her hands and waited.

The man known on at least three continents for being cool, calm, and collected then stumbled over his explanation. "It's the state of your eggs and I'm not going there and my sister-in-law told me I'm not being fair to you."

Annabelle blinked. "And you discussed my eggs with your sister-in-law?"

Where is my gun?

"They wanted to invite you to go to the spa with them today."

Her blood heated and her smile went cold. "And for that, you want to divorce me?"

"No, dammit. I don't want to divorce you. I liked what we had just fine. But you want children!" He hesitated and shot her a look that might—just might—have held a tiny ray of hope. "Unless you've changed your mind?"

She wanted to lash out at him. The man still wanted to sleep with her. He'd happily schedule sex all over the globe. That's what he wanted. That's *all* he wanted. Casual sex. No home. No kids. No strings. Mark Callahan couldn't handle strings. He'd hang himself with them.

"No," she said softly, swallowing the hurt. "I haven't changed my mind."

That truth told only half the story. What she had wanted from Mark was emotional involvement, but apparently that asked for too much. Mark Callahan was the most closed-off person on the planet.

She'd witnessed and respected his detachment during the years they'd worked together, and she'd strived to maintain a similar state herself. With their occupation, a degree of detachment had been necessary to survive. But when they married, they no longer worked in the unit. They had the freedom to want, to care. To love.

But he couldn't. Wouldn't. Wasn't capable.

It had taken Annabelle time and a late period to figure that out. That weekend in New York before it all fell apart, she had come to understand that she wasn't just ready for emotional involvement—she was already there. She'd cared about Mark Callahan. She had been in love with Mark Callahan.

When he'd celebrated the negative test and rejected even the idea of making a family with her, he'd shown her that his walls were still firmly in place.

But Annabelle never had been one to give up easy. Once she got past the hurt, she had reassessed. The man's walls were higher than hers, thicker than hers. She had thought that maybe he simply needed more time for those walls to come tumbling down.

So she'd waited. One month. Two. Twelve. Somewhere along in there, she had told herself she didn't love him anymore. Didn't want him anymore. If he was too blind, stubborn, and hard-hearted to take what she had offered him, then it was his loss.

Nevertheless, she had continued to wait. He was still her husband, and she was loyal to that.

Until now.

You had your chance, Callahan. You blew it.

Annabelle took a business card from her desk and handed it to him. "Have your lawyer send the papers here. Now, I have an appointment I need to get to."

His eyes widened ever so slightly. His jaw hardened. "You're awfully calm about this."

She arched a single eyebrow. "You would prefer histrionics?"

"No . . . no . . . of course not. I just thought . . ." He blew out a heavy breath. "It's better this way, Belle. I can't give you what you need."

"That's right." She smiled coldly. "You can't. And I can't give you what you need."

"I don't need anything," he protested.

"Exactly. And I didn't do anything wrong, which makes this whole thing easier. I'm clear, you're clear, and we walk away. Clean and easy. Just like that Texas expression you used to say when we finished an operation—calf rope. It's done."

She picked up her purse and waited expectantly.

After a moment's hesitation, he walked to the door and stepped outside.

Annabelle called upon years of training to conceal her emotions, to hide her breaking heart. This could well be the last time she ever saw him. He was leaving for good this time and she had to let go. She had to let *him* go.

Calf rope.

He stopped, turned around. His gaze locked on the blooming plants in her flowerpots, and his voice came soft and low and troubled. "Annabelle . . ."

"Have a nice trip home, Callahan. Have a nice life." With that, she closed the door.

Chapter Four

Seattle
Seven months later

"Got 'em." Mark switched off his computer and rose from his desk, satisfaction washing through him. Days like today were the reason he continued to work rather than spend all his time salmon fishing. The cyber-sting operation he'd developed at the request of an old friend who was now the police chief of a Denver suburb had gone off without a hitch. Tonight, a ring of child pornographers faced spending a big chunk of their lives in prison due in part to his efforts. Made a man feel good.

He grabbed a beer from the fridge, then wandered into the living room of his downtown condo, where floor-to-ceiling windows provided a multimillion-dollar view of Puget Sound and the Olympic Mountains. Outside, the sun was shining and the breeze was gentle, so he stepped out onto the small balcony to enjoy the afternoon.

He'd bought this condo, which occupied half of the thirty-second floor of the high-rise, after his dot-com investments had made him rich, but before he had separated from the army. He'd wanted a place far away from Texas and his father, and the Pacific Northwest had felt right. Since he did the majority of his work on a computer, he could work from anywhere. His only real regret was living so far from his brothers.

He sipped his beer and gazed out across the sound at the pleasure boats skidding across the water. If the weather held, maybe tomorrow he'd take the *Sea Breeze* out, catch a few fish, and call Matt to brag. Ordinarily this time of year, Matt and Torie would be traveling the world on one of their so-called Great Adventures, but this year they'd nested down in Brazos Bend to await the birth of their baby. Matt had been downright obnoxious about the good striper fishing at Possum Kingdom Lake of late when he and Mark had last spoken. He deserved to be scoreboarded over pounds of fish caught.

The landline in his office rang and he decided to let the answering machine pick up. Moments later, a woman's tearful voice said, "Hello, Mr. Callahan. This is Frances Russo."

Mark's radar went on full alert. Russo called him from time to time, but never his wife. He set his bottle down on the patio table, then moved back inside and over to his desk. He picked up the receiver as she continued. "I'm Jeremy's wife. You came to our wedding. I need to speak with you—"

"Hello, Frances. It's Mark. It's nice to hear from you. What can I do for you?"

At that, she burst into tears. *Ah, hell.* Mark propped a hip on the corner of his desk and tried to catch the words she managed through her sobs. He picked up a few that he wished he'd misunderstood.

"Jeremy . . . *mumble, mumble* . . . dead . . . explosion. *Mumble mumble mumble* . . . accident. They're wrong." She let out a long, hard sob. "Wrong!"

Mark closed his eyes and took a few seconds to mourn. Jeremy Russo had been a good man and a fine soldier, and he knew his way around explosives like nobody else. For Russo to have made a fatal mistake, he would have needed to be seriously distracted.

Or seriously unhappy. Mark stared out the window at the spectacular view without really seeing it. He could picture Russo committing suicide by bomb easier than he could see him killing himself by mistake. But the Russo Mark knew wouldn't take the coward's way out and do himself in. No, something was very, very wrong here.

He walked around to his black leather desk chair and took a seat. "Frances, what exactly happened? Can you tell me?"

"It *wasn't* an accident!"

"I tend to agree with you. Jeremy wouldn't have made a mistake like that."

She settled down a bit then and told him about Russo's backyard workshop and the wood-carving hobby he'd taken up. Mark recalled Russo sitting beside a campfire on a mountain in Serbia, whittling a stick. Yeah, he could see him with a workshop. Frances Russo next described how she and her husband had sat down for supper and talked about the trip to Vegas they had planned for the following month.

"He was excited about going, Mark. He'd won the Super Bowl pool at work and had stuck the money away for gambling. He wasn't depressed or anything. He was happy. We were happy. We had decided to start a family."

Mark blew out a heavy breath. "Where has Jeremy been working?"

"At Martindale Junior High. He earned his teaching certificate and he's the shop teacher. He loves it. Loved it."

She broke down again then, and while Mark waited

her out, he wondered just what was going on. Why would a woodshop teacher have explosives in his work shed? When he judged she'd collected herself, he asked again, "What can I do to help you, Frances?"

"I want you to show the police. Prove it to them. Someone did this. Someone murdered my Jeremy and I want you to find him and make him pay. You're a private investigator—Jeremy told me. I want to hire you. He had some life insurance, so I'll be able to pay you—"

"Wait. Hold on, honey. Jeremy was my friend, part of my unit. I will look into it, but I won't take your money. You hear?"

"But you will find out who did this?"

"Yes, Frances, I will. You have my word." He grabbed a notepad and a pen from his desk. "I need a few details. First, have you scheduled services yet? If so, when and where?"

They spoke for another few minutes; then Mark disconnected the call. Immediately, he punched in another number. The phone rang twice and a man's voice said, "NetJet."

"Hi, Jim, it's Mark Callahan. I'm gonna need the Citation at six a.m. tomorrow for a flight to Philly."

"Sure thing, Mr. Callahan. She'll be ready and waiting for you."

He hung up, retrieved his beer, and briefly debated the idea of getting something stronger. *Damn, Jeremy. What the hell happened?* His thoughts drifted back to the three years when he had lived and breathed the unit.

God, he'd loved it. Russo had been the one to tag them as the Fixers. They'd been a team of a dozen, nine men and three women, from different services, agencies, and departments in the government, each with unique talents, assigned to special duty beneath the direction of Colonel Greg Warren. Special covert duty. Warren had an office at the Pentagon and an official title, but they had little to do with his real job. Colonel Warren and his team functioned as freelance troubleshooters for everyone from the army to the CIA.

The Fixers worked all over the world representing Uncle Sam's interests through espionage efforts aimed primarily at criminal organizations involved in the drug trade and arms smuggling. Upon occasion they coordinated with the Company and spooks like Matt if foreign governments figured into the equation. The unit had done good work, provided vital information, and survived some hairy scrapes to boot. He'd never forget that time in Colombia when Annabelle—

"Annabelle." Mark stiffened. If Frances Russo contacted the rest of the Fixers, then Annabelle would be there. She would come to Russo's funeral. He would see her again.

His ex-wife.

Maybe she'd bring her new boyfriend with her.

"Well, shit." Mark drained the rest of his beer.

Philadelphia

Sitting in her car in the parking lot of Devlin's Funeral Home on a blustery spring day, Annabelle flipped her cell phone shut with a trembling hand. The conversation had confirmed the fear that had been growing inside her since she'd begun making the calls for Frances Russo yesterday. Four members of the unit were dead, three of those recently. She couldn't reach four others. What was going on?

Had somebody targeted the Fixers?

It was an incredible thought, but nothing else made sense. Dennis Nelson had died in a car wreck almost two months ago in Europe, so that one might well be unrelated. But in addition to Russo's implausible death, for Terry Hart to die in a rock-climbing accident, and most unbelievable of all, for Melanie Anderson to commit suicide, all within a span of three weeks?

No. Uh-uh. Too much coincidence to be believable.

Add in the fact that she couldn't reach Rocky Stanhope, Jordan Sundine, Rhonda Parsons, and Vince Holloway, and she knew without a doubt that the unit had trouble.

Annabelle was heartsick over the deaths. The years they'd worked together had created a real bond between teammates. She regretted that they had drifted apart in the years since the Fixers disbanded, but that fact didn't negate her sense of loss. Or her concern for the surviving members of the unit.

Like Mark.

She suppressed a shudder. Had Frances Russo not informed her that she'd spoken to Mark before calling Annabelle, she would have been frantic. She might have divorced the man, but she had yet to figure a way to evict him from her heart.

Though she had made a real effort to do so. She'd stayed busy and tended to her social life. She'd dated. Annabelle *wanted* to fall in love.

Despite a real and concerted effort, she had yet to find a man to replace Callahan. When Paulo Giambelli spent two weeks in Hawaii for the stated purpose of winning her heart, she'd tried to accommodate him. Paulo had opined that she'd never move forward until she took another man into her bed, and of course, he'd volunteered for the job. But Annabelle's core values hadn't changed, and in spite of his charm, his wit, his drop-dead-gorgeous features, he couldn't convince her to make that leap. When he announced his intention to woo her for a third week, she'd gently sent him home, telling him she simply wasn't ready for serious romance. Since then they had settled into a habit of twice-weekly flirtatious calls, which she admittedly enjoyed.

Maybe if she'd jumped into romance with Paulo, the prospect of seeing Mark again wouldn't bother her so much. But now she not only had to see him—she would have to talk to him. Maybe work with him again. They could not ignore these deaths and disappearances.

"Lord, help us all." She tucked her cell phone in her purse and exited her rental car. Checking her watch, she saw that the viewing had begun forty minutes ago. A chilly wind whipped up the hem on her new navy coat and she scanned the area with a watchful gaze as she crossed the street to Devlin's. She kept her hand perched on the opening of her shoulder bag, ready to plunge inside and grasp her SIG if need be.

Devlin's Funeral Home was a converted Victorian mansion. Under other circumstances, Annabelle might have taken time to study the architecture. She had a thing for that era, from the style of the buildings with their gingerbread and dormer windows to the crocheted doilies on parlor chairs. It was a side of herself she kept hidden—soft and girly—but someday when the time was right, she'd have her Victorian on the hill with a picket fence and a dog and a swing set in the backyard.

Unless whoever was finishing off the Fixers got to her first.

Oh, jeez. She walked up the sidewalk and stepped onto the porch. At the door, she paused and drew a bracing breath. As much as she dreaded facing Mark, she couldn't deny her gratitude that his broad shoulders could help carry some of this burden.

She opened the door and stepped inside. The foyer was filled with people dressed in dark suits and subdued dresses. Jeremy's family and friends had come out in force. Annabelle glanced around the dimly lit room, anxiously looking for familiar faces.

There. Some of the tension inside her eased as she spied the two team members she had been able to reach. Tag Harrington stood talking to Noah Kincannon. Tag wore a sport coat and gray slacks; Noah a dark suit. Both men were tall with broad shoulders and military posture. Tag's red hair had darkened over the years to a deep auburn. Noah's hair was still dark brunet. They appeared handsome and somber and fit. They looked wonderfully alive.

That just left . . . she stiffened as she tangibly felt his gaze. "Mark."

He stood beside an open doorway, a little behind Frances Russo. He wore a charcoal Armani suit, a patterned tie, and dress shoes with a military shine. His eyes glittered like emeralds until their gazes met, at which point they went studiously blank. The knife he'd sunk into her heart months ago twisted a bit.

She gritted her teeth. She wanted more than anything to speak to Tag and Noah and delay approaching her ex, but good manners dictated that she pay her respects to Jeremy's widow first. She took a step forward, then stopped when a gruff voice said, "Annabelle?"

She noted the uniform right away, then the warm blue eyes that gleamed at her from beneath bushy salt-and-pepper eyebrows. Lines aged his face, but his steely jaw remained the same. "Colonel Warren!"

"Annabelle, it *is* you." He wrapped his arms around her and gave her a hard hug. "Good Lord, woman. You're a sight for sore eyes."

"You, too, Colonel," she replied with a smile. She was surprised to see him. As the Fixers' commanding officer, Colonel Greg Warren had been the driving force behind their missions, though his position prevented him from being a true part of the team. She had left a message about Russo's death with his assistant as a courtesy. She had never expected he would make the trip for the funeral, but she was thrilled that he had. He might have information about the trouble. Perhaps that was why he was here. "I guess you received my message?"

"I did. Such sad news. Russo was a good man. It's always hard to lose a man, but to lose someone so young and in such an unfortunate manner . . . well . . ." He shook his head, then glanced over her shoulder and smiled. "There you are. Honey, I'm sure you remember my old friend and colleague Annabelle Monroe. Annabelle, my wife, Lala."

A wife? The last she knew, Colonel Warren had been a widower. Annabelle turned to see a woman who could be Catherine Zeta-Jones's sister, a woman who looked vaguely familiar. Extending her hand, she said, "Hello."

Lala Warren smiled pleasantly as she accepted Annabelle's handshake. "It's a pleasure to see you again, Ms. Monroe. I wish it were under happier circumstances."

Annabelle considered trying to fake her way through the moment, but she decided to confess. "I'm sorry," she said, offering an embarrassed smile. "I'm having a brain freeze. I don't recall where we met."

"The Fixers helped my first husband and me escape from Iraq. I believe you piloted the helicopter?"

"Oh, yes." Now she remembered. The husband had been a brilliant scientist, a biologist, who didn't want to work for Saddam Hussein. That extraction was one of the first missions the Fixers ever completed.

"My Stefan died four . . . almost five years ago now. An automobile accident. Not long after Greg's wife passed away."

Colonel Warren patted her arm. "Lala and I have

been married for two years now. I am blessed to have had two wonderful women in my life."

"I'm glad for you, Colonel," Annabelle told him honestly. He was a good man and she was pleased to see him happy.

"It's a shame it takes an unfortunate incident like this to bring us together."

Annabelle gave him a sharp look. Did he know that Jeremy's manner of death was more murderous than unfortunate? She couldn't tell, and now was not the time to ask. "Yes, it is. If you'll excuse me, I need to speak to Jeremy's wife."

"Of course, Annabelle. Lala and I were just leaving. We'll visit more tomorrow at the funeral."

Annabelle then threaded through the crowd, slowly making her way toward the widow. After acknowledging Mark with a brief nod, she took hold of Frances's hands and gave them a comforting squeeze. "Hello, Frances."

"Annabelle, thanks for coming." Her voice was strained, her complexion pale and translucent in the room's soft lighting. "Thanks for helping to make calls. Jeremy is surely looking down from heaven, happy to see members of the unit here." Her voice cracked as she added, "You meant so much to him, you know."

"He meant a lot to us, too, Frances."

"Everyone loved him." The widow's eyes grew teary, but she bravely blinked the moisture away. Then as a bit of a line formed behind Annabelle, Frances Russo gestured toward the viewing room where Jeremy's flag-draped casket was on display.

The scent of gardenia hung heavy on the air as Annabelle moved reluctantly into the room, grateful it wasn't an open-casket event. She didn't do dead bodies well, especially not ones that had been drained and dressed for planting. She traced her phobia back to her great-uncle Ray's funeral and The Accident. At seven, she'd been inquisitive, bold, and . . . foolish. It had been her bad luck that the church had a staircase to the choir loft that allowed her to lean over the casket to get a better look. Lean too far over. So far that she lost her balance and fell.

She closed her eyes and willed away the memory.

A hand took her elbow. "You okay?" Mark asked, his tone a low, respectful rumble.

I was. Not so much now. "I'm fine."

"You look flushed."

"I'm fine," she repeated, tugging her arm from his grip.

"All right. Then let me introduce you to Jeremy's mother. She is anxious to meet members of the team."

Annabelle recalled that the groom's mother—a traditional Italian Catholic—had boycotted the Las Vegas wedding in protest. Frances had told her that mother and son took a year to reconcile. Bet she regretted that lost time now.

Mark scanned the room and frowned. "We're still missing a lot of folks. Were you able to get hold of everyone?"

Annabelle didn't want to go into the situation here, so she simply said, "None of the others will be coming. I need to talk to all of you about that."

"About what?"

"Not here."

Mark shot her an inquisitive look, then said, "Tag suggested we get a drink at the bar around the corner when this is over."

"Good." She worked to keep her expression as blank as his. "Introduce me to Mrs. Russo."

Annabelle spent the next half hour meeting Jeremy's entire family. At some point, Noah and Tag joined her, and Mark slipped away. When Tag wandered off for a moment, Noah leaned toward her and asked, "What's up, Anna-B? What's bothering you?"

Noah always did have good instincts. She gave her head a little shake and said, "It'll wait until later."

Darkness had fallen by the time they exited the funeral home, but the surrounding area bustled with activity. When Tag suggested they walk to the bar, Annabelle didn't protest. She honestly didn't think anyone would be so bold as to gun them all down in the midst of so many potential witnesses. Nevertheless, she remained watchful during the brief walk and didn't relax until they'd been seated at a quiet round table in the upstairs dining room.

The air inside Murphy's Pub was thick with the scent of fries and yeasty beer, but the place had the homey feel that made a neighborhood bar work. After draping her coat on a rack next to the window, she'd made certain to take a seat where she could keep an eye on both the staircase and the street below. It was well past the dinner hour, and at the only other occupied table upstairs, the couple had just received their check. Without consulting a menu, all three men ordered a hamburger. Annabelle would have choked on anything more substantial than the ale she requested.

With her concentration focused on their situation and surroundings, she found herself caught off guard when Tag turned to her and asked, "So, Annabelle, what have you been up to since I last saw you? Do you have a husband and two-point-three kids?"

Viciously, she stifled the instinct to look at Mark and kept her gaze solidly on Tag as she replied, "I'm not married."

"Dating anyone? You know, my brother still talks about you. You've been his fantasy woman ever since our paths crossed that time in DC. He's single again. Maybe . . . ?"

"I don't think so." Then, because she was a woman

who did have her pride, she smiled and added, "I'm seeing someone."

It wasn't exactly a lie. She recently had two dates with a friend of her brother's, a lawyer who had come to the Islands on business. The fact that he had gone home to Kansas didn't mean they would never have another date.

She asked Tag about his love life, which led the conversation down a similar path with Noah. Through it all, Mark kept maddeningly silent. Had Annabelle been a weaker woman, she would have allowed the tension, stress, and sadness boiling inside her the outlet the emotions craved. However, she'd rather give up chocolate for the rest of her life than cry in front of Mark "Cold-Heart" Callahan.

The next best thing to a good cry was a chat with her mother. She sipped her ale and wondered if it was too late to call home.

I'm seeing someone, Mark repeated in a silent sneer, his mind drifting away from the conversation taking place around him. *Isn't that special?*

He told himself to be glad that at least she didn't bring the sonofabitch with her. This situation blew as it was. He sure as hell didn't need to watch her cooing up to the man she'd replaced him with. He needed to keep his mind on the business at hand—discovering the truth about Jeremy Russo's death.

Kincannon and Harrington questioned the police findings, too. They'd each taken him aside during to-night's viewing and expressed their disbelief at the idea that Russo had accidentally blown himself up. That's when he'd decided to meet with the team and share his intentions to investigate the matter.

Even though he'd rather chew tenpenny nails than sit across the table from his oh-so-sexy ex.

She looked like a million dollars tonight. Like she'd

told him that night on Lanai, black *was* a great color for her and the conservative cut of her dress only accentuated her curves. She'd done something different with her hair since the last time he saw her that day in her office. It looked . . . bouncy. And she had big honking diamond studs in her ears.

What's up with that? Annabelle had never worn diamonds. Never been much on jewelry of any kind, from what he recalled, except for that cheap-ass wedding band he'd bought at the Vegas wedding chapel. That she had worn on every one of their "weekends" until it slipped off while they snorkeled in New Zealand. He had intended to buy her another, but he'd never followed through.

Looked like his replacement didn't hesitate to drop the big bucks on bling. She could have bought the ear rocks for herself, true, but knowing Annabelle, he doubted it. Much better odds that the boyfriend had given them to her. The idea made him a bit nauseous.

Mark knew that his reaction was stupid. He had expected her to hook up with someone. That was the whole idea of legally splitting the sheets, wasn't it? Yet when he'd called her home phone the day their divorce was final and a man had answered—at six freaking a.m. her time—the reality of it had been a punch to the gut. He hadn't liked listening to the bastard's voice then, and he didn't like looking at proof of his existence now.

It made him almost glad to turn his attention to something as disturbing as murder.

Small talk continued as a waitress served their drinks; then just when Mark decided to share Frances Russo's request with his friends, Annabelle spoke up. "Guys, I have some news."

A note in her voice warned him. Mark looked at her hard and put the pieces together. She had contacted the others. *Someone else is dead. Well, hell.*

"It's bad and it worries me," Annabelle continued. Once she had everyone's attention, she announced, "I think we have trouble. Russo isn't the only Fixer we've lost. Nelson, Hart, and Anderson are dead, too. Hart and Anderson just in the past two weeks. Plus, I couldn't reach Stanhope, Sundine, Parsons, or Holloway."

While Annabelle spoke, Tag Harrington froze with his beer mug halfway to his mouth. Noah Kincannon set his scotch on the table. "What was that?"

"Hart fell while climbing, and Melanie . . ." She briefly closed her eyes, then finished, "The ME classified Melanie's death as a suicide."

"Screw that!" Harrington declared.

Kincannon set his mouth in a grim smile. "I don't believe that for a minute. What about Nelson?"

"He died a couple months ago in a car accident in Europe."

Mark drummed his fingers on the table. "Tell me about the others."

"Holloway's number has changed and I wasn't able to track him down before I had to catch my plane. Rhonda Parsons is apparently on a white-water-rafting vacation. Stanhope lives in some remote mountain cabin in Colorado and doesn't answer his phone, and Jordan Sundine . . ." She blew out a heavy breath. "Jordan hasn't shown up to work in almost a week."

While Kincannon and Harrington grappled with the news and peppered Annabelle with questions, Mark mentally connected the dots and reached an undeniable conclusion. During a pause in the conversation, he lobbed it out like a grenade. "We're being targeted."

Conversation around the table abruptly died. Annabelle licked her lips, then nodded. "Yes. I think so, too."

"Holy crap," Harrington breathed. He sat back in his chair hard.

Kincannon tapped his fingers against the battered and aged tabletop, his brow knit with worry. "Why now? We haven't worked together for seven years. It makes no sense."

Annabelle didn't say anything for a moment, a worry line creasing the skin between her finely arched brows. "I intend to investigate these deaths and disappearances. In the meantime it's imperative that we all take measures to protect ourselves."

"I'll help you, Annabelle," Kincannon said.

"We had better all help." Harrington picked up his beer and tossed back a swallow. "Sounds like our asses are on the line."

"I've already started," Mark said, smiling grimly. "I told Frances when she called me in Seattle that I would find out what really happened to Russo. I've spent much of today hounding the police."

"What have you learned?" Kincannon asked.

"Not much. The police still say accident. Honestly, if I didn't know Russo, I would have reached the same conclusion as the cops. It was a classic flammable-gas explosion. I suspected someone held a personal grudge against Russo. Now with Annabelle's news . . . I have to reassess."

"What do you want me to do, boss?" Harrington asked Mark. "I may be rusty at fieldwork, but I do remember how it's done."

Mark noted the annoyance that flashed across Annabelle's face. The role of subordinate had always chafed her, even before the team disbanded, before the two of them married. After Las Vegas, she quietly asserted herself as an equal in their relationship. Reverting to old roles wouldn't be easy for her, but their roles *would* revert. Mark had always been the über-alpha in this pack filled with alphas, and that would not change. He was the leader of this team.

So he assessed his assets. He had three team members—the Fixers' sniper, their ghost, their siren—and himself, their e-man. Tag Harrington, the shooter, had spent the past few years as head of security for a high-end retailer—not exactly the occupation to keep his skills sharpened. Noah Kincannon ran a company that specialized in providing security systems to art galleries and museums. He'd told Mark earlier that the systems his people installed weren't considered finished until Kincannon attempted to breach them and failed. No rust on his skills.

That left Annabelle. The siren, the distraction, the Woman-as-Weapon. She could sidle up to a target and take him down without chipping a nail because, generally, they were too busy gawking at her assets to take a look at her hands.

She practiced her skills without even trying every time she went out in public.

Not a bad team to have at his back. Not bad at all. Mark exhaled a heavy breath. "First priority is to track down the others and warn them of the potential danger. After that, we need to look into each one of these deaths. If we're right and they are murders, whoever is behind this will have left a footprint somewhere—whether it's electronic or physical. Now, has anything crossed y'all's desks that could in any way be related to our old work?"

The others took a moment to think. Then the men gave their heads a negative shake. Annabelle slowly nodded and Mark raised an eyebrow and met her gaze.

"Boris Radovanovic," she stated quietly.

Mark scowled.

"Who's that?" Kincannon asked, frowning. "Russian? Was he part of that god-awful insertion we did in Kazakhstan?"

"No." Mark shook his head. "My dealings with this particular dirtbag were a long time after the Fixers' days." He gave a brief sketch of his history with Rad, including events in Hawaii last year. "Even if he broke Annabelle's cover and somehow connected the two of us, it's a stretch to think he'd go after the team."

With the subject of Rad leaving a sour taste in his mouth, Mark fished in his pocket for a peppermint. "That said, we can't afford to ignore anything at this point. Annabelle, has he contacted you at all since that night?"

He popped the piece of hard candy into his mouth as she thumbed a line of moisture dribbling down her glass. Quietly, she said, "Yes, I've heard from Rad. He appreciated the job I did that night. He paid my invoice and . . . sent me roses."

Mark damned near swallowed the peppermint whole. Roses. From Radovanovic. Jesus.

Because he suddenly needed to move, he pushed to his feet and crossed the room to the dartboard, where he grabbed the steel-tipped darts from the corkboard. Events of that night in Hawaii flashed through his mind as he took a warm-up throw. His mouth flattened in a grim smile when his dart hit the triple ring at 10. "I'll put my brothers on Radovanovic."

She frowned. "I could—"

"No," he snapped. He whipped his head around and glared at her. "You're done with him."

Her eyes widened, then narrowed. She snapped her mouth shut and he could hear her toe begin to tap against the hardwood floor.

Kincannon and Harrington shared a droll look. Then Harrington observed, "It would be nice if you two learned to work together without bickering, but in a way, it's good to know that some things never change."

Mark shot two more darts in rapid succession. "Tell us everything you know about the others, Annabelle. Where did Parsons go to raft? Where are Stanhope's cabin and Holloway's workplace? I want details."

He could all but hear her grind her teeth before she opened her mouth and gave a succinct and thorough report. As she talked, his concern deepened. He didn't like this one bit. When she was done, he plucked his darts from the board and dropped them onto the table. "Sounds like you've done everything possible with the information you have so far. When I get back to my hotel, I'll get on my computer and see what else I can ferret out."

Annabelle opened her mouth to comment, then abruptly shut it. Kincannon gave her a sidelong look and murmured, "He *is* a gold-star hacker."

Mark blazed ahead, rapidly making plans. "If I find anything we can move on tonight, I'll yell at one of you. Tomorrow before the funeral, I'll speak with Colonel Warren and get his take on all this. I'll ask him to review our mission files and see if he can connect anything from those years to something going on now."

"I know this is a bit off topic, but how about his new bride?" Harrington asked. "Day-yum! I've always admired the colonel, but now . . . he's a god."

Kincannon and Mark gave him an amused look while Annabelle said drily, "It's reassuring to know that you haven't changed, Tag."

Kincannon smirked at that, then observed, "I had heard that Stefan Jankovic died. He was a brilliant mind and doing some important work for the Defense Department. It's a shame we lost him so young."

"The DOD's loss, our commander's gain."

"You're a pig, Tag," Annabelle said.

Harrington winked at her, scooped up the darts, and handed Kincannon three of them in a wordless challenge. He took a place behind the strip of green tape on the worn wooden floor and lined up for his first throw.

"So, what do you think, boss?" Kincannon asked, frowning as Harrington hit the bull's-eye. "We have a lot to cover. Are we going one-on-one on this?"

"I've already done some follow-up on Dennis's death," Annabelle interrupted. "The accident happened in Tuscany. Paulo Giambelli offered to help me look into it."

I'll just bet he did. Again, the image of Radovanovic and red roses flashed through Mark's head, only this time, the Italian Stallion stood right beside the Croat, holding a bouquet of his own. Annoyed at his own nonsense, Mark spoke testily. "We'll work in pairs. Kincannon, you and Harrington can take Parsons, Sundine, Anderson, and finish up here with Russo. Annabelle and I will cover Stanhope, Holloway, Nelson, and Hart. Let's connect after the cemetery service tomorrow morning and we'll go from there."

"Sounds like a plan," Harrington said as Kincannon nodded his agreement. They all exchanged cell phone numbers, and then the two men returned their attention to the dart game.

Annabelle sat staring down into her half-full beer. Mark watched her and knew he'd have been better off to pair her with one of the others, but he couldn't make himself do it. Though he trusted both Harrington and Kincannon, if somebody was gunning for the team, then he wanted to be the one watching Annabelle's back.

He needed to say something to ease the tension between him and his ex. Trouble was, anything he said to her was liable to make her mad. Still, he had to try. "Annabelle . . ."

As she glanced up, a ring tone sounded. She fished in her bag and pulled out a cell phone. He saw a smile flicker on her lips as she checked the number. "I need to take this," she said. "Excuse me."

She rose and left the table, crossing to a window on the far side of the room. Her gaze shifted between the street and the staircase as she carried on a conversation that lasted a good five minutes. During her call, Mark tried to concentrate on the mission before them, but time and time again, his attention drifted to the woman he'd left behind.

Damned if she didn't giggle into the phone. Mr. Diamond-Ear-Stud Giver must be a real comedian to get a laugh out of her under these circumstances. She'd been on edge from the moment he saw her walk through the funeral home door.

Fool that he was, Mark resented the fact that the boyfriend was the person in position to relax her. After all, he knew just what position relaxed her best. Annabelle wore herself out when she was on top.

He stuck a fry in his mouth and scowled. Now even salt tasted sour.

"Doesn't count." Harrington's voice intruded into his brooding. "The dart must stay on the board for at least five seconds after your final throw to count."

"You're the one who can't count," Kincannon replied. "That was five seconds."

Annabelle shook her head over their bickering as she returned to the table, a faint grin on her lips. Even as he opened his mouth, Mark knew he was making a mistake. "So, does your new boyfriend give you flowers along with diamonds for your ears, or it is just gangsters who do that?"

That took the smile off her face. Temper snapped in her big brown eyes, but she kept her voice cool as she spoke in a voice pitched low so the others couldn't hear. "Hold it right there, Callahan. We'd better get this straight right from the outset. You aren't my husband anymore, so you don't get to make those sorts of remarks to me. You don't get to comment on my personal phone calls, my social life, my jewelry, or my freaking hairstyle."

"Look—"

"No, you listen. I didn't plan on ever seeing you again, but since I want to be alive to spend Memorial Day with my family, and I'd just as soon not have to go to another funeral for one of our team—even yours—I'm willing to put my personal druthers aside. We need to figure out who is after us, and we need to do it without egos or pride or tape measures."

Tape measures! For God's sake.

"I'll accept you as team leader, but that's as far as it goes. You signed away any right you have to play alpha male with me beyond the mission. So, what do you say, Callahan? Can you bridle your tongue long enough for me to help save your ass?"

Mark knew he should defend himself. He knew he should probably apologize. He knew without a doubt that he should get his mind back on business and leave it there. For good.

Instead, all he could do was stare at her and imagine her naked. Imagine her sinking down on top of him, taking him into her sweet, slick heat. Riding him, her head flung back, her eyes closed, the tip of her tongue centered at the top of her lip. Her full, coral-tipped breasts swaying. The throaty moans of pleasure she made when she came.

"Well, Callahan?"

He blinked. Came hurtling back to reality. She looked angry as a wet hen in a wool basket.

I am so screwed.

He opened his mouth to apologize, but was saved by the scream.

* * *

The noise came from downstairs and immediately, the four Fixers shifted into work mode. Four guns appeared. Four former team members silently took position as shouts followed the scream. Tag and Noah lined up on either side of the staircase, and Mark took point with Annabelle directly behind him, ready to provide cover. Four pairs of eyes connected. Then Mark nodded and started downstairs.

Bar fight, Annabelle confirmed at first glance at the scene. From her spot overlooking the street, she'd watched these thugs arrive just about five minutes ago. They hadn't worried her. Experience convinced her that any threat to the Fixers would come from a more subtle source. Behind her, she heard Tag ask, "So when did biker gangs start frequenting Irish pubs in Philly?"

Annabelle tuned in to the shouts flying around the bar's interior and replied, "Since an Irish-pub waitress started dating a Southern-fried do-rag, apparently."

"They're probably all corporate executives playing dress-up," Noah observed.

"Or dress down," Tag fired back.

"I doubt it," Annabelle said. "Too many piercings and tats in places you can't cover up."

She counted seven grimy, leather-wearing thugs who hadn't been there when they'd arrived. They were breaking glass and shouting at patrons, but so far it didn't appear as if fists had started to fly. Yet. Their leader was a big bald guy with bad teeth and gold chains who had to be cold wearing a black leather vest with no shirt. The focus of his ire was the manager of the pub, a woman about Annabelle's age who called the biker "honey" and begged him not to throw the chair in his hands at the mirror behind the bar.

Mark glanced back over his shoulder, an unyielding set to his jaw. "This has nothing to do with us. Let's go."

The Fixers put their guns away and continued downstairs. There, Mark paused to pay their tab by shoving a hundred at a terrified waiter as Annabelle and the others threaded their way toward the door. She had just begun to think that they would make it outside without incident when the biker sent the chair flying, then made a terrible mistake. He grabbed a handful of the manager's dark hair with his left hand and punched her face with his right.

"Well, hell," Annabelle muttered, knowing what that meant.

Mark immediately changed directions and sailed into the fray, Tag and Noah on his heels. Annabelle took a second to analyze the situation—seven against three, no real challenge for her teammates there—and zeroed in on the manager.

As she guided the sobbing woman away from the fight, she couldn't help but watch her ex-husband in action. His movements were lightning-fast and graceful, practiced and controlled. Mark spun and kicked and dropped first one attacker and then the other with seemingly little effort. Then he picked up a pool cue and whirled to block the idiot coming after him with a knife.

The injury wouldn't have happened had a bystander not tried to help. A young corporate type foolishly decided Tag needed help. He rushed into the fray and into the path of Mark's kick, which gave the idiot time to move close enough for his knife to draw blood. Mark's blood.

Literally and figuratively, Annabelle saw red.

She registered a few facts immediately. The blade had caught him during a turn and sliced, not punctured, just below his ribs. Mark was still on his feet.

The biker went down on his ass.

Nothing too serious, then, Annabelle decided as the corporate type's buddies escalated the brawl by joining in. "For heaven's sake," she muttered with disgust as she shoved the manager into the kitchen and ordered, "Stay."

If the corporate crowd was going to get involved, then she would, too. This might be just a normal bar fight, but who's to say that Russo's killer wouldn't take advantage of the moment? The sooner the Fixers got out of here, the better.

Anticipation caused her blood to pound and tension gripped her muscles, but when she turned back to the fight, her teammates had the situation under control. Tag was grinning like a fool, waving his fingers in a come-at-me taunt toward a pasty-faced biker in a yellow bandanna do-rag who was backing toward the door. Noah was shoving a pair of button-downs back into their seats, while Mark took the last fighter down by slamming the blunt end of the pool cue into the guy's solar plexus.

She was almost disappointed. Her blood was up and humming and the events of the past two days had her feeling a bit mean. The sight of the red bloodstain against the white cotton of Mark's dress shirt didn't help matters one bit.

So when she spied one of the downed badass wannabes slipping a knife from his knee-high leather boot, she took great pleasure in rearing back and kicking it away, giving the offending hand a good whack in the process. The fool yelped and she smiled down at him. "Don't make me draw my gun."

As color drained from the biker's complexion, Annabelle addressed the Fixers. "You high-speeds ready to roll?"

"We're gone," Mark replied.

Outside, Annabelle smothered the impulse to ask Mark about his wound and responded in turn to her ex-husband's question about each of the Fixers' accommodations. Of the four of them, Annabelle was the only one who'd already checked into a hotel.

"That's where Colonel Warren is staying," Noah told them.

"Let's all get rooms there," Mark said. "We can meet for breakfast and I'll ask Colonel Warren to join us. I prefer that we hang close until we get a better handle on what's going on."

A little over an hour later, after she'd showered and pulled on her favorite sleep shirt—the University of Kansas basketball jersey her dad had given her following KU's Final Four appearance this year—she'd just pulled back the covers to climb into bed when her phone rang. "Hello?"

Mark said, "I'm next door and I could use a bit of help. I've already unlocked my side of the connecting door. Would you come here for a minute, please?"

Her gaze flew to the door in question. Stupidly, she repeated, "You're next door?"

"It'll just take a minute. I just . . . well, crap. My hand gets too slippery with blood to hold on to—"

Annabelle didn't hear the finish because she slammed down the phone and headed for the connecting door.

Mark stood in the bathroom facing away from her, wearing only a towel around his waist, and when he twisted his torso, her pulse jumped and she sucked in a breath at the sight.

He could have been a muscle jock posing for the cameras. The twist of his broad shoulders revealed cords of muscle that bunched beneath his tanned, toned, and battle-scarred skin. His dark hair, still wet from his shower, curled at the nape of his neck and dripped water slowly down his spine. Her gaze snagged on the exit-wound scar high on his torso. That had happened not long before their blowup in New

York, when he'd tangled with a tango out to kill the woman his brother Matt loved.

So many scars, she thought. And not all of them on the outside.

Her stare drifted lower, noting another new scar across his rib cage, then past his narrow waist to where he held a washrag against the small of his back. The damp towel clung to his buttocks, and her palms all but itched as she recalled running her hands over those firm, muscled cheeks. He stood with his feet apart and Annabelle knew she was in trouble when she realized that even his high-arched feet looked sexy to her tonight.

She cleared her throat. "What's wrong?"

Green eyes flicked to her reflection in the mirror. "Damn cut. The shower started it bleeding again. I could use some help with the butterflies."

He lifted the white washrag away from the cut and Annabelle sucked in breath to see the bloodstain. "Jeez, Callahan. If it's still bleeding that much, you probably need stitches."

"Nah, it's a side effect of the medicine I'm taking."

"Medicine for what?"

"I was on a job in Malaysia a few weeks ago. Caught a bug. Here." He gave her a handful of bandages. "I'll hold it together if you'll keep it dry so that the butterflies stick."

She frowned and gave him another once-over, this time keeping clinical about it. He hadn't lost weight, didn't appear pale or wan. The man looked healthy. In prime shape. Fit for anything.

At that point, clinical observation failed her and her traitorous mind continued its dangerous assessment. Fit for exercise. Strenuous exercise. Horizontal exercise.

Dear God. What was wrong with her? She had divorced this man. She didn't much like him anymore.

She certainly didn't trust him. He'd stolen her heart and stomped all over it!

It had to be the hotel-room phenomenon. The two of them and a hotel room were a dangerous combination.

She dragged her thoughts back where they belonged and hoped that he'd blame the flush in her cheeks on a reaction to the lingering hot steam from the shower. He was on something for a bug. With any luck, it gave him gastrointestinal issues. *That thought should keep my libido in check.* "Is it contagious?"

"The bug? Nah. Don't worry." When she still hesitated to approach him, to touch his bare skin, he said, "Annabelle? Are you going to let me bleed to death?"

Chapter Five

Mark thought he had quit playing with fire the night he and his brothers accidentally burned down the boot factory in Brazos Bend and put a quarter of the town out of work. Looked like he'd been wrong. He'd damn sure struck a match when he'd picked up the phone and called the room next door.

He'd known exactly what he was doing, too.

The why of it was more of a problem.

She'd challenged him back there at the bar. *You don't get to comment on my personal phone calls, my social life, my jewelry, or my freaking hairstyle.* And *We need to do it without egos or pride or tape measures.*

Tape measures. Since she was the one who'd brought up the subject of his penis, he figured he'd show her tape measures. She'd all but asked for this. And he was getting to her, he could tell.

Not that he intended to do anything about it, because he didn't. Really. He just wanted to show her that walking the walk was more difficult than talking the talk where the two of them were concerned, and that she shouldn't be all sanctimonious when it came to dealing with him.

Because Mark knew her. He knew that no matter how many men she'd taken to her bed since their split, he would always be special. He was her first. He didn't doubt that he was her best.

God knew she was his best. He'd had more than his share of women all over the world and better simply didn't exist.

I've missed you, Belle. I've missed us.

The words remained unspoken. He knew better.

She glanced down at the butterfly bandages he'd given her. "Wait a minute. I'll be right back."

He scowled as she turned and fled, and he gave the cut another look in the mirror. He could use her help. Surely he hadn't scared her away. He hadn't said one single suggestive word.

Of course, with Annabelle he didn't need to say anything aloud. She knew him as well as he knew her.

She returned carrying a travel-sized first-aid kit and wearing an impersonal expression. Yet, when she stepped all the way into the bathroom, awareness thickened the air like steam from a hot shower. "Put down the washrag, Callahan."

He dropped it onto the counter and worked not to reach for her. Focused on the slice in his skin, Annabelle didn't notice. "The cut is longer than I realized," she said. "He got you during a spin, didn't he?"

"Yeah."

She set her kit on the counter, then removed a two-inch square pack. She tore it open and unfolded an alcohol wipe. "Lift your arm."

Her instruction didn't register with Mark because she'd moved close to him, which allowed him to see down the gaping neckline of the basketball jersey. The sight of those full magnificent breasts sent his blood rushing south. *That's what I needed to stop the cut from bleeding.*

He hissed when she slapped the wipe against the wound with an ungentle hand. "Stop it, you perv."

Not even the bite of alcohol on an open wound was enough to distract him from those perky, coral-tipped globes just made for his mouth. Nothing perverted about it. He was a man. She was a woman. They were in a hotel room. . . .

"Callahan!" she warned, slapping her hand against the neckline and interrupting his visual feast.

He dragged his gaze away from her, grabbed hold of the granite counter's rim, and stared into the mirror.

And remembered making love to her in front of a mirror in a hotel in Hong Kong.

Shit. Maybe this wasn't such a good idea at all. He clenched his jaw and closed his eyes, but immediately opened them again, looking for a distraction from the memory played in living color across his brain. "You sleeping with college boys now, Annabelle?"

Her incredulous gaze flicked up to meet his in the mirror. "What?"

"Where did you get the jersey?"

Her hand stilled. The alcohol stung. "Nick Koldus played at Kansas."

She's with a pro basketball player now? "He's with Seattle."

A devilish smile played about her lips. "He has good hands."

Witch.

She finally decided she'd tortured him enough with alcohol and brought out the antibiotic cream. The first soft brush of her hand against his skin both soothed him and stirred him. This had been a dumb idea.

He sucked in a breath and smelled . . . Annabelle. While he always used whatever shampoo the hotel provided, Annabelle brought her own along with a lotion of the same tropical scent. It was subtle, yet earthy. Exotic. Erotic. Annabelle.

This had been a spectacularly dumb idea. He should have slapped a bandage or five on the cut and gone to bed.

The bathroom seemed to shrink to the size of a closet. He closed his eyes and forced himself to think about other things. He mentally made a shopping list for the Seattle condo. Debated the breed of dog he'd get when his lifestyle would allow one. Considered what to get Luke and Maddie's twins for their next birthday.

He heard the rip and tear of paper and opened his eyes. "Gauze? Can't you just use the butterflies?"

"I know you consider a Z-Pak and butterfly bandages as your medical cure-alls, but this cut requires something more. Turn around, Callahan, so I can reach."

He hesitated, knowing he couldn't hide the tent in his towel if he did as she asked. Then their gazes met in the mirror and he saw the knowing in the warm brown depths of her eyes.

He saw knowing and a vulnerability he'd never seen in her before.

She licked her lips and said, "Let's just get this over with, please?"

Mark turned. She stood mere inches away, so close he could feel the heat radiating from her body. Unable to stop himself, he lifted a hand and brushed back the silky fire of her hair, tucking it back behind her ear so that he could see her face. He skimmed his fingers down the softness of her cheek and spoke a hollow truth that went beyond the moment. "I don't want it to be over, Annabelle."

Her hand trembled as she gently pressed a pad of gauze against the seeping cut in his skin. She was so close, so warm, so soft, her deliciously erotic fragrance teasing his senses. Mark almost threw away the last of his good intentions at that point and bent his lips to taste her.

Even as instincts propelled him forward, she grabbed hold of his hand, of the fingers stroking her skin, and wordlessly moved his hand to the gauze and stepped back. Quickly and efficiently, she tore strips of tape from the roll and fixed the bandage to his skin. Stepping back, she drew a deep breath, then looked him in his eyes. "To quote Mick, you can't always get what you want. See you in the morning, Callahan."

Then he was alone.

Again.

As always.

Annabelle watched rainwater drip from a stone angel's trumpet. What an awful day to be standing around a cemetery. Yet better to be standing than lying like poor Jeremy.

The storm had rolled in during the funeral mass and cold, steady rain brought solemn, dampened moods even lower. Frances Russo sat sobbing beneath the shelter of the graveside tent. Her stoic mother-in-law patted the distraught widow's knee as the priest lifted his hands to the sky and announced, "Heaven weeps with happiness today to receive such a fine man as Jeremy."

Standing beside Annabelle, Tag leaned over and murmured in her ear, "As long as he's the only one of us heaven gets today, I'll be happy."

Annabelle's lips twisted with a rueful smile. Actually, she wasn't worried about their safety at the moment. Mark had hired private security for this event—extensive private security who had established a perimeter that would make the Secret Service proud.

She was glad of the respite. This was the first time since she'd realized the Fixers had a problem that she felt able to relax, able to mourn. Listening to Russo's friends and family talk about his plans and hopes and dreams created a lump in her throat the size of a baseball. Hearing them talk about his "accident" made her mad. Jeremy deserved better.

Her gaze drifted to Mark, Tag, Noah, and Colonel Warren, and determination dissolved the lump in her throat. Jeremy would have better, by God. They'd catch the person who killed him if it was the last thing she ever did.

Now, there's a positive thought.

Annabelle choked back the hysteria-edged giggle that wanted to bubble from her mouth. Her emotions pulsed with turmoil today. Funerals for friends tended to make a woman both cranky and a little crazy.

Having to hang around her ex-husband placed the freaking cherry on top.

And yet, that stubborn part of her psyche made her determined to quash everything but the professional within her. She refused to allow anyone to see her fear or her fury. As far as the feelings Callahan stirred inside her . . . well . . . maybe this contact would help her rid herself of those last few tenacious tentacles of attachment.

Mark Callahan had proved difficult to get over. While she lectured herself against comparing other men with her ex, she found herself doing it every single time she dated someone new. No one measured up, not enough to intrigue her beyond a few dates, and certainly not enough to go to bed with—even after she'd relaxed her standards in that regard. The day her divorce was final, when she'd been weak and lonely and afraid, she'd poured too many glasses of wine and the whole miserable story to her brother, Adam, who'd been visiting with his family at the time. He had promised to keep her secret if she promised to listen to his advice.

Sleep with someone, Annabelle, he'd told her. *Just once. I know you have an old-fashioned outlook in that area and I can't believe that I'm actually telling you to do it, but after listening to you today, I'm afraid it's going to take that for you to get beyond Mark Callahan. The man is not a god—*

He is in bed, she'd drunkenly moaned.

—and you need firsthand proof.

Remembering now, she sighed. The woman standing beside her handed her a tissue, and Annabelle realized that a pesky tear had indeed overflowed to dribble down her cheek. Dammit. She wiped away the tear, then saw that Tag, Noah, and Mark had witnessed the betrayal. Great. Wonderful.

That's what you get for thinking about sex at a funeral.

Death. Life. Procreation. Divorce. Death. Good Lord, she was losing it.

"Excuse me." She turned and threaded her way to the back of the crowd. She needed to move, to walk off some of this nervous-energy edge. Jeremy would understand. The man had understood the ins and outs of explosives—both the physical and emotional kind.

She opened her black umbrella as she stepped from beneath the tent and strode away from the grave site, walking blindly, ruining her shoes in the sopping grass in the process. At some point she grew aware of a presence behind her. She prayed it wasn't Mark.

St. Mary's was a large, old cemetery with ornate monuments and sepulchres that dated back over two hundred years. Under other circumstances, she might have enjoyed exploring the place. Right now, she simply wanted out of here.

The hand on her shoulder told her that wasn't to be. "Hold on, Annabelle."

She halted and turned in relief. "Colonel Warren."

"Are you all right?"

"Yes. I'm fine. I just . . . too much sugar at breakfast, I guess."

He slipped his hand to her elbow and guided her to a covered bench nearby. "I wanted to speak with you and I feared you were leaving. Sit down, please."

Annabelle waited while the colonel took a seat beside her. As usual, he got directly to the point. "Callahan brought me up-to-date with recent events. I'm concerned about the Balkan connection, and I'd like to hear your take on it."

"Balkan connection?"

"Ćurković. Radovanovic."

Annabelle frowned. "Sir, I don't think that situation has anything to do with this one. Mark's brother was kidnapped and killed after the unit disbanded. That syndicate has no reason to move against the Fixers."

"Callahan seems to think it's possible and he believes you might be the catalyst. He mentioned a relatively recent event in Hawaii?"

She ground her teeth, then said, "I was undercover on a job and I have absolutely no reason to believe that my cover was blown. Callahan is paranoid when it comes to the Eastern European Mafia. He doesn't see straight when anything is even tangentially connected to his brother's death. Sir, if we are correct in our assumptions and the unit is being targeted, then the perp is connected in some way to the unit, not the Callahan family. Otherwise, Mark might be burying one of his brothers today instead of Jeremy Russo."

"I hope you are right, Monroe." The colonel blew out a heavy sigh, his lantern jaw set hard as he stared out over the graveyard. "It's bad enough we have to fight the damned drug, gun, and human traffickers in the Balkans. I'd hate to think they are so entrenched that they are killing our people here in America in their own suburban workshops. After they retired! If that's the case, we will never be able to relax our guard."

"Whoever is doing this has a personal grudge, Colonel."

"I tend to agree. However, we can't afford to ignore any possibility. I told Callahan I'd try to find out what Ćurković's heirs have been up to of late. To that end, can you brief me on your involvement with Radovanovic?"

"Certainly, sir."

She took a minute to organize her thoughts, then gave a succinct report of the happenings in Hawaii. After a few follow-up questions, he said, "Hmm . . . as much as I despise the drug runners, I hate the sex traffickers the most. I wish your Italian friend much success in his efforts."

"I'll pass that along next time I talk to him." She expected Paulo to call this afternoon.

Colonel Warren continued. "Now, I intend to stay in contact with the team until this situation is resolved, so you'll be hearing from me. In the meantime, I trust you to be my eyes in the field just in case Callahan is correct. If you uncover even a hint of involvement by Radovanovic, I want to know."

"Yes, sir."

The colonel put his hands on his knees and rose to his feet. "I'd best get back to my wife before she thinks I deserted her. You take care of yourself, Monroe. That's an order. I don't want to attend one of these events for you."

"Yes, sir," she repeated, smiling.

"Are you returning to the grave site or are you staying here?"

Looking past his shoulder, she saw Mark waiting a short distance away, slowly twirling his umbrella. She sighed. "I guess that depends on my team leader."

The colonel frowned. "He looks to have a burr up his butt, doesn't he?"

Annabelle took a closer look. The colonel was right. Anger glimmered in Mark's eyes, and his lips pressed in a grim line. Oh, no. This wasn't good. A sense of dread swept over her as she stepped out into the rain. "What is it?"

"I had a phone call. We have another body. It's Rocky Stanhope."

The colonel muttered a curse, and Annabelle's stomach sank. "What happened?" she asked.

"I'm not sure. A woman he has been seeing called me. She was hysterical. She said that right before he died, he told her to call me rather than the authorities."

"Did this just occur today?"

"I'm not sure. I couldn't get much out of her. We need to leave immediately. I told her we would be there this afternoon."

"Be where?" the colonel asked.

"Colorado," Mark replied. "Stanhope lived—and died—in a mountain town in Colorado."

As his private jet winged its way toward Colorado, Mark decided he didn't have second thoughts about his decision to partner with Annabelle during the investigation. He figured he was going on at least thirty-seven thoughts by now. Never before had he found it so difficult to keep his mind focused on the business at hand.

His team was dying, and instead of concentrating on the data he'd collected overnight as part of his attempt to learn why, his attention kept drifting to the woman who sat on the opposite side of the plane.

They'd both changed clothes for the trip. He wore jeans and a polo. She'd donned jeans and a white oxford shirt. She sat with her legs crossed, subconsciously kicking her foot, which allowed her slip-on canvas flat to slip off her heel and dangle from her toes. It drew his gaze like a magnet. The familiar scent of the lotion she used on her skin teased him, and that little moan of pleasure she made when she indulged in an afternoon piece of chocolate tormented him. As a result, by the time the Citation landed at Telluride Regional Airport, he'd worked his way through only half of his research and he departed the jet feeling grouchy and a little bit mean.

If he didn't get his wits together, he was liable to get them both killed.

He took a look around, pausing a moment to appreciate the majestic beauty of the San Juan Mountains. "I'm not surprised Rocky settled in the mountains. He had a passion for snow skiing, remember? Skiing in the winter and fishing in the summer. The man knew how to live."

"And now he's dead," Annabelle replied.

Mark grimaced. Man, did that suck.

"We have to catch this guy, Callahan."

"We will." He pictured his old teammate as he'd last seen him at Russo's wedding, his head thrown back with laughter at something Anderson had said. "We damn sure will."

The rental car Mark had arranged for was ready and waiting for them. As they climbed in a four-wheel-drive SUV and fastened their seat belts, he handed her a file folder. "Rocky's lady friend owns an art gallery, and she asked us to meet her there. You want to navigate for me?"

Annabelle opened the manila folder and scanned the top page. "Take this road down the hill until it dead-ends at the highway. Turn right."

Mark waited for her to say more, but when that didn't happen, he started the engine and drove out of the parking lot. He should be accustomed to the cold-shoulder treatment by now, since she'd barely spoken to him all day. Annabelle's words and actions toward him had been all business.

At the funeral, she'd spent her time talking to Harrington and Kincannon. During their three-hour plane ride, she'd studied her own research and notes.

He told himself he was glad for it.

He knew he was lying.

They reached the bottom of the hill and he turned onto the highway. Annabelle glanced back at the directions. "Go about three miles into town. Then you'll take another right on Pine. Mercer's gallery will be in the second block."

They were close. Mark felt that familiar buzz of anticipation. Stanhope's girlfriend claimed she might have seen the killer. Aloud, he mused, "We might have caught a break with Brooke Mercer. A physical description of the killer could confirm Rad's involvement."

Annabelle opened her mouth, then reconsidered and shut it without speaking. Annoyed, Mark snapped, "You are underestimating that organization, Annabelle."

"No. I think it is much more logical to believe that whoever is killing off our team members has a grudge against the unit."

Mark rolled down his window to breathe in the fresh mountain air, hoping it would wash away his frustration. He could admit that at times he wasn't exactly reasonable when it came to the likes of Radovanovic, but his family had underestimated the bastards in the past and look how that had turned out. His youngest brother—the only innocent one among them—had paid the ultimate price.

Poor, snakebit John—he'd never caught a break. Being punished for the mistakes of others had turned out to be his lot in life. For instance, he had been an innocent bystander the night his three older brothers got liquored up and carelessly set that god-awful fire. Only thirteen at the time, John hadn't been drinking that night. Instead, he'd tried to stop his older brothers' foolishness and had been rewarded for his efforts by being banished from Brazos Bend just like Mark and Luke and Matt.

At least the old man had sent John to military school rather than wash his hands of him like he had done with his older sons. Well, that's what Mark and his brothers had believed at the time, anyway. Only recently had they discovered that Branch had arranged for someone to be watching over each of them without their knowledge. "Damned manipulative bastard," Mark muttered.

"Excuse me?" Annabelle asked.

"Sorry, I was thinking about something else." He slowed down as they entered the old mining town with its quaint Victorian houses and downtown area. With ski season over and the summer tourist season yet to begin, traffic was sparse on both the road and the sidewalks. "What's the name of the street again?"

"Pine." Her cell phone rang just as she spoke. She checked the number and smiled as she flipped the phone open. "Hi, Mama."

Annabelle held the phone slightly away from her ear, and as a result, Mark heard both sides of the conversation. The first thing her mother asked was when she was coming to Kansas.

"I don't know how long this job will take, Mom, but I promise that the minute I'm finished, I'll head for home."

"What sort of job is it again?" Mrs. Monroe asked. "Your father said something about finding a deadbeat dad? That's not dangerous, is it? You promised me you wouldn't do anything dangerous anymore."

Mark glanced at Annabelle and saw her close her

eyes. "Mother, you don't have to worry. Now, what's the latest with Aunt Polly? Has she given up the idea to run for mayor or is she still causing trouble?"

With that, she successfully distracted her mother, and Mark quit listening quite so closely to the conversation. Locating Pine, he made the right turn and spied the sign for Mercer Gallery in the next block. Despite the lack of tourists in town, parking spaces were at a premium and he drove around a few minutes looking for one while Annabelle finished her call.

"I've gotta go, Mom. I'll call you tomorrow. Yes. Yes. Me, too. I love you." She flipped her phone shut and said, "There's a parking place. Around the corner. See?"

Mark knew he shouldn't comment on the call, and as he made the turn, he tried to keep his trap shut.

He failed.

"Still lying to your mother, I hear," he casually observed.

He could see the torque in her jaw as she gritted her teeth. When she failed to respond, it just egged him on more. "I guess you probably haven't told her about the divorce . . . since you never got around to telling her that we got married."

She whipped her head around and sneered. "That's rich coming from you. Your brothers filled me in on your history. At least I've only kept one spouse secret, not two."

Mark pulled into a parking space, shifted into park, and stifled his smile. It was contrary of him to intentionally annoy her, but dammit, he didn't like being frozen out. "But I didn't lie to my mother. That's a much bigger deal."

She gave him the Annabelle Monroe version of the evil eye. "You seem to have forgotten the discussion we had at the pub, Callahan. You don't get to talk to me about personal things."

Mark switched off the engine and unbuckled his seat belt. "At risk of sounding childish, what are you going to do to stop me?"

Her mouth gaped a bit in disbelief as he pressed on. "If we are going to work as a team, we need to be able to talk to each other. You and I aren't comfortable the way things are, and that could work against us in an emergency situation. It could work against us in this interview if Ms. Mercer senses a problem and holds something back as a result of it."

"I don't believe you." Annabelle shoved an errant lock of hair behind her ear. "Now you're trying to tell me that in order to be a professional, I have to let you into my personal life? You have more nerve than a broken toe, Callahan."

His lips twitched as he opened the SUV's driver's-side door. "Just how is your family doing these days, Belle? Are your sisters still mad because you didn't want to come home and help run the bakery? Did your dad get that heart problem taken care of?"

"I am not talking to you about my family." She yanked at her seat belt and gathered up her purse.

He climbed out of the SUV and waited for her. Sunshine glistened on her hair and distracted him for just a moment. Then she lifted her chin and her snooty attitude got to him. He slipped his hands into his pants pockets and shrugged. "I'm just curious since I gave you my mother's secret muffin recipe to bribe your sisters with, not to mention the fact that I compiled all that research about doctors, procedures, and facilities to help your father make his decision."

She drew a deep breath, then blew it out on a heavy sigh. "Lissa and Amy mostly are over being angry about my choice of career. The lemon muffins sell out every day. Dad had the surgery . . . oh, it's been eighteen months ago now."

"He's doing well?"

"Very well." She hesitated, then added, "Thank you."

Now he couldn't hold back his smile. *That was like pulling teeth.* "You're welcome. I'm glad it all worked out. Whatever happened with that tavern your brother-in-law was thinking about opening? Did he follow through on it?"

She gave him a long look, then surrendered. "Jason opened the Flying Saucer almost a year ago now. It's doing phenomenally well. Adam still works the farm with Dad, and he and his family are all doing well. That catches you up on the Monroes. Now, shouldn't we discuss our interview with Rocky's friend? Do you want to ask the questions or shall I?"

Before he could answer, her cell rang again. She checked the number and smiled. "Paulo! *Pronto.*"

Mark grabbed the phone away from her. "She's working now. She'll have to get back to you."

"Dammit, Callahan!" she exclaimed as he flipped the phone shut.

He continued as if the Italian Stallion had never called. "You take the lead. You know what to ask, and that way if she gives us a description of Radovanovic or one of his goons, you can't say I influenced the description."

"But—"

"Focus, Monroe."

She snapped her mouth shut and nodded. Minutes later, they arrived at the art gallery. Mark noted the CLOSED sign in the window, but tried the door anyway. Locked. The interior of the building looked dark.

He checked his watch. They were well within the time frame he'd given the woman when she called. "I don't have a good feeling about this."

"What time did you tell her to expect us?"

"I gave her a two-hour window. We're right in the middle of it."

Annabelle shielded the sides of her eyes with her hands and peered through the plate glass window. "I see movement. Someone is inside."

Mark rapped on the door loudly. Annabelle said, "Here she comes."

The lock *snick*ed and the door cracked open. "Yes?"

"I'm Mark Callahan. This is my partner, Annabelle Monroe."

"Thank goodness you are finally here." The door swung wide and a woman ushered them inside, then quickly locked the door behind them. She immediately moved to the back of the room.

This was one frightened woman, Mark thought. One drop-dead gorgeous frightened woman, too, he amended when she switched on the track lighting to a soft, low glow. This woman was a classic, classy brunette with angular features, a long, lean build, and a hundred-dollar haircut. She wore black slacks and a gray silk shirt and pearls. He caught a whiff of Chanel and hid his surprise.

She was not what he had expected. The women he'd seen Stanhope go for in the past had been outdoorsy, earth-mother types. "Ms. Mercer?"

"Yes. I'm Brooke. Please call me Brooke. Thank you so much for coming. I've been so afraid. Rocky . . . oh . . . I can't believe . . ." She closed her eyes and her breath gave a little hitch. "I'm just so . . . I don't know. . . ."

Annabelle reached out and gave Brooke Mercer's hand a quick, comforting squeeze. "I know this must be a trying time for you. Rocky was a special man. He had a way of coaxing a smile out of you even under the most difficult circumstances."

"He loved to make me laugh. He loved me and I loved him." She grabbed a tissue from a box on the desk at the back of the gallery and dabbed at her watery brown eyes. "This has been such a nightmare."

"I'm sure it has," Mark agreed.

He waited a bit impatiently for Annabelle to jump right in with questions about Rocky. Instead, she chose to approach the subject slowly. "You have a wonderful space here. Are these local artists?"

"Colorado artists. We like to showcase our own." She managed a wobbly smile. "I have two of Rocky's works. Would you like to see them?"

Annabelle and Mark shared a look of surprise. Then Mark asked, "Rocky painted?"

"Yes, of course. That's how he and I met." She led them around to a side wall where two abstract paintings hung. One was dark and disturbing, a study of shapes. The other was an explosion of color. "He was brilliant."

He was troubled, Mark realized, recognizing the import of the gold chain depicted in the painting on the left. He glanced at Annabelle and saw that she had made the connection, too. On the team's last mission in the field, their Pakistani mountain guide had been a thirteen-year-old boy with a ready smile and an unpronounceable name. Since his most prized possession was the gold-link necklace he'd worn around his neck, everyone called him Goldie. Goldie liked to laugh, throw a football with Stanhope, and eat chocolate.

One night he disappeared from camp. They came across a headless body nailed to a tree two days later. They recognized the boots and the gold necklace.

Stanhope never got over it.

"If the paintings are still for sale, I'd like to buy this one," Mark said, deciding on the spur of the moment. "The colorful one."

Brooke Mercer's face registered surprise, but she nodded. "Yes, of course. I'm sure Rocky would like that."

She named a price that Mark considered fair and he peeled off hundred-dollar bills from his money clip,

then withdrew a card from his wallet and handed it
to her. "Call this number and ask for Frank McGee.
He will give you a purchase-order number and the
shipping address for my condo in Jackson Hole."

He noted curiosity quickly banked in Annabelle's
gaze. He'd bought the Wyoming mountain home since
they'd split. In fact, he'd bought three vacation places
since the divorce was final. Luke's wife, Maddie, said
there was a message in that for him, but he didn't
see it.

"Perhaps we could ask you a few questions now?"
Annabelle inquired.

"Yes, of course. Let's move to the back. I'd rather
we not be interrupted."

She led the way into a small office at the back of
the building. She moved behind a Queen Anne desk
and gestured for them to take seats in the chairs on
the opposite side. A crystal water pitcher and a selec-
tion of soft drinks sat on a credenza behind her. She
nodded toward it and asked, "Would you care for
something to drink?"

They declined and the art dealer took a seat across
from them. She folded her hands and met first Annabelle's, then Mark's gaze. "I know you've traveled a
long way to ask me questions, but I need to ask you
a few things first. Rocky directed me to do this as he
lay dying."

His former colleague's caution didn't surprise Mark.
He expected Ms. Mercer to request proof of identity—
a piece of knowledge rather than a driver's license.
Instead, Brooke Mercer asked, "In the past three
months, has either of you been contacted by another
member of your team?"

Mark pursed his lips. The arch of Annabelle's brows
signaled her surprise. She asked, "What sort of
contact?"

"Any sort. Phone calls, e-mails, personal visits— anything."

"No, I haven't," Mark told her. "Not prior to Russo's funeral, anyway."

"I spoke to Melanie Anderson a couple months ago," Annabelle shared.

Interest lit the other woman's dark eyes. She didn't appear quite as fragile as she'd looked a few moments before. Leaning forward, she said, "You did? Please tell me about the conversation."

"She called me on my birthday," Annabelle responded with a shrug. "We've exchanged birthday calls for years. I don't recall anything unusual about the conversation. What are you looking for?"

"A message," Brooke Mercer replied. "Did she perhaps mention any other team members? Maybe she was in contact with one of the others?"

Annabelle thought for a moment, then shook her head. "Not that I recall."

Mark's patience had run thin. He hadn't rushed to Telluride to face the third degree and be told nothing in return. Annabelle might be willing to let this drag on for hours, but he wasn't. "I'm a little lost here. What is it Rocky told you to do before he died? How did he die? What did you see?"

The gallery owner winced. "Just bear with me another minute, please? I have one more question. Have you been contacted by anyone outside of the team regarding current activities of team members?"

"No," Mark snapped. "Now, what is this about?"

Brooke Mercer stared at Annabelle until she shook her head. "No, I haven't, either." Annabelle's voice took on a familiar note of steel. "Please, Ms. Mercer. Talk to us."

Just as Mark was ready to lose his patience and say something he shouldn't, the woman visibly reached a decision and nodded. "I believe you. You are not connected to this. Rocky suspected as much—that's why he gave me your number to call, Mr. Callahan—but he made me promise to question your involvement before I told you his story."

She drew in a deep breath, then blew it out in a rush. "I guess I should start with the phone call. Your phone call, Ms. Monroe."

"I didn't reach Rocky."

"No. We were away for a few days camping and he listened to your message when we returned. He was going to call you after dinner. Then he received another call. It was from another one of your team members."

"Which one?" Annabelle asked.

"I don't know. Rocky didn't say. He went out for a long walk and when he came back, he sat down at the computer, wrote for a while, then printed his work." A sad smile flickered on her face. "It was the first time I ever heard him grumble about not having Internet access at the cabin."

Mark had a dozen questions on his tongue, but he held them back. This woman would tell her story at her own pace, and then he'd give Annabelle a go at her. What he'd told his partner on the way here was true. He didn't want to influence Brooke Mercer's responses.

"Rocky said we needed to go to town. I went upstairs to shower and change. I had been upstairs twenty minutes or so when I heard the car. I glanced out the window and that's when I saw him."

The killer? Mark tensed and leaned forward. Annabelle placed her hand on his knee and squeezed a silent warning to keep quiet.

The art dealer closed her eyes and lifted a trembling hand to smooth back her hair. "He appeared ordinary. A man in a T-shirt, jeans, and sneakers. I thought he was a tourist who had taken a wrong turn and needed directions. I turned away from the window and went back into the bathroom to put on my makeup."

She paused and licked her lips. "I never heard the gunshot. Never heard Rocky cry out. Never heard the car leave. When I went downstairs, he was lying on the floor. Blood was everywhere."

Now a tear spilled from her eye and trailed slowly down her cheek. "He told me to call you and not the police. He said you would know what to do. He told me to leave him lying there just like he was and to hurry back to town. I wasn't to talk to anyone until you arrived. Then I was supposed to ask you all those questions. He said you'd understand why."

Mark sat back in his chair. His old friend had been wrong as hell about that.

"What about the killer?" Annabelle asked. "Did Rocky give you a name?"

"No! I asked, but he never answered that."

Annabelle glanced at Mark. "This doesn't make sense to me. If the shooter were one of us, why not say his name? If he wasn't one of us, why bother with those questions?"

Mark shook his head. He didn't have a clue.

Annabelle thought for a moment longer before asking, "Then what happened, Ms. Mercer?"

The art dealer closed her eyes. Swallowed hard. "He died. My Rocky just lay there and died."

Mark couldn't hold his tongue *and* sit still, so he shoved to his feet and paced the small office. Annabelle waited a respectful moment, then said, "Rocky Stanhope deserved better, Brooke. His killer needs to be brought to justice. With your help, Mark and I will make sure that happens."

"I know you will try, but . . . ." She shrugged.

"We don't fail," Mark said. "We *won't* fail."

Annabelle nodded her agreement, then continued. "So, what did you do next?"

The art dealer laced her fingers atop the desk, clasping them so hard that her knuckles turned white. "I covered him with a blanket. I know he said not to touch anything, but I couldn't just leave him that way. I couldn't! Then I ran to the car and drove home. I had blood all over me and I needed to get it off."

"Of course you did," Annabelle said in a soothing tone.

Brooke Mercer shuddered. "I was so frightened. I didn't know what to do, whether to call you like he'd asked or to call the police. I worried that the killer had seen me and would come after me. I sat in my house all night thinking about it, trying to decide what to do." Tears swam in the eyes she lifted toward them. "Last night was the worst night of my life."

"It's terrible you had to go through that." Annabelle gave the woman's hands a comforting pat. "But you know what? The worst is behind you now. Mark and I will take care of everything."

"Thank you. Thank you so much." She blew out a heavy breath. "I should have called you from the cabin. I'm sorry I hesitated. At first I couldn't think. Then all I did was think and I got confused."

Mark cleared his throat. "I would have done the same thing."

"Now," Annabelle said, her voice brisk and businesslike, "I'd like to ask you a few questions. First, let's talk about the killer. Was he inside the car when you saw him, or outside?"

For the next ten minutes, Annabelle took the woman through her story in a thorough, yet gentle, interrogation. Mark admired her effort. His ex-wife had a deft touch in this respect. She knew just when to be tough and when to cajole. She pulled much more out of Brooke Mercer than he would have managed.

As a detailed picture of events began to emerge, Mark's spirits lightened. They had a place to start—

Stanhope's computer. The document he'd printed and left in his hidden safe at the cabin. His phone records. And Ms. Mercer herself.

Annabelle reached into her tote and withdrew the envelope filled with photographs that Mark had requested before leaving Philadelphia. Mark braced himself as she handed the art dealer the stack of photos that had been waiting for them along with the rental car. "Could one of these men be the man you saw outside of Rocky's cabin?"

Brooke Mercer worked her way through the pictures that included the other nine Fixers, Colonel Warren, Boris Radovanovic, and a half dozen random, unrelated faces. "I don't think so, no."

He let out a breath he hadn't realized he'd been holding. While Ms. Mercer had not ruled out the possibility that someone in the unit had turned on his former teammates, she hadn't confirmed it, either. And despite the fact that he had included Rad's photo, he never really expected her to finger that bastard. Radovanovic would have sent goons to do his dirty work.

Annabelle glanced at Mark. "Do you have anything to add?"

He gazed out into the gallery toward Stanhope's paintings. "Do you have a clue why he wanted you to contact me instead of the police? Is there anything up at the cabin I'll need to . . . sanitize . . . before we call in the authorities?"

"You mean . . . anything illegal?" Mercer asked. "No. However, in his studio you'll find one stack of paintings that might concern you. They are graphic, and I recognized some of the faces you just showed me from that stack of paintings." She paused and added, "Actually, I recognized you both from the paintings."

Mark arched a questioning brow, but she shook her

head. "They are something you will have to see. I can't really describe them."

With that, she pulled a piece of paper from the desk drawer and rose to her feet. "You had best be going if you want to make it up the mountain and back down by dark. Here are directions, and the combination to the safe I told you about. You shouldn't have any trouble finding the cabin."

"You're not going with us?" Annabelle asked. "The police will need to interview you. They won't like it that you called us instead of them."

She nervously smoothed her slacks. "I realize that, but this is a small town. They know me and they know where to find me. They'll understand that I was hysterical yesterday and can't bear to go back up there today."

"Can't say that I blame you," Mark said, taking the map and giving it a quick once-over. "Thank you for your help."

"Just find the person who did this." A lone tear spilled down her cheek and she impatiently wiped it away. "I don't want Rocky to have died in vain."

"Neither do we," Annabelle assured her.

They shook hands, then departed the gallery. Mark heard the door lock behind them. He and Annabelle didn't speak as they returned to the rental SUV. Once they were inside, he slipped the key into the ignition, glanced at her, and asked, "Well, what do you think?"

"What do I think?" Annabelle repeated, her tone dripping with scorn. "I don't think. I know. That woman was lying like a rug."

Chapter Six

Annabelle expected him to scoff. After all, Brooke Mercer was a beautiful woman, and Annabelle hadn't missed the flash of male appreciation in her ex-husband's eyes when he first met the gallery owner. She waited for him to dismiss her suspicions out of hand, especially since instincts alone had led her to her conclusion. Instead, Mark surprised her.

"She did go from hysteria to calm pretty damned fast," he observed after he'd started the car and pulled back onto the main street.

"Too fast." Annabelle wordlessly declined the mint he offered. "That woman did not have a loved one die in her arms yesterday. I don't care how pretty you are—that shows up on your face."

"So what are you saying? She didn't love Stanhope or she is making the whole thing up?" Mark popped a peppermint in his mouth.

Annabelle idly wondered when he'd gotten himself hooked on hard candy. "Her story rang true. Her tears and sorrowful expressions appeared genuine. Still, I didn't pick up vibes of grief. If anything, I thought a time or two that she was coming on to you. Her body language raised my hackles."

Mark opened his mouth, then abruptly shut it. Annabelle realized she'd fed him a straight line, and that he'd been smart enough not to take advantage of it.

They drove for a time, each of them lost in thought until Mark observed, "Stanhope liked the ladies, but she wasn't his type."

"He liked the girl-next-door," Annabelle agreed. "Friendly and outgoing. Brooke Mercer is beautiful, but she's a little too . . . upscale. I picture him doing business with her, but dating the lady who runs the saltwater-taffy shop."

Mark slowed the vehicle in order to turn off the main highway, then handed her Brooke Mercer's hand-drawn map so she could continue her navigator's job. "It was probably just sex."

"That's what I think," Annabelle agreed. "But I can see how the role of tragic lover left behind would appeal to that woman."

Mark arched a brow. "Didn't care for her much, did you?"

"She wasn't mourning my friend."

With that, Annabelle turned her attention to the surroundings. Their path had taken them out of the box canyon that nestled the town of Telluride and up a twisting, turning narrow mountain road that provided stunning views.

Annabelle gazed at the craggy, snowcapped peaks and realized she'd missed these mountains. During her childhood, her best friend had invited Annabelle along on her family vacations to Colorado. She'd looked forward to that one summer week for the entire fifty-one others. She'd often thought that it was the trips to the Rockies that had instilled within her the need to see and do and experience. That need had eventually pulled Annabelle away from the family farm and small-town life and steered her into the military.

Now as her ears popped with their ascent, she found herself wanting to share the thoughts with Mark. She couldn't do it, however, because that would mean cracking open a door she'd intended to leave shut for good.

Of course, when she'd formed her intentions, she didn't anticipate traveling with him alone in the middle of nowhere on their way to face the body of a man they had once considered a good friend.

Maybe under these circumstances, I could relax a little, she thought as she guided him through a series of turns that took them down one hill and up the next. What would hurt? A little conversation might make this trip easier to bear.

Besides, opening her mouth differed from opening her heart. That wasn't in danger of happening.

Neither would she open her bedroom door. She wasn't stupid. Anxious, yes. Maybe even a little nervous. Not stupid. Never stupid.

God, she hoped she wasn't stupid.

She cleared her throat and attempted to distract herself from her thoughts by observing, "The word 'remote' doesn't do Rocky's place justice."

"I'd hate to have to take this road in the dark."

Annabelle caught a glimpse of a sapphire blue lake below them. "I had a chance to buy a house on a hill above Honolulu, but the hairpin curves changed my mind. So much of the work I do is at night."

He nodded and pursed his lips. A moment later he asked, "Why Hawaii?"

"What do you mean?"

"Why did you pick Honolulu as the place to build your business? Last time you and I talked about it, I thought you were thinking about Dallas or Denver or Oklahoma City—somewhere closer to your family.

Picking Hawaii, you might as well have kept Europe as your home base."

Great. She should have kept her mouth shut instead of taking a stab at conversation. Right away, he jumped in a direction she didn't want to go. "I decided to take up surfing. So, who do you pick to win the World Series this year?"

He slanted her a look that said he knew she was dodging the question, but thankfully didn't pursue it. Instead, they talked baseball, then eased into college football until she spied a national-forest sign. "Okay, that's it. We're entering the little stretch of private land. The turnoff to Rocky's place will be on the left. It's marked by a—"

Mark laughed. "Bullwinkle. Damn, I'm going to miss that man."

Annabelle glanced up to see an eight-foot-tall plastic cartoon character standing beside a narrow dirt road. "Okay, that makes me want to cry."

Mark turned onto the path that snaked through the forest of conifers and aspen. The tall trees all but blocked the sun, casting shadows that swallowed the car and turned the atmosphere eerie. Almost ominous. Annabelle peered into the trees, looking for elk or deer or Bigfoot. Maybe zombies or some creature created by Stephen King.

The map indicated they were getting close. Dread sat in her stomach like a fried pie. She had encountered her share of bodies over the years, but never that of an old friend who had died violently and aged for a day in a cabin in the middle of nowhere.

The SUV clattered over a small wooden bridge that stretched across a bubbling mountain stream into a clearing about a half acre in size. A two-story wooden cabin nestled against the side of a mountain. "Fishing in his front yard," Mark observed. "Bet Rocky was happy as a clam up here."

Mark stopped the SUV just beyond the bridge, avoiding the two sets of tire tracks leading to and from the cabin. He didn't need to tell Annabelle that he did it to avoid further contaminating the crime scene.

"At least it didn't rain last night or this morning. The locals will be unhappy enough as it is." He gave Annabelle a sidelong glance. "You ready for this?"

"Not really. Are you?"

"Hell, no."

With that, they both started forward.

The stench of death hit her before they ever reached the door. She spied what must have been Brooke Mercer's bloody shoe prints along with some sort of animal tracks on the wooden porch in front of the door, and Annabelle sent up a silent prayer of thanks that the woman had shut the door behind her. This would be hard enough as it was. If animals had gotten to Rocky . . . she shuddered. She simply didn't want to think about it.

Mark opened the door and they stepped into the cabin, where a red and blue plaid blanket covered the body on the floor. Annabelle instinctively wanted to hold her breath, but training taught her to breathe naturally, since the stench would numb her sense of smell after a few minutes.

She started to follow Mark toward the body, but he held up a hand. "Why don't you take the safe."

"Chivalry in action, Callahan?"

He gave a wry smile. "I know better than that with you, Annabelle. No, I think, knowing Stanhope, he'd prefer you didn't see him this way."

Not chivalrous, but sensitive. And right. Rocky always tempered his language and maintained his privacy around the female members of the team. "I'll head upstairs."

Brooke Mercer had given them the combination to Rocky's safe and told them they'd find it in the attic

studio behind a painting of Telluride's Bridal Veil
Falls. Annabelle climbed the stairs to a room brilliant
with afternoon sunshine.

Windows lined both the eastern and western walls,
offering views beautiful enough to give Hawaii a run
for its money. Paintings filled the space on the north
and south walls—landscapes, still lifes, portraits of
both people and animals. Furnishing the studio were
an antique chaise lounge, two ladder-back chairs, and
a rocker. The air smelled of turpentine, and multicolored paint flecks splattered the wooden floor.

This was a side of Rocky Stanhope she'd never
known existed.

Giving the walls a second look, Annabelle spied the
painting of the falls. She pulled the slip of paper con-
taining the combination from her pocket, but before
she moved toward the safe, a canvas propped upon
an easel set to catch the morning light snagged her
attention.

It was a portrait of an infant—a fat little cherub
with blue eyes and blond hair and a single tooth. Her
heart gave a twist. "Oh, Rocky," she murmured.
"With all this talent, why did you ever join the army?"

Next her gaze caught a stack of paintings leaning
against the wall. They were the Fixer paintings the art
dealer had mentioned, and they, too, diverted Annabelle from her task. There were five of them—three
depicting incidents in Bosnia, one in the jungles of
Brazil, one in the sands of Oman.

"We need to take these with us," she murmured.
These particular paintings should remain classified for
the time being.

That thought dragged her back to the business at
hand, and she crossed the studio to the waterfall painting. Shifting one corner to see behind it, she spied the
metal face of the safe. She lifted the painting off its
hook and propped it against the wall at her feet. She

double-checked the combination and reached for the dial. Mark's sharp, urgent voice stopped her.

"Stop! Don't touch that, Belle."

"What's wrong?"

"I found another body. A woman. She's in his bedroom. I think she had just finished showering before she died. She's wearing a towel."

"What? That doesn't make sense."

His gaze met hers, his emerald eyes diamond hard. "It does if she's the real Brooke Mercer, and you and I had tea with a killer."

Annabelle froze. "No."

"The woman in the bedroom is the girl-next-door. Think about it, Belle."

Rocky's type. Annabelle's mind whirled and she spoke aloud as she thought it through. "That woman was the shooter? Why would the killer meet us? . . . Oh. All those questions. She wanted to find out what we knew."

"That's the way I see it."

Annabelle stared at the portrait of the child without really seeing it. "But why send us out here? She had to know we'd find the second body and figure her out." Then, before he could respond, she made the connection. "She didn't care. We're not supposed to leave here alive."

Mark nodded toward the safe. "Remember the explosion in Russo's shop."

"You think the safe is rigged to explode?"

"It makes sense. This second body casts doubt on everything that woman said. Her call lured us to Colorado. Meeting us at the gallery to ask her questions, then sending us here gives her plenty of time to get away even if we did call the authorities before we opened the safe."

"Which she set us up to do with her story about what Rocky said and did," Annabelle mused.

Mark studied the safe. "Nothing is obvious, but then, it wouldn't be. This operation isn't being run by a fool—or fools. They've taken down at least four of us already—if not more."

Annabelle's teeth tugged at her lower lip. "She could have some connection with the Fixers. It doesn't have to be more than one person."

"Or we could be under siege by a team. You know whose team I'd put at the top of the list."

She set her teeth against a sigh. She refused to voice Rad's name.

"Stanhope didn't die yesterday, either," Mark continued. "Neither of them did. The bodies aren't that fresh."

"We need to ID the woman we met today."

"Yeah, but something tells me her prints won't show up either here or in the gallery."

"Unless we're wrong and she really *was* Rocky's girlfriend." She looked into Mark's troubled eyes. "We need to call the locals. They'll know if this dead woman is Brooke Mercer or not."

"Yep."

"But if we *are* wrong, bringing them in before we've accessed the message Rocky supposedly left for you might cause us some grief."

"I think that's a chance we have to take. I also doubt any message from Stanhope exists."

Annabelle nodded her agreement as Mark pulled his cell phone from his pocket and checked the service. "Nothing. And the landline is out. Lovely. Just freakin' lovely."

"If we're going back to town, let's recon these first." She gestured toward the stack of paintings that depicted the unit. Mark glanced through them, and whistled softly. "It's like being there all over again."

He handed her a painting to carry, then took a second look as he picked up another one. "Whoa. This one's not a canvas." He checked the back. "No wonder it's so heavy. Looks like steel." Of the remaining three, one other was a painted metal sheet. He waggled his brows hopefully. "You want to carry them?"

She rolled her eyes, knowing from experience that his Texas good-old-boy upbringing wouldn't allow it.

He handed her the three regular canvases, then hoisted the other two and exited the studio. Annabelle detoured into the master bedroom to check the woman's body for herself. Seeing the freckled-face woman—definitely Rocky's type—who'd died wearing only a towel and an expression of surprise stirred her anger. "This just has to stop."

She continued downstairs, where she paused at Rocky Stanhope's blanket-covered body. "We'll find out who did this, Rock," she said softly. "I promise."

Annabelle's heart was heavy as she stepped out onto the porch and took a grateful gulp of fresh air. Mark set his burden down long enough to fish the keys from the pocket of his jeans. He let out a grunt as he lifted the paintings once again, then started down the porch steps. Annabelle followed behind him, slightly to the right.

The same instant she heard the gunshot, pain zinged across her left arm.

Shit.

Even as he felt the round hit the steel plate in his hands, experience and training had Mark reacting instinctively. He processed their situation in an instant. Shooter in the trees to his left. The paintings shielded him, but Annabelle was vulnerable. He stepped between her and the line of fire.

"Get down and stay behind me," he ordered even as more shots rang out and pinged against the paintings. He couldn't draw his weapon without dropping the shield.

Annabelle didn't have that problem. "On your right," she said, then fired a shot toward the trees. "Go go go!"

She fired twice more as they dashed for the cover of the car. There, crouched by the front grille, he set down the paintings and reached for his own gun. "You okay?"

"Winged."

He whipped his head around. Red blood stained her white sleeve. He took it like a punch to his gut. "Goddamn . . . how bad is it?"

"Just a scratch. Did you see anything?

"Not really. Trees are too thick. I placed one shooter at ten o'clock. You?"

"Same." Annabelle touched her bloody arm and winced. "Do you think it's her?"

He knew she meant the woman from the gallery. "I don't know. This is sloppy. Why would she follow us up here? Why didn't she do us in the gallery? Hell, we were sitting ducks for her."

"Maybe she wanted just one kill spot. As remote as this place is, it could be weeks before anyone found us."

Annabelle had a point. If he had been carrying regular canvases instead of steel ones, the shooter would have gotten her heart shot. Or if Annabelle had walked out in front of him, she would have suffered more than a graze.

Mark went cold inside at the thought. "Screw this. Cover me."

He started to rise, but Annabelle grabbed his shirt and held on. "Wait. Get a grip, Callahan. There could be a team out there. You could be right and Radovanovic could be waiting for you! Don't be stupid. You're never stupid. What's wrong with you?"

The feelings of frustration that had been simmering inside Mark ever since he'd received the phone call

from Russo's wife heated to a boil. "Be damned if
you die on my watch, Belle."

"Oh, for God's sake." She whacked him on the side
of the head. "Don't go Texan on me now."

Mark scowled at her. "Well, we can't stay here like
this. The murdering bitch is probably working her way
through the trees for a better angle right now!"

"Then let's get into the car and drive out of here."

Mark contemplated her suggestion. He hated running when he was the one doing the chasing, but
maybe if they considered it a strategic retreat . . .

"There is only one way down this mountain," he
mused. "We could pick our ground."

"Now you're thinking."

He readied the door key. "Cover me."

This time she didn't argue. But even as she flexed
her muscles to rise, another round of gunshots rang
out. Six . . . eight shots from a position just to the
left of where they had come from earlier. Mark and
Annabelle glanced at each other, then smoothly
switched into team mode.

"One, two, three," she said, rising and firing toward
the spot where the shots originated.

Mark scrambled toward the driver's-side door, noting the flat tire on the back wheel. Damn. He took
half a second to check the other back wheel. Flat, too.
Dammit to hell.

All right, change in plan. His mind raced as he
slipped the key into the ignition. They wouldn't get
far on two flat tires, but they could get out of range
long enough to regroup and develop a strategy. He
cranked the key and the engine fired. He motioned
for Annabelle to join him.

Instead, she held up her hand, palm out. "Listen.
That's a car. She's leaving!"

Mark followed her lead and listened intently. Annabelle was right. Sound carried in the hills, and a vehi-

cle of some sort was hauling ass down the mountain. Nevertheless, the moment still called for caution. "Go ahead and get in the car, Belle."

"I think the tires are flat."

"I know the tires are flat. We're only going around behind the house."

Keeping low, Annabelle made her way around to the door behind Mark and climbed into the car. "I think she was alone. I think she decided that since she'd lost the element of surprise, she couldn't take us out. She shot out the tires to give herself time to get away."

"Yeah," Mark agreed, dragging his gaze away from her bloody shirt as he put the car in gear. "Let's give it a few minutes to make sure, though."

He maneuvered the car around behind Stanhope's cabin, then switched off the engine. "Back door?"

"Sure."

"Let's go." He exited the car and covered her while she dashed toward the cabin.

Annabelle tried the doorknob and found it locked, so she used the butt of her gun to break a glass pane, then reached inside and flipped the dead bolt. Seconds later, they entered the cabin's kitchen.

Mark did his best to ignore the scent of death that hung on the air as silence settled around them. Slowly, the tension inside Mark eased and he let out a long breath.

He felt like an idiot for having walked into an ambush. Last time he'd managed that dumb move, he'd been in a jungle in Jakarta. "This is the craziest damned situation. . . ."

"My knees feel like Jell-O." Annabelle smiled wryly and added, "It's been a long time since I've been under fire."

"Let's have a look at your arm."

Annabelle glanced down at her left sleeve and winced. "It didn't hurt until you reminded me of it, Callahan. Thanks."

She tugged at her sleeve, trying to yank it above the wound, but the cuff made that difficult. She hesitated, darted him a look, and muttered, "Wonderful."

She turned her back to him, worked the buttons on her shirt, and slipped it off. Mark couldn't look away from the delicious sight of her peach-colored bra against the tanned skin of her long, lean back. He recalled smoothing his hand across that skin, trailing his tongue down the indentation of her spine. His fingers itched to touch her once again.

Then his gaze settled on the angry red slash across the side of her arm, and anger chased away the lust. "That's ugly."

"Gee, thanks." She twisted her head to look as he stepped toward the cabinets and hunted in drawers for a clean dish towel. Finding one, he dampened it with water from the kitchen faucet, then gently took her arm. "C'mere."

He cleaned away the blood and his worry eased. "You were right. It's just a scratch."

She scowled at him. "It hurts."

Her skin smelled of peaches and he wondered if she chose her lotion to match her bra. "You've had worse from a tree branch." He touched an old scar on her shoulder. "Remember?"

It had been the one time they'd crossed the line while teammates, an event they'd never mentioned even during the time they were together.

The insertion into Uzbekistan took place back in 2000. As they'd parachuted in on a moonless night, Annabelle got caught in a crosswind that carried her into a grove of olive trees. Ordering the others ahead toward the target, Mark delayed to cut her down.

Upon hearing her suck in a breath, he'd discovered the wicked, two-inch tear in the skin above her collarbone from a branch.

He'd cleaned and bandaged the wound, then done something totally unprofessional and totally out of character for him. He had leaned over and kissed it better.

Caught up in the memory, he bent his head to repeat the action. Annabelle swayed, closed her eyes, and shuddered. "Don't, Mark. Please."

Her voice broke the spell. He let go of her arm and stepped away. Clearing his throat, he said, "I'll go look for a bandage. He's bound to have some in his bathroom."

"Thanks."

Mark exited the kitchen and headed straight for the stairs, avoiding the great room, where his friend's body lay, and using the time to wrestle his thoughts back under control. Being with Annabelle was playing havoc with his head. He needed to focus on matters at hand—like how they'd get off this damned mountain with their car out of commission.

He found a tube of antibiotic cream, a bottle of aspirin, and a box of Band-Aids in Stanhope's bathroom medicine cabinet. Returning to the kitchen, he impersonally treated the gash and never once took a look at her breasts.

Okay, maybe he sneaked one quick look, but she didn't catch him at it.

He turned away as she slipped her injured arm back into her blouse, and scanned the kitchen for a key rack. "Stanhope has a truck in his garage. You want to help me look for the keys?"

"Sure." Her manner was crisp and businesslike, and the sexual tension that had hummed between them seeped away.

At least, that's what he told himself.

She located keys in the mudroom, and they entered the garage. Mark eyed the ceiling and spied the automatic door opener. Good. That made this just a little easier. They'd been inside for less than five minutes and he did believe the shooter had decamped, but he'd rather be ready to roll the minute the door lifted just in case.

They climbed into their seats; then he asked, "You ready?"

"Yes. Definitely. I've had all this place I care for."

"Me, too." He motioned toward the garage-door remote hanging on the visor. "When I say go, hit that button."

He turned the key, and the motor . . . clicked. He tried again. Nothing. Gritting his teeth, he yanked the hood release and climbed out of the car. When he opened the hood, he let out a string of curses. The hoses and exposed wires had all been cut.

Annabelle walked up beside him. "This truck isn't going anywhere, is it?"

"Not anytime soon."

"Lovely. Just wonderful." She blew out a heavy breath, then glanced back toward the door that led into the cabin. "Callahan, I'm not spending the night here. Not with two dead bodies."

"Won't have to. We have a spare and so does Rocky."

Twenty minutes later as Mark tightened the lug nuts on the second wheel, Annabelle said, "Uh . . . Callahan? Something's dripping. Look."

He rolled back on his heels and looked toward where she pointed. His stomach sank. "Brake fluid. Bullet must have nicked the line."

"We can't drive down this mountain without brakes," Annabelle said, stating the obvious. "Can you fix it?"

Mark stared at the plate-sized puddle on the ground

and considered the hairpin turns that awaited them. "I could jury-rig something, but I don't know that I'm willing to trust our lives to it. We're better off hiking down the mountain."

Annabelle pursed her lips. "We won't make it before dark. We'll have to camp."

"Rocky is sure to have equipment we can use."

"All right, then. Let's do it. Honestly, after the past few days, a walk in the woods sounds like heaven."

Heaven? Mark smothered a snort. Obviously, the woman hadn't thought it through. They wouldn't make it down the mountain before dark. They'd have to camp overnight. Just the two of them, all alone, beneath a starry sky. He and his ex-wife. Emphasis on the *ex*.

It would be a long, lonely night.

Sounded like hell to him.

Chapter Seven

Two hours into the hike, Annabelle paused and re-arranged the pack on her back. It was a man-sized rig and didn't fit her properly, so the weight kept shifting. She rolled her shoulders, then murmured, "At least it's mostly downhill."

"And we don't appear to have a gunman on our asses," Mark responded.

Thank God for that. She'd had all the gunfire she wanted for today, thank you very much. And while she wished she had a pack that fit, her comment was more whine than complaint. A blue sky stretched above them, the temperature hovered in the fifties, and Mark had found insect repellent with the camping supplies, so she didn't have to worry about chiggers. Her bullet wound stung slightly, but didn't really bother her. All in all, she considered herself a lucky woman.

Shortly after leaving the cabin, Mark had found the spot where the shooter had parked her car. Footprints in the dirt pegged her as a woman and 9mm shell casings suggested they had indeed found their assail-ant. Confirming that the shooter had left the immediate area had taken a huge weight off Annabelle's shoulders.

The exercise and clean mountain air had proved to be just what she'd needed to shake off the tension that lingered following the day's events. The farther they traveled from Rocky's cabin, the lighter her mood grew.

Annabelle was an outdoor girl at heart. She still liked hiking and fishing and cooking over a campfire. Between their own suitcases in the SUV and the supplies they'd found in Rocky's cabin, they had managed to equip themselves quite well for the hike back to civilization. The idea of spending the night in the woods sleeping in a tent didn't bother her in the least.

Well, except for the fact that they had only one tent.

One small tent.

That's okay, she told herself, trying to think positively as she stopped to observe a pair of squirrels scampering from tree to tree. After all, the side of a mountain wasn't a hotel. Hotels were what got her and Mark in trouble. They needed a bed to be bad. Or at least a wall. A shower. A bathtub. A floor. A beach. She'd never forget that night on the private beach in New Zealand.

They wouldn't be sleeping on a white sand beach tonight. They would be sleeping on dirt. Moist, rich, fertile soil.

Fertile. Annabelle frowned and scowled at Mark Callahan's back. All of a sudden she didn't feel so chipper.

They continued their march down the mountain, mostly following the road, but taking a wilder route upon occasion as they headed toward what they both recalled as being the closest sign of life—a ranch house positioned a little more than halfway between Telluride and Rocky's cabin.

Every fifteen minutes or so, Mark dragged his cell phone from his pocket and looked for a signal. Annabelle knew he was wasting his time. She also knew better than to point that out.

The man was acting strange. Jittery. Antsy. Similar behavior in another man would earn the term "nervous." Mark Callahan didn't get nervous, so what was up with him? Did he know something she didn't? Was he hiding something important from her?

Or was he suffering from the same malady as she? Was he thinking about the coming night? Remembering all the nights gone by?

Was Mark Callahan being led down the hill by the divining rod in his pants? Or, to use one of his terms, the Top Gun? The Heavy Artillery? The Seven-Star General?

"Why is it that men feel compelled to name their penises?" she muttered.

A short distance in front of her, Mark tripped over a rock. "What did you say?"

"It's just stupid. It's childish." And it had nothing to do with that old joke about men wanting to be on a first-name basis with the brain that made most of their decisions.

"Do you need to stop, Annabelle?" He watched her warily.

"I'm fine."

"Are you drinking your water?"

"I'm *fine.*"

He scowled at her, but kept on walking.

Annabelle followed along behind him, trying to regain her pleasure in the day. Curse him for being antsy. Curse him for making her think about his penis. Curse him for making her think about how lonely she'd been since that day in New York.

She frowned at his back, then got distracted by his buns. The man did wonders to a pair of jeans.

You'd better find a cold mountain stream to dunk yourself in before you go off and do something stupid.

Like have sex with your ex.

Luckily, Mark paused in the trek long enough to make an observation that jerked her mind back where it belonged. "You know, Annabelle, I've been thinking. Rocky and the woman were killed with a forty-five. The shots fired at us were nine-millimeter. What if we're dealing with two different shooters here?"

"You don't think the woman from the gallery killed Rocky?"

"I don't know. I'm just thinking aloud. If Radovanovic—"

"Stop!" She wanted to scream, but instead she put her hands on her hips and declared, "You are trying to fit a square Croat into a round hole. Quit trying to force Boris Radovanovic into these crimes."

"Okay, forget Rad. I'm just wondering, why use such a different methodology for these murders than with Russo and the others?"

"What do you mean?"

"Someone went to a lot of effort to make Russo's death look like an accident. Anderson's 'suicide' and Hart's climbing accident—those were subtle takedowns."

"Nothing subtle about what we found at Rocky's cabin."

"Exactly. This shooter committed out-and-out murder and included a nonteam member to boot. It would have been fairly easy to make Stanhope's death look like murder-suicide or a lovers' triangle gone bad, but this killer didn't even try. It's different from the others. Why?"

"Because the killer knows we've made the connection to the team, so now he's in a hurry." Annabelle stepped carefully over a fallen log. "Or maybe Stanhope's killing isn't connected to the others."

"No, they're connected. Otherwise, why the interview at the gallery? Look. I believe the team is being targeted by either someone with a grudge or someone who thinks we know something they don't want us to know."

Annabelle had reached that conclusion, too. "I agree."

"But what if it's both?"

"Two killers?" She gave a pinecone lying on the forest floor a kick. "That's a stretch, Callahan. Kinda like Rad being one of the players here."

Mark shifted his backpack to redistribute the weight, then continued. "I know it's a stretch. This theory might be all wet, but as we look into the other deaths and disappearances, I think we should keep it in the back of our minds. If we have one killer and the killer is the woman from the gallery, then why all the questions?"

"Maybe she asked the others questions before she killed them, too. She certainly intended to kill us at the cabin. Nothing subtle about that. It fits the 'some-one who thinks we know something' scenario."

"Yeah. But that business inside the cabin . . . sure had the feel of a grudge killing to me." Mark took a sip of water from his canteen, then silently offered her a sip. While she drank, he mused. "We need an ID on Gallery Gal. At least we have somewhere to start now."

"This whole thing makes my head hurt, Callahan." She shoved her fingers through her hair, pushing it away from her face as weariness washed over her. Too much had happened over the past few days. Too much uncertainty still existed. While it generally wasn't in her nature, this time she wouldn't mind making like an ostrich and burying her head in the sand. "Maybe we should just stay up here on this mountain. It's nice. It's peaceful. The wildlife doesn't carry guns."

"Obviously you don't watch *The Hillbilly Bears* on the cartoon channel," Mark said with a snort. He glanced up at the western horizon, then added, "Speaking of bears, we'd best see about picking out a campsite. It'll be dark before we know it."

Annabelle turned her head and listened hard. "I hear running water. You want to head that way?"

A few minutes later, they found a burbling mountain stream, which they followed downhill until they discovered the perfect spot for a campsite. The flat, packed-dirt area was about the size of a small bedroom and shielded by a rock wall on two sides; the forest bounded the third, and the stream the fourth. Mark pitched the tent while Annabelle gathered wood for a campfire. Once she had it burning brightly, crackling and popping and throwing off cedar-scented smoke, she fished in her backpack for the freeze-dried meal pouches she'd taken from Rocky's pantry.

"Do you want beef stew or chicken teriyaki?" she asked, though she knew him well enough to know he'd choose the beef.

"The stew sounds good. Maybe if I get lucky, we can have trout for breakfast."

She glanced over to see him standing beside the creek, a collapsible fishing pole extended and baited with a fly, his expression alight with anticipation. She couldn't help but smile at the sight. She'd seen this man fish in spots all over the world. Tag Harrington used to say that Mark would fish in a dog's water bowl if given the chance. "Sounds good."

She sat on a rock and watched him work the fly line while she ate her chicken and rice. The man moved beautifully, his motions practiced and precise and . . . sensual. Lulled into relaxation by the music of a burbling mountain stream, the pleasing scent of burning wood, the fatigue of well-used muscles, and the comfort of a full stomach, Annabelle lowered her defenses and lost herself in the moment.

She allowed herself to feel.

Desire flowed through her, warm and thick and real. In a moment of brutal honesty, she admitted that she wanted him. She'd never stopped wanting him. Mark Callahan was a fever in her blood that neither distance nor divorce had doused.

She'd tried. Lord knew she'd tried. Up until now, she'd thought she'd made real strides toward putting him behind her. Apparently, she'd been lying to herself.

Or maybe not. Maybe this was nothing more than proximity and a long dry spell. Who's to say that if another All-American Hunk stood before her, flexing his pecs, she wouldn't feel the same way?

He let out a chortle of satisfaction and pulled a wriggling fish from the water. He turned to her like a conqueror flush with victory, a grin on his lips and a gleam in his eyes. "Am I good or what?"

Alarm bells clanged. Danger signs flashed. Enough. Annabelle rolled to her feet and gathered up a change of clothes, soap, and a towel. "I'm going to wash up. The water is hot for whenever you want your pouch of stew."

"Thanks," he called over his shoulder as he put his fish onto a stringer. "I'll eat in a bit. Stay within ear-shot, would you?"

"Sure." She walked downstream less than a hundred yards and found a shallow pool. She kicked off her sneakers, then dipped her toe in the water. Ice-cold. "Brr . . ."

Movement across the stream caught her attention. A doe and her fawn moved out of the trees and up to the bank of the creek. Annabelle held still and watched them. So pretty. Mama and baby. Nature . . . life. It made her think of her own mom and a yearning to hear her mother's voice washed through her. Too bad she didn't have cell service. She could use a dose of Lynn Monroe's common sense right now.

"Wouldn't Mama be shocked to hear me say that?" she murmured. Her mother didn't think Annabelle listened to anything she said, but she was wrong. Just because Annabelle's dreams had taken her off the farm and away from Kansas didn't mean she didn't share her parents' values or value the lessons they had tried to teach her.

For instance, her mom would be pleased to know that she'd been a virgin on her wedding night. Too bad Annabelle couldn't tell her, since that would mean spilling the beans about the Las Vegas Lunacy, and her mom would never forgive her for that.

Maybe it was good she didn't have cell service after all. What would she do, call up her mom and ask, "How do I quit lusting after my ex?"

Annabelle stripped off her shirt, wincing at her thoughts as much as at the soreness of the wound on her arm. She understood part of the problem. When a person has a brush with death, she wants to reaffirm life. Annabelle had it time and again during her years in the service. She'd never indulged that urge in the past and she wouldn't indulge it tonight.

Really.

She wouldn't.

Absolutely not.

She slipped out of her jeans, grabbed her soap, stepped into the icy water, and soaked herself.

Mark was feeling pretty cocky as he returned the stringer to the water. He'd landed three speckled trout for breakfast. While the freeze-dried pouches provided decent food—the beef stew had proved downright tasty—fresh trout at sunrise couldn't be beaten.

He decided to follow Annabelle's lead and wash off some of the stink. He peeled down to his skin and got wet.

He'd just stepped from the water and reached for

his T-shirt to dry off when Annabelle came marching into camp. She stopped abruptly. "Oh, you dirty dog."

"Huh?"

"This is not a hotel, Callahan."

He gawked at her, then glanced around. What was she talking about? "No, it's not a hotel."

"We are not married!"

Oh. He pursed his lips. Now he understood. She was thinking about sex. Thinking about sex and looking a little wild. "No, we're not."

"Okay, then." Her gaze raked him up and down. She closed her eyes, grimaced, and whirled around. "Okay."

Mark's lips quirked in a slight grin. Well . . . well . . . well. Heat surged into places diminished by the mountain stream's icy chill and as his body stirred to life, he glanced down, halfway expecting to see steam rising off his pecker. But no, just the Seven-Star General stiffening to attention.

"Put your pants on, Callahan."

"Hey, you're the one who came busting into camp before I was finished with my bath." Unlike Annabelle, he hadn't packed an entire change of clothes for the trek down the mountain. He did, however, have a pair of gym shorts, which he'd figured to sleep in, since he avoided the confinement of denim while he slept if possible. While he tugged them on, he considered how he wanted to play this.

If he put his mind to it, he could probably seduce her, though it wasn't guaranteed. Annabelle was a strong-minded woman, not the type to be swept away by her hormones.

Well, except for that night in Las Vegas. And the one in Paris. Melbourne. That afternoon in Madrid. Holy crap. The beach in New Zealand.

Come to think of it, the woman had no control whatsoever.

It wasn't unheard of to have sex with your ex. In fact, he was pretty sure he'd seen the topic touted on a magazine cover. Maybe even a book cover. Surely they had a segment on Lifetime TV about it.

His gaze drifted over her. She'd changed into sweatpants and that basketball jersey and piled her hair on top of her head. Damp tendrils escaped the rubber band and danced in enticing curls at her neck.

Need grabbed at him with sharp, tearing claws. When she glanced at him over her shoulder, heat flared as if a half dozen logs had been tossed upon the fire. "Belle . . ."

It was there, hovering between them—the chemistry, the past, the knowledge of the pleasure each could give to the other.

"Honey . . ."

"No."

For a one-syllable word, it sure came out shaky. Uncertain. It wouldn't take much to change it to a yes.

He took a step toward her. "I'm working on a long dry spell here, Annabelle. The last time I had sex was with you in New York."

That gorgeous mouth of hers gaped. "You are kidding."

"Nope. You're a hard act to follow." He took another step toward her. "You pretty much spoiled other women for me."

She moved back. "You are so full of it, Callahan."

"No. Not about this. Never about this. After we split, I went looking a time or two, but my heart wasn't in it."

Emotion flashed in her eyes, a flicker of hope that, once recognized, she quickly doused. She lifted her chin and scoffed. "That never stopped you before."

He clicked his tongue. "Now, Annabelle. You wound me."

"As if."

"So, tell me." He ran his tongue around the moist inside of his mouth. "Has it been different for you? Have you found what we had with someone else? Do your other men make you sizzle and shake and scream?"

"I'm not going to tell you anything."

"It makes me crazy thinking about you with other men, you know."

She opened her mouth to protest, but he held up his hand palm out. "I know, I know. I have no right. I gave up my rights where you are concerned. That doesn't mean I don't miss how right it was between us."

She laughed bitterly. "How right it was?"

"It was perfect, Belle."

"It was physical attraction and sexual tension. That's all."

"You're wrong."

"Am I? I don't think so. We could have had more, but you wouldn't let that happen."

"For me it *was* more," he said, his tone soft and sincere.

Annabelle closed her eyes. "Don't do this."

"Do what? Tell you the truth?" His mouth twisted in a wry smile and he deliberately pushed one of the buttons he knew so well. "Grovel at your feet?"

"Seduce me. You're trying to seduce me."

"Is it working?"

She closed her eyes. Closed him out. "I'm tired. It has been a very long day. I'm going to sleep now. Alone."

He was close enough to smell the soap she'd used— something coconut. One more step, and he could touch her. If he touched her, he could have her. He knew it and he wanted it. He wanted her. Desperately.

But dammit, she had said no. A weak no, but no nonetheless. "Are you sure?"

The moment's hesitation gave him hope, but finally, she nodded. "I'm sure."

Crap.

She walked over to the two-man tent, bent, and began to pull her sleeping bag from inside. "Don't do that, Annabelle. Rain is headed this way. There's no need for you to sleep outside. I won't touch you. You're safe with me."

When she shot him a doubtful look, he twisted his mouth in a rueful grin. "Like you said, this isn't a hotel."

When she still hesitated, he added, "I give you my word."

She let that hang in the air for a moment, then said, "Thank you."

She climbed inside the tent and closed the flap.

Mark let out a long sigh, then turned away and began to tend their camp. As time passed, he kept an eye on the sky. Rain might miss them after all. He sat beside the fire, stirring it with a stick and adding more wood when the flames began to die.

Fatigue dragged at his bones and he counted it as a blessing. It was hard to maintain a raging hard-on when he was dog-ass tired.

Clouds rolled in as dusk deepened into night, and as intermittent raindrops began to spatter onto the fire, Annabelle's voice came from within the confines of the tent. "Have you honestly not had sex since our divorce?"

He straightened. "No."

A minute passed, then two. Just when he decided that she'd said all she intended to say, she spoke again. "Me, either."

Those two little words all but knocked the air from his lungs.

The flap on the tent whisked back and Annabelle crawled from inside, then rose to her feet. Mark would have stood, too, but he seemed to have lost the ability to move . . . to swallow . . . to breathe.

Because she grabbed the hem of her blue and white jersey and whisked it over her head.

"Don't take this wrong, Callahan. We're just two healthy, unattached adults with normal human drives." She shimmied out of her pants. Now she stood before him wearing only a hot pink thong. "This is nothing personal."

Bullshit, he thought as his gaze burned over her. It *was* personal. Very personal. The epitome of personal. That she would attempt to claim otherwise totally pissed him off.

"We've had a difficult few days," she continued, "and we're likely to have a few more. We're stressed."

Stressed? This wasn't stressed. This was chemistry. The chemistry that had propelled them first into a wedding chapel in Vegas, and then into hotel rooms all over the world. It was chemistry that he'd never found with another woman and that, apparently, she'd never found with another man.

"It is like the guys on the team always used to say. Sex is the best stress reliever around. If we do this, we'll be able to sleep. We need to sleep to concentrate. We need to concentrate so we can put a stop to any more murders."

"Sex to solve a murder?" Mark laughed. "Hell, babe, the police academies will be overrun."

Her eyes looked a little wild. "As long as we're up-front and honest about it, I don't see what a little casual sex will hurt."

Casual sex. Mark's jaw hardened and in two steps he stood before her. "Annabelle?" He reached for her uninjured arm and dragged her against him. "Shut up."

Then he crushed his hungry mouth to hers.

He devoured her with lips that ravaged, with a

tongue that plunged and plundered and took. It was a kiss fueled by more than two years of anger and frustration. Two-plus years of loneliness and guilt. And she responded, by God. She shuddered. She moaned. She whimpered. *Nothing personal, my ass.*

His teeth nipped into her at the base of her throat, a little savage, a tiny bit mean. "Casual sex," he growled. He jerked his head back. His gaze burned down into hers. "Fuck that. Nothing about us has ever been casual."

He noted a flicker of apprehension before bravado filled her eyes and she lifted her chin. "This will be."

It was waving a red flag in front of a bull. "You think so? You think you get to call all the shots? Well, think again, darlin'. You came to me. You asked for this. This time . . . tonight . . . we're doing this my way."

He picked her up and backed her against the rock wall, then held her there with his body as he punctuated his declaration with another blistering kiss. The blood boiled in his veins, fueled by anger and by passion and by regret.

I'll show you personal.

He allowed her feet to slide to the ground; then he grabbed both her wrists, eased her injured arm above her head, yanked the healthy one up. She gasped and struggled against him a bit as he secured both wrists with one large hand. Her doe eyes glittered in the firelight. In their depths, he saw excitement, arousal, and a bit of apprehension.

His hand slipped beneath the minimal barrier of her panties and tested the soft flesh between her legs. Oh, yeah. She was wet for him. Ready. He could take her now—fast and hard and hot—and release the tormenting pressure.

That's what she wanted. Relief. Mindless, physical release.

Right at the moment, it sounded pretty damn good to him, too, but he ruthlessly resisted even as she arched and rubbed herself against his hand. Speed wouldn't do. Speed might be what Annabelle preferred, but not Mark. He wanted more.

He wanted everything. And he wanted it to last all night long.

Who knows if I'll ever get the chance to have her again?

He yanked his hand from between her legs and she let out a little whimper of loss. "My way," he murmured, locking gazes with her. "We're gonna do this my way."

Surprise flickered in her eyes. "Mark, I don't—"

"First, I'm going to eat you up." He brought his fingers up to his mouth and slowly, thoroughly, licked away her delicious honey. "Mmm . . ."

She drew in a ragged gasp and closed her eyes. It was, he knew, surrender.

He skimmed the backs of his fingers down her cheek and across her neck, then filled his palm with the soft, heavy heat of her breast and rubbed his calloused thumb over its turgid nipple. She visibly trembled. He nipped her chin, then moved lower, replacing his thumb with his teeth, raking them across her hard tip, before sucking her into his mouth.

She whimpered, thrashed, and tried to pull her hands from his grip, but he held her tight. While his mouth worked first one breast and then the other, his mind went spinning into madness. *Belle, Belle, Belle.*

His blood burned. His heart pounded. His cock was hard as steel.

"Please, Mark," Annabelle groaned, her hips canting forward. "Please."

He released her breast, captured her mouth, and thrust his hand between her legs, his two middle fingers into her hot, slick sheath.

"Is that what you wanted, Annabelle?" he asked as he stroked her, worked her.

"Yes . . . no . . . ah . . ."

Her thighs clamped around his hand and she ground herself against him. Her head was flung back and her eyes closed. A moan escaped her throat.

The familiarity of it shuddered through him. God, how he'd missed this. How had he survived without it? How in hell would he live the rest of his life without it? Without her? *Not personal, she says. Casual . . . something she wants to forget?*

Like hell. He was raw inside at the idea of this being anything less than incredible for her.

"Is this casual enough for you?" He reached higher inside her. Let his fingers dance. Ground his palm against her clitoris. "Just sex. Nothing personal?"

She murmured incoherently.

"How about this?" He removed his fingers from inside her, and sank to his knees. With one hand on her ass, he grabbed her thong's thin line of elastic and ripped it away.

Then he leaned in and licked her. And licked her again. And again and again and again. She put her hand on his head and made a halfhearted effort to push him away. But when he slipped his hands palms out between her legs and pushed her thighs apart, allowing him better access, her fingers threaded into his hair and held on.

He buried his mouth in her damp sex and probed with his tongue, rasped with his teeth, and sucked that hard little nub that made her shudder and shake and share her soft, liquid heat.

God, she was sweet.

Casual, my ass.

Lord, I'm gonna die, Annabelle thought as the climax slammed into her, a hurricane's wind that sent her reeling, flying, soaring. It must have knocked her off her feet, because she found herself lying on her back, writhing. He wouldn't leave her alone. Wouldn't let it end.

It was the most electrifying sex she'd ever had in her life.

He'd taken control. Powerful and strong, he gave no quarter, showed no mercy. His fingers clenched on her hips, holding her still while he continued to use his mouth, driving her onward and upward incessantly. Anger hummed through him into her, giving their lovemaking an edge that was new and different.

He was a male staking his claim, and to her inner feminist's shame, she found it utterly thrilling.

Surrender, she discovered, excited her. It was primal, honest, and real. Feminine. Completely, gloriously feminine. He'd taken command and her body no longer belonged to her. It was his. Only his. And to her surprise, she loved it.

When the second orgasm hit her, she collapsed, spent, sobbing out his name.

And Devil Callahan rolled back on his heels and showed her a smile that was all teeth.

"What do you say, Annabelle? That impersonal enough for you?"

Annabelle closed her eyes and returned to reality. She'd really touched a sore spot, hadn't she?

"Look at me," he demanded. He moved, straddling her hips, his sex jutting out before him, huge and straining. A bead of moisture glistened on its tip.

He put his palms against the ground on either side of her head and stared down at her. His green eyes glittered like a mountain cat's. A hungry mountain cat about to pounce. "Answer me."

But Annabelle's dalliance with surrender was done. Such a thing could get out of hand, she decided. Exerting some control of her own, she opened her legs, arched her hips, and declared, "No."

.

With a growl, he thrust inside her. Filled her. Her body clenched, gripping him hard. He pumped and thrust, ramming into her with a feral intensity that left her gasping, stoking the cinders of her desire back into flame. She matched his rhythm, that reckless, relentless need building . . . building. *I've missed him. Oh, how I've missed him.*

He hissed, he snarled, he angled her hips so that he could drive deeper. As he hammered himself into her, Annabelle sensed it coming, another tidal wave of pleasure. She strained toward it, reached—and she screamed as it broke over her, sucked her down into a swirling vortex of sensation.

Only then did he throw back his head as if in pain. His hard body jerked and went rigid and he shuddered . . . shuddered . . . shuddered.

And called out her name.

Chapter Eight

Annabelle's first conscious thought the next morning was that she needed an aspirin. Her head threatened to explode.

Slowly, she cracked open her eyes and saw not the ceiling of her home on Oahu, not the ceiling of an anonymous hotel, but nylon. Sky blue nylon.

She smelled fish cooking.

Her eyes flew open wide as memory came rushing back. Dear God. She sat up, bumped her head on an aluminum pole, and stuck her head outside the tent flap. Her gaze flew to the fire ring where foil-wrapped fish sat over glowing coals, then scanned the rest of the campsite. Mark was nowhere to be seen. Thank God.

She brought her fingertips to her temples and gently massaged. She let loose a little moan. Not only did her head pound, but her body ached all over. If sex hangovers existed, then she had a doozy of one.

Memories of the previous night rolled through her mind like a bad dream. A hot, mind-blowingly erotic bad dream, but a bad dream nonetheless. What had she been thinking?

"I'm a cliché," she muttered. A pathetic cliché. You read about it in magazines all the time. Sex with the Ex. Surely Oprah had done a show about it. How many times had she scoffed at women who fell into this trap?

And it wasn't just sex with the ex. She'd had mind-blowing, superorgasmic, incredibly amazing sex with her ex. Why the hell didn't Oprah warn her viewers about that?

Oh, God. She had satisfied an urge and sacrificed her self-respect. Because she didn't have it in her to detach herself from emotion and simply focus on the way sex with Mark Callahan made her feel. No, she wasn't that kind of girl.

Which meant she'd thrown away all the emotional work she'd done over the past two and a half years—especially the last seven months—for an orgasm. Well, orgasm*s*. Plural. Multiple. Heat rushed right to her as the memory of straddling atop him returned full force.

Oh, Jesus save me. I'm in trouble. I AM that kind of girl. Who the hell am I kidding? Were Mark to climb into this tent right now, I'd jump him.

Annabelle rolled to her feet, grabbed her clothes and the bottle of aspirin from her purse, then headed for the privacy of the downstream pool she'd found the day before. When she returned washed and dressed ten minutes later, Mark had the tent down and packed away, the fire doused, and her breakfast sitting on top of a rock.

She had never felt this awkward. Not even on the morning after their wedding night when she'd awakened in his arms. That morning, he'd nuzzled her neck and spoken gentle words of reassurance. Made love to her again. Today, he didn't speak. Barely even looked at her. Was he feeling as uncomfortable as she?

"Hurry up, Monroe. Be damned if I'll spend another night on this mountain."

Well.

Not uncomfortable, but unhappy. Apparently Callahan was no more thrilled about what transpired last night than she. She'd expected his familiar postsex grin. Face it. She'd *wanted* to see it. At least something about this whole ordeal could be normal, couldn't it? Instead, he was acting like . . .

Someone who'd been used.

That took her aback. What did he have to be pissy about? He was a man! Men loved sex with no strings.

"I'm ready," she snapped back. "I'll eat my breakfast while we hike."

"Fine."

"Fine." Goody goody peppermint gumdrops fine.

He frowned down at the fresh bandage she'd put over her wound. "How is your arm? Do you need help with your pack?"

"It's good. I'm good." She would have died before she let the wince show on her face as she hefted the pack up onto her back. *Actually, I'm a basket case.*

She pondered the situation while she snacked on the delicious trout and a handful of trail mix and followed him downhill. What did he have to be cranky about, anyway? He got laid, didn't he? Wasn't that the bottom line for men?

Annabelle snarled at his back. Leave it to Mark Callahan to look at matters differently from the average guy.

She could live to be a hundred and she'd never figure him out, so why waste her time and brain cells trying? Better to spend a few hours attempting to discern what weakness of character made her susceptible to Mark Callahan in spite of all their baggage. That way if—God forbid—they ever spent another night alone together, she would be able to resist flinging off her jersey and jumping him.

Her mother would blame it on hormones. Of course, her mother blamed everything on hormones these days.

Yes, hormones were part of it. Heaven knew she'd been a walking hormone around Mark ever since that first night in Las Vegas, but Annabelle knew it was more complicated than that. Even though they'd never officially lived together, while she and Mark were married she'd always felt an emotional connection to him. She'd missed having that with another human being. With a man.

Her desire for a child had not waned. She'd spent the last seven months trying to move forward in order to further that particular goal. Early on in the process she'd realized that reaching for the future meant letting go of the past, but doing so proved easier said than done.

Because only after he was well and truly gone had she realized how much she had counted on his staying.

Now she had last night to deal with. Without a doubt, last night had set her recovery back months. Maybe when this was all over, she'd see about getting some help. She wondered if a twelve-step program existed for idiots who wanted to go to bed with their ex. If not, maybe she could start one. She could contact all of Mark's old girlfriends . . . probably pull in his brothers' old girlfriends, too . . . and have enough brokenhearted bodies to form a national organization. They could meet online. Maybe hold a convention once a year in Vegas. Or maybe a spa somewhere. A cruise. The Callahans Anonymous cruise—the Anti-Love Boat.

She let out a little self-mocking giggle.

Mark glanced back over his shoulder and frowned at her. "Something the matter?"

"Oh, no. Everything is great. Wonderful. I have blisters on my feet and a bullet wound on my arm and a bug bite on my butt. Life is peachy keen, Callahan."

"Well, aren't you Miss Mary Sunshine?" he observed.

"Bite me, Callahan."

"I already did, Monroe. So shut the hell up."

Hiking with a hard-on was a bitch.

Mark figured he could have passed for a grumpy old bear lumbering through the forest right about now. You'd think that last night would have done him for a while. Instead, it appeared to have awakened the sleeping beast.

No, *she* had done it. This was her fault. She came at him. She put it out there and tempted him to take it. This was all about her.

But then, for him, it had always been about her. Call it chemistry or lust or brain lapse—no other woman did it for him like Annabelle.

He could jump her again right now. Every sound she made scraped across his nerves. The slightest whiff of her scent had him going on point. He didn't need to look at her to want her because the image of her naked and hungry and lying on the forest floor was burned into his brain.

It royally pissed him off.

He wasn't the type of man to be ruled by his johnson, goddammit. He had a well-earned reputation for icy control. Why did it take no more than one come-hither look and a disappearing basketball jersey to take him from ice to boiling? Hell, even as a swinging-dick eighteen-year-old when he started courting Carrie, he'd had more control than that. This was damned humiliating.

The sooner he could solve his teammates' murders, the better. Otherwise, he was liable to find himself back in the sack with Annabelle again, and that wasn't healthy for either one of them. They were divorced. They didn't need to be in each other's pockets or each other's pants. Period.

But the idea of her in another guy's pants made him snarl. Then a small voice that sounded suspiciously like Torie's said, *Well, what do you expect her to do? Wait forever for something that you won't give her?*

Damn it all. Why did letting go of Annabelle have to be so fucking hard?

It would be easier if he didn't like her so much. If he didn't respect her. But dammit, Annabelle Monroe was everything a woman should be, everything a man could want. If only she hadn't been so set on settling down and having . . .

"Holy shit." His heart all but stopped. He rounded on her, demanding, "Tell me you're on the Pill."

"What?" Frowning down at her shoe where she worked to free a stone, she repeated, "What did you say?"

"The Pill!"

"What pill? I don't take any . . . oh." Her eyes went round as saucers. "Oh, dear."

Oh, dear? His gut dropped to his toes. "You're not on it."

She threaded her fingers through her hair, pushing back the thick auburn tresses. Worry dimmed her eyes. "No . . . I'm not. It hasn't been an issue with me."

His blood churned. Panic sizzled along his nerves. "Because you want to get pregnant!"

Her chin came up. Her hands fisted on her hips and she took a step toward him. "Because I haven't been having sex, you jerk!"

"Well, you did last night."

"I know that."

"If you're not on the Pill, then we had unprotected sex."

"I know that, too!"

His throat closed and his question came out rough and raspy. "Did you plan it, Annabelle?"

You'd have thought he'd hit her, the way she reared back. For a long moment, time hung suspended as they stared at each other. Panic churned through him. Panic and a big black cloud of dread. He could see the hurt in her eyes, but the ugly emotions churning inside him prevented him from caring.

Then she pushed past him and in a scathing tone said, "You ass."

He wouldn't argue that point. He knew she hadn't planned the sex. She'd been swept up in the moment just like he had been. The problem was that Annabelle would welcome the result of their carelessness, while he . . . he . . . oh, crap.

He didn't want a child.

Downhill from him ten yards or so, she suddenly stopped and turned. "You know . . . I let you do this to me once before. That day in New York I was so shocked that I let you sputter and spew without calling you on it. You know something? I've regretted it ever since."

"Look, Annabelle."

"No. Let's do 'Look, Mark' instead, shall we? I have a few things I want to say to you. I think right here and right now is a right fine time to say them. So here we go. First"—she held up her thumb—"I want children, yes, but not at the cost of my honesty and integrity. That was true when my period was late two years ago, and it is true today. For you to suggest otherwise is both insulting and blind. Second, I don't know what your hang-up is regarding children, but based on comments you've dropped in the past, I suspect it has something to do with your relationship with your own father. Frankly, Callahan, you need to do something about that."

"Now, wait one minute."

She made a sweeping gesture with her hand and said, "Hush. It's still my turn to talk. Your father must be, what . . . in his seventies? Maybe his eighties? You'd better deal with your issues while he's still around, Callahan. Otherwise, one of these days you'll wake up and it'll be too late."

As always when the subject of Branch Callahan came up, Mark clamped his jaw shut. Children were one thing; his father was quite another.

Annabelle held up another finger. "Third, and pay attention, Callahan. This is a big one. Third. As upsetting as our lapse of good sense last night is, we can't let it interfere with the purpose at hand. Someone wants to kill us, to kill all the Fixers. We need to keep our focus on finding that person."

He knew she was right . . . about that last part, anyway. He sucked in a deep breath, then nodded curtly. But just as he decided that he could keep his mind on murder, she had to go and distract him.

"And finally, fourth, if I turn up pregnant, we'll deal with it then. There's no sense worrying about it ahead of time. So I suggest you put whatever hang-ups you have back in the closet, as we don't have time to deal with your issues along with everything else." With that, she continued down the hill.

Mark stared after her, her words echoing like thunder through his brain. Deal with it then . . . hell. He *couldn't* deal with it. She didn't understand.

In that moment, he wanted her to understand. For the first time ever, he wanted to share with her that sad, secret story that only a handful of people knew. His brothers, their wives. His goddamned father.

Maybe he should have told her that weekend at the Waldorf or that day at her office in Hawaii, but it was just so private. He told his brothers only because pain meds loosened his tongue. Hell, even all these years later, it was still a kick to the nuts just to think about what happened.

But maybe if he told her, she'd finally get it. The subject would be done with. Over. Finis. *Until her test stick turns blue.*

Crap.

Hell, if his luck went that bad, then he'd probably be better off if she knew the score. Easier to tell her now than to do it then. God knew he wouldn't be feeling as calm as he was right now if she came to him and said that cursed word: "Daddy."

Shit.

So nut up and do it, Callahan. Drag your heart out of your pocket and show her.

Mark closed his eyes, drew a bracing breath, then pulled his wallet from his pocket and started after her. "Annabelle, wait."

"I've said all I have to say."

"Well, I haven't." He grabbed her arm and yanked her to a stop. "I have something to show you. Someone, actually. Just keep your mouth shut and let me get it over with, okay?"

Before I lose my nerve.

As always, a lump the size of Texas formed in his throat as he pulled the picture from behind his driver's license. He looked down at the photograph. The scrunched-up face and the Cindy Lou Who curl atop her head. Big, serious blue eyes. He thumbed the edges, swallowed hard, then handed it to Annabelle. "This is Margaret Mary, although I think of her as Maggie."

Her quizzical look lasted only a few seconds before her eyes widened and her gaze flew up to meet his. "Maggie . . . Callahan?"

Annabelle always had been quick. He licked his lips and nodded.

Shock sharpened her tone. "You have a child?"

"Not anymore. She's dead. She and my wife are both dead."

Almost imperceptibly, Annabelle stiffened. She licked her lips. "I don't recall you ever mentioning that you'd been married before."

"I don't talk about it."

"Obviously." She brushed a finger over the photo. It was a newer copy of the old faded and tattered version he'd carried around for years. Torie had sneaked it from his wallet one day, worked some photographer's magic on it, then gifted him with this one. Her tone soft and sad, Annabelle said, "She was a beautiful baby."

"She was born during Desert Storm while I was deployed. She died before I ever had the chance to see her."

Annabelle's big brown eyes softened with sympathy and pity. "Oh, Mark."

She touched his arm, but he pulled back. Closed off. Shut down. He took the picture away from her and returned it to his wallet.

"What happened to her? To her mother?"

He clenched his teeth. Even after all these years, this was still so damned hard.

"Mark?"

He brushed his thumb across the soft leather of his wallet. "They were killed in a car accident. My father was responsible."

"He was driving?"

"In a manner of speaking." He shoved his wallet into his back pocket. "Look, none of that matters. . . . I'm telling you about Maggie so you'll see why the idea of having another child leaves me cold."

She stared at him for another few seconds, her eyes moist. "I'm sorry for your loss, Mark. I can only imagine how difficult that must have been for you."

"So you understand my position."

Again, another pause, then, "It was a long time ago."

Anger whipped through him like a hot desert wind. He'd heard that before from his brothers and their wives and it pushed all his buttons. "No one has the right to tell someone else how long to grieve."

"That's true." She studied him, her smile just a shade toward pitying. "If I thought grief was the problem here, I'd be a little more sympathetic."

"What the hell does that mean?"

"I've stood beside you in a gun battle in Bosnia. I've followed you into the Colombian jungle to rescue a hostage from a drug lord. I watched you infiltrate a meeting between gun runners, gangsters, and terrorists in the Swiss Alps with no other weapon than your mind. I never took you for a coward, Callahan, until now. The prospect of fathering a child, of being responsible to a child, doesn't leave you cold. It scares you to death!"

Mark's jaw gaped. He gave his head a little shake. He couldn't believe what he'd just heard. "Did I just hear you call me a—"

"Coward. Yes. That's what I said. That is exactly what I said." Annabelle gave her head a toss. "If this had happened last year, in the last few years, I wouldn't argue that it was grief. But more than fifteen years ago? It's an excuse, Callahan. A few minutes ago I suggested you had issues to deal with. Well, let me put it a little plainer. You need a shrink."

Anger roared through him and he grabbed her arm. "Where the hell do you get off saying something like that?"

She yanked away from him. Anger glittered in her eyes. "Because it's my life, too. The child I could have had. The child we *should* have had. I loved you, Callahan. You should have told me."

"I don't talk about it. I can't."

"Not good enough."

"It's the truth. You don't know what it's like. Losing so much. First my mother, then my brother. Then my wife and daughter. It's just too damned much. This is how I deal."

"Deal? My God, Mark. That's not 'dealing.' That's avoiding. You need to quit living in the past."

"I'm not. I'm merely controlling my future."

"That's a cop-out." She threw out her hands in frustration.

Mark clenched his fists. "You don't understand."

"You are right about that. I *don't* understand. Maybe I could if you were still a teenager, but you're a grown man. You need to face this like a man."

She gazed at him with a look of scornful disbelief. "I swear, I've seen you under fire. I've watched you face certain death without blinking. I thought you were the strongest, most courageous man I've ever known. But you're not strong and you're not brave. You're hiding in the past and that . . . weakness . . . of yours stole my future. You stole *my* family, Callahan. Damn you for that!"

With that, she turned and marched away, descending the hill without sparing a single glance back.

Mark stared after her, the emptiness inside him yawning in his heart like a big black hole.

She'd called him a coward.

Damned if she wasn't right.

The Telluride cops followed standard procedure when they separated Annabelle and Mark for questioning. She was dirty, tired, hungry, and still damp from the rain that started falling ten minutes or so before the tourist from Texas had stopped his car and given them a ride into town. Nevertheless, she'd never been so thankful to be escorted into an interview room in her life.

To call the mood between her and Mark strained was like saying the weather in hell was rather warm.

They'd exchanged maybe two dozen words since their altercation on the mountain, and the words had been curt. He was furious at her, but Annabelle didn't really care. She was pretty furious herself.

How could a man be so physically courageous and such an emotional wimp?

She'd bet her bottom dollar that it went back to that family of his. To his crazy father. Back during the Fixer days, Mark had let slip little snide remarks about the man from time to time. Then during one of their weekends after they married, she had invited him to attend a volunteer dinner where she was to receive an award. He begged off, explaining that it conflicted with the Callahan brothers' annual get-together in memory of their youngest brother, John. When she'd asked what the brothers did to mark the occasion, he'd replied that they usually spent the weekend fishing and cussing their father's name. The venom in his voice when he'd said it had taken her aback.

Now as Annabelle waited for the police to begin their interrogation of her, she wondered just what Branch Callahan had done to make Mark hold him responsible for the car accident that killed his wife and child.

Mark's wife. She wanted to know the other woman's name, how long they'd been married, everything. They had to have been young—barely twenty, if even that—for the timing to work with Desert Storm. Had they been high school sweethearts? Or had Mark met her after Branch Callahan exiled him from his hometown?

Branch Callahan. Now, there was a man whom she'd like to slap upside the head if she ever had the opportunity to meet him. From what she could tell, he was the one who put the "dys" in the dysfunctional family.

The door opened and a cop walked in. "Ms. Monroe? You are free to go."

She frowned at him. "But you haven't questioned me."

"It's not necessary. Mr. Callahan gave us a rundown of what transpired."

Annabelle opened her mouth, then shut it. She knew she should keep it shut, stand, and make her exit, but she couldn't hold back the words. "And you believe him? Just like that?"

"We got a call from the Pentagon that backed up everything Mr. Harrington said. We were preparing to begin a search for you and Mr. Callahan when you arrived here. Now we'll start looking for the woman who impersonated Brooke Mercer."

Annabelle's mind snagged on the name. "Harrington? Tag Harrington called you?"

"No, ma'am. He's—"

"Here." Tag stepped past the policeman into the room. "I'm here."

The solemn look on his face had her stomach sinking. "What's wrong?"

"Noah and I couldn't reach you. We were afraid you had run into . . . trouble."

"We did."

"So I understand. That's a bitch about Rocky."

He shoved his hands in his pants pockets and she waited, knowing there was more. Who was it? Noah? She braced herself as he opened his mouth, but nothing could have prepared her for the words he spoke.

"Annabelle, we got a call from Kansas yesterday. There are no fatalities, but there's been an attack on your family."

Everything within her froze. "Excuse me? What did you say?"

"He hit your family farm. Apparently it was someone's birthday and a crowd was there. Something exploded in the kitchen. Luckily, almost everyone was in the dining room and escaped with only cuts and bruises."

Annabelle reached out and grabbed the back of a nearby chair for support. "Almost everyone?"

"Honey . . ." Tag's blue eyes offered both encouragement and concern. "Your dad went back to the kitchen for more hot gravy. He's expected to pull through, but the blast banged him up pretty bad."

Once it sank in, Annabelle couldn't control a little hysterical giggle. "Mama always said his love for gravy would kill him."

"Ah, Annabelle." Tag crossed to her and took her in his arms. She buried her face against his shoulder and wrapped her arms around his waist and held on as tremors shook her. He murmured gentle words of comfort and pressed kisses against her hair. "It'll be okay, hon. It'll be okay."

Annabelle's mind spun. So much to do. She had to call Mom. Find the quickest way to Kansas.

Tag had said it happened yesterday. Though she guessed it was physically possible that the gallery woman hit Kansas after leaving Colorado, it didn't seem probable. That meant that the gallery woman probably had a partner.

Someone attacked her family. Oh, dear Lord.

"We have to find these bastards, Tag. We have to stop them."

It wasn't Tag who answered, but Mark. "We will."

Annabelle looked up. Her ex was watching her with a blank, unreadable stare, though his left hand was fisted at his side. Tag glanced from Mark back down to her, a question in his gaze.

Annabelle ignored him, ignored them both. She didn't have the time or the energy for rooster barnyard posturing.

"Mark, my dad . . ."

"I just got off the phone with the hospital. My pilot is filing a flight plan as we speak."

Cold fear washed through her. "Is he . . . ?"

"He's stable, Annabelle. I spoke with a doctor named Ellis."

"He's our family doctor."

"He said to tell you that your father's hard head came in handy for once. You are not to worry, that he has every expectation that your father will make a full recovery."

"How badly is he injured?"

Mark's gaze flickered away. "HIPAA laws . . ."

"Mark, please." She knew the man better than that.

"They operated to stanch some internal bleeding, and he came through that just fine. He had a couple broken ribs, a concussion. They're a little concerned about his blood pressure, but they're monitoring him closely."

"That's all? You swear?"

"You have my word."

"Good." She shut her eyes. "That's good."

Reassured, she started thinking again. She glanced up at Tag. "Is Noah with you?"

"No. He flew to Florida. His parents retired to Captiva Island, but he couldn't reach them by phone. He'll rejoin us once he makes sure everything is fine in Florida."

"Your family?"

"My parents have been gone for years, and I was an only child. Not an issue with me."

Annabelle raked her fingers through her hair. "Who are these people? Why would they go after our families? What's—" She broke off abruptly. "Your brothers, Mark."

"I've already called 'em. They're fine and they know how to take precautions." He crossed the room and smoothly separated her from Tag. "C'mon, Belle. We need to grab a shower and something to eat before we leave. Harrington has some calls to make. He'll meet us at the plane."

"You're coming with us, Tag?"

"Yeah." He shrugged. "You have a large family. We figure having an extra gun around can't hurt."

The weakness slowly began to leave her and anger flowed in to take its place. "I hope there's a special level in hell for whoever is doing this."

"And I hope we make sure they get to visit it ASAP," Tag added.

Twenty minutes later, Mark unlocked the door to a hotel room and ushered her inside. She spied a change of clothing for both of them lying on the bed—jeans and T-shirts and underwear. Two sets of inexpensive sneakers sat on the floor. "The sandwiches I ordered should be up anytime. You want to hit the shower now or after you eat?"

"Now." She'd been hungry following their trek down the mountain, but her appetite disappeared once she'd heard the news about her dad. At the moment, she didn't care if she ever ate again.

She gathered up the clothes and carried them into the bathroom, where she checked the sizes. Everything was perfect. Leave it to Mark Callahan to remember the details.

The luxuriously equipped bathroom offered a separate shower and tub. A long bath sounded lovely, but she couldn't afford the time, so Annabelle opened the shower's glass door and turned on the hot water, then stripped bare and dumped her torn and dirty clothes in the trash. Steam billowed and she adjusted the temperature to just below scalding and stepped into the stall.

Water cascaded over her. As the heat slowly permeated her skin, she twisted the spigot and increased the pressure. At some point, the pounding heat warmed her enough to melt the cold chill inside her and Annabelle began to cry.

She didn't cry very often, so when she did, the tears came from the very depths of her soul. Events of the last few days overwhelmed her and let loose a hurricane of emotions. Fear. Despair. Guilt. Regret. Grief. She buried her head in the crook of her arm, leaned against the shower tile, and sobbed.

She cried for her daddy, for her family home, for Rocky and his lady and the Russos. She cried over blistered feet and bug bites and broken hearts. She cried for the child she wanted so desperately, but had to hope did not result from her impetuousness last night.

She cried hard and she cried long, and at some point she became aware of the naked arms wrapped around her and of the soothing words being murmured into her ear, of the tender kisses being pressed against her brow, her temples, her lips.

"Hush, now, baby. It's okay. It'll be okay."

His hand stroked over her naked skin and she melted against him. Slowly, she turned and leaned against his familiar form. Reaching down, she touched the tips of her fingers to his beneath the spray. He laced their hands without another word and pulled her closer.

There was no question about what he wanted, no question about what she needed. His naked and aroused body spoke for him as he gently pressed her against him. His mouth sought hers and Annabelle was lost.

So sweet. So soft. The warmth of the water sluiced over them as he whispered her name amid hot, open-mouthed kisses that stole her breath. Her heart slammed against her chest, and somewhere deep in her brain, Annabelle knew she shouldn't be here, shouldn't do this. . . .

Yet she needed it so badly. Needed *Mark* so badly that she could no sooner stop this than cease breathing.

Make it go away. The pain, the worry, the fear, the confusion. Raising her eyes to his, Annabelle made a silent plea for him to pull her into a place where she didn't have to think.

Blinking away the emotion, she reached up and kissed him again, not wanting to think about babies or bombs or even tomorrow. Especially tomorrow. He took her cue and deepened their connection, his tongue plunging in and out as prelude of what was to come.

He ran his hands down over her body, over her breasts, her stomach. His fingers teased against the juncture between her legs and she lurched up with a gasp. A shiver made her hot and cold at the same time, and the steam radiating from the shower only enhanced the heat between them.

He knew where to touch. Where to kiss. Where to arouse. He buried his face in her shoulder and nipped along her neck as he eased one finger up inside of her.

Her head lolled back as he trailed his mouth downward, settling on an extended nipple. He drew on her with soft pulls, his tenderness more affecting than she could bear. Stroking his hair, Annabelle sighed and arched her body farther, moving against the rhythm his hand created, letting him take her into the sweet bliss of oblivion.

But she wanted him. Didn't want to go alone. Needed the connection. Needed Mark. Pulling back, she reached down blindly, tugging him to her, aligning his body with hers. In one stroke, he entered and Annabelle nearly cried with relief.

Lifting her knee, she brought him deeper, feeling her body tighten and climb the ladder, rung by rung. Her senses reeling, her mind vacant of all save him, she rocked against the tide and came apart with a throaty sob.

Gasping, trembling, she looked up at him in the dim light of the shower stall, his eyes glittering with a myriad of emotions as he pulled her closer, driving himself to the hilt.

He held her in place and made such sweet love to her that Annabelle cried more silent tears against his shoulder. Her Mark. Her husband. The only man who would ever hold her heart. He'd known she needed him and he'd come to her.

Cradling her in his arms, Mark murmured words that had no meaning and found heaven himself.

Chapter Nine

Annabelle remained quiet as they left the hotel and headed for the airport. She fell asleep before the plane was airborne. During the flight, Mark attempted to focus on the phone calls and faxes that had piled up during the time he'd been out of touch, but his gaze kept returning to Annabelle.

Exhaustion added a fragility to her beauty that he'd never seen in her before today. Despite the exposure to the sun during their trek down the mountain, her complexion appeared pale and almost translucent. She had dark circles under her eyes and a little furrow of worry between her brows even as she slept.

Annabelle Monroe was just about the strongest woman he'd ever known, and seeing her this way, hearing her sobs earlier, tore him up. As he watched her now, he silently swore that when he finally tracked the killer down, the bastard would pay for every tear this woman had shed.

"So what's with you two?" Harrington asked.

Mark jerked his attention to the man seated across from him, who now stared at Mark with a penetrating gaze. Mark tried to fake it. "What do you mean?"

"Guess you two worked out whatever differences you had in Philly. How long have you been sleeping with her?"

Mark scoffed. "What in the world gave you that crazy idea?"

"Crazy? I don't think so." Tag Harrington shook his head and clucked his tongue. "It's written all over your face, Callahan."

"The hell you say."

"The chill in the air around you two in Philly led me to suspect that it was an affair gone bad. It's not cold around you anymore. Besides, the look you gave me when you walked into that interrogation room and saw her crying on my shoulder gave the game away."

Mark knew then that there was no sense in fighting the inevitable. "It's complicated."

"Considering that some nutjob has a hard-on for us all—including our families—I'd say so."

Harrington's mention of families brought Mark's thoughts back to the Monroes and he grimaced. "You need to keep this to yourself while we're in Kansas. Annabelle's family doesn't know about us."

"*I* don't know about you. What's the deal?"

Mark hesitated, not knowing just how to respond. He tried to think strategically, but as his gaze drifted again to Annabelle, that unusual and still-growing sense of protectiveness washed through him once again. The main question in his mind became, how much would Annabelle want him to reveal?

She's tough. She's brilliant. She's worldly.

At her core, she's still a Kansas farm girl. Her teammates' opinions matter to her.

"We . . . uh . . . were married."

Harrington couldn't hide his shock. "You're shittin' me."

"Emphasis on *were*."

"You're divorced?"

"Yeah, but her family doesn't know about any of it, and she will want it to stay that way."

"Details. Give me details."

"No." Mark rubbed the back of his neck. "What did I do to give us away? I need to make sure I don't do it again."

Harrington's mouth twisted in a wry grin. "You'll probably be okay as long as you never look at her or speak to her. Better not stand next to her, either. I swear, the air sorta sizzles between you two."

"That's nonsense."

"Hey, it's your funeral." Tag no sooner said the words than he winced. "Sorry. Bad choice of words, under the circumstances, but you get my drift."

Yeah, he did. To Mark's consternation, Harrington had it right. He couldn't look at Annabelle the same way he'd done before they were married. He couldn't look at her differently now that they were divorced. He wanted her too much. Way too much. Still.

"I'm screwed."

"Obviously. That's the problem."

Well, it was a problem he had to solve. Annabelle didn't need family drama on top of everything else.

Mark drummed his fingers on the table in front of him and muttered, "This is ridiculous. I can fix this. I can act the way I need to act, hide what I need to hide. I've successfully worked undercover in some of the most dangerous places in the world. I surely can do it in Kansas!"

Harrington snorted. "Seems to me that it's your undercover work that is the problem here."

Deciding he was done with the conversation, Mark gave his friend a sneering smile, flipped him the bird, then turned his attention to the faxes.

He had a killer to find.

He made calls to Texas, DC, and the security firm in Kansas he'd hired during the flight to Wichita. Annabelle didn't open her eyes until he shook her awake after the plane had taxied to a stop at the airport. The two hours of sleep had eased the dark shadows beneath her eyes just a bit, but she still looked like hell. Well, as much as a beautiful woman could look like hell.

The car he'd hired met them at the plane. Annabelle didn't speak during the ride to St. Joe's, but she opened the passenger door before the car rolled to a complete stop at the entrance. "Wait," Mark admonished, placing a hand on her arm. "Give the security guys a chance to take their places."

She climbed out of the car anyway. "This is home. My family is inside."

"Dammit, Annabelle." Mark scrambled after her, Harrington right behind him. He tensed, anticipating a sniper's shot, as they hurried toward the front door.

They made it inside safely, and Annabelle went straight to the lobby desk, where she addressed the candy striper, "Intensive care?"

"Five North."

Annabelle waved her thanks and headed for the elevator, where she waited for the car to descend, tapping her toes, impatiently slapping her denim-clad thigh. Mark's hand hovered at the ready to reach for his gun as a man in a suit approached them. "Mr. Callahan?"

Mark relaxed. "Yeah."

"You're all clear here."

"Thanks. I'll—" He broke off abruptly when Annabelle took off for a door marked STAIRS. "Sonofabitch."

Mark and Tag sprinted after her, not catching up until they'd climbed to the fifth floor and she stopped abruptly at the swinging metal doors below a sign marked ICU. Tag asked, "Annabelle?"

"I'm scared."

"No, you're not. You are never scared."

"I am this time." She put her hands against her chest as if holding back a terrible pressure. "This is my fault."

Mark scowled and took her chin, forcing her to meet his gaze. "Don't be stupid. You know better."

"They'll blame me. I blame myself."

"The only person to blame for this is the a-hole who is doing it. That's the truth, honey, and they'll see it. If they don't, I'll explain it to them."

Her teeth gnawed worriedly at her lower lip.

He leaned down and wiped that sign of worry away by giving her a quick hard kiss. "Go see your family, Annabelle. We're right here with you."

She nodded, blew out a heavy breath, then opened the door that led directly into the ICU waiting room.

The place was crowded with people, but Mark picked out the Monroes right away. Two women who bore a startling resemblance to Annabelle sat on either side of an attractive older woman. The man standing behind her was a masculine version of Mark's ex-wife. The expressions on the faces of all four as they caught sight of Annabelle gave his heart a little twist on her behalf.

Her mother's eyes softened with relief and love. One sister smiled with welcome; the other's face went stony with anger. Her brother looked like he'd choke her if given half the chance.

Mark took a protective step closer to Annabelle.

"Oh, baby." Her mother lifted her arms. "I'm so glad you are here."

Annabelle crossed the room in three long strides, dropped to her knees before her mother, and buried her head on the older woman's lap. "Mama, I'm so sorry."

The angry sister—the youngest, Mark guessed—snapped, "Well, I certainly hope you are."

"Come on, Lissa," said the other sister.

"Don't 'Come on, Lissa' me. I'm not the problem. I'm not the one who worried Mom and Dad half to death by disappearing for months on end with my job. I'm not the one who broke their hearts by deciding to live in Hawaii."

"Save it, Lis," her brother said, glaring down at Annabelle. "Not in front of Mom."

"Not anywhere," the first sister fired back. Mark decided he liked her.

The brother added stonily, "We'll visit with her at home."

Mark's fingers literally itched to reach out and pop him one. Under other circumstances, he might have done it. He opened his mouth to put in his two cents' worth when Annabelle's mother said, "Stop it. All of you." She stroked Annabelle's hair. "Your sister served her country—her father and I are proud of her for it, and you all know it. What happened isn't her fault. She didn't set that explosion. So just hush. We will stand together as a family here. No squabbling, especially in public. That's the way your father would want it."

At that, Annabelle lifted her head, glanced at her sisters and her brother, and repeated, "I'm sorry."

The angry sister, Lissa, appeared to crumple. "Me, too. I'm sorry, too. It's just been . . . scary."

"How's Daddy?"

Her brother spoke. "Better. They're running a couple tests now. . . . That's why we're all in the waiting room. You'll be able to go in and see him soon."

"Does he know what happened?"

"We don't even know what happened," the sister who'd smiled said. "Or who these . . . interesting . . . men are who accompanied you."

Annabelle glanced back over her shoulder as if she'd forgotten Mark and Harrington were there.

"Oh . . . um . . ." She climbed back onto her feet, then gestured to Mark, then Harrington. "Mark Callahan, Tag Harrington, meet the Monroes. My mother, Lynn, my brother, Adam, and my sisters, Lissa and Amy. Guys, Mark and Tag are colleagues of mine. They're gonna help us find out who did this to Daddy."

Adam Monroe stepped out from behind his mother and, ignoring Mark, shook Harrington's hand. "Sorry to involve you in family drama. Everyone around this is a little uptight right now."

"Understandable," Harrington said, waving it off.

Mark wasn't quite so willing to let it go. He didn't like this guy and judging by the look in his eyes, Adam Monroe didn't care for him much, either. It made Mark wonder what, if anything, he might know about Mark's situation with his sister.

But that was a discussion for another time. Annabelle was all that mattered now and she was why he inserted himself into the fray. "Annabelle hasn't exactly had it easy lately herself. In fact yesterday—"

"Mark," she interrupted, glancing over her shoulder, her brown eyes big and pleading. "Don't. It's okay." Then brother and sister wrapped their arms around each other for a hug, proving the fact of her assertion.

Her sisters greeted both Mark and Harrington with a handshake. Mrs. Monroe stood up and gave them both a hug, saying, "Thank you so much for bringing my baby girl home safe and sound."

For a split second, Mark catapulted back in time, back into his own mother's arms. Dear God, he missed her. How different his life would have been had she not died so young. He cleared his throat, met Lynn Monroe's gaze—Annabelle had her eyes—and made a solemn promise. "I intend to make sure she remains safe and sound."

At that point, a group of a dozen or so people entered the waiting room and Mark and Harrington were introduced to aunts, uncles, cousins, and neighbors who had returned from the cafeteria with a positive report on the quality of the supper menu. Annabelle's siblings urged their mother to go have a meal herself, but Lynn refused and a gentle argument ensued, interrupted a few minutes later when a nurse opened the unit's inner doors. "Mrs. Monroe? We're done. Two of you can come back now."

Lynn held her hand out to Annabelle. "Come with me, baby. Your shining face is just the medicine your daddy needs."

Annabelle cast one quick panicky glance toward Mark, then followed her mother. As Mark stood and watched the metal doors swing behind her, an elderly woman—Great-aunt Polly—said, "So, young man. How long have you been sleeping with our Annabelle?"

A giant wave of guilt rolled over Annabelle as she entered the ICU cubicle where her father lay sleeping, hooked up to tubes and electrodes and machines that hummed and beeped. On the left side of his head a bandage covered a shaved section of his salt-and-pepper hair. One arm was folded across his chest, a line taped into place on the back of a hand whose skin appeared black-and-blue and paper thin.

"Oh, Daddy," she murmured.

His eyes opened, blinked. He looked around, found his wife, and smiled wearily. "Lynnie."

Lynn Monroe stepped next to the bed and gently took his hand, then motioned to Annabelle. "Look who's here, honey."

Annabelle blinked away her tears. "Hi, Daddy."

Light brightened his blue eyes. "Little Bit. You came."

"Of course I came. How are you feeling?"

"Not too bad, considering." He thumbed the motor control on his bed and raised his upper body into a seated position. Then, his voice stronger than before, he cleared his throat and added, "I knew I could get you home if I blew myself up."

She closed her eyes and shuddered as she imagined the scene. "Oh, Daddy, I'm so sorry this happened. It tears me apart to know . . . well . . ." She swallowed hard. "You are in that bed because of my job. If I had known then what I know now, I would have gone to beauty school like you wanted."

"Oh, stop it. You would have been a disaster at cutting hair. Now, what I would like is an explanation. Your mother was skimpy with details. Someone is going around killing people you worked with?"

Annabelle brought her parents up-to-date with a short, succinct report that provided the information they needed and deserved while leaving out details that would cause them extra worry. She ended by saying, "We are going to find the people responsible and make them pay. And in the meantime, we'll keep everybody safe. I promise, Daddy. You have my solemn word. I brought team members with me and we're hiring extra security for everyone in the family until whoever did this is caught."

"Even Aunt Polly?"

A smile flickered on Annabelle's lips. "Even Aunt Polly."

"You better pick out your toughest man to guard her."

Annabelle had a quick mental vision of Mark attempting to tell Aunt Polly what to do. She would shake her finger in his face and stomp her cane to punctuate her comments. Then she would do what she wanted to do anyway. "Or the man with the most patience."

Frank Monroe nodded. "You do have a point. You say you brought people with you?"

"Yes."

"Who is in charge? I want to meet him."

Annabelle glanced at her mother, then said, "Visitors are limited to family, aren't they? Maybe once you are out of ICU."

"Tonight, Annabelle," Frank Monroe instructed. "Now."

She hadn't expected to have to introduce Mark to her father and she wasn't prepared for it. She attempted to put him off by saying, "I don't know that either Mark or Tag is any more in charge than I am, Daddy. If you want—"

"Mark? Wasn't your team leader named Mark? Mark Callahan?"

"I guess the concussion didn't hurt your memory at all, did it?"

"Go get the man, Little Bit."

Annabelle had never disobeyed that tone of voice in her life.

She returned to the waiting room, but Mark was nowhere to be found. She looked at Amy. "Mark?"

Aunt Polly piped up. "He couldn't take the heat and got out of the kitchen."

"He went down to the gift shop to buy me a pack of gum," Amy explained.

Annabelle shot a querying look to Tag, who stood guard at the ICU outer door. He fought a grin as he shrugged. "Your aunt is a pistol, Anna-B."

He didn't have to say more. Experience had taught her long ago that Aunt Polly had never met a question too personal to ask. It was obvious that Mark had run for cover.

"I like him," Amy said.

"I don't," snapped Adam and Lissa simultaneously

just as Mark shoved open the waiting room door and stepped inside.

He gave Amy a tight smile as he handed her the pack of gum. "Thanks," she said.

"Thank you," Mark responded before glancing at Annabelle. With his jaw set and his body vibrating with tension, he asked, "Are you ready to leave now?"

"No. My father wants to talk to you."

Mark nodded, then hesitated. He shifted his gaze toward Aunt Polly. "Is she related on your father's side of the family or your mother's?"

"My dad's. Why?"

Aunt Polly said, "He's afraid that your daddy will see what I saw."

Mark took her arm and led her out of the waiting room. "Let's go, Annabelle. Now."

Aunt Polly's voice followed them. ". . . that you and that young man are having S-E-X."

Annabelle closed her eyes and groaned.

"You might have warned me, Annabelle," Mark said through gritted teeth.

"What did you say to her?"

"Nothing! Not a damned thing! What is she . . . some sort of witch?"

"Just shoot me," Annabelle muttered. "Just shoot me now and put me out of my misery."

"You know, right now is probably not a good time to be using that particular expression." Mark dropped his hold on her arm and raked his fingers through his hair. "I need a Sitrep here. What does your father want from me?"

"Reassurance, I think."

"About our sex life?"

"About his family's safety."

"Oh. Okay, that I can do."

Annabelle led him past the nurses' station, holding up her hand to ward off their protest. "He's the man guarding the family. I'm just going to introduce them and leave."

Mark wore a solemn expression as Annabelle presented him to her father. The two men spoke briefly about Frank Monroe's injuries and anticipated recovery, and then her father asked Mark how he intended to guarantee the safety of the Monroe family.

"I brought one of my best men with me, sir, and I've also retained the services of the best personal-security firm in Texas. I've worked with them in the past and I can assure you that they are good people. They're due to arrive before morning, and they'll make sure nothing more happens to your family."

Annabelle's mother said, "This is all just a nightmare. Why would anyone do something like this?"

"I don't know, Mom, but we'll find out." Annabelle held up a finger, gesturing "one more minute" to the nurse.

Mark said, "Mr. Monroe, I'd like to hear your description of what happened the other night."

"So would I," Frank observed. "Unfortunately, I can't recall a blessed thing after saying grace over our meal two days ago."

"Would it help to hear it from my perspective?" Annabelle's mother asked.

"Yes, certainly," Mark replied.

While Lynn Monroe couldn't describe what had happened in the kitchen, she did fill in enough of the blanks for Annabelle to note the similarities between this explosion and the one that killed Jeremy Russo. "Mama, have you had any unusual visitors to the farm recently?"

"Bart Torbush is damned unusual," her father offered.

Annabelle grinned at her father's mention of the

local Methodist preacher, while her mother scoffed, "Oh, Frank."

It was good to see that his sense of humor was still intact. "I meant any visitors you didn't already know. Any strangers."

Her parents looked at each other. Frank said, "The photographer."

"A woman?" Mark asked.

"No. A man." Annabelle's mother frowned. "I considered him myself, but he was such a nice man, at the farm two full days before the accident."

It wasn't a freaking accident, Annabelle thought.

"It's not difficult to delay a detonation, Mrs. Monroe," Mark said. "With a thorough investigation, the authorities should be able to pinpoint a trigger. If they can't, we have access to people who can."

Annabelle asked, "Who was he? Why was he there?"

"His name was something plain. . . . Hmm." Lynn Monroe thought a minute. "Johnson. Bob Johnson. He said he was doing a coffee-table book about farmhouses. It's supposed to be published next year by a New York publisher. He spent the better part of two days around the place taking pictures both inside and out."

Mark asked, "Did he carry a camera bag around with him?"

"Yes, two of them, in fact."

"Were you with him all the time?"

"Oh, heavens no. We showed him around, then went about our business."

"Can you describe him for us, Mama?"

"I can try." She thought a moment, then said, "He's about your age, Annabelle. About your height, Mr. Callahan. He wore cargo pants and a T-shirt and a photographer's vest. Sneakers on his feet."

Frank Monroe added, "He wore an earring. A gold

stud. I thought that meant he's gay, but he talked about his wife and children, and your sister says that earrings aren't a gay thing anymore." Shooting a sharp look at Mark, he added, "What about you? You got an earring, boy?"

"No, sir," he said with a smile, before meeting Lynn's gaze. "Do you recall complexion type? Hair color? Eye color?"

"He had fair skin and his hair was cut very short—a flattop, we called them back in my day. His eyes were brown. I remember because I noticed his eyelashes. The man had the thickest, longest lashes."

"What are you doing noticing another fella's eyelashes?"

Lynn lifted her gaze to the ceiling and sighed. "Adam met him, too. You might see if he remembers more."

Annabelle asked, "And you never saw a woman with him?"

"No."

At that point the nurse lost her patience and stepped into the room. "I've allowed this to go on long enough. One of you must leave now."

"My cue." Mark spoke up, shifting toward the door. "We can finish this later, ma'am."

Annabelle's mother studied her husband and gently brushed his hair away from his brow. "Actually, I think it's time we all leave. You are tired, honey. I am, too. We both can use some rest."

"You'll go home like you promised?" he asked, catching her hand and bringing it to his lips for a kiss. "You won't try to spend the night up here again? You need a good night's sleep."

"I'm going home. Adam has offered to stay the night here, and I'll be back here first thing in the morning."

Frank scowled. "Adam doesn't need to stay. I'll be fine. Tell him to go home to his family."

Lynn pursed her mouth. "Are you sure?"

"I'm going to take that sleeping pill the doctor ordered and saw logs. Y'all go on now."

Both women kissed Frank Monroe good night, then joined Mark, who waited in the hallway. "He looks good, don't you think?" Lynn asked her daughter. "His color is better. I think he's better. I think he'll be fine."

"I know he will," Annabelle replied in a reassuring tone. She believed it, too. Seeing him had made all the difference. "I'm not worried at all, Mama. Not anymore."

Not about this attack, anyway, she thought as she turned her attention to preventing another. The photographer was the key. He had to have been the one to set the explosives.

They'd walked halfway back toward the waiting room when Annabelle slowed. Something was bugging her. Something her mom had said. She couldn't quite put her finger on it.

She put that issue away as they returned to the hospital waiting room, and she was forced to run interference between Mark and Aunt Polly by falling on the proverbial sword and asking her aunt about her bunions. She watched her siblings' jaws drop because they all knew that the question had invited a twenty-minute harangue.

At least they wouldn't ask her about her sex life in front of Mom. She couldn't say the same if it were just Aunt Polly.

Aunt Polly moved on to gallstones when the family doctor sauntered through the doors, his relaxed air easing the tension still humming inside Annabelle. He discussed the results of the latest tests and agreed that no family member needed to stay overnight. Annabelle thought her mother might burst into tears when he predicted that, barring any unforeseen complications, he would discharge Frank Monroe in two days.

Relieved, her family scheduled hospital visits for the following day, after which Mark and Tag discussed security arrangements. Though it took creative maneuvering, Annabelle managed to escape the hospital without confrontation about her sex life from any of her oh-so-nosy relatives.

Her thoughts returned to the photographer during the hour-long drive out to the farm in the rental car Tag had arranged. What was bothering her? What clue had her mother provided that she couldn't quite put her finger on?

"I need to clear my mind," she said as she turned off the highway onto the road that led to the Monroe family farm. "Wish I had real running shoes instead of these Keds. I'd go for a run."

Mark glanced at her. "You do have athletic shoes. Running clothes, too. I asked the Telluride police chief's wife to buy us a little of everything to replace what we left at Stanhope's place. I made sure you had workout clothes, since I know you prefer exercise to popping Xanax to deal with stress. They're in suitcases in the back."

"Thank you." Annabelle wasn't surprised. The man knew her too well. As soon as she got home she'd . . .

"Why wait?" she murmured before steering the car off the road and onto the narrow shoulder. She pushed the button to release the trunk. "The house is about six miles straight up this road. Yellow paint with white shutters. You can't miss it."

Tag's brows winged up. "You're going running? Now?"

"You know, that is an excellent idea." Mark opened his car door. "I'll go with you."

"I'll be fine by myself."

"I know, Annabelle. It's my drug of choice, too."

She shrugged, then spoke to Tag. "The first house on the left is my brother's place. Keep going past it for another half mile. Do yourself a favor and say yes when my mom offers you chocolate cake."

"Isn't her kitchen blown to hell?"

"Won't matter. She'll have it. It's my grandmother's recipe and my sisters sell it in their bakery in town. One of them will have sent some home."

She climbed out of the car and walked back to the trunk. Guessing that the pink suitcase was hers, she unzipped it, then removed running shoes, socks, a sports bra, and wind shorts. When she whipped her shirt over her head and reached to unfasten her bra, Mark muttered, "Good Lord." Then he reached for his own suitcase and called out, "Eyes forward, Harrington."

Five minutes later, the car's taillights were pinpoints in the distance and Annabelle and her ex-husband ran side by side on the asphalt road. It was the first time they'd been alone since the shower sex, but she didn't expect him to bring the subject up. She and Mark had been running partners for years, and they each knew what the other wanted while they ran—silence. Lovely, peace-bringing silence.

Annabelle picked up her pace as the endorphins kicked in. The moon had yet to rise, and as the evening darkness deepened, stars flickered into sight in the sky above like freckles on a face. She filled her lungs with fresh country air. With the scent of home. And she ran a little faster. Her muscles strained, and her breathing labored. Her mind went blessedly blank.

And suddenly she remembered.

Chapter Ten

Mark was thinking about fire ant hills and wondering if the pesky insect that terrorized Texas had made it as far north as Kansas when Annabelle pulled up short. "Eyelashes!"

He halted forward progress but continued to run in place as he asked, "You have something in your eye?"

"No, in my brain. Eyelashes!"

He wished the moon would rise. He could barely see her. "Honey, I think you've cracked."

"Think back, Callahan. Remember when Colonel Warren was assembling the team? He brought on a guy that lasted two months, maybe three? He and Noah despised one another. Remember? He had the most beautiful eyelashes I've ever seen on a man."

Mark rubbed the back of his neck as he thought for a moment. Kincannon had despised a lot of people. Finally, he shook his head. "Eyelashes on a man aren't something I tend to notice, Annabelle."

She snapped her fingers repeatedly, searching for the memory. "What was his name? C'mon, Callahan. You remember him. You didn't like him any more than Noah did. One of the first things you did after the colonel named you as team leader was to give the guy the boot."

Since it was obvious she wasn't going anywhere anytime soon, Mark stopped jogging in place. "Why did I kick him off? What did he do wrong?"

He watched the shadow that was Annabelle brace her hands on her hips and stare at the ground. "I'm not sure. Oh, man. It was so long ago."

"Almost ten years," Mark said. "I've met a lot of people in that amount of time."

"Me, too."

"Which makes me wonder if your eyelash guy is the same guy as your mother's eyelash guy. Maybe you two just have a thing for eyelashes. Ten years is a long time for someone to nurse a grudge without doing something about it."

"So, something had to trigger it. I wonder what." Without warning, Annabelle started running again. "We need to get to a phone and you need to call Colonel Warren. Ask him to get us a list of everyone who washed out of the program. Dad has a fax at home or the colonel could e-mail it. Whichever is easier. If I see the name, I'll remember it."

Hidden by the darkness, Mark gave her a smart-ass salute.

An hour later, showered and dressed in a fresh T-shirt and jeans, Mark checked the fax machine and then his e-mail in her father's office. Nothing on the fax, but his in-box had a message from the colonel. He opened the e-mail and read the list of names. He could recall some of the men; others he blanked on entirely. As he printed the list, the fax number rang and the first of the photographs came through.

Those would take a while, Mark knew, so he carried the list of names toward the dining room, where he heard Annabelle speaking with her sister.

"Mmm . . . ," she moaned ecstatically. "Nothing on earth is better than Nana's chocolate cake."

"Are you sure about that?" Amy asked. "And here I was thinking that you'd rate sex with Sergeant Steamy as number one."

Just out of sight beyond the doorway, Mark halted. He peered through the crack between the door and its frame to see his ex-wife seated at her mother's dining room table sharing a double-sized slab of chocolate cake with her sister.

Color flushed Annabelle's cheeks as she closed her eyes. "What's with this sudden fascination everyone has with my sex life?"

Amy shrugged. "You always made such a big deal out of holding out for marriage. I'm just glad to know they won't be asking you to star in the sequel to *The Forty-Year-Old Virgin*."

"Look, he's a colleague. That's all." She paused as Amy snorted in disbelief, then added, "And he never was a sergeant. He was a lieutenant."

"Lieutenant Luscious, then. Man, oh man . . . those shoulders, those six-pack abs." She waggled her brows and pretended to swoon. "Tell me he has a package to match?"

"Amy! Excuse me, but what would your husband say about your ogling another man?"

She waved a dismissive hand. "I can blame it on hormones. That gets me out of all kinds of trouble these days." She glanced toward the staircase, then said, "Mom has gone to bed, right?"

When Annabelle nodded, she leaned close and said in a low tone, "We haven't told the folks yet, but I'm pregnant."

Mark's stomach sank. *Shit. That's all Annabelle needs.*

Outwardly, Annabelle reacted exactly how her younger sister would have wanted. Smiling widely, she reached over and hugged Amy hard. Mark knew her well enough to see that inwardly, though, she took it as yet another blow.

Her baby sister was going to have a baby.

"Ah, Amy, that's wonderful news!" Annabelle bubbled. "I'm so happy for you. When are you due?"

"Christmas. If we have a girl, we're going to name her Holly."

Mark decided that now was a good time to intervene. He stepped into the doorway and cleared his throat. The women looked up. Annabelle's chin lifted high as the old resentment rushed back into her eyes. "Do you need something?"

Mark suspected she'd like to throw her cake at him.

He crossed the room, all business, as he handed the printed e-mail list to her. "Here are the names from Colonel Warren. He's faxing the pictures now."

His hair wet from his shower, Harrington entered the dining room as Annabelle studied the list. "William Ronald Kurtz," she said. "Ron Kurtz. That's him, Callahan."

Ron Kurtz. Didn't ring a single bell. Mark glanced at Harrington. "Do you remember him?"

"No." His old friend shrugged. "The name doesn't ring any bells for me."

"Me, either. But Annabelle's instincts are good. I think we might be on to something here."

Amy rose from her seat. "Should I go wake Mom?"

"No, let her sleep," Annabelle decided after a moment's thought. "They said Adam met the photographer. Let's call him instead."

Adam Monroe drove a utility cart from his place up to the farmhouse, arriving just as the fax of Ron Kurtz's image began to emerge from the machine in his father's office. Mark clasped the paper the moment it was free and studied it. "Okay, yeah. Now I remember him."

He handed the page to Adam, and Annabelle held her breath.

Her brother frowned, then slowly nodded. "Yes, that's the photographer. He's the one who did this?"

Annabelle's eyes gleamed with fierce exultation. "Yes, he's the one who did this."

"Why?" Amy asked. "What does he have against you?"

"I don't know." Annabelle pursed her lips and considered it, then glanced up at Mark. "I also don't know how he is connected to the impostor at the gallery."

"I intend to find out," Mark replied, his voice hard and determined. "Before anyone else gets killed."

Captiva Island, Florida

Ron Kurtz couldn't understand why all these old geezers liked to collect seashells. The way he saw it, somebody who had the cash to retire to a place like this should collect something cool like classic cars or guns.

Gun collecting would be fine. That's what he would collect if he had the money. Antique firearms. Colt revolvers and Elgin cutlass pistols. A Remington Creedmoor rolling-block action rifle.

Hell, he got hard just thinking about it.

Instead, these old farts strolled along the sand looking for pieces of old dead animals.

If you could call what they did strolling. More like tottering or weaving. He was glad the Kincannons had been the active type. Otherwise, Noah Kincannon might have considered his parents a burden and would have been glad to see them gone. That would have ruined everything.

Kurtz lifted the baseball cap from his head and rubbed a hand over his hair, wiping away the sweat.

He didn't like wearing hats. Always made his head hot. But once he'd heard Noah's most recent phone message and realized he had a few more hours to kill, he'd decided to get out of the house and the cap was part of his disguise.

Not that he figured any of these geezers would pay a bit of attention to him. Their gazes were all locked on the beach, looking for their treasures.

Hell, he should have stayed at the house. He'd walked down here hoping to spy some eye-candy pussy sunning in string bikinis. Instead, all he'd found were wrinkled-up prunes spoiling the scenery.

Goddamned Land of the Retirees, Florida. Why hadn't Noah sent his parents to a California beach?

Whistling the Beach Boys' "California Girls" beneath his breath, Kurtz turned and started back toward the Kincannon house, a short five-minute walk from the beach. He'd turn on the television and see who Oprah had on her show. Maybe he'd bake some cookies. While rummaging for breakfast in the pantry this morning, he'd noticed the old lady had the makings for chocolate-chip cookies. Bet old Noah would appreciate being met with the scent of fresh-baked cookies on the air when he walked through the front door.

Besides, it would make his own wait more pleasant, since it would help cover up the stench of blood.

Happy at the thought, Kurtz hitched his canvas supply bag over his shoulder and walked the short block to the white house with its pink plantation shutters. He wondered how Noah had liked his folks having pink shutters on their house.

"Pretty damned gay if you ask me," he murmured. He'd be embarrassed if it were his folks' place.

Just looking at the house pissed him off. Property like that had to be worth over a million. Probably a million five. Back in the day, Noah Kincannon didn't come from money. None of the Fixers did. Well, technically the a-hole Callahan did, but nobody knew it at the time. It was their stint in the unit that made everyone rich, gave them the skills and experience and contacts they used to rack up the big bucks once they left the service. Made it possible for Kincannon to set his parents up in highfalutin digs like these.

That's what Callahan had taken away from him when he kicked him off the team. Taken away his future. Taken away his prosperity. He'd had to work his ass off all these years while they sat around and got rich. The bastard said he didn't have what it took. Said he lacked discipline and the mental intensity to make it.

Then that fucker Dennis Nelson had the balls to show up at his workplace and accuse him of turning on his country. Accuse him of being a goddamned traitor! Of all the nerve.

It still chapped Kurtz's ass that Nelson died before he could get to him.

"Well, I'm teaching the rest of them, though, aren't I?" Kurtz smiled, then burst into a laugh. "I'm teaching all of them."

Access to the Kincannon house was a piece of cake, with the lush vegetation shielding the view of any potentially nosy neighbors. When he'd arrived last night shortly before the Kincannons themselves returned home from a last-minute trip to Orlando—and why did old folks want to go to Disney, anyway?—he had picked the lock and waltzed inside slick as snot.

The first thing he'd done after determining that no one was at home was to note the blinking light on the answering machine. Listening to the increasingly worried messages from the old geezers' son had made him smile. In fact, he'd been so pleased by the stir he'd created that he took pity on Mom and Dad and waited until they came home and went to sleep before he shot them.

Offing the old folks hadn't given him quite the charge as doing Stanhope's girlfriend in front of him. It paled in comparison with thinking about his little surprise for the Monroes.

"Annabelle Monroe," he murmured. "That bitch." He chuckled at the idea of what she must be feeling right about now. He wondered how many of her family members died. With any luck, every last one of 'em. Maybe after he finished up here, he would stop by the local library or an Internet café and see what the Kansas papers had to say. Unfortunately, the Internet was down on the Kincannons' computer. "That must needle Noah, too."

Kurtz startled as the phone began to ring. He waited it out until the answering machine clicked on. "Mom? Dad? You there?"

Noah. Kurtz's eyes widened and he grinned with delight.

"Hello! Mom? Dad? Pick up the phone! Mrs. Wilson next door said you came home last night, so I know you're there. I've been trying to track you down for a day and a half."

Kurtz followed the sound to the room that served as a study for the old geezer, and the telephone sitting on the whitewashed desk. He was tempted . . . oh, so tempted . . . to answer and have a little conversation with dear old Noah.

He heard mumbled curses coming from the machine, then a heavy sigh. "Mom, Dad, we need to make some changes. I know how much you two enjoy your impromptu trips, but you need to let somebody know where you are going and how you can be reached."

"Not gonna be a problem any longer, Noah," Kurtz said into the empty room.

From the machine, Kincannon's voice continued. "I'm on my way there. It's been one travel delay after another, but the weather finally lifted in Atlanta, so I'll arrive by lunchtime. Anyway, I need you to do a favor for me and stay home until I get there. I've sent someone over to keep an eye on things until then, so don't be nervous when you see him sitting outside."

"They won't be nervous," Kurtz told the phone. "They were dead before the pitiful excuse of a security guard you hired arrived. Really, Noah, I know the pickings are slim around here where muscle is concerned, but you could have done better."

"Mom? Dad?" Noah Kincannon let out another heavy sigh. "Good-bye. See you soon."

"Yep. Yes, you will." And Ron Kurtz chortled.

He returned to the kitchen, where he set out ingredients for cookies and imagined Kincannon's arrival. God, this was fun. So much more fun to drag it out, to make them suffer before he killed them, than to off them outright.

While he creamed shortening, sugar, and eggs in a stand mixer, he pictured Noah Kincannon wailing and gnashing his teeth. He'd measured out a cup of flour when an unexpected sound caught his attention. The doorbell. Someone was at the door.

Quietly, Kurtz moved to a window that allowed him to see the front porch. A woman. Mid-thirties, attractive, classy. She dressed well in a tailored jacket and slacks. Definitely not Florida-casual attire. She could be a neighbor woman on her way to work. More likely, she could be another security person. Maybe even a cop. That jacket was unnecessary for the temperate weather this morning. It could be concealing her weapon.

The bell rang again. Kurtz debated whether to invite her in or wait her out and see if she went away. He decided it was better to speak to her. He could deal with one person easily. If she yanked out a cell phone and called in a squad of cops, he'd be up shit creek.

He turned the mixer on low, grabbed a tea towel to wipe his hands, then walked to the front door. "Hello, can I help you?"

The woman smiled. "May I speak with Mr. or Mrs. Kincannon, please? I'm an old friend of their son's."

Kurtz flipped the towel over his shoulder and smiled broadly. This wasn't a cop. He opened the screen door, saying, "Sure, come on in. I'm Jack Watson with Comfort Keepers Elder Care. I hope you weren't standing here long. I'm in the kitchen baking cookies. Mr. K. sure does have a sweet tooth."

The woman stepped inside and glanced around with polite curiosity. "Are the Kincannons in the kitchen, too?"

"No, they're at their morning water-aerobics class." He made a show of glancing at the clock. "They'll be home in another twenty minutes. Would you like to wait in the kitchen with me? I just made a fresh pot of coffee."

"That will be lovely. Thank you."

Kurtz led her toward the kitchen, saying, "So, you are a friend of Noah's? I'm sorry, I don't believe I caught your name."

She offered a friendly smile and said, "I'm Annabelle. Annabelle Monroe."

A warm rush of excitement washed through Ron Kurtz's blood, the predator on the scent of prey. This woman wasn't Annabelle Monroe. How interesting that she would claim otherwise. Who, then, could this person be? What did she want with Noah's parents?

In the kitchen, Kurtz motioned for her to take a seat at the table. He removed an ironstone cup from a cabinet and poured her a cup of coffee. "Cream or sugar, Annabelle?"

"Neither, thank you."

"Let me get these cookies in the oven—then we'll chat," he told her as he set her cup on the table and returned to the mixer. With the motor turned to low, he quickly and efficiently added the dry ingredients to the bowl and then the chocolate chips. When his cookie dough was ready, he removed the bowl from the mixer and carried it to the table. "Would you like a spoonful of dough? I have to admit it's my favorite part."

"No, thank you." Again, she gave a polite smile, then added, "The coffee is delicious."

"Thanks. I'm afraid I am a coffee snob. The first thing I did when I went to work for the Kincannons was to dig out their coffee grinder from the depths of the pantry. At least they kept beans in the freezer."

Kurtz filled a cookie sheet with little balls of dough, then slipped the pan into the preheated oven. He set the timer, washed his hands, and carried the cookie jar over to the table. He smiled warmly at "Annabelle" as he reached into the glazed pottery jar with his right hand.

He pulled out his gun. Took aim at her head.

As her eyes widened in alarm, he dipped the index finger of his left hand into the mixing bowl. His mouth made a popping sound as he sucked chocolate-chip-cookie dough from his finger. "Now, Ms. Whoever-You-Are. It's time for you to come clean. I need to know who you are and what your connection is to the Fixers. I suggest you be truthful and talk fast and convincingly."

He chambered a round and added, "You see, when my timer goes off, I'll decide whether you live or die."

The stress caught up with Annabelle. She had an awful time getting to sleep, but once she finally drifted off, she didn't awake until midmorning. "Oh, great," she muttered when she caught sight of the time. She'd catch grief from the sibs for this. She couldn't believe nobody woke her.

Rolling out of one of two twin beds in the bedroom she'd shared with Amy while growing up, she quickly showered and dressed, all the while wondering what she would find downstairs.

Maybe the reason no one woke her was that everyone was busy with their normal daily activities. Although her sisters did not intend to reopen their bakery until Dad was released from the hospital, Amy had mentioned something before she went home last night about bookkeeping issues that needed tending. Lissa had planned to spend the morning at the hospital and Adam had a million things to do here at the farm. That left Mom, who was probably chomping at the bit for Annabelle to get downstairs and take her into town to visit Dad.

And she couldn't forget Mark. Knowing that man, she would bet he'd rolled out of bed by six a.m. and started working the phones before his first cup of coffee—never mind that he'd worked late into the night and had less sleep than she over the past few days.

She wondered how long he and Tag had continued to work after she'd thrown in the towel and gone to bed last night. While Tag had been outlining a surveillance plan to the leader of the Texas team who Mark had brought in, her ex had been cursing her dad's computer equipment while he attempted to hack into databases in search of Ron Kurtz.

Downstairs, all was quiet. She peeked into her father's office first and found it empty and the computer turned off. Her mother was not in the ruins of the kitchen or in the master bedroom or bath. She did, however, find a note to her from her mother lying on the dining room table.

Annabelle: Your friend Tag is taking me to visit your father. You'll find a load of towels in the washer. Please put them in the dryer for me. Mark told me the news. I'm so excited!! See you this afternoon. Love, Mom.

"News?" she murmured. "What news?"

And where was Mark?

She walked out onto the porch and scanned the area. She waved to one of the men from Texas assigned to patrol the farmhouse. The chug of an engine drew her gaze to the field to the west, where she spied Adam perched atop the seat of the John Deere tractor. Still no Mark.

Back inside, she called, "Callahan?"

No response. Frowning, she gave the first floor another quick search, then climbed the staircase. She found him in her mother's sewing room, sound asleep in her grandmother's old padded rocking chair, one leg propped upon the matching ottoman, the other sprawled out on the floor. A magazine lay open on his lap. He held his cell phone clutched in his right hand.

He let out a soft snore.

The sight and the sound suddenly catapulted Annabelle back to a moment in their past when he was working out of DC and she was based in San Diego.

For a change of pace, when it was his turn to choose the spot for one of their getaway weekends, Mark had forsaken the glitz and glamour of the city and rented a cabin on a lake in the Ozark Mountains. Her flight had been diverted due to weather and she was late arriving. Four or five hours late, as she recalled. She had arrived midafternoon and instead of finding him fishing like she had expected, she'd walked into the cabin and interrupted his afternoon nap.

Ordinarily when they were together, whether on a mission or later during their marriage, Annabelle dropped off to sleep first. She had never caught him napping, never heard him snore. That day, she achieved both. He'd been stretched out on a couch with the sports page draped across his chest, sawing logs so loudly that he didn't hear her come inside. It was the first time, the only time, she ever managed to sneak up on him.

He'd looked boyish in sleep that day, softly relaxed, a lock of hair curling down over his brow. Then he'd opened his eyes and smiled at her, a slow, steamy flash of teeth.

There was nothing of the boy in that smile, in that look in his eyes. No softness in the man whatsoever.

He had crooked his finger at her. That's it. Just lifted a hand and wiggled that index finger and put her into some sort of sexual trance that had pulled her like the moon pulls the tides.

He never said a word. The entire time, everything he did to her, everything they did together, was accomplished without a single word being spoken between them.

She closed her eyes, remembering. The ripple of muscle beneath naked bronzed skin. The earthiness of his scent. His salty, masculine taste. The dark power of his touch as he compelled her to respond, as he freed her of all her inhibitions.

It had been rough, raw, and erotic. Fantasy sex. Forbidden sex. The kind of sex she could never have admitted she wanted. The kind of sex that brought shivers to her skin even now at the memory of it.

My God.

Now years later, here in her mother's sewing room, she felt herself sway as she experienced that pull once again. Opening her eyes, she found Mark awake and staring at her. This time there was no wicked smile of welcome, but the look in his eyes, the heat in his eyes, was as familiar to her as . . . her dreams.

"What are we going to do about this, Annabelle?" he asked.

She might have tried to deny she understood him, but she didn't have the energy to lie. "Nothing has changed. We can't keep rolling the dice. I don't want to be a single mother."

He put his feet on the floor and sat forward, his elbows propped on his knees, his head resting in his hands. Annabelle took a step backward, preparing to retreat. They could start this day over again later downstairs, where the mood wasn't so personal. Then he stopped her with a pair of world-rocking words. "You won't."

Everything inside her tensed. "What do you mean?"

After a long moment, he lifted his head. Still, his eyes didn't quite meet hers. "If you're pregnant, we'll remarry. I don't run from my responsibilities."

For a long moment, she felt nothing. Then pain whipped through her like a windstorm. Did the man intentionally mean to hurt her, or was he simply stupid like a . . . a . . . a man? "Why do I suddenly feel like the Irish waitress in *Caddyshack*?"

Callahan blinked, obviously caught off guard. Then she could see him mentally reviewing the movie, saw when he recalled the scene where the waitress's period was late and the caddy took the news on the chin, then stoically said, *We'll just get married.*

"Gee, Noonan," she said, sarcasm dripping from her tongue as she continued in *Caddyshack*-speak. "You hit that right in the lumberyard, didn't you?"

Now she'd made him mad. He shoved to his feet. "Dammit, Annabelle, don't—."

"No." She cut him off. "*You* don't. I'm tired of your attitude, Callahan. This hot and cold thing simply doesn't work for me."

"Attitude has nothing to do with it. We're talking about a child here. Our child."

"You mean the child you didn't want two and a half

years ago? The child you still didn't want yesterday up on that mountain? That child?"

"Yes, that child," he fired back. "Look, you are right. I admit it. I *am* a coward. The idea of father-hood scares the crap out of me."

That shocked her. She never dreamed he would admit it. The Mark Callahan she knew would never admit to such weakness. For some weird reason the fact that he had admitted it only stoked the fires of her temper hotter.

"But guess what?" he continued, his voice frustrated and accusing. "The thought of giving you up again is almost as frightening. Been there, done that. Hated it. I'm in a bind here, Annabelle, and I don't know what to do about it because I haven't had the chance to think about it. I've been too busy trying to find a killer to even sleep, much less solve my relation-ship psychoses."

"Is that what I am?" She put her hands on her hips. "A relationship psychosis?"

He froze. Seconds ticked by. The he blinked and flashed a grin that laughed at them both. "Honey, you are not a psychosis—you are a disease."

He reached out and grabbed her wrist, then yanked her against him. "You are in my blood, in my bones, and I have finally realized that you are there to stay."

But she wasn't ready to let it go. Petulantly, she muttered, "So I'm an incurable disease. Lovely. I—"

He swooped down and hushed her with a kiss—a long, deep melding of mouths that drained her of her temper and left her feeling raw and confused.

"It will be okay, Belle," he said against her temple. "I promise. We will figure it all out. We just need to give it a little time."

"Nothing is easy, is it?"

"You and I aren't the type of people to go for easy. We are all about challenge."

She nuzzled against him, inhaling his familiar scent, enjoying the comfort of his arms. They stayed that way for a good five minutes before a rumble from his stomach made her laugh. "Do you need breakfast, Callahan?"

"Lunch. I had breakfast with your mother."

With that, the moment of intimacy was behind them and Annabelle returned her attention to matters that required immediate attention. Like her own need for coffee.

"Speaking of my mother, what 'news' did you tell her and why were you sleeping in her sewing room?"

"Oh." Mark snapped his fingers. "I almost forgot."

He scooped up a magazine and his cell phone off the floor beside the rocker. "The kitchen she likes is in this issue and the magazine was up here. I sat down to make my calls and that's all it took. That chair, Annabelle. It doesn't look all that comfortable, but once you sit down . . . wow. Do you think she'd sell it to me?"

"She'd rather sell one of her children," Annabelle replied, a note of dryness in her tone. "What calls? Something about Ron Kurtz?"

"No. The kitchen. Turned out to be pretty easy, since the exact setup was already assembled and ready to ship to a builder in Florida. All I had to do was change the receiving address and expedite shipping."

She put the clues together. The news her mother's note referred to was kitchen news. Always interested in countertops herself, Annabelle grabbed the magazine. "Which one is it?"

"Page twenty-seven."

She flipped the pages to a beautiful French country kitchen. "What part is she getting?"

"The kitchen." Mark pressed by her and exited the sewing room.

"What part of the kitchen?" Annabelle asked as

she followed him downstairs, mentally reviewing just what in the kitchen was salvageable. The fridge was fine. She needed a new stove and one entire section of cabinets.

"The whole thing."

Annabelle mentally tallied the costs, then frowned. "My parents can't afford this."

"The unit's insurance will pay for it."

"What unit insurance? There is no unit insurance."

"Sure, there is. It's private insurance."

Private insurance? Then suddenly, she knew. Callahan Casualty, no doubt. "But—"

"Annabelle, think." His green eyes bored into her. "Your mother told me that your father is a proud man. The damages to your mother's kitchen happened because of the unit. I'm the unit commander. I'm the head Fixer. Let me fix this."

"Head Fixer? You?" She snorted even as a warm rush of affection flowed over her. For all his faults— of which there were many—Mark Callahan had always had a generous heart. "I guess that when it comes to kitchens, the Fixers could follow a 'don't ask, don't tell' policy."

"Exactly." He grinned at her, then added, "Well, except when one Fixer tells another where to find the kolaches your mother mentioned before she left?"

A short time later she sipped from her cup of freshly brewed coffee and refused his offer of ten dollars for the last fruit-filled pastry, the single one she'd claimed from the entire plate now empty but for crumbs. Only then did she feel up to facing the day.

"Were you able to find out anything more about Kurtz after I went to bed last night?"

He nodded. "I prepared a dossier. Made a copy for you." He pushed back from the table, saying, "Let me get it."

Annabelle watched him walk away, knowing she

should keep her mind on the business at hand, but unable to look away from his very fine butt. She took a bite of her sweet roll and sighed.

A minute later, he tossed a butterfly-clipped, two-inch-thick stack of papers in front of her. "Whoa. All this? What time did you go to bed last night?"

He shrugged. "I don't know. I lost track of time."

She flipped through the pages. "Does anything in here say where he is right now?"

"That I couldn't find. If he's flying, he's using false ID. I found no rental cars, no current credit cards, but get this. He was last seen at his current address in up-state New York four months ago. That was just a couple weeks after he had a visitor." He paused, waited for her to meet his gaze, then said, "Dennis Nelson."

"Our Dennis Nelson?" When he nodded, she took another sip of coffee and considered. "That's the trigger."

"Yep. I suspect so."

Annabelle drummed her fingers on the table. "Now that we know who we are looking for, we will find him, right? People can't hide in this day and age. Not for long, anyway."

"We'll find him, Annabelle."

The farmhouse telephone rang then, and Annabelle rose to answer it. Her sister Lissa called with the news that she was bringing lunch from one of their favorite restaurants in town. Annabelle knew better than to tell her that she'd just finished breakfast. While the sisters chatted, Annabelle noted that Mark had wandered over to the framed pictures that crowded one wall of the entry hall—her mother and father's proud "Hall of Fame."

Annabelle visualized what he saw. Adam at bat at T-ball, his eyes scrunched shut. Lissa in her ballerina costume at Halloween. Amy poised to dive into the pool at her first swim-team race. Annabelle was up there, too, of course. In the high school drama club's production of *Our Town*. Riding her bicycle with her best friend, playing cards clothespinned to the spokes of their wheels to turn them into "motorcycles." In front of the army recruiting office with Sergeant Harwell the morning she left for basic training.

She watched the smile on his face slowly fade as he reached the north end of the wall. The baby section. Annabelle and her siblings, Adam's three children, and Lissa's four. Her mother grouped the babies together because she loved to point out the family resemblance between them all.

Lissa's voice came over the receiver. ". . . Daddy's color was putrid. I swear, Anna-B, what is wrong with Aunt Polly?"

"If I try to answer that, we will still be talking when it's time for my shift at the hospital tonight."

Lissa laughed and declared she was on her way. They said good-bye and Annabelle hung up the phone.

Mark stood in front of the babies, his hands shoved into his pockets. The strain on his face made her heart break all over again.

Looking for something . . . anything . . . to distract him, she said, "Lissa is on her way with lunch. You have to promise me not to tell her that I just ate breakfast."

He grabbed on to her conversational distraction like a lifeline. "Oh yeah? What's it worth to me?"

Before she could answer, his cell phone rang. He pulled it from his pocket, checked the number, then answered, saying, "Hey there, Noah."

He turned away as he listened and Annabelle slowly became aware of the subtle stiffening of his stance. She moved around to see his face.

His brow was furrowed, his eyes closed. He wasn't happy about something. "Mark?"

He opened his eyes, and met and held her gaze as he said, "Christ, Noah. What the hell is going on?"

Chapter Eleven

Three dead.

Noah Kincannon had found three people dead in his parents' house. Three *strangers*.

"This whole thing is just getting weirder by the minute," Mark muttered a half hour after Kincannon's call had come in. He checked his e-mail one more time before joining Annabelle and her sister in the dining room. Lissa had arrived a few minutes before with takeout that smelled delicious, but Mark had told the women to start without him. He was waiting to hear from half a dozen people about a dozen different items.

Mostly he wanted to get a look at the crime-scene photos Kincannon was supposed to send in order to see what clues, if any, he could pick up from those.

He could only imagine what Kincannon had felt when he walked into his parents' home and discovered the woman's body in the kitchen along with a plate of freshly baked cookies, a glass of room-temperature milk, and a note to him waiting on the kitchen table. Tough, cold-blooded Noah Kincannon's voice had trembled when he relayed the contents of the note to Mark.

Welcome home, Noah. Go upstairs and say good night to your folks.

Kincannon had described climbing the staircase braced for the worst and discovering the two bodies in his parents' bed. He said it had taken him a full minute to really see them, to comprehend that the bodies were not those of his mother and father.

He had called Mark while waiting for the police to arrive in answer to his 911 call. The minute they had disconnected their call, Mark had fired off a flurry of e-mails, bugging everyone from Colonel Warren in Washington to a computer hacker even more talented than he for updates on previous requests he had made for information about Kurtz.

With nothing of import in his mailbox, Mark followed the women's voices to the lunch table. Pasting a smile on his face, he greeted Annabelle's sister and gestured toward the Styrofoam container on the table in front of an empty chair. "Is this mine?"

"Yes. The best meat loaf, green beans, and garlic mashed potatoes you'll ever eat," Annabelle replied, a question in her eyes.

She wanted to know if he'd heard from Kincannon, Mark knew. With her own loved ones protected, Annabelle had seen no reason to worry them further, and she had asked that they keep news of this latest attack from her family for the time being. He answered her silent inquiry with a surreptitious shake of his head. "Great. I'm starved."

Lunchtime discussions focused on lighter subjects as the sisters caught up on local gossip, the plans for Lynn Monroe's new kitchen, and Lissa's summertime plans with her family. Mark mostly listened while he shoveled the best meal he'd had in days into his mouth and in doing so saw a side of Annabelle's sister that she had kept hidden yesterday at the hospital. As she laughed about something one of her children did, he realized she reminded him of his twin's wife, Maddie. Annabelle's sister was fierce as a lioness when it came to family.

Mark's cell rang and he checked the number. Matt. "It's my brother," he said, aware of Annabelle's sudden tension. "Excuse me."

Stepping out onto the porch, he flipped the phone open and said, "Whatcha got?"

"A bruise on my chin after laughing at my wife when she tried to climb out of her chair. She looked so damned comical I couldn't help myself. Torie has a good right hook."

"You are a dumb-ass, Matthew. Did you call looking for sympathy or do you have information for me?"

"Dammit, Mark. You always take her side. Just for that, I might not tell you my news." He paused a moment before saying, "I've found Vince Holloway."

Mark braced himself. "He's dead?"

"Nope. Very much alive. Alive and working on the side of the angels in Pakistan. He sends his best to you and says to get the bastard."

Mark blew out a heavy, relieved breath. "Excellent news. For that, I'll give Torie a call and tell her she needs to kiss your bruise better."

"Hell, if I'd known that was the reward, I wouldn't have dodged when she tried to knee me in the junk."

"What about Holloway's family?" Mark asked, his thoughts moving forward.

"None to concern yourself over, according to Holloway. You can cross him off your worry list, brother."

"Good. That makes my job easier." Mark took quick mental stock of the current situation. Of the twelve members of the team, he could now account for ten of them. "That leaves only Rhonda Parsons and Jordan Sundine."

"Who do you want me to work on next?"

Mark considered what he knew so far about his missing teammates. "Parsons, I think. Sundine has always been a free spirit. It wouldn't be unusual for him to pick up and take off. Parsons is more of a worry. Being out of pocket this way is unusual for her, according to her brother. We really need to find my last two teammates."

"Are you still worried this Kurtz asshole might make a go at the families?"

"Oh yeah." Mark told his brother about the phone call from Kincannon. He didn't bother to suggest that Matt beef up security at home. His brother was a pro. He would do what needed doing.

"So who are the vics?" Matt asked.

"I'm waiting on that information myself. With any luck, the cops clear that up fast. Noah needs information about his family. The uncertainty is driving him crazy."

"I can certainly understand that." Matt waited a beat, then said. "All right, then. You better hang up the phone so I can track down your friend. I'll give you a call back soon. Probably won't take me any time at all to find these folks, since we both know I'm twice the investigator you are."

"Bite me." And with that pithy comment, Mark hung up and rejoined the women in the dining room, where conversation had moved on to the topic of their aunt Polly. Mark listened in amazement as the Monroe sisters discussed the sex lives of seniors at the assisted-living center where good ol' Polly lived. When they giggled over Aunt Polly's comments about her "current squeeze's package," he grew indignant on the gentleman's behalf. "Why, she's nothing more than a dirty old woman."

"Are you just now figuring that out, Callahan?" Lissa asked, a laugh in her voice.

He quit listening to them then and dug into the dessert she'd brought—a piece of heaven otherwise known as apple pie. Lost in the pleasure of it, at first he didn't notice Annabelle's and Lissa's expectant stares. "I'm sorry. What did I miss?"

Annabelle said, "Since Dad has been moved out of intensive care, the questions are starting. They'll be worse when he comes home and people come to visit and see for themselves what happened. We need a family plan on just what we should say. I asked for your opinion."

Mark licked his fork and considered the options. "I don't know how tenacious reporters are in this part of the world, but we don't need anyone to come snooping around. We don't want Kurtz to learn that we are on to him."

"Or for the Gallery Girl to be certain that she got away clean," Annabelle added.

"Why not call it a butane-tank malfunction and leave it at that?" he suggested.

"That's the simplest story," Lissa agreed. "Certainly better than Adam's suggestion." When Mark arched a querying brow, she explained. "He said we should say Mom got careless in the kitchen and blew the place up. Mom didn't think that was funny."

Annabelle winced, then said, "I'm wondering if it wouldn't be nice to have extra eyes on the situation here. We could float the story that someone from my old army outfit has post-traumatic stress syndrome and has targeted my family in order to hurt me. A good thing about living in a small town is that people watch out for one another." Glancing at Mark, she added, "That way if we need to go to Florida for Noah . . ."

Lissa straightened, her expression growing stormy.

"You are leaving? Already? For crying out loud, Annabelle, you just got here. Do you want to break Mom's heart? I can't believe you—"

"Kurtz killed three people this morning," Annabelle interrupted. When Lissa abruptly snapped her mouth shut, she continued. "We think Kurtz did it, anyway. It's a little early to be sure. It happened in our team member's parents' home."

"In Florida?" her sister asked, subdued.

"I don't think we will need to make that trip," Mark said. "Kincannon will be able to do the footwork there."

"Unless he is too busy looking for his parents."

Lissa asked, "Do you think this Kurtz guy hurt them, too?"

Annabelle abruptly set down her fork. Mark addressed the question. "We don't know enough to know that yet. Of course we hope that's not the case, but until they turn up one way or the other, we simply can't be certain."

Lissa chewed at her lower lip, a nervous habit Mark had watched Annabelle do a thousand times. Finally, her gaze direct and demanding, she asked, "Are we still in danger?"

Mark glanced at Annabelle, whose expression had taken on a grim cast. "Until we interrogate Kurtz and find out if this actually is a case of PTSD or something else . . . we just won't know for sure."

Annabelle rose from her seat and carried her lunch cartons to the kitchen. He heard the rattle of plastic as she dumped the remains of her lunch in the trash.

Mark met Lissa's gaze. "That said, I honestly believe Kurtz took his shot at y'all and won't come around again until he has a check by the name of everyone on the team. Lissa, the people we have watching over you are extremely good at their jobs.

Even better, your sister is on the case. I've worked with a whole lot of people over the years, and Annabelle is simply the best."

Lissa sat back in her chair and drummed her fingers on the table. After a moment, she snorted. "Don't let her fool you, Mark. She might be good at cloak-and-dagger stuff, but when it comes to kolaches, I leave her in the dirt."

"In your dreams," Annabelle said as she cleared her sister's and Mark's cartons, too.

With that, the mood lightened. Lissa invited Mark and Annabelle to walk with her down the road to Adam's house, where she wanted to coordinate Little League car pool with Adam's wife. "Better not," Annabelle told her. "I have a stack of reports to go through before I go into town to see Daddy."

A few minutes later as he watched Lissa stride down the front walk, Mark observed, "I don't think she hates me as much today as she did last night."

"Callahan charm strikes again," Annabelle murmured. "Besides, she didn't hate you. She hates the work. That's what you represented. Adam, on the other hand, hates you. He knows about us."

"What? I thought you hadn't told your family."

"Just Adam. He was visiting me when the divorce was final. I . . . um . . . had a few drinks."

Mark recalled the man who had answered when he had phoned that day. Not a boyfriend, but her brother. Well . . . well . . . well. Apparently he had obsessed over nothing. "No wonder he looked like he wanted to kill me."

"I wouldn't get too close to him if he has a pitchfork in his hand if I were you." She turned toward her father's office and changed the subject. "Why don't you check your e-mail? Maybe Noah has sent us something by now."

Mark dragged his gaze away from the barn into

which Adam had moments earlier disappeared. He sauntered into the office and moved the computer mouse. Four new messages.

Kincannon's had an attachment. "Here we go."

Annabelle moved to stand beside him and they read the message together.

> *My family is safe. Located at condo in Branson, Missouri, as part of a house-swap vacation. Deceased couple identified. A case of wrong place, wrong time. Woman in kitchen remains a mystery.*

Mark clicked on the first photo. A man, seventies, single shot to the head. Same for the woman beside him in the bed.

"Those poor people," Annabelle murmured.

He opened the third picture and froze. Beside him, Annabelle gasped. "It's her. The woman from the gallery."

They both stared at the photograph for a long minute. Then she added, "I don't get it. I don't get this at all. What connection does she have to Kurtz? Was she working with him and he turned on her?"

"Or was she after him, too?" Mark recalled the theory that had occurred to him up in the mountains of Colorado. "Did she or whoever she worked for figure out what Kurtz was doing and try to stop him?"

"If that's the case, then why try to kill you and me?"

"We won't know anything until we figure out who the hell she is."

Mark flipped open his cell phone and dialed Kincannon. He answered on the first ring. "Any ID on the body downstairs?" Mark asked.

"No. Nothing. No purse, no car keys. Not a blessed thing." Mark communicated the news to Annabelle with a shake of his head.

"We need that information," he said into the phone. "She is the shooter who came after us in Colorado."

Kincannon took a moment to digest that before replying in a dry tone, "That's interesting."

"To put it mildly. We need a name and to know what connection she had to Kurtz. Are the locals giving you access? Do you need some help from Washington?"

"I met a little resistance. I've already called the colonel, so that's been handled."

"I need copies of her prints ASAP," Mark said, mentally choosing where and how he would run them. Any name that the Florida cops attached to the woman would need vetting through a number of databases not available for access by just anyone.

Annabelle waved her fingers in a silent request for the phone. Mark handed it to her and she asked Kincannon about his parents. Then the two spent a few moments commiserating over the fear they'd both experienced due to this turmoil having touched their families. Then she asked, "So the killer believed the couple upstairs were your parents? Your mom doesn't have family photos sitting around the house?"

Mark saw her gaze go to her parents' wall of photos while she listened to Kincannon's response. "Wow. Stupid of him." A smile played across Annabelle's mouth as she added, "I'd pay money for copies of those, Noah."

"Copies of what?" Mark asked once she'd ended the call, laughing.

"Nude photos."

He frowned. "Of his parents?"

"No, stupid." She rolled her eyes. "Of Noah."

He shot her a look. He knew she'd been teasing, and figured out the photos must be baby pics, but he still didn't like it. Grumpy, he returned his attention to the photograph of the dead woman. Tracking down

Kurtz wouldn't be enough. "Who were you?" he murmured.

"And what was her connection to the Fixers?" Annabelle added.

"We had better find out." Mark tossed the photo on Frank Monroe's desk and took a seat at the computer, prepared to get to work with the information they had. "That's the only way we will ever be safe."

Four days later Annabelle carried a laundry basket full of wet sheets out to the clothesline behind the farmhouse and went to work hanging them to dry. Though tossing them into the dryer was easier, she agreed with her mother's belief that sheets dried by sunshine and fresh air made the best beds. Besides, to Annabelle, climbing into a bed made with line-dried sheets meant home.

She knew her father would feel that way, too. A fever had delayed Frank Monroe's homecoming, but earlier this morning Adam had called with the news that doctor had okayed an afternoon discharge. Lynn Monroe joyously canceled her daily trip to the hospital to spruce up the house for the special event and prepare a celebration meal in her brand-new kitchen.

Annabelle grabbed a clothespin from the bag, then fixed one end of a blue-and-beige-striped pillowcase to the line. After days of dividing her time between the hospital and the investigation, doing mundane, mindless chores provided a welcome break.

She'd spent her hours at St. Joe's running interference with visitors, which served to remind her of how much neighbors and friends liked and respected her family. The support for the Monroes had been both overwhelming and eye-opening for Annabelle. For the first time in years—actually, for the first time ever—the idea of Kansas living began to appeal to her.

Maybe she should reconsider her decision to live in

Hawaii. Maybe it was time to come home to Kansas. The divorce made it easier to look her parents in the eyes again, since she no longer kept her marriage secret from them. She had made a mistake by eloping with Mark, true, but she'd cleaned it up afterward. Confessing the truth at this late stage would do more harm than good.

At least, that's what she told herself.

She bent over to grab another sheet from the basket and heard a wolf whistle from the direction of a pickup truck where Tag helped the flooring contractors load the last of their scraps into its bed. Annabelle paused to blow him a theatrical kiss.

Having Tag around the farm in addition to Mark had proved to be an added blessing because he deflected family attention away from her ex. Tag went out of his way to be friendly and charming, while Mark remained friendly but reserved. As a result and despite Aunt Polly's sharp eyes and loud mouth, they had managed to keep her family in the dark about her and Mark's history. If anything, her mother and sisters were trying to play matchmakers with her and Tag.

She could tell Mark liked that about as much as he liked Paulo Giambelli's continuing calls. He had been downright cranky when her mother suggested he switch guard-duty positions with Tag today so that Tag could spend more time with her.

Annabelle heard the slam of the pickup's tailgate, then the crank of the engine. That meant they were done with the kitchen and Mom could count on cooking for Daddy tonight.

"Good," she murmured aloud, speaking around a clothespin. Maybe positive results on the home front would trend over into the investigation, where progress had slowed to a crawl.

Since the bloodbath in Florida, Ron Kurtz appeared

to have dropped off the face of the earth. The Gallery Girl remained unidentified. Her prints had come back clean and the identification she'd used to secure a rental car proved false. Last night during a meeting around her mother's dining room table, Annabelle, Mark, and Tag, together with Noah on the speakerphone, had hammered out a plan on what to do next.

They still had missing Fixers to find. Mark had the Callahans looking for Parsons. Tomorrow after her father's return home simplified security arrangements here in Kansas, Tag would head for Sundine's place in Boston. Once he stashed his parents somewhere out of reach, Noah was off to Europe to take a hard look at Dennis Nelson's death. Colonel Warren had taken charge of tracking down the identity of Gallery Girl.

Annabelle and Mark would concentrate on Kurtz and unless he showed up on the radar in the next day or so, they figured the best way to find him was to lure the man to them. Once her family was settled and safe, Annabelle and Mark planned to set themselves up as bait. They'd stayed up late last night working the phones, their connections, and the computer looking for the perfect spot to spring their trap.

"Annabelle?" Lynn Monroe's voice called. "Are you almost done there?"

She glanced into the laundry basket, then went up on her tiptoes and peered over the clothesline to spy her mother standing on the back porch, her eyes gleaming with excitement. "I have two more pillowcases to hang, Mom. Is everything okay?"

"Everything is wonderful. Come into the kitchen when you're done, would you?"

"Sure." Annabelle made quick work of her task, then hurried inside where her mother was belting out a Rodgers and Hammerstein show tune into a wooden spoon. "Mom?"

Lynn flung her arms wide and said, "Look, darlin'.

Isn't this the most beautiful kitchen you've ever seen? Why, if I'd known I'd get this out of the deal, I'd have blown the place up myself years ago."

"Mom!" Annabelle protested with a giggle.

Lynn winked and said, "Sit down and keep me company, Annabelle, while I break out my new pots and pans."

"You got new pans, too?"

"I sure did. Look." Lynn slid open a deep drawer beneath the Thermador cooktop and pulled out a frying pan. Reverently, she said, "It's All-Clad."

"Oh, wow." Annabelle was suitably impressed. Leave it to Callahan to supply the best.

"I know it probably seems silly to you, but having a kitchen like this with granite counters and Thermador appliances and two sinks and hot water on demand . . . it's a real dream come true. Me walking into this kitchen is like Lissa being offered the keys to the New York City Library along with all the time in the world to read, or your daddy being turned loose in the John Deere dealership with a fairy godmother on his shoulder. It would be like you getting a . . . a . . . what's the most superior gun on the market? One you've always wanted and would never buy for yourself?"

Annabelle knew her mother didn't mean to hurt her. Nevertheless, her words punched her like a roundhouse to the stomach. A gun? Her mother thought the thing that would please her most would be a gun?

She felt her throat go tight, and pressure built at the back of her eyes. From out of nowhere came words she never meant to say, especially not to her mother. "I want a Mountain Buggy jogging stroller."

Lynn Monroe slowly lowered her frying pan. "Annabelle? Are you pregnant?"

She had to force the word past the lump in her throat. "No. No, Mama, I'm not."

Her period had started right on time three days ago. She'd told herself to cheer the fact that she and Mark dodged that particular bullet. Honestly. She didn't want her child to go through life wondering if she was an "accident."

"Does this have something to do with your sister's news? I know that Amy thinks she's keeping her pregnancy secret, but I figured it out a week ago."

Annabelle had to be careful with her words here. She didn't want to confirm or deny her sister's condition. That was Amy's prerogative. Instead she said simply, "I'm not married."

Her mother leaned against her new black granite countertop, folded her arms, and raised her eyebrows. "And what does that have to do with anything?"

Annabelle wanted to curl up in a little ball, but instead she squared her shoulders. "You know about the promise I made when I was sixteen. It was a vow and I took it seriously."

"I know that, dear. It gave me quite a bit of comfort as you were growing up, I have to tell you. You were always the most strong-minded thing. You made a decision and you stuck to it come hell or high water. That's why when you came to us and told us you had decided to join the military, I told your father not to bother arguing with you, even though the idea scared us both to death. But I knew you'd be successful at it. You are successful at everything."

"No, I'm not, Mama." The truth about her marriage hovered on the tip of her tongue, but Annabelle bit the words back.

Her mother continued as if she hadn't heard her. "But, Annabelle, you aren't sixteen anymore and I am no fool. You might have waited until marriage if you'd married young, but at your age . . ." Lynn Monroe shrugged.

"Now, babies are something different. I admit to

being old-fashioned in that respect in that I do think it's best for everyone involved to wait for marriage before having children. But, darling, if you are pregnant and afraid to tell us, you needn't be. It's not like you're sixteen anymore."

"I'm not pregnant, either, Mom! I told you that."

"Then what's wrong? What is it you are afraid to tell me? Don't say 'Nothing,' because I've known since I saw you in the hospital that something was eating at you."

"Of course something was eating at me! Daddy almost died in an explosion an enemy of mine set!"

Lynn dismissed that with a wave of her hand. "No, it's something personal. What is it, honey? You can tell me. Is it something to do with Tag?"

Annabelle began pacing the brand-new slate tile floor. "What are you planning for supper, Mom? Can I help? Do you want me to peel potatoes or something?"

"I want you to spit out your secret, Annabelle Diane. Why did you say you wanted a luxury baby stroller if you're not expecting a baby?"

Annabelle halted midstride and declared, "I'm not pregnant, Mama. I'm divorced!"

The wooden spoon slipped from Lynn Monroe's fingers and clattered against the floor. "What did you say?"

Annabelle grabbed her head in her hands. Oh, for crying out loud. Could this have gone any worse? Why did she have to go and open her mouth now? Right in the middle of her mother's new kitchen?

"Annabelle?"

At that, the words came pouring out. "Oh, Mama. We were at a wedding in Las Vegas and I just . . . I just . . . I just wanted him so bad and the chapel was right there and . . . oh, Mama. I fell in love with him. Truly, madly, deeply in love. And I wanted the house and the nursery and the Mountain Buggy stroller, but he didn't. He doesn't. So why can't I quit loving him? Why can't I quit wanting him? What's wrong with me?"

"Oh, Anna. My poor darling Anna." Lynn crossed to her daughter and wrapped her arms around her. "You know, it's a measure of my love for you that I'm willing to hold off the scolding you have coming over this. A secret marriage . . . for goodness' sake. What's the matter with Tag? I need to give that boy a piece of my mind."

"It's not Tag, Mama. It's Mark. I was married to Mark Callahan."

Lynn Monroe sighed. "Mountain Buggy strollers and haunted-eyed Texans. Leave it to you to choose the ones that cost the most. The stroller will break the bank . . . but the man, he'll break your heart."

"He already has, Mama. He already has."

Her mother clicked her tongue, then stepped back. "Sit down, dear. Let me pour us both a drink and you can tell me all about it."

Annabelle expected her mother to pull the jar of iced tea from the refrigerator. Instead, she went straight to the liquor cabinet and pulled out a bottle of single-malt scotch. She poured two fingers into two glasses and carried them to the table.

Annabelle laughed. "Mom, I love you."

Chapter Twelve

Ron Kurtz pulled his car into the parking lot of Six Flags Over Texas and followed the line of vehicles to a row of empty slots. The park was open on weekends this time of year and the beautiful weather had brought the fun seekers out in force. Since Kurtz had some time to kill, he figured he would join them.

He found a parking space and cut the engine of the sweet Caddy he'd picked up in Orlando. Ordinarily, he'd have purchased something sportier, but with a long drive to Texas in front of him, he'd decided to give a luxury sedan a try. He'd made a good decision. It was a damn shame that he'd have to abandon this ride for the next leg of his journey.

Brazos Bend, Texas. Podunk town, Texas.

End of the Line, Texas.

He chuckled as he double-checked that his weapons remained stored out of sight, then exited the car. Strolling toward the front gate, he stuck his hands in his pockets and whistled the theme from *Jaws*. Damn, but revenge made a man happy. If he'd known just how much he would enjoy the work, he would have indulged his desires a long time ago.

Kurtz bought his ticket, grabbed a park map, and headed inside, looking forward to a day riding roller coasters. He'd heard this park had some great coasters and that's why he'd decided to stop. Except for killing, nothing offered up an adrenaline rush like topping the hill of a particularly long drop on a fast ride.

He loved the rush. He had come to crave it. What was the term for it? Adrenaline addict? No, adrenaline junkie. That's it. That's him. He believed in only natural highs.

Kurtz kept his body fit and his mind sharp. He didn't do drugs. Didn't drink alcohol. He ran five miles a day and spent an hour on the gun range five days a week. He worked crossword puzzles in the evening.

His discipline had paid off in Florida.

As he opened the park map and debated which coaster to choose first, he absently rubbed the fading bruise on his right forearm where the bitch had kicked him. The Texas Giant? Judge Roy Scream? The Flashback? Hmm . . .

The Titan. That suited him. He had been a titan battling that woman. Nada Marić. "Nada No-More," he murmured with a laugh.

Kurtz whistled beneath his breath as he eyed a bevy of scantily dressed teenage girls who giggled as they licked pink cotton candy off their fingertips. He appreciated youthful tits and asses as much as anyone, but these little lovelies couldn't hold a candle to the memory of the dear, departed Nada.

Tangling with her had been the most fun he'd had in quite some time.

She had taken him by surprise with the kick that knocked the gun from his hand. Whoever provided her martial arts training had done an excellent job; she had come close to taking him down. If not for his own years of training, he might well have been the

one to stay down. The woman had put up a good
fight. At least, until he'd hurt her. She'd been a wuss
when it came to real pain.

The crowd around Kurtz thickened as he approached the ride. He glared at a teenage boy who
jostled him, and reached down to steady a little girl
who bumped into him while distracted by the ice-
cream cone in her hand. The scent of funnel cakes
drifted in the air along with the sound of screams from
the roller coaster as he entered the line for the Titan.
Excitement warmed his blood.

Nada Marić had screamed as he . . . coaxed . . .
information from her sweet lips. She'd spilled a gold
mine of information and answered a number of questions he'd entertained since the day Dennis Nelson
showed up at his office full of accusations. He'd allowed his temper to get the best of him when he discovered that she had already rained on his parade by
doing Nelson, Anderson, and Russo, but she'd deserved the punishment he gave her. Her partner deserved worse. He took delight in imagining the real
traitor waiting anxiously for Ms. Nada No-More's call.

Amazing, really, that he'd lived this long and never
realized just how much anticipation heightened a
man's pleasure. No wonder women liked foreplay so
much.

A preteen boy with freckles and a wild mane of red
hair interrupted his reverie. "Hey, mister? Have you
ever ridden this roller coaster before?"

"No, son, I haven't. Have you?"

"Yeah. It's the best ever." The kid rattled on about
crazy twists and nightmare drops and high speeds.
"It's awesome, mister. Just wait. You've never had a
rush like it."

"I wouldn't be so quick to say that," Kurtz said, his
mind drifting back to Florida and the delicious moment when he'd stood hidden from sight and watched

Noah Kincannon enter his parents' house. Without so much as touching his dick, he'd come close to shooting his load right then and there.

And now he got to anticipate the next particular pleasure—taking revenge upon the head Fixer himself.

"This is gonna be fun," he said to the boy, an anticipatory smile playing about his lips.

When he originally decided to pay his teammates back for their sins against him, he had intended to save Callahan for last. That changed after his little tête-à-tête with Nada Marić in the Kincannon kitchen.

He'd given careful consideration to how to use—or not use—the identity of the traitor in Callahan and company's midst. At first he'd been ready to move the partner to the top of his hit list. Ron Kurtz was a patriot, after all, and treason was a capital offense. But once he gave the matter some thought, he changed his mind. After all, if not for the traitor, he wouldn't have started down this road of death and destruction. He enjoyed the hunt, pleasured in the payback. Hell, if he'd known he would enjoy vengeance this much, he would have started killing the Fixers years ago.

So the traitor remained on his list—but at the bottom.

Callahan's family moved to the top.

Ron Kurtz reached the front of the line for the roller coaster and took his designated seat. As the car slowly climbed the ride's initial hill, delicious anticipation built in his veins.

"Are you ready, mister?" the redheaded kid asked.

"I'm ready," he replied, his tone humming with glee. "Oh, yes, I'm ready," he repeated, his blood pounding with excitement as the coaster reached the apex of the climb.

Ready to destroy Mark Callahan.

Ron Kurtz laughed maniacally as the roller coaster shot over the hill.

*   *   *

The Monroes declared their patriarch's homecoming a holiday and the entire family showed up for supper. Ten minutes into the onslaught, Mark considered jogging out to the road to check for a sign that read BRIGADOON. That or FANTASY ISLAND.

When his family got together, they laughed. They played. They teased one another. This family Laughed, Played, and Teased. Their joy in the moment, delight in their reunion, and pure unadulterated pleasure in being together created a knot of emotion in Mark's gut. Grief for the family he had lost with the deaths of his mother and John, homesickness for the family he had now with his brothers and their wives and kids, and knowledge that he'd thrown away the promise of family with Annabelle—it was enough to make him want to run off to Zanzibar.

Or at least, leave for the Keys a few days early.

After much debate and discussion, they had decided to spring their trap for Ron Kurtz on a private island he'd purchased during his vacation-home buying spree. Located twenty-five miles from Key West, Melody Key offered the basics he required to set up this particular ambush—an isolated location, limited access, and a sparse population. He had no intention of ever telling Annabelle that the reason he'd chosen Melody Key over his place in the Rockies was the opportunity to see her in a bikini.

Annabelle. Coming here with her had been an eye-opening experience for him. Seeing her interact with her family had revealed a vulnerable side he'd never guessed she possessed. It also helped him understand the source of her desire for picket fences and Pampers. Annabelle had left the farm to live big and she'd accomplished that. Now, though, she was ready to return to her roots. Home. Family. It wasn't all that different from what Luke and Matt had done.

So where does that leave me?

Maybe he wouldn't have to figure that out. Maybe Annabelle would turn up pregnant and the choice would be made for him. That way he could keep her, and he'd be forced to face his phobias.

God, Callahan, you're a chicken-shit.

"There it is," Lynn Monroe said, tugging an ice pack from the back of a kitchen cabinet. "I couldn't remember where I put it. It will take me a little time to grow accustomed to all this storage room I have."

She walked over to the refrigerator and filled the bag with ice, then handed it to him with a smile that didn't quite reach her eyes. Mark thanked her, then made a quick departure from the kitchen.

At times throughout the evening he had sensed Lynn Monroe's troubled gaze upon him and it left him uneasy. Had she figured out that he had bankrolled her kitchen rather than the insurance policy he had invented out of thin air? Mark couldn't tell.

On the other hand, he knew exactly what Adam Monroe's angry glare meant.

Annabelle's brother didn't like him, didn't want him around his family and especially not his sister. Mark couldn't exactly blame him. Still, did he have to peg him with his hardball during the after-dinner baseball game?

"How's the arm?" Frank Monroe asked from the porch rocker as Mark wandered onto the porch, holding the ice bag against his right wrist. His host had a blanket over his knees and a bowl of peanuts in his lap. Broken shells littered the porch floor around him.

"Sore, but not broken."

"That's good. Adam has a wicked fastball. Made All-State pitcher in high school."

"I believe it." Mark gazed out toward the yard where the Monroe siblings and their spouses, children, cousins, and other various family members remained embroiled in fierce competition. From the kitchen came the voices of Annabelle's mother and two aunts, who, with KP behind them, sat at the table, laughing and lingering over their coffee and desserts.

Out on the makeshift baseball diamond, Annabelle came up to bat. Both Mark and her father remained silent as she took the first two pitches, then swung hard. Ball cracked against bat and went sailing into the outfield. As her opponents scrambled to retrieve the ball, Mark watched her long legs chew up the bases. And he yearned.

"So," her father said in a conversational tone. "I understand that you married Annabelle in order to sleep with her."

The ice bag slipped from Mark's grasp and thunked against the porch's painted wood floor. "Uh . . ."

"Then you divorced her rather than live with her and give her babies."

"Ahhh . . ." *Thanks for the warning, Annabelle.*

"And after that, you seduced her while the two of you were stranded on a mountaintop."

Mark opened his mouth to defend himself, then abruptly slammed it shut. This was a no-win situation.

Frank Monroe motioned to the empty rocking chair beside his. "Sit down, boyo." He passed the bowl toward Mark, adding, "Have a peanut."

Mark didn't want to sit and he didn't want to shell peanuts. But the man still wore his hospital bracelet and the look in his eyes reminded Mark of his drill sergeant during basic training. He sat down. "Mr. Monroe . . . I, um . . . this is awkward."

"I expect so."

"If she's pregnant, I intend—"

"She's not. She talked to her mother this afternoon. Poured her heart out."

She's not pregnant. Mark sat back in his chair hard.

He waited to feel the expected wave of relief. It never came.

Frank Monroe cracked a peanut shell. "I'm in a difficult position here. I'd love to kick your ass, but my doctors won't let me try. I'd like to lay into you with a tongue-lashing I'm certain you deserve, but my wife made me promise not to do that, either.

"So about all that leaves us with is for you to sit there and explain to me just what on earth you plan to do to heal my little girl's broken heart."

"Annabelle's heart isn't broken."

Frank held up a nut and said, "It's plain as this peanut that it is, and if you can't see it, then you don't know my Annabelle. You don't deserve my Annabelle. She loves you."

Mark leaned forward, rested his elbows on his knees, and hung his head. "She's not thinking straight. Look at what has happened in the past couple of weeks. It's been one emotional blow after another. She's confused, that's all."

"You actually believe that nonsense coming out of your mouth? Hell, maybe that fastball bounced up and hit your skull."

"Look, Mr. Monroe—"

"I have looked. That's why I think you love her, too."

Mark opened his mouth to deny it, but the words just didn't come. "I'm confused, too, okay? One thing I do know, though, is that I'm not good for her."

Frank popped a peanut in his mouth. "No man is good enough for her. Nevertheless, she chose to give her heart to you."

Mark shoved to his feet. "I can't believe I'm talking to you about this. Men don't have heart-to-hearts about their emotions. We talk about football!"

"It's baseball season. Almost time for the College World Series. You want to talk baseball?"

"Sure. I love baseball." And anything was better than this.

"We can talk baseball after we finish talking about Annabelle." Frank fished through his bowl of empty shells looking for a nut he'd missed. "Nothing is more important than the women in my life. Having a brush with death brought that point home with a vengeance." Frank found an intact nut and cracked the shell, saying, "Don't get me wrong. I love my Adam, too, but a father's relationship with his son is different from that with his daughter. I try not to butt into my boy's life."

Mark couldn't help but snort at that. "What I wouldn't have given to have had a father like you."

"Your father must have done all right. You have your good points."

"My old man never did anything right."

Frank gave him a considering look. "Annabelle told her mother that you and your father are estranged."

Jesus. "I knew she hung out sheets this morning. Didn't realize she'd hung out all my dirty laundry, too."

"Apparently, she did a Mount Saint Helens explosion." Monroe's mouth twisted in a rueful smile. "Told my wife all sorts of things—every secret she's been keeping for half her life. Told her some things I'd just as soon not know, to be honest."

Mark closed his eyes. "Look, Mr. Monroe. I didn't set out to hurt Annabelle. I never intended to get married. I acted impulsively."

"You're saying it was a mistake?"

"Yes. No. I don't know. It was wrong. Wrong for me to do that to her. Wrong for me to expect . . ."

"What?"

"I don't know what I expected. All I know is that I don't regret marrying your daughter."

"Then fix it."

"I can't. She knows that. I've had two families and I've lost them both. I'm just not up for a third round."

"Yes, Annabelle told my wife you lost your first wife and child years ago. That's a hard thing, son."

Damn right, it is.

"Still, I wouldn't have taken you as a coward."

Fury surged through Mark. He grabbed the porch rail and squeezed hard enough to dent the wood. "Goddammit, I'm not a coward! I just don't want the wife and child and picket fence. All right? Is that a crime?"

"Nope. Not at all. Not as long as you don't string Annabelle along."

"That's why I gave her the divorce."

"Then why are you keeping hold of her heart?"

"Are you a farmer or Dr. Phil?"

Frank Monroe's chin came up. His eyes flashed with temper. "I'm Annabelle's father."

Hell.

"And I'll be damned if I'm going to let some gutless fool tear apart what's left of her heart."

Mark propped both hands on the porch rail and leaned his weight against it. For a long moment, he heard only the creak of Frank Monroe's rocker and the pounding of his own blood. Then a shout from the baseball diamond caught his attention and he looked up to see Annabelle running hard to catch a fly ball hit to left field. "You are right, Mr. Monroe. I do love her. But that doesn't mean I am right for her. I just don't know what to do about it."

"I'll tell you what you do about it," Lynn Monroe declared. The screen door squeaked opened, then banged behind her. She marched up to Mark, braced her hands on her hips, and said, "Ordinarily I wouldn't stick my nose in your business, but Annabelle's father has done a poor job of it—"

"Lynn!" Frank protested.

"—so here I go. It's plain as the nose on my face what the problem is. You don't have an ounce of forgiveness in yourself, do you, Mark? Not for your father and not for yourself. Have you ever thought that maybe your father's admittedly misguided actions were motivated by love?"

Mark closed his eyes and gritted his teeth. The Monroes could say whatever they wanted about Annabelle and he would listen—that was their right. But he'd be good and goddamned if he'd listen to anyone defend Branch Callahan.

"Excuse me, Mrs. Monroe. I don't wish to be rude, but you need to leave my father out of this. You don't know anything about him and what he did—"

"I know enough." She pointed a finger toward the empty rocker and said, "Sit down, Callahan. Annabelle told me the whole tragic story."

"Annabelle doesn't know the whole tragic story! She doesn't know that he threatened to use his money and his power to steal our baby from my wife while I was stuck overseas and couldn't do a damn thing to protect her. She doesn't know that my wife and baby were running away from my father when a drunk driver killed them."

"Oh, dear."

"Yeah. Oh freaking dear."

"That explains a lot of your anger, doesn't it? Nevertheless, I am going to talk and you are going to listen. Do you know why? Because I like you."

"Because I gave you a kitchen," he muttered beneath his breath as he took his seat.

"No, because you are a man with principles. You're a man with honor and integrity and loyalty. You are a man of great passion."

"I don't want to hear about passion," Frank Monroe grumbled.

"If I hadn't been so distraught about Frank, your

misdirection with Tag would not have fooled me. It's obvious that you care deeply about our daughter and that she cares deeply about you. That said, unless you change a few things, you are going to throw away any chance of happiness the two of you have. Now, let me speak plainly."

He kicked at a peanut shell on the porch's floor. "You weren't already?"

She folded her arms and clicked her tongue. "Mark, Mark, Mark."

In that moment, he heard his own mother's voice. She'd have kicked his butt for that smart-ass remark.

"Let's talk about your wife and child," Lynn Monroe continued. "What were their names?"

"Mrs. Monroe, I don't want to talk about—"

"Their names, son?"

He blew out a sigh. "Carrie. My wife was Carrie, my daughter, Margaret Mary."

"You need to stop living in the shadow of what happened to Carrie and little Margaret Mary. It's a horrible, horrible thing, but you've punished yourself long enough. You need to forgive yourself for not being there. And you need to forgive your father for his part in the accident. You need to make peace with your past in order to go on with your future, Mark. It's as simple as that."

"Simple?" he scoffed. "I don't think so."

She folded her arms, tilted her head, and studied him. "I'm not the first person to tell you this, am I?"

Mark's thoughts went to his brothers and especially their wives. "No, ma'am."

"That's good. It's not a new idea, then. That only makes your current confusion more telling. You know I'm right. You know what you must do." She walked over to Mark and slipped her arm through his. "Look out there. At Annabelle. She's your future, if you're smart enough, brave enough, to reach for her."

At first, Mark didn't say anything as the conversation replayed through his mind. Make peace with his father? "I'll never forget. I don't want to forget. They were my family."

Frank Monroe spoke up. "You don't have to forget, son. You just have to forgive. With forgiveness comes peace."

Mark didn't know what to say after that, so when his phone rang a few minutes later, he reached for it like a lifeline. "Hello?"

His sister-in-law Torie said, "Mark? Where are you?"

Trepidation gripped him. "I'm in Kansas. What's wrong?"

"Kansas. Good. That's not too far. Do you have your plane?"

"Yes. Torie! What's wrong?"

She laughed. "Nothing's wrong, Callahan. Everything's right. Or it will be right by sometime tomorrow. Get your butt home. I'm having your brother's baby and you need to be here. Matt needs you here. I need you here. Come home, Mark. Hurry."

Annabelle watched Amy set up in the batter's box, then glanced toward the porch at the sound of her name. Mark waved her in, calling for Tag, too. The ball cracked against the bat, but she allowed Amy's hit to sail right past her as she took off for the farmhouse. Something was up.

Five minutes later, the three Fixers congregated in her father's office, discussing the change in plan. Mark looked troubled as he sank down into the chair and rubbed the back of his neck. "I don't have to go to Texas."

"Yes, you do." A shout of laughter out on the field drew Annabelle's attention and she moved to the window. "Your family wants you there. You owe it to them to go."

Tag propped a hip on one corner of the desk, picked up the rabbit made from painted rocks she'd made for her father in the fifth grade, and added his two cents. "She's right. You should go."

"Will you come with me, Annabelle?" he asked.

Her brows arched in surprise. "Wouldn't it be better for me to go straight to the island and work on the setup there?"

"If you are comfortable leaving here, I'd rather you come with me."

Annabelle took a moment to think about it. Could she in good conscience leave Kansas now? Her father was home, the farm was guarded like a fortress, and the security guys from Texas kept excellent watch over her sisters and their families. They had intended to leave in another day or two, anyway.

Yet, the idea of packing up and going tonight left her feeling a bit sick to her stomach.

She blamed the reaction on Ron Kurtz, of course. It had nothing to do with the fact that Mark had asked her to accompany him to the Callahan hometown to mingle with the Callahan family while a Callahan bride gave birth to a Callahan offspring.

"Just shoot me now," she muttered as she gently banged her head against the window glass.

Mark frowned. "Annabelle, if you're worried about your family . . ."

"No. I'm not." *Suck it up, Annabelle.* "I'm really not. I have complete faith in the Texans, and I also think the odds of Kurtz coming back to Kansas are slim—especially once we launch our media blitz."

Tag returned the rabbit to its place, picked up a pencil, and began to bounce the eraser against the telephone receiver. "I hope I get the chance to meet these sisters-in-law of yours someday, Callahan. I have to say I'm impressed with how fast they put that whole media thing together."

Mark grinned. "They are pretty impressive. Maddie's father was happy to help the cause—Blade loves to create a scandal—and Torie's paparazzi friends are salivating at the notion of racking up big bucks with those money pics." Meeting Annabelle's gaze, he added, "Let's not forget who came up with the idea. Annabelle is impressive *and* brilliant."

Annabelle accepted the compliment with a graceful nod. Her idea *had* been inspired, she thought. Once they had decided to bait their trap at Melody Key, they'd faced the problem of how to make sure that Kurtz got the word about where to find them. While his intelligence about the Fixers had been spot-on so far, without knowing how he got his information, they feared leaving it to chance. That's when Annabelle got the idea to use Mark's connections and create some tabloid fodder.

With Maddie Callahan's father's blessing, they planned to "out" his recent but still secret marriage to a sixth wife, a bride who would scandalize the celebrity world. News that the aging rock star Blade had married the former Kathy Hudson, owner of the Dairy Princess in Brazos Bend, Texas, would make the front page of the tabloids on every supermarket shelf in America.

As soon as Mark gave the word, half a dozen hand-picked paparazzo photographers were set to receive a family photo of the event: Blade; his bride, Kathy; Blade's daughter, the infamous rock princess "Baby Dagger," aka Maddie Callahan; and her husband, Luke Callahan—Mark's identical-twin brother.

One special friend of Torie's would even get video for the cable-TV folks. Everyone would receive a press release of sorts that included the news that the entire Callahan family planned to prolong the festivities by vacationing on the private island where the wedding had been held, Melody Key, for the next two weeks.

"Ron Kurtz will have to be dead to miss the news," Tag observed.

"I hope the idea doesn't prove to be more bust than brilliance." Annabelle moved away from the window and swiped the pencil out of Tag's hand, then returned it to the pencil cup. The man fiddled with things like a five-year-old. "We weren't planning on Torie's baby coming this early. It's going to be difficult for your family to hide out with a brand-new baby. If word leaks out that they're still in Brazos Bend, it will ruin everything."

"It'll be fine," Mark assured her. "Matt and Luke have that problem covered. It helps that Torie wanted to have her baby at the lake house. From what Luke said, Matt has turned the place into a veritable hospital. They wanted time to themselves after the kid is born, anyway, so it all works."

"You're not worried about Kurtz sneaking past the perimeter?" Tag asked.

"No." Mark's green eyes gleamed with determination. "We made that mistake once before at Four Brothers Vineyard. It won't happen again. Matt has put in a security system that the Secret Service could take pointers about."

Annabelle slumped into the chair opposite the desk from Mark. "What worries me most is the thought that we might be too late already. He's had time to get to Texas."

"True, but he's not in Brazos Bend yet, according to Matt. That's a good thing about living in a small town where everybody knows everybody. Add in the DEA roadblocks Luke arranged, and no one is getting in or out of the county without the Callahans knowing about it. He might well be on his way, but right now, it's clear."

They all glanced toward the window when a rousing cheer arose from outside, signaling the end of the game. Tag said, "Now that Frank is home, I think we're good to go. The sooner the better, in my opinion."

Mark drummed his fingers against the desk. "Matt's baby coming early actually helps our timetable. When Torie realized she was in labor, the family made a big production of leaving town to attend Blade's wedding. I figure we'll be in and out of Brazos Bend in a matter of hours—Torie does everything fast. She'll drop that kid lickety-split and we can be wheels up tomorrow afternoon."

"Drop the kid?" Annabelle repeated. "Jeez, Callahan, she's not a goat."

His mouth twisted ruefully. "You're right. I should have said 'drop the kit.' Our Torie is a lioness."

While Annabelle rolled her eyes at that, he continued. "I intend to be on Melody Key by sunset tomorrow. We'll send the photos out the minute we're on the island, and with any luck we will have Kurtz in custody by the end of the week."

"With any luck," Tag repeated as the Monroes filed into the house, the winners giving the losers a hard time on the way to the kitchen for their after-ball-game ice cream.

"Well, then. We'd better get moving." Annabelle rose and wiped her suddenly damp hands on her shorts. "I guess it's time to say good-bye."

Chapter Thirteen

Meacham Field
Fort Worth, Texas

Twenty minutes after the Citation landed at the airfield, Mark walked across the tarmac beside Annabelle and eyed his brother Matt's sweet Bell 210 helicopter, their transportation for the short final leg of their trip. The prospect of flying in the bird with his ex-wife as pilot didn't bother him. The idea of flying to Brazos Bend made him want to throw up.

He hadn't been back since his discharge from the hospital after tangling with Torie's stalker, and the intensity of his reaction caught him by surprise. He had thought he had a handle on his feelings for his father. Branch was dead to him. Period. So why was his skin clammy and his stomach sour?

"Maybe I'm getting sick." His gait slowed; then he stopped. If he was coming down with something, he shouldn't go to Brazos Bend and expose Torie and her baby to illness.

Annabelle noticed he had fallen behind. "Something wrong, Callahan?"

"Yeah. I don't feel so good."

She walked back toward him and, in that maternal way women had, tested his temperature by placing the back of her hand against his forehead. "No fever. What's the matter?"

He looked deep inside himself and came up with the truth. Maybe he was the coward the Monroes claimed him to be. "Nothing. Not really. I'm just not looking forward to this trip."

She made an offended snort. "Excuse me, but who was the helo pilot for the Fixers? Who supplemented her income by piloting tourist flights on Oahu?"

He laughed at himself as much as at her. "It's not the flight that bothers me, Belle. It's the destination."

"Why? Are you afraid your sister-in-law will ask you to deliver her baby?"

"Not hardly." He inhaled deeply, then exhaled in a rush. "I'm afraid my father will be there. I haven't seen him since he faked a heart attack and almost got me and Torie killed."

"Well." Her eyebrows shot up. "I haven't heard that story."

He waved a dismissive hand. "It's not worth wasting my breath over. Suffice to say, when the day was done, none of his sons wanted anything to do with Branch Callahan. He's still a real sore subject with me, so we don't talk about him. I don't know if the others have anything to do with him now or what. I didn't think to ask Torie when she called."

"You aren't exactly rational when it comes to your father, Callahan. You do realize that?"

He heard the echo of her mother's voice in his mind. *Forgive your father. Make peace with your past to go on with your future.* "Yeah, I realize it."

"Just how sick to your stomach are you? Think you'll throw up in my bird?"

"It's my brother's bird."

"Not when I'm the pilot." She slipped her arm though his and tugged him toward the helicopter. "How old is your father?"

"Mid-eighties."

"Is he healthy?"

"I haven't a clue. I told you we don't talk about him."

"He was healthy last time you saw him?"

"Healthier than me, considering my ass was shot up." He shrugged and added, "He walks with a walker. Was goofy over a new little ankle-biting dog he owns."

"A walker, hmm?" Her lips twitched. "Tell you what, Callahan. If that big bad bully is there, I promise I'll protect you."

"You think this is funny."

"No, actually, I think this is sad."

Personally, Mark thought it was pathetic. "Let's go get this over with. How long does it take to have a baby, anyway?"

She slanted him a look and in a tone as dry as West Texas in August said, "I wouldn't know."

Mark winced. *Way to go, dumb-ass.*

The flight to Brazos Bend took less than half an hour, and as Annabelle brought the bird down with a deft touch on the helipad beside Matt and Torie's home, Mark spied the Callahan welcoming committee gathered on the lake-house porch. Luke and Maddie, Matt and . . .

"Torie? They're letting her walk around? Outside? Shouldn't she be in bed if she's in labor? What the hell is Matt thinking? What if she has the kid standing up?"

"Why are you asking me all these baby questions?" Annabelle snapped. "Which reminds me . . . you're off the hook, Callahan. I'm not pregnant." She flipped switches with sharp, angry movements as she shut down the bird.

While the rotors slowed, he hesitated, wondering how to respond to that. Should he tell her that her parents already spilled those particular beans, or should he keep his mouth shut? "Annabelle . . ."

She blew out a sigh as she went through the procedure to shut down the helo. "I'm sorry. That was unkind of me. It's your turn for neurosis. Is your father here?"

"Look, we'll talk about this later, okay?"

She closed her eyes, gave her head a little shake. "Introduce me to your family, Callahan. I'm curious to meet them."

Mark knew for a fact that his brothers and their wives were more than curious to meet Annabelle. When he called to tell them he was on his way, he mentioned he'd be bringing company. He hadn't expected the welcoming committee. He'd figured they would all be inside pacing the floor while Torie did the baby thing. To find everyone—including Torie—on the front porch waiting left him more than a little uneasy. He didn't see Branch anywhere, thank God. If he'd spied the old man standing on the porch with the others, he would have taken control of the stick and lifted this bird off the ground the minute Annabelle set her down.

They exited the helicopter and started toward the house. His brothers and their wives met them halfway with Torie waddling in front of the others. "Mark!" she exclaimed, wrapping her arms around him in a hard hug. "You made it."

"Apparently in plenty of time."

"Yeah." She pouted like one of Maddie's twins. "My contractions stopped. It's looking like it was a false alarm."

Before he could comment on that, Maddie stepped up to Mark and gave him a quick kiss. "I think she was just waiting for you. Mark, introduce us to your guest."

He stepped back, widening their circle to include Annabelle, then gestured toward each person as he introduced them. "Annabelle Monroe, meet the Callahan clan. The fat one here is Torie—" He took her punch to his arm with a grin. "She's Matt's wife."

Torie said, "Welcome, Annabelle. Did I see you flying that helicopter? That's so cool! It makes me downright jealous. I've been trying to get Matt to teach me how to fly and he totally refuses."

"That's because the last time you sat copilot in a chopper, Shutterbug, you shot me." Matt winked at Annabelle and said, "Hi, Annabelle, I'm Matt. After our adventure in Hawaii, I feel like I know you, but it's nice to finally meet you."

"*Finally* being the applicable word," Maddie interjected, shooting Mark a chastising look.

"The sweet-talker is Maddie, my brother Luke's wife."

Maddie's smile was warm and her brown eyes gleamed with pleasure as she said, "We're so glad you came."

"Welcome to Brazos Bend, Annabelle," Luke said.

"This isn't Brazos Bend," Mark insisted, the detail being a sore spot with him.

Maddie and Torie each slipped a hand through Annabelle's arms and began to usher her toward the house. Mark winced to hear Maddie say, "Torie and I debated how to play this. Then we decided to lay our cards on the table. We are curious as can be about your marriage to Mark, but we're not going to pepper you with questions. However, any details you care to send our way we'll be happy to listen to."

"Thrilled to listen to," Torie added. "It's possible

we could be of some help to you. If anyone on earth understands the trials and tribulations of being involved with a Callahan man, it's Maddie and I.''

"That said, we want you to be relaxed while you're here. You won't need to worry we're going to launch a nosiness sneak attack." Maddie patted Annabelle's arm and added, "Though we'll listen if you want to talk."

"We'll definitely listen," Torie agreed.

"Don't you have a baby to deliver or something?" Mark called out.

Torie glanced back over her shoulder. "My plan is to become distracted from every twitch in my belly so that I relax. I've decided I'm too tense. Once I relax, labor will resume."

Maddie sighed and spoke an aside to Annabelle. "Thus speaks a woman who hasn't been through labor yet and doesn't quite get that she has absolutely no control over the timing of it."

"Hey, what does it hurt for me to think positively?"

Annabelle smiled wanly, then glanced back at Mark as if hoping for rescue. He abandoned his brothers and stepped toward the women. He knew his sisters-in-law and he owed Annabelle his support. Had he known he would be bringing her into the lions' den, he'd have prepared her for it. As it was, dumping her into a coffee klatch with Maddie and Torie was like dropping her into a hot LZ with no backup.

Moving up beside Maddie, he asked, "How are the girls? Are they here?"

"They're fine. They're wonderful. They're little demons like their daddy. They're asleep in the nursery. Breaking in the baby's bed."

"I'm second-guessing that decision," Luke said. "Samantha is liable to chew through the crib slats by morning. We had to switch to a metal bed for her. Maddie gave birth to a chipmunk."

It provided a fine distraction. As they entered the cabin and she led them upstairs, Maddie rattled out a rundown of his nieces' latest antics. As always when he greeted the little ones, Mark had to brace himself. His first sight of the twins invariably gave the old knife in his heart a twist. It had gotten easier as they grew older and didn't look so much like the photograph in his wallet. Still, that first glance was always a What-Could-Have-Been kick in the gut.

Tonight was no different. As he walked into Torie and Matt's nursery and spied Maddie and Luke's little girls, that old wave of grief rolled over him. When one of the twins lifted her head from the mattress and aimed a smile their way, he nutted up and smiled back.

The baby climbed to her feet and said, "Da Da Da Da."

"Shush, Kitty-Cat. You'll wake your sister," Luke said, moving toward the crib. Catherine lifted her arms and her father picked her up. When he turned back toward the doorway, Annabelle gasped.

Mark looked at his identical twin holding a brown-eyed, redheaded little girl and knew exactly what Annabelle was thinking.

Well, shit.

That could be our little girl.

Emotion rolled through Annabelle, a cold combination of pain and confusion and anger. The need to escape overwhelmed her and she backed away from the door's threshold, bumping into Mark, brushing against Maddie. She needed out of there *now*.

She turned and rushed downstairs headed for the cabin's front door. She vaguely noted Matt and Torie sharing a look of concerned surprise as she rushed out into the night and took the first path she came to. She wanted to run, to exercise her body, to exorcise her demons, and she wished she wore sneakers rather than sandals.

"Annabelle!" Mark called from the porch.

She picked up her pace, not caring where she was going as long as it was away.

She followed the twisting stone pathway lined by solar lights that threaded through a stand of trees and sloped gently downward. Emerging from the trees, she saw that the trail ended at an elaborate boathouse. Security lights illuminated an attached swim dock that included a diving platform with a rope swing and a slide. Beyond the boathouse stretched a black empty expanse of water. Perfect.

The heels of her sandals clacked against the metal walkway as she crossed onto the dock. She halted at the edge, breathing heavily, tension pounding through her blood.

"Why did I come here?" she muttered. "I shouldn't have come to Texas. Why do I keep putting myself in this position? I'll never get over him. I'm such a fool."

Hearing Mark following behind her, she did the only thing she could. Annabelle kicked off her shoes, tugged off her shirt, and shimmied out of her pants, then executed a racing dive into the lake. The cold shocked her system and when she surfaced, she gasped in a breath.

"Dammit, Annabelle!"

She struck out in a crawl, kicking hard and digging her strokes deep as she swam parallel to the shore, fleeing the haunting image of Luke Callahan and his Catherine. Fleeing the pressure in her chest. Fleeing Mark. She swam in fifty-stroke laps over and over until the water's chill seeped into her bones and cooled her temper, and the exercise drained her of tension and despair.

She drifted in the gift of a dark, numb void until a thought bumped her like a shark beneath the surface.

Something about that scene up in the nursery was wrong. What was it? The brown-eyed, redheaded baby in "Mark's" arms could have been her child, their child. True. But what about the picture didn't fit?

Annabelle pulled up, treading water, reaching for the knowledge that seemed to hang just beyond her reach.

Mark interrupted her. "Annabelle? I threw a boat cushion and it's at your six, probably five strokes away. If you don't go get it, I'm coming in after you."

She wanted to growl at him, but the fatigue in her muscles told her to cooperate. She turned and spied the white square and swam toward it. She tucked the buoyant pillow beneath her breasts and rested, floating beneath a star-filled sky as suddenly, brilliantly, the answer flashed like a comet.

She didn't crave that baby.

It was true. Seeing that sweet little girl with her own hair and eyes in the arms of a man who looked exactly like Mark was a shocking sight, but it didn't break her heart. It hadn't shot arrows of longing into her soul. She had not looked at little Catherine and silently wailed, *She should have been mine!*

Instead, she'd run. Why?

Could it possibly be that despite what she'd been telling herself for years, what she had wanted from Mark wasn't a child?

She blew out a breath and gazed back toward the boat dock, where she could see her ex-husband standing there watching her, no doubt ready to dive to the rescue if he decided she needed it.

What she needed was to think this through.

She looped a hand through the strap on the boat cushion and rolled over onto her back. Moving her arms and legs just enough to remain afloat, she gazed up at the starry sky while staring deeply into her own soul.

Until she'd realized her regular-as-clockwork period was late, she had been perfectly happy with her childless state. Growing up, while her sisters gazed into their futures by planning their weddings and choosing names for their babies, she'd imagined herself as everything from a dolphin trainer to an archaeologist to an astronaut. She'd planned trips to Tibet and studied the ecosystem of the rain forest. When she and her sisters played house, Lissa and Amy argued over who got to be Mommy. Annabelle always wanted to be the daddy who went off to work flying airplanes or driving race cars or spying on foreign governments.

Babies had never been on her radar until the calendar introduced the idea. But from the moment she had shared the possibility with Mark and he'd reacted so violently against it, she'd been convinced that she wanted a child . . . his child . . . more than anything else.

It wasn't true.

"You've been lying to yourself, Monroe."

In that moment, she finally saw the truth. It wasn't the *baby* she had wanted from Mark. What she'd wanted was the commitment the baby represented.

"Holy Moses."

The idea stunned her and left her reeling, but it made perfect sense. For two years, she and Mark had been having what amounted to a legalized affair—spectacular sex in exciting cities with next-to-no commitment. She'd wanted more. She'd needed to give more. She'd needed to receive more.

To her Kansas-farm-girl psyche, more came in the way of a baby. Babies were the ultimate commitment. Not just for Mark Callahan, but for Annabelle Monroe, too. She hadn't wanted the child; she'd wanted the marriage. A real marriage. That's what she'd been ready for that day in New York. That's what she'd waited for until that day in her office on Oahu.

"How could I have been so blind not to see it?"

At that, exhaustion claimed her and all her limbs felt like hundred-pound weights. She knew she'd best return to dry land before she drowned. Pushing the cushion in front of her, she swam for the dock. Upon reaching the swim ladder, she grabbed hold with one hand, threw the soggy boat cushion onto the dock, and climbed from the water.

Mark met her with a fluffy white beach towel. Without speaking a word, he wrapped it around her and tucked one end between her breasts. Then he reached for a second towel and used it to dry her hair, gently squeezing strands between its absorbent folds with a tender touch.

She wanted to run from him, but she couldn't quite make her feet move. Why couldn't this be forever? Why couldn't this work? They worked in so many ways . . . but not the most important one. They didn't trust. *I don't trust him and he doesn't trust himself.*

"If this isn't the damnedest situation. I expected we would land in the middle of Torie's having the kid and all the focus would be on her." He finger-combed her hair, smoothing it back away from her face. His face was a solemn study of shadow and light as he stared down at her and said, "I don't know what to say to you."

He knew what to say. He just didn't want to say it.

A wisp of a cool night breeze swirled around them and Annabelle shivered, whether from that or the chill inside her soul, she didn't know. "Don't say anything, Mark. Just don't say anything."

He made a low growl of regret and wrapped his arms around her, sharing his warmth, and she was so numb that she let him. His hands stroked her, up and down her back, over the damp chill bumps on her arms, massaging the taut muscles at the base of her neck.

The first brush of his butterfly kisses against her temple barely registered, so lost was she in the whirlwind of self-discovery.

What an idiot she'd been. When she first suspected she might be pregnant, she had not jumped for joy. Not that she'd considered it a disaster, either, because after all, they were married and in their thirties and it was time. That reaction should have told her something, shouldn't it?

Mark's mouth moved over the whorl of her ear, licking, nibbling. Instinctively and unconsciously, she tilted her head to allow him better access to her neck.

Instead, she had ignored that big red light and decided she wanted children more than anything because he so obviously did not.

"Ah hell, Annabelle." He tightened his hold on her and captured her mouth in a long, deep, peppermint-flavored kiss.

That broke through the numbing chill and finally got her attention. Warmth spread throughout her body, then collected in the core of her as she kissed him back, her body humming with need and hunger and heat. He molded his body against hers, his erection hard against her belly. She lifted her arms and sank her fingers into the hair at the nape of his neck.

Dear God, she loved this. Loved him.

"I want you so damned much."

And that, she realized, was it in a nutshell. She loved. He wanted. Two different things. Same song, second verse.

She wrenched herself from his arms. "No. I'm not going to do this. Not again. I deserve more."

Mark muttered a curse and shoved his fingers through his hair. He stared at her, baffled, confused, and a little wary. *He realizes he's not going to be able to fix this.*

He did try, however. "I know. I know you do, honey. I'm making an effort here. You need to know that. If you'll just give me a little time."

"Time? I've given you time, Callahan. All you did was take advantage of me."

"Hell, Annabelle. I never intended that. You have to know that." He rubbed the back of his neck, his expression grim. "I'm sorry. I'm so goddamned sorry."

She grabbed her shorts and slipped them on, then looked around for her shirt. Where was it?

Mark picked it up from behind a Sea-Doo and handed to her. "Look, Annabelle, your mother said something to me . . . told me I needed to make peace with the past in order to look to the future. It got me thinking. Maybe she's right. It's just . . . now isn't the time for me to stretch out on the analyst's couch. Not when we have a killer after us. Maybe once we've dealt with Kurtz, I can tackle my . . . um . . . demons."

Annabelle yanked on her shirt and shoved her feet into her sandals. "Maybes and wants aren't enough, Callahan. I don't—"

"I love you, Annabelle," he interrupted.

She closed her eyes as the words echoed in her mind, her heart, her soul. "You know what?" she said slowly, finally. "I think I believe that. I think you probably do love me, as much as you are capable. The problem is . . . I don't trust it. I don't trust that it will be enough. I don't trust you to battle your demons for me, Mark. I guess I believe you fear them more than you love me. And I'm done waiting for you."

A muscle in his jaw twitched. His hands fisted at his sides, but he did not comment.

He might be a hero, but he can't face his own dragons. Not even for me.

Annabelle closed her eyes and reached deep for the

strength that had sustained her for so long. "I think I'll go to bed now. Tomorrow, I'll go on to Melody Key and do what I can to bait our trap for a killer."

"I can't believe there is only one way in and out of this crappy-ass town," Ron Kurtz muttered as he studied a Texas road map. He sat in his car in the parking lot of the public observation area of the dam at Possum Kingdom Lake and wondered if it was just his bad luck that today some numb-nut bureaucrat had decided the road through Brazos Fucking Bend was the primo spot to catch smugglers bringing illegals into the country. Or was it possible that Callahan expected him and this was a setup? A trap?

He hoped so. That meant his plan was working. Kurtz stared out over the lake and imagined the asshole pacing the floor as he worried about his family. He grinned with delight.

This was so damned great. His decision to slow down his attack, to give Callahan time to wait and anticipate and worry, was risky but right. So what if it took extra effort to circumvent whatever defenses he erected? The challenge was half the fun of it.

He drummed his fingers against the steering wheel and considered his next step. He needed to get a better map. There had to be farm roads or something leading in and out of that place.

He also needed to don his disguise. Even if Callahan had identified Nada Marić by now, he wouldn't know whose payroll she'd been on. He wouldn't know that through her partner, she had given Kurtz the heads-up that Annabelle Monroe's mama had fingered him as their bomber. Callahan would expect him to arrive in his family's little burg as himself. If the roadblock he'd spied up the road a bit was a means to search for him, he needed to go in as someone else.

Kurtz twisted his mouth and scratched his jaw.

Good thing he had anticipated this possibility and come prepared.

"Right, Killer?" he murmured to the part of his costume that had four legs and a tail. He'd picked up the small Heinz 57 at an animal shelter in Fort Worth. She was the perfect accessory for his disguise.

He snapped a leash onto the dog's collar, then opened his door and exited the car. Immediately, the furry mutt put her head down and sniffed out a place to piss. Once her business was done, he strolled over to the concrete display that held a brass plaque, and read the information about the building of the dam. "Possum Kingdom Lake," he observed. "What a goofy-assed name."

The dog let out a whimper and held up a paw. Kurtz spied sticker burrs embedded in the tender flesh and he knelt and clucked his tongue. "Poor thing. Sorry about that."

He liked dogs. He'd had a couple of his own he'd been forced to give away when he began this quest for vengeance. That's another thing he owed Callahan and his buddies for.

With the burr disposed of, he glanced around the parking lot, taking inventory of the other visitors. One older couple and a younger couple and their six-year-old or so child. One uniformed type who was getting into a vehicle marked BRAZOS RIVER AUTHORITY and who never glanced Kurtz's way.

Kurtz surreptitiously watched the young family a few moments and decided they were so wrapped up in one another that he'd need to set a bomb off to get their attention. Excellent. Next he studied the older couple and judged them to be an observant pair. He'd wait on them a bit.

He spent ten minutes playing fetch with Killer. When the gray hairs loaded up into their car to leave, he sauntered back to the car and coaxed Killer into the backseat. Then he thumbed the trunk release on his key fob and removed the duffel bag full of supplies. He ambled toward the restrooms and, after making certain that Mom's and Dad's and kiddie's attention remained elsewhere, ducked into the ladies' room.

Fifteen minutes later, an attractive woman in her early sixties strolled out wearing brown polyester pants and a long cotton tunic in a paisley print, a gray wig, glasses, and a nice rack of tits.

She climbed into his car and batted thick, mascara-coated lashes at the growling dog. "Now, Killer, calm down. It's just me."

She started the car and exited the parking lot. A few minutes later, she pulled back onto the highway headed north, toward the roadblock. "Brazos Bend, here we come."

Chapter Fourteen

Murder was the topic of the day as Matt Callahan gave his brothers a tour of the trellises at Four Brothers Vineyard. Amid intermittent talk of fruit production and root disease, they discussed bodyguards and electronic security monitors and enemies out of their collective pasts. Luke's career with the DEA, Matt's with the CIA, and Mark's with military intelligence gave them plenty of names to discuss as they attempted to figure out how the dead woman in Noah Kincannon's parents' house could be connected to Ron Kurtz.

"We had, what, three missions that overlapped over the years?" Luke observed.

"Four, if you count Ćurković." Matt studied the sticky yellow paper the size of a note card positioned at the end of one row of vines, which helped him and his partner, Les Warfield, monitor the state of insect infestation in the vineyard. "He might be dead, but his organization continues to thrive."

"I've thought from the beginning that our Balkan friends might be involved in this. Annabelle claims there's no logic to that suspicion, and that I have a blind spot where Radovanovic and his goons are concerned." Mark gave a fist-sized rock at his feet a kick. "That sonofabitch sent Annabelle flowers."

Matt and Luke shared an incredulous look; then Luke commented, "The hell you say."

"I thought she maintained her cover in the aftermath of the business in Hawaii," Matt said.

"The flowers weren't a threat. He wanted to date her."

"Holy crap." Luke gazed across the vineyard to Matt's house. "Maddie said some Italian called her bright and early this morning, and that Annabelle said she'd meet him in Paris after this thing with Kurtz is done."

Mark stiffened at that news and damned if his brothers didn't notice. Matt and Luke shared a look. Then Luke said, "You're going to let your wife go to Paris with an Italian?"

"Ex-wife."

"She's only your ex because you're a dumb-ass," Matt observed.

"Drop it."

He wasted his breath. "Why the hell are you letting this happen, Mark?" Luke continued. "That woman is the best thing that's ever happened to you."

"Don't start."

Matt shook his head. "Your personal life is—"

"Personal," Mark snapped.

"—a wreck. Haven't you learned anything from Luke's and my mistakes? You'll avoid a lot of grief if you'll just fix things with her now."

"It isn't that simple."

"It never is, not with women. But it's worth it. You need to stop being such a hard-ass. I always thought Branch won the prize for granite head in the family, but I think you might just win that contest, after all."

Mark was already strung tight as skin on a sausage.

He didn't need this now. "Look, y'all. Annabelle and I—"

"Help!" The feminine cry brought all to a halt. "Luke! Help us!"

The three brothers took off running for the house. Mark drew his gun. They'd taken no more than five steps when Annabelle burst through the front door and headed in the opposite direction. "What the hell? Belle!"

His brothers continued sprinting toward the house as Maddie shouted from inside. "Luke! Matt!"

Mark veered off toward Annabelle. She hadn't drawn her gun, he noted. Fear lodged in his throat and he put on his afterburners attempting to catch up. But his ex-wife ran like a rabbit and she'd jumped in the helicopter's pilot seat and started flipping switches by the time he reached her. "It's Torie. She's hemorrhaging."

Mark holstered his gun as he pivoted and raced toward the house. He sprinted up the porch steps as a grim-faced Matt exited the door carrying a pale and wan Torie in his arms. A streak of bright red blood stained her clothes and his arms. Mark understood the plan without being told and he turned right around and dashed for the helicopter. There he opened the passenger door and took Torie from Matt so that his brother could climb into the passenger seat.

"Hang in there, sweetheart," he told her, giving her forehead a kiss as he handed her back to her husband. He slammed the door shut and backed away as Annabelle took the bird up.

The noise of the rotors prevented him from hearing the engine of a car, so he was caught unaware when Luke and Maddie's SUV roared out of the garage, then stopped in front of the house. Maddie came down the front porch steps, a daughter in each arm.

He ran for the car, reaching for his cell phone. He

dialed the Brazos Bend hospital from memory. When the operator answered, he said, "The Callahans are en route by helicopter with a hemorrhaging woman, nine months pregnant. ETA approximately five minutes. Her doctor is—" He glanced at Maddie, who looked up from buckling one of the twins into the car seat.

"Dr. Jarrell."

Mark repeated the name, then added, "Have a stretcher ready to meet them at touchdown and have the ER ready for her."

As Mark spoke into the phone, he heard Luke conversing with security guards on the radio. Two minutes after the helicopter took off and with Luke behind the wheel, Mark, Maddie, and the twins were on the road headed for town. The security firm's SUV fell in behind them.

At that point, Mark asked, "What the hell happened?"

Sitting in the backseat between her two fussing children, Maddie replied, "We were in the kitchen talking. Torie, Annabelle, and me. She was in labor, but wanted to wait a bit to say anything. She reached into the freezer for a bag of ice chips she had ready, and as she lifted the carton of Blue Bell, she gasped and bent over double and then the bleeding started. I was ready to run for the car, but Annabelle said, 'No, we'll take the helicopter.' I was a basket case, but she stayed calm and controlled. Smart. I'm so glad she was there!"

After a moment of quiet, Luke asked, "Torie hurt herself lifting a carton of ice cream?"

Maddie said, "No. I imagine it's a problem with the placenta."

Mark glanced back over his shoulder. He didn't want to ask the question, but he and Luke needed to know what they could expect. "That's what keeps the baby alive, isn't it?"

Maddie's teeth tugged worriedly at her lower lip as she nodded.

Mark closed his eyes and prayed.

Once in a Philippine jungle, Annabelle hid beneath a pile of brush within spitting distance of the gun-toting terrorists searching for her with the intention to kill. Another time she'd faced three armed drug runners with rape on their brains, with only her wits as a weapon. She'd even climbed up onstage and sung in public at a USO show in Germany.

But never in her life had she been as afraid as she was at this very moment.

She couldn't hear what Torie Callahan murmured over and over, but she could read the woman's pale lips. "The baby. They have to save the baby."

Matt looked as if he'd been carved from stone.

"That's downtown?" Annabelle asked, spying a collection of buildings ahead.

"Yeah." Matt's voice sounded gravelly and tight. "The hospital is that three-story building at two o'clock."

"Got it."

"There's no helipad, but you can use the park area to the north of it for an LZ."

"I'm all over it." Seconds later, she was.

Annabelle spied the stretcher and people in hospital greens waiting as she brought the bird down gently. She glanced at her former brother-in-law, and his emotionless expression reminded her so much of Mark on the battlefield as he'd gathered himself seconds before entering a firefight. Her heart went out to him and his wife. "God be with you, Matthew," she murmured as the stretcher arrived and a flurry of activity erupted.

Alone, she blew out a heavy breath, then methodically shut down the helicopter, flipping switches and turning dials with hands that betrayed a slight tremble. The coppery scent of blood tainted the air and suddenly, nausea rolled in her stomach and threatened to erupt. She threw open the door and stepped out into the fresh, just-cut-grass-scented air. She took three deep breaths and her stomach finally settled.

"Wow," she murmured. That was unusual. She'd wallowed in blood and gore more times than she could count, and she'd always had an iron stomach. But something made today's event different from anything she'd ever experienced before.

That something, she thought, was love. Love had lived and breathed and swirled in the air of the cockpit during that short trip. Love—Matt's for his wife and child, Torie's for her husband and child—created a tangible force more powerful than any she'd witnessed on the battlefield.

A truth hung just beyond her reach. Something about Mark and the child he'd lost . . . about her and Mark and the child the two of them never created. Commitment. Love.

Fear of commitment.

Had she been just as guilty as Mark in that respect?

The sound of cars careening into the hospital parking lot jerked her back to the moment. As they approached the Emergency entrance, she jogged to meet them. The lead car screeched to a stop and doors flew open. Luke and Mark emerged from the SUV and shot her identical panicked hopeful looks. "So far, so good," she reassured them.

As the bodyguards exited their vehicle, they looked to the Callahan brothers for orders. Seeing a way she could help, Annabelle took control. "Mark, you and Luke go on inside while I park the car. Maddie, stay with me and I'll help you with the girls." She gestured toward the bodyguards and said, "You guys are with us."

The Callahan brothers nodded and headed for the door. They spoke simultaneously when they said, "Hurry."

"We will," Maddie assured them as Annabelle climbed into the driver's seat. Once the doors were closed and Annabelle put the SUV into gear, she asked, "Was that the truth? She made it there alive?"

"Yes. Torie was holding on." Annabelle licked her lips and added, "I don't know about the baby, though."

"Oh, God."

"That's nothing necessarily bad," Annabelle hastened to say as she pulled the vehicle into a parking spot. "I truly know nothing. You have more experience with this sort of thing than I."

Maddie shrugged as she released her own seat belt, then attended to one of the twins. "My experience says this is a bad thing. We should know by the time we get inside. Let's hope our guys greet us at the door with news of a healthy C-section birth. If not—dear God—I don't think any of us will be able to bear it."

She passed Samantha to Annabelle, then pinned her with a warning gaze and said, "And, Annabelle? If the worst happens? I don't care what problems you and Mark have had in the past—you'll need to be there for him. Mark would take the loss of another Callahan baby extra hard."

Annabelle momentarily bristled at the implied criticism, then shrugged it off. If she were in Maddie's shoes, she'd probably say the same thing. "He may not be my husband anymore, but Mark is still my teammate. I won't abandon him on the battlefield or in a hospital waiting room."

Maddie gave a brief smile. "I like you, Annabelle.

I truly do. Now, let's nut up and go see what sort of trouble we're facing.''

"Nut up?" Annabelle repeated.

Again, a quick smile. "A girl's gotta grow a pair if she's gonna hang with the Callahan boys." Then Maddie glanced toward the security guys who'd pulled up next to them. "Are we good to go?"

"Yes, ma'am," the guard wearing a cowboy hat and aviator sunglasses replied. "My partner here will lead the way."

Annabelle's pulse pounded as they approached the hospital and she experienced a moment of déjà vu. This time it wasn't her family waiting within the hospital walls, but Mark's. It didn't make it much easier, she decided.

"I'm getting tired of hospitals," she said to the little girl currently batting at Annabelle's hoop earring. "Let's just hope this visit turns out as good as the last one, though, and I'll be happy."

The automatic doors whooshed open. Annabelle let Maddie lead the way. She took a corridor to the left that led them to a nurses' station. "Torie Callahan?"

A nurse looked up from a chart. "They took her straight into delivery."

"Thanks." Maddie jerked her head to the right. "This way."

She led them through a maze of corridors to an area whose sign read BRAZOS BEND WOMEN'S CENTER. "The labor and delivery waiting room is at the end of this hall," Maddie informed them. As they approached the doorway she'd indicated, Maddie reached out and gripped Annabelle's free hand.

Mark and Luke paced an otherwise empty waiting room. At the women's entry, they looked up. Identical faces wore identical expressions of abject worry. Annabelle's stomach sank and Maddie squeezed her hand even tighter, then asked, "Any news?"

Mark and Luke shared a look. Then Mark cleared

his throat and replied, "They were going to deliver the baby right away. It should be over with by now. The fact that we haven't heard . . . that Matt hasn't let us know . . ."

"Oh, dear Jesus," Maddie said. She went to her husband and gave him a one-armed hug. When that wasn't enough for either of them, she set her toddler on the floor and embraced him fully.

Upon seeing her sister free to roam, the girl in Annabelle's arms started squirming. She set her down beside her sister, then crossed the room to Mark. "Can you use a hug, too?"

He opened his arms. "C'mere."

The minutes dragged by like hours until a woman appeared in the doorway. Her expression serious, her tone guarded, she asked, "Callahan family?"

"Shit," Mark muttered.

"Fuck," Luke said.

Maddie sank into a chair.

Annabelle stepped forward. "Yes? That's us."

"My name is Linda. Your brother has asked you to join him. If you'll come with me?"

Mark's voice emerged in a croak. "Torie? How's Torie?"

"And the baby?" Luke added.

Linda said, "Mrs. Callahan is still in surgery. We need to go this way."

Mark shot Annabelle a look filled with fear. None of them had overlooked the fact that the nurse had avoided the question about the baby.

"Let's get this over with," Luke said grimly, clasping his wife's hand and all but dragging her toward the door.

"The girls . . . ," Maddie protested.

Annabelle was torn. She hated to leave Mark—that tick in his jaw told her he needed her—but . . . "I'll stay and watch them."

"We can handle the little-bits," one of the body-guards, picking up on the problem, said. "I have three of my own. You go on. We'll be fine."

Maddie nodded, and the four of them followed Nurse Linda through a pair of swinging metal doors and down a hallway. She stopped in front of a door and gestured them inside.

Luke and Maddie entered first. Annabelle heard Maddie gasp. Mark all but crushed her fingers with his hand as they stepped into the room.

Matt Callahan stood framed by a window, sunlight haloed around him, a single tear rolling down his face. He held a child cradled in his arms.

The newborn wore a little blue cap and he sucked the middle two fingers of his right hand. Matt cleared his throat and said, "He's healthy. He's perfect. We're naming him John."

Mark wondered if his heart might just pound right out of his chest. He cleared his throat. "Torie?"

"They made me leave. I don't know what's going on. The only reason they let me see the baby being born is that everything happened so damned fast they didn't kick me out in time." He closed his eyes and added, "This is America. She can't die having a baby in America."

"She's not going to die," Maddie declared fiercely. "Not because this is America, but because she is Torie. Think about it, Matt. Your wife is stubborn, she's a fighter, and she has wanted to be a mother for so long. Add all that to the fact that she's head over heels in love with you—she won't let this beat her. I know it in my soul.

"Now. Let me see my nephew." She stepped forward next to Matt and smiled down at the baby. "Ah, he's beautiful, Matt. Look at that little bow-shaped mouth! Hello, Johnny. I'm your auntie Maddie."

Then she looked up at her husband and said, "We need to call Branch."

"Shit." Luke's troubled gaze locked in on Mark. "I know we don't talk about him to you, but he's made a real turnaround since our girls were born."

"He's old, Mark," Maddie added. "Old and sad and filled with regrets he's trying to fix before he dies."

Mark felt Annabelle's hand slip into his in a silent show of support. He knew they wouldn't call him if he said no. They hadn't called on the way to the hospital, partly because of the rush, true, but Mark knew it was partly because of him, too. They put his feelings first.

When Matt glanced up from his baby's face, his expression bearing the sign of one burden too many, Mark knew the time had come to return the favor. For Matt. For Torie. For Luke and Maddie.

Well, crap. Here he was smack-dab in the middle of Brazos Effing Bend, Texas, the one place in the world he'd sworn never to visit again. What was one more broken vow?

"I'll call him."

Under other circumstances, the shock on his family members' faces would have made him smile. Right now, though, he had to suck it up and swallow the poison on behalf of the people he loved.

And as Annabelle gave his hand a hard squeeze, he silently added, *Hell. And maybe, just maybe, for me, too.*

He stepped out into the hallway to make the call, dialing the number from memory. Some things you never forgot.

It rang four times before the old fart said, "Hello?"

Mark's reaction was instant and visceral. For a moment, he couldn't force the words past the knot of anger that lodged in his throat.

"Who's there?" Branch Callahan demanded.

Mark heaved out a sigh. "This is Mark. Torie had a problem and she's in surgery. The doctor delivered her baby. He's fine. We're in the maternity waiting room. I'll call the security company and have your driver bring you here. How soon can you be ready?"

"Mark? Did you say you were Mark? My Mark?"

He closed his eyes. Swallowed bile. "Yeah."

"Oh, God. Torie. She must be dying if you are willing to call me."

"No, dammit. She will not die. That's not gonna happen." Fear and fury lay behind his next words. "Just get your bony old ass up here and meet your new grandson. For some godforsaken reason Matt wants you here. I'll tell the driver you're leaving in twenty minutes. Be ready."

"I'll be ready in ten," Branch said as Mark lowered the cell phone from his ear and punched the disconnect button.

He made a call to the bodyguard assigned to watch Branch, and arranged for a redistribution of resources, then leaned against the corridor's wall, his head tilted back, and closed his eyes. A moment later, he sensed a presence. Annabelle. Damn, but the woman was a comfort to him. "I swear I'd rather take on a hundred Taliban single-handedly and weaponless than do this."

"You did the right thing."

He shrugged. "Matt wants him here, so he'll be here."

"They're wondering if you will stick around."

"I'm not going anywhere. Not until we know Torie is gonna be all right." He sighed heavily, and levered himself away from the wall. "At times like this, families should be together. I'm glad you are here with me, Annabelle."

She rose on her tiptoes and pressed a quick kiss against his cheek. "Anything for a Fixer," she said lightly.

A Fixer. Not a husband. He guessed he had that one coming.

They rejoined the others in the waiting room and Mark explained the arrangements he'd made. Maddie excused herself to go check on the girls, and Mark and Luke flanked Matt in order to better inspect their newborn nephew while distracting the baby's father from his worry about little baby John's mother.

"No wonder Torie has been looking like she was toting around a keg," Luke observed. "This kid is huge for a newborn."

"Nine pounds, six ounces." Matt shifted the baby so that his brothers could get a better look.

Mark said, "Gonna be a ball player, for sure."

"See how he's sucking those middle two fingers?" Luke asked. "Kid will probably grow up to play quarterback for the Longhorns. Doing the 'Hook 'Em Horns' sign already."

"Nah," Mark disagreed. "He's an Aggie through and through. See? He's saying, 'Texas sucks.' "

A grin flickered on Matt's lips. "You are both wrong. Look how big his head is. The boy is all brain. John will be an Ivy Leaguer all the way. Princeton. Maybe Yale. Maybe Princeton undergrad and Harvard B-school."

They continued to discuss their ideas regarding young John Patrick Callahan for a while. Maddie returned to the room and begged the opportunity to hold the newborn. Mark noted that Annabelle slipped in and out of the room from time to time, but he kept his focus on his brother. Tension radiated out of Matt like heat from a charcoal grill, and Mark knew the best thing he could do for Matt was to keep him occupied.

Minutes dragged by like hours. Luke took a turn at holding the baby. Even Mark got in on the act after

Maddie demonstrated how to support the baby's head, then just plunked John into his arms.

Mark gutted his way through this new experience. He'd been halfway across the world backtracking a Filipino terrorist cell based in Cleveland when Luke's girls were born, and they'd been staring at their one-month birthday before he'd made it back to the States to see them. When he first held them, they'd had some bulk to them. Cradling this little guy scared the bejesus out of him.

It also caused one of those What-if moments that he had to shake off quick. Now was not the time to wallow in the past.

Hell, maybe those times were gone for good.

Holding this little guy in his arms took his thoughts toward the future. As soon as he and Annabelle dealt with the Kurtz and company problem and Torie was back on her feet—which *would*, by God, happen—the focus of the family needed to turn to this next generation of Callahans. Catherine, Samantha, and little John here.

As the scent of baby lotion teased his nostrils, he wondered why it had taken him so long to see it. The Callahan family needed to quit looking backward and start looking forward.

The baby let out a little mewling noise, and Mark's lips twisted in a rueful smile. *Callahan family, hell. Matt and Luke aren't the problem here. I am.*

Matt and Luke had moved on. They did look forward. They'd stopped living in the past. Of the three of them, Mark was the lone holdout.

Why? No secret there. His brothers had told him. Their wives had told him. Annabelle's parents had told him. Annabelle, too. He'd heard them, but he'd never listened to them. Not *really* listened. Not to the extent that he truly comprehended what they were saying.

As he looked down into the face of the peacefully sleeping child, he told himself that maybe today that had changed.

A noise in the doorway had him glancing up in hope of seeing the doctor standing in the doorway with a big smile on his face. Instead, Maddie stood in the threshold and warned, "Branch is here."

Even as Mark braced himself, she stepped away and his father appeared in the doorway. Mark couldn't hide his shock. He had not seen Branch Callahan since the sonofabitch had circumvented nurses and invaded Mark's hospital room during his recovery from a gunshot wound—yet another injury that could be laid at the old man's feet. Leaning heavily on a wheeled walker, his formerly thick, silver hair now a thin, limp white, his complexion mottled, his limbs palsied, he seemed to have aged ten years in two.

On the heels of shock, Mark felt that old soup of emotions that had defined his feelings about his father for so long—fury, rage, pain, betrayal. Also, a new ingredient swirled in the mix this time, and he wasn't quite sure what to call it. Not forgiveness. He wasn't there yet. Sorrow? Pity? Compassion?

Hell, maybe it was a combination of all those things.

Branch captured Matt's gaze and asked, "How's our girl?"

"We haven't heard a goddamned thing. I'm about ready to go hunt someone down to give us a report."

"Let me do that," Luke volunteered. "You have someone to introduce to Branch."

Mark turned, ready to hand the baby back to Matt, when Matt surprised them all by saying, "Branch, this is your number two son, Mark. Mark, that's your father, Branch. I'd be honored if you would introduce my son to his grandfather."

Well, shit. Under the circumstances, how could he refuse?

Mark stepped forward, cleared his throat, and spoke directly to his father for the first time in years. "Branch, you need to meet the newest addition to our family. This is John Callahan."

"John? Well . . ." He choked up. Tears overflowed the old man's eyes and spilled down his face. He reached out and touched the newborn's cheek, his mouth stretched in a wistful smile. "He's a fine-looking boy, Matthew."

Branch touched Mark's arm. "A fine son."

Ten minutes later when Torie's doctor showed up wearing that smile Mark had wanted so badly to see, tears spilled from the eyes of all the Callahan men.

Chapter Fifteen

Nerves prickled Annabelle's skin as she paced the hospital's hallway. Four hours earlier, Torie's doctor had sat the Callahan family down and explained the details about her uterine rupture—a rare event for a woman of Torie's health and medical history. He'd credited God's grace and the speed of her arrival to the hospital for saving her life and the baby's life. He gave himself credit for saving her uterus.

Meanwhile, word had spread throughout town of the Callahans' mad rush to the hospital. As a result, too many people had appeared to express their concern for Torie, to visit Matt, to share in the joy of a new Callahan baby. And, Annabelle deduced, to mine for gossip about why the family had pretended to leave town, but hadn't done so.

While the bodyguards Mark had hired appeared to be on top of the situation, she simply wasn't comfortable. There were too many strangers and too much activity around this place for that.

Not with a killer on the loose and targets painted on the backs of the Callahans.

"Hey, Annabelle."

She turned back to see that Mark had emerged from the ICU. "Hi. How is she doing?"

"She's cranky when she's awake. Wants more time with the baby than they're giving her. All in all, though, she's doing just fine."

"Good. I'm so glad. . . . I know you two are close."

He smiled. "Maddie gets in your face and makes you love her. Torie is sneakier about it. She calls me on Maggie's birthday."

"They're both exceptional women."

"Yeah. And speaking of that . . ." Mark stepped up beside her and took her arm. "I want to talk to you about—"

He broke off abruptly, frowning toward a group of women who emerged from the elevator at the end of the hall. Pivoting, he led Annabelle in the opposite direction. "That's our old Sunday school teacher, one of the gossip queens in town. I don't have patience enough for her right now."

He opened a door marked EMPLOYEES ONLY and grinned, then tugged her inside.

A hospital linen closet? Annabelle rolled her eyes. "What is this . . . a soap opera? *As the Brazos Bends*?"

"Very funny."

But when the scent of his aftershave teased her senses, she couldn't help but remember other times they'd shared a closet. On that Lanai estate. In a hotel in Amsterdam. At a restaurant in Atlanta. He flipped on a light switch and jerked her back to the present.

"I haven't had the chance to thank you for the quick thinking this morning. The few minutes you saved by taking control of the situation saved her life, Annabelle."

"I'm glad I could help. I just wish we could have done this whole thing a little quieter. Have you seen the waiting rooms?"

Grimacing, he nodded. "Luke and I both spoke to the guys from Saunders Security. They have reinforcements on the way."

"Good." Annabelle breathed a sigh of relief.

"They also mentioned that you had already called requesting more men."

She shrugged. "Y'all were understandably distracted. I thought a few extra precautions were in order."

"Like arranging for a private family ICU waiting room? That was good thinking, too. That's made it easier for security to do its job."

"It freed up eyes to man the hospital entrances." She laughed mirthlessly and added, "I've spent so much time in hospitals of late that it was easy to recognize the need."

"This hospital trend definitely has to stop. I say we do resort hotels from here on out."

Annabelle smiled a bit wistfully. "I'm worried, Mark. We have Matt shifting between Torie's room and the nursery, and Luke and Maddie can't keep their twins cooped up for hours on end. I know your brothers can take care of themselves and their loved ones, but it's obvious to me that all of you are a bit off your marks today. If Kurtz gets into the hospital . . ."

"That won't happen," Mark declared in a hard, flat tone. "The guys on the door are good. They have a recent picture of Kurtz and he won't get past them. Look, we considered sending Maddie and the girls home, but until the extra help arrives, we think it's safer to keep the family together."

"I know. It's just that I'd feel better about everything if not for the near-constant parade of Brazos Bend friends come to pay their respects. And bring baby gifts. And flowers for Torie."

Mark brushed her cheek with the pad of his thumb

and grinned. "I understand you threw a bit of a tantrum when Sara-Beth Branson came looking for pictures and quotes for the local newspaper."

Annabelle didn't try to hide her snort of disgust. "The woman noticed the security guards and decided she had a scoop on her hands. I couldn't talk her out of it. Maddie couldn't, either. Luke had to promise her an exclusive once this is all over to get her to back off."

"Luke has a way with Sara-Beth. She was his girlfriend in high school."

"He told me we can trust her word, so I'm not worrying about it anymore. Still, she was awfully nosy about me. I'm hoping that things will calm down for a bit now that the nurses have closed the nursery blinds until evening visiting hours. That should give us some time to regroup."

He tucked her hair behind her ears and with admiration warming his voice said, "You are something else, Annabelle. I don't know what I would have done without you today. You were there for us with Torie, there for me with Branch. I can't thank you enough."

"You did a good thing by calling your father. I know it wasn't easy for you."

"Damn straight it wasn't, and I'm glad you noticed. See, I did it for Matt, but I also did it for you. Yesterday you told me that you were finished waiting for me because you didn't trust me to battle my demons. Well, I took on one of the biggest a few hours ago when I made that phone call. I hope that demonstrates to you that I don't fear my old ghosts more than I love you."

Annabelle closed her eyes. She wanted to believe him, but . . . "Look, Callahan. I don't think either of us needs 'us' to be an added distraction right now."

"I won't say another word . . . as long as you promise me that you'll reconsider what you said yesterday about not waiting for me."

She blew out a sigh. "All right."

"I love you, Annabelle."

"That's another word, Callahan."

The gleam in his eyes warned her and her heartbeat quickened. "So is this."

Tugging her against him, he kissed her. Just like always, he wove a sensuous spell around her. She couldn't stop her pulse from pounding when his tongue flicked over her lips. She couldn't still the vibration in her skin when his hand skimmed down her back. She could not stay the damp heat of desire that pooled between her legs as he pressed himself against her and rocked, his hard length finding that spot that ached . . . ached.

Annabelle hardly noticed when he reached down and locked the door, then pressed her back against it. What was it about this man that defeated every defense she attempted to erect? His touch made her forget her doubts. The taste of him awakened a craving within her so intense that she disregarded all her misgivings. And worst of all, the words he murmured over and over and over again . . . against her ears . . . against her throat . . . against the breasts he bared to his seeking mouth . . . those three little words seduced her to his will. Totally. Completely.

He entered her with one hard thrust. "I love you."

And Annabelle knew that, like it or not, she was his, now and forever.

But before she could put the thought into words, he moved. Ruthlessly, relentlessly, he took her, and Annabelle threw her head back and rocked against him, everything but this vicious need he'd created within her wiped from her mind. He drove her up until she quivered helplessly, poised at the precipice. Writhing. Waiting. Begging.

And then she fell; she flew; she soared, riding a wave of pleasure so intense that she was only vaguely aware when his hard body went rigid. When his body shuddered. When he muffled a groan against her neck.

She collapsed against him, her breathing rapid, her heart clubbing the walls of her chest; she was wishing they could stay as such forever when his lips said yet again, "I love you. I love you. I love you."

He loves me. I love him. He's mine. My Mark. My husband. Annabelle put all thought of killers and hospitals and babies born or yet to be conceived from her mind and concentrated on the moment. On the reality of their love.

And that maybe, just maybe, he loved her enough.

In the aftermath, Annabelle struggled to orient herself. She was . . . where? She blinked twice and made herself focus. A hospital linen closet. Her shorts were gone; her panties were in tatters. Her bra hung open, its front clasp undone, but she still wore her shirt and her sandals.

"Oh, for God's sake, Callahan. What did we just do?" She glanced around and took in the stacks of towels, a mop, a bucket, and a pile of tabloids the maids had collected.

In a thick, sleepy drawl, he said, "If you don't know, then I didn't do a very good job of it."

"I can't believe this," Annabelle muttered. "Of all the stupid, idiotic, unconscionable things to do."

"Unconscionable?"

She grabbed her panties, surveyed the tears, then gave up on them and pulled on her shorts commando. She shoved the tattered panties into her pocket. "Yes, unconscionable. For all we know, Ron Kurtz could be standing outside this door ready to take a shot at us."

"Well, if that's the case, then I feel even better about what we just did." He yanked up his pants and Annabelle was mortified to realize that he'd never taken them off. They truly were depraved. "And I have to tell you, sweetheart, I'm feeling pretty damned good right about now."

Annabelle paused from fastening her bra long enough to snarl at him, though she was trying hard not to laugh.

"Oh, darlin', don't beat yourself up. In a way, we had a brush with death today, and it's only natural to want to reaffirm life in a mutual expression of love."

She instinctively made a fist and had to stop herself from swinging. "You know something, Callahan? I've forgotten how chipper you get after you've been laid. Did I ever mention how obnoxious that is?"

He winked, grinned, and said, "I love you, Annabelle."

She made a growl of frustration and reached for the doorknob. After giving it half a turn, she paused and glanced back over her shoulder. "You didn't use a condom."

"You're right."

"I could get pregnant."

He waited a beat, stared into her eyes, and said, "Annabelle, that wouldn't bother me one bit."

Holy hell. She didn't have a clue how to react to that, so what she did was throw open the door to flee. "I'll go check on the twins in the playroom."

Damned if she didn't hear his laughter follow her down the hall.

Once away from him, Annabelle waited for the doubts and regrets to grab her. Instead, she discovered a buoyancy to her step as joy and hope crept into her heart.

Maybe, just maybe, they had a future, after all.

Dead meat walking.

From his position in the doorway of the public ICU waiting room, Ron Kurtz watched Annabelle Monroe stride down the hospital corridor, looking a little mussed following her interlude in the closet with Callahan. So, the two of them were an item. Talk about an unanticipated, but welcome, turn of events. It opened up all sorts of intriguing possibilities.

Callahan himself stepped out of the closet, and as rage flared in his veins, Kurtz's hand went instinctively to his handbag. These big tote bags women carried now certainly came in handy when a man dressed in a dress needed a place to stash his .45, not to mention his knife and his knuckle-duster.

With his prey so close and unaware, the urge to precipitously end the game almost overwhelmed him, but this new development where Monroe was concerned stayed his hand. If Monroe was more to Callahan than an easy lay—and from what he remembered about Annabelle, he doubted "easy" had anything to do with it—then taking her out along with part of his family would turn Callahan into a raving loon. He'd be killing two birds with one stone, so to speak.

"I love it," he said softly as he watched Mark Callahan pause and speak to the guard at the door of what served as the family's private waiting room. Then, after a subtle adjustment to his wig, he hooked his handbag over his shoulder and followed Monroe.

He caught up to her while she stood in front of the elevator. The button with the arrow pointed down glowed yellow.

Kurtz decided to use the stairs. He took them two at a time and paused on the second-floor landing. Peering through the small window, he watched the elevator pass two headed for one. He exited the stairwell just behind Annabelle Monroe and indulged himself in the pleasure of watching her walk. Damn, but the woman had curves. Maybe he should incorporate a little private time for the two of them into his plan before he did her. *I could do her, before I do her,* he thought with a smirk.

She turned down a hallway marked WOMEN'S CENTER, and he figured she must be going to check on Callahan's brother's wife. Toward the center of the hallway, he spied a burly guy in a suit standing in front of a door. Another obvious member of security—a woman this time—held position in front of a set of double doors at the very end of the corridor. Hmm. Must have family in both places.

Some ten steps or so from the male guard, Monroe paused to speak to an old geezer wheeling his way down the hallway on a metallic blue walker. Kurtz slowed his steps and tuned in his ears.

The old guy was saying, ". . . my boys say you saved my daughter-in-law's life by getting her here so fast."

"We were fortunate to have the helicopter available," Monroe replied as Kurtz walked past.

He sensed her gaze upon him and gave his purse a little hitch as a distraction. By then he stood parallel to the male guard and he stole a glance past him into the room. Plastic toys in bright, primary colors. A children's playroom. A door connecting to an outdoor playground.

Aware of the wary gazes on his tail, Kurtz turned into the first hospital room he came to as if he belonged there. Luckily, the occupant of the private room's bed was asleep and sawing logs.

Kurtz kept the door cracked and put his ear to the space. Annabelle was saying, ". . . looks like your granddaughters are having a good time with those wooden blocks."

"Old-fashioned toys that don't go out of style."

The geezer had to be Callahan's father, Kurtz decided. This just kept getting better and better. And the granddaughters Monroe referred to must be the twins he'd heard about when he'd stopped in that coffee shop searching for gossip and a turkey sandwich for lunch.

"Hmm . . . ," he murmured. "So much family. So many choices. What's a girl to do?"

He waited until he heard Monroe and old man Callahan enter the playroom; then he closed the door and took a few minutes to sketch out a plan.

The easiest thing would be to kill them all and that particular idea did have some appeal. He could go in slick and quick and get out before anyone knew he'd been here. He imagined how Callahan would react when he walked into that playroom and found his lover, father, and nieces dead, knowing he'd failed to protect them, aware that their deaths could be laid right at his feet.

It'd kill him.

But it would be quick. Too quick.

Kurtz reached down and readjusted the padding for his boobs and considered the situation further. Callahan needed to hurt. He needed to anguish and ache and be ripped into painful little pieces. He needed to be tortured.

Kurtz's gaze flickered over to the old lady snoring in the bed. He plotted; he planned. He pulled his gun from his purse and screwed the sound suppressor onto its barrel.

Then he ducked into the patient's bathroom and touched up his makeup. When he decided his disguise would hold, he winked at his reflection in the mirror. "Torture Callahan? I know just how I want to do it."

Annabelle sat cross-legged on the floor, accepting blocks from Catherine and Samantha. She used the multicolored blocks to build two towers, which the girls knocked over with flailing arms and squeals of glee. Branch Callahan sat in a chair behind her, helping his granddaughters choose which colors to add to the stack next.

"I'm feeling blue, Mitten," his voice boomed.

"Papa boo. Papa boo," Samantha babbled.

Annabelle's eyes widened as the toddler picked up a blue block and chucked it at her grandfather. Demonstrating quick instincts for a man his age, Branch caught the blue wooden cube inches before it would have hit his nose. "Whoa. Look at that. We need to get that girl a softball right away."

"And gloves for the rest of us," Annabelle replied with a laugh.

Branch chuckled and gazed at his granddaughters with eyes filled with tenderness and love. He wasn't what she'd expected. Instead of a powerful, patriarchal villain, she saw a simple old man with arthritic joints who sincerely cared about his family. Watching him interact with Catherine and Samantha, Annabelle couldn't help but think of another of Branch Callahan's granddaughters. Considering that his actions all those years ago continued to have a real effect on her own life today, she wouldn't mind hearing his side of the story.

His thoughts might have traveled in a similar direction, because the next time he spoke, he said, "I understand that you and my son Mark are close."

Her lips twisted wryly. "Sometimes closer than others."

"You know, he would hate to hear me say this, but of all my boys, Mark is the most like me."

She couldn't help but laugh. "You're right. He would hate to hear you say that."

"I know, but it's true. We are both stubborn cusses with heads hard as stone."

Annabelle wouldn't argue with that.

"I like to think I'm a little softer now than I was back in the day, but Mark . . ." He sighed. "Damn near impossible to move him off a position once he's taken a stand."

She wouldn't argue with that, either.

"I've made a million mistakes in my life, missy. Hell, probably a billion. It's the mistakes I made with my boys that top the list of my biggest regrets. I'd trade my life to change them, but . . ." He gave his shoulders a weary, weighted shrug. "Some things . . . you just can't fix. Some things are beyond a man's power, and other times trying to fix 'em would only make 'em worse. I think that's one of the harder lessons I've had to learn in this old life. By nature, I'm a fixer, Ms. Monroe. It's been a bitch kitty to accept that there are some things in this world I just can't fix."

A fixer. Annabelle couldn't help but smile at the irony. *Like father, like son.* She wondered if he had any clue about Mark's work with the team. Probably not.

"Mark told me about his wife and child, Mr. Callahan."

"So you know, then." He closed his eyes and shook his head. "Hell. If I could only live those decisions over again. I never guessed he'd take it so hard."

He raked his hand through his hair, repeating the gesture she'd seen Mark do countless times. Compassion melted a corner of her heart.

"Before I die, I hope . . . I pray . . . he'll let me explain," Branch continued. "Not excuse, mind you, but explain. I feel a powerful need to make it right with him, but I'm afraid. . . ."

"Mr. Callahan."

"Call me Branch, please. And, Annabelle? Just in case that doesn't happen, I want you to know that I've written him letters. Been writing them for years. They tell the whole story. If after I'm dead and buried, hell freezes over and he changes his mind . . . well . . . it'll be there for him."

"Actually, Branch, I think there might just be a cool breeze knocking at the door to Hades now."

He sat up straight. "What?"

"I think there is a chance he might be mellowing a bit."

The old man's eyes widened and filled with hope. "Really? You think he'll listen to me?"

Annabelle's teeth tugged at her lower lip. She didn't want to give the man false hope. "I don't know that he's ready to sit down with you right now, but—"

"The letters." Branch gripped the arms of his chair and pushed himself to his feet. "The letters. Maybe he'll read the letters. That's the best way, anyway. I say it all there. Everything. About his wife and the baby. About John."

"Papa, Papa, Papa," little Catherine said, holding her arms up for him to lift her.

"Later, Kitten. Papa's gotta go now." He grabbed his walker and wheeled himself toward the door, speaking to his assigned security guard as he exited the playroom. "C'mon, Jeeves. We need to make a quick run home."

"Papa!" Samantha cried out, her bottom lip extended in a pout. "Papa."

"Uh, oh." Annabelle winced. She knew an unhappy toddler when she saw one.

"Want Papa."

"I know, sweetie. He'll be back soon, though." She reached for a red rectangular block. "What color is this, Samantha?"

"Wed." She plunked her thumb into her mouth. "Want Papa."

Catherine joined in. "Papa, Papa, Papa."

"What color is this, Catherine?" Annabelle held up a blue block.

"Boo." *Sniff . . . sniff.*

Annabelle tossed a "Help me" glance toward the

security guard, but he simply shrugged his shoulders and started to turn away as she grabbed a yellow block. "Your turn, Sam. What color is—"

She broke off abruptly when the guard stepped back into the room, his hand reaching. . . .

It all happened in an instant. *Pftht. Pftht.* His body jerked. Splotches of red. Annabelle reached for the weapon . . . she wasn't wearing. The guard fell at the same time the security guard who'd been stationed at the door to the maternity area entered the playroom, followed by a woman. *Pftht. Pftht.* The second guard fell as the woman shut the door behind her.

"Yellow," said the voice from out of her past. "It's yellow, Annabelle. I'm not. Wasn't then. I'm not now. You and your boyfriend made a big-assed mistake."

"Kurtz," she said, seeing past the disguise. Those eyelashes!

"You got it in one. Now . . ." He stepped over the guard's body, swooped down, and picked up Samantha, who let out a surprised and unhappy yelp and squirmed to be put down. Kurtz put the muzzle of his gun against her tummy. "Get the other kid."

Annabelle's mind raced as she reached for Catherine. She didn't have many options at the moment. Were she by herself, she would try to overtake him. If only one child were in danger, she might still give it a shot. But with the lives of two children at stake, she needed to be very careful.

She took one calculated risk when, hidden by the process of settling a squirming Catherine in her arms, she slipped her hand into her pocket and pressed the call button on her cell phone. At the moment, she couldn't recall the last person she'd phoned. Was it Tag? Noah? Either one would notice her number, listen to the call, then phone Mark. At least, with any luck, that's the way it would happen.

In order to hide any sounds coming from the phone and to communicate the problem, she asked, "Why are you doing this, Kurtz?"

"Keep your mouth shut until I tell you differently, Monroe." He stooped and disarmed the dead guard, then crossed the playroom and peered outside into the fenced playground. "Where's the key to unlock the gate?"

Both twins began to cry, so she lifted her voice and said, "I don't know. I certainly don't have it. Please, Kurtz. The gun is scaring the babies."

"Smart girls." He pondered the problem a moment, then said, "All right, then. Here's what is gonna happen. There's an exit sign above a door to the right. You will walk directly there. Make eye contact with anyone, make a sound, and this little redhead goes the way of her bodyguard. Now, move."

Hoping her call went through, Annabelle patted Catherine's back and murmured in a calm tone, choosing words that could convey the seriousness of the situation to Tag or Noah without tipping Kurtz off. Either Tag or . . . oh. She bit her lip. It wouldn't be Tag or Noah. She'd called Paulo Giambelli last. *What time is it in Rome right now?*

She took one step, then stopped. "Leave the children here, Kurtz. You don't need them. Taking me will make Mark Callahan hurt plenty. He loves me. Losing me will tear him apart."

"All right. Put her down. I'll kill them both now. That crying is kinda gettin' on my nerves anyway."

"No! We're moving." She stepped out into the corridor and headed for the door marked EXIT, praying that Luke would decide to check on his twins or that Matt would pick that moment to leave Torie's bedside in order to spend some time with his newborn son.

She didn't dare look around to check, however, but

went right through the door and into another short corridor that led to another door with a sign that read EMERGENCY EXIT ONLY.

Annabelle halted. "If we use that, we might trip an alarm."

"Good try, Monroe, but they would have a warning sign for that."

She opened the door and realized they'd entered the emergency-room area. Kurtz moved closer and murmured, "Keep going. . . . Keep going."

A woman wearing blue scrubs said, "Can I help you?"

Kurtz spoke in a falsetto tone while heading directly for the outside doors. "Just got turned around trying to take the babies outside. Sorry. We'll be out of your way quick as a minute."

The automatic doors swished open in front of them, and Annabelle stepped outside into the hot afternoon sun.

She'd never been so cold in her life.

Chapter Sixteen

Mark was in visiting Torie when the cell phone in his pocket vibrated against his hip. He checked the number and frowned. Not one he recognized. "Sorry, sweetheart," he said to Torie. "I hate taking a call here, but under the circumstances . . ."

"Answer it," she said.

He thumbed the connect button and brought the phone to his ear. "Hello?"

Static. Lots of static. Then, ". . . Giambelli . . . in trouble."

The phone went dead as the call dropped.

"Strange," he murmured. He thought the guy said "Giambelli," but the only person he knew by that name was Annabelle's Italian Stallion. Why would he . . . ? Wait . . . Noah. Noah was in Europe. In trouble. Shit.

"I need to find a spot that has better reception. Be right back."

His thoughts raced as he exited the ICU and headed for the elevators with the intention of leaving the building. He didn't like this one bit. Why would Kurtz have followed Noah to Europe when he had easier targets here in the States?

More likely this call had nothing to do with Kurtz and Kincannon. Could be Annabelle called Giambelli to explain that she and Mark were back together and when the Italian mentioned "in trouble," he was making a wussy, long-distance challenge.

Weak, Callahan. Something's wrong. As he waited for the elevator, the phone vibrated again. Same number. "Hello?"

"Do you know where Annabelle is?" the Italian demanded.

"She's with me."

"So you are both being held at gunpoint?"

Mark froze. "Say that again?"

"It's a call from her phone. . . . Words are muffled. Sounds like she has a child with her." He explained about receiving the call in the middle of the night, noting Annabelle's number, and the pieces of conversation he'd been able to decipher. "I think she might have a rental car. Said something about Hertz."

Not Hertz. Kurtz.

For a moment, Mark stood frozen in fear before his mind and feet started working again. A child. Luke's girls were in the nursery. Mark gave up on the elevator and hit the stairs, flying down as fast as humanly possible.

Hold on, Annabelle. Just hang in there. Help is on the way.

With her arms wrapped tightly around Catherine while she kept a watchful guard on Samantha, Annabelle studied her surroundings, hoping to identify an opportunity for escape. Ron Kurtz had directed them to follow the drive that went around behind the hospital, their destination a parking lot on the opposite side of the building from the emergency room.

Heat radiated up from the asphalt, and perspiration dribbled down Annabelle's spine. She tried to ignore the "if only's" running through her mind, but they persisted. If only the extra security had already arrived. If only she'd realized that she needed to wear her gun in the children's nursery. If only they had considered the idea that Ron Kurtz might disguise himself as a woman. If only Torie hadn't—as Matt put it—busted a gut.

Regrets were a waste of time and energy, neither of which she could afford. *Think, Annabelle.* It was difficult to do with squirming, crying children in stereo.

When the girls paused to suck in a breath, Annabelle heard a car coming up behind them. She glanced over her shoulder.

"Don't even think about it," Kurtz said, stepping closer.

Oh, she thought about it. Especially when the car slowed and a window came down. "Whoa, there," said a man wearing a minister's collar. "Somebody isn't happy. Do you ladies need help with the little girls?"

Kurtz smiled and shook his head. Annabelle felt the gun barrel against her back. "No thanks," she told the driver. "It's nap time. They'll be fine once they sleep."

"Poor things. Those are Luke Callahan's daughters, aren't they? I went to high school with the Callahan brothers. I understand Matt's wife had an emergency today."

Kurtz pulled out his falsetto voice. "Yes, but thank heavens she's doing great. If you'll excuse us, sir. We truly do need to get these sweethearts down for their naps."

"Certainly. Certainly. I need to move along, myself. I'm supposed to give Communion to Martha Howard in ten minutes and if I'm late, she'll never let me hear the end of it. Y'all take care now."

Annabelle tensed, visualized throwing Catherine through that open window as she kicked behind her and brought Ron Kurtz down. The car drove forward even as she decided, *No, too risky.*

"Good job, Monroe. You get to live a little longer. Now, see that white van? That's where we're going."

Annabelle licked her lips. She absolutely, positively couldn't allow this killer to get them into the vehicle. As they crossed the hospital's north-side parking lot toward the van parallel parked on the street, she glanced around, hoping to see something—anything— she could use to get the drop on him.

She spied three vehicles slowly crossing the parking lot, two trucks and a black Cadillac. Out on the street where the van was parked, steady traffic rushed in both directions. SUVs. Fords. Nissans. A trash truck.

A trash truck.

Her gaze shifted to the Dumpster positioned beside the street some ten feet ahead of them. A *metal* Dumpster with a lid up. They'd pass it on the way to the van.

Okay. Okay. It'll have to do. Might be dangerous for the girls, but if we get into that van, we're dead.

She had no choice. Annabelle patted Catherine's back, then slipped her hand lower onto the toddler's diapered bottom. She slowed her steps. She'd have to time this just right. She needed to keep Ron Kurtz close.

Almost . . . almost. Annabelle drew a deep breath, tensed her muscles, and said a quick prayer that neither twin would get hurt. "Yah-eee!" she yelled at the top of her lungs as she pitched Catherine into the Dumpster, and rounded on Kurtz with a hard, high kick.

A gunshot sounded. Pinged off the metal. Her kick connected and she, Kurtz, and little Samantha went down.

Kurtz held on to the gun.

*   *   *

Mark blasted through the door from radiology into the emergency room, shouting his question as he ran toward the outside door. "Did a woman come through here? With two girls?"

The ER personnel looked up from their work with alarm. "Hold on there, mister."

"Two down in the playroom. Gunshots. One is still alive. Did my wife come through here with my twin nieces?" He was almost out the door. "With a man?"

"With another woman," someone called after him.

Outside he paused long enough to survey the area. Nothing. Not headed for the helicopter like he'd thought. He looked right, then left. Kurtz had to have a car. He'd take them around back. Less traffic. Mark took off running again before he'd completed the thought.

His feet pounded the pavement and he turned the corner at the back of the hospital and spied them. Walking. Alive. She carried one girl, Kurtz the other. Oh, God. Please, God.

He put on a burst of speed. One hundred fifty feet away. One forty. Pulled his gun. Could take a shot at fifty.

Kurtz's back was a big fat target, but Mark dared not risk it. He had hollow tips loaded into his .45. Couldn't risk the round going all the way through the bastard into the baby.

Shit. Shit. What to do? Get close enough and shout? Trust his partner to react? Yeah. That was a plan. This was Annabelle. Beautiful, brilliant Annabelle. His teammate. His soul mate. *My wife.*

One hundred feet. Hell, she probably expected him to show, likely already had this figured out and was just waiting on him to make his move. Eighty feet. They'd almost reached the street.

Mark took a breath to shout.

And Annabelle screamed.

Time slowed to a cold-molasses pace. He saw Catherine go flying, heard the gunshot. Saw his wife, niece, and Kurtz fall to the ground.

Sixty feet.

Samantha scrambled up, screaming. On wobbly legs she darted away from the struggling couple on the ground.

Toward the street. Toward the traffic.

"Samantha!" he cried. "Honey. This way!"

Another gunshot. Annabelle! "Oh, Jesus. Jesus Jesus Jesus. Please!"

Forty feet. Samantha dashing into . . . oncoming traffic. Screaming. Screaming. Into the path of a speeding car.

Twenty-five goddamned feet too far.

Something flew from a black car. Someone. Shoved the baby to safety. Squealing brakes.

A third gunshot.

A crash on the street. Mark saw his father go down. Traffic stopped.

Closer, Annabelle and Ron Kurtz quit moving.

"Oh, God." Fifteen feet.

He heard stereo screams as people rushed into the street. "Belle? Belle? Annabelle!"

Ten feet. Two still figures and a spreading pool of blood. Kurtz lay on top of her. Mark couldn't see her. "Belle . . . Belle . . . please!"

There. He was there. Down on his knees. Yanking Kurtz off her. Shoving Kurtz's gun beyond reach. The sight and smell of blood and of gunpowder made his stomach roll. "Belle?"

She opened her eyes. Blinked once, twice. "Girls?"

"They're okay. Are you hit?"

She winced, moved, and grimaced. "No. Not my blood. Kurtz?"

For the first time, he looked at the killer. Kurtz's

eyes were open and aware. Blood pumped from a
wound in his leg. A lot of blood. Femoral artery?

Annabelle sat up. She looked toward the street and
smiled, then turned her attention to her wounded ad-
versary. "He's bleeding out."

"Let him," Mark replied, even as he reached to put
pressure on the wound.

Kurtz grinned, his breathing labored. "Fuck you,
Callahan."

"I'm not the one who's fucked here."

Damned if Ron Kurtz didn't laugh at that. "Sure,
you are. I'm not the only one out to get you, but I'm
taking that name to my grave. Believe me, Callahan.
Monroe. You're screwed."

Mark and Annabelle stared at each other over
Kurtz's prone body. Then the medical people and
frantic Luke, Maddie, and Matt spilled from the door-
ways. Within moments, Ron Kurtz was loaded onto a
stretcher and headed for the ER. Luke rescued an
unscathed, but stinky, Catherine from the Dumpster
while Maddie ran sobbing toward Samantha, who sat
safe on the side of the road.

In her grandfather's arms.

"We're okay," the old man said. "We're fine."

Maddie went down on her knees, bursting into
tears, wrapping both Branch and Samantha in her
arms and rocking them all back and forth. As Mark
and Annabelle approached, Branch met his son's gaze.
A tear rolled down his cheek. "I did it. I made these
damned knees move. I saved her."

Mark cleared his throat. "Thank God." He swallowed hard and added, "Thank you, Dad."

Ron Kurtz died on the operating table.

The knowledge of who else was after the Fixers died
with him.

In the aftermath of the shooting, doctors treated

Annabelle and the girls for minor cuts and abrasions. Branch received similar care in addition to some tests ordered by his cardiologist and an orthopedic specialist. General consensus around the hospital credited adrenaline with his ability to move the way he had, and dumb luck that he'd fallen so violently without suffering any bone breaks. The Callahans considered it another miracle for which they were grateful.

Now in a large, family-style maternity suite, Branch rested in an overstuffed recliner in the sitting room area and waited along with Matt, Mark, and Annabelle for Luke and Maddie to join them after putting the girls down for a nap in the bedroom. Though Torie remained in ICU for now, hope remained high that she would be moved into the suite soon.

Annabelle could tell that despite his breakthrough out on the street, Mark wasn't exactly comfortable sprawled on a love seat, making small talk with his father. The topic was dogs—Branch's little Pomeranian named Paco and the darling little mutt discovered in Kurtz's van who was currently the subject of an adoption tug-of-war between a policewoman and a nurse.

Mark and Branch needed to shut themselves away somewhere to clear the air, she thought, watching father and son grope for things to say. That would have to wait until later, however. First she needed to share with the Callahans what she'd learned from the day planner recovered from Kurtz's van.

Luke and Maddie tiptoed out of the bedroom and silently shut the door behind them. Maddie dropped like a rag doll onto the sofa next to Annabelle and closed her eyes. "Just so that everyone knows, I'm calling for a moratorium on emergencies at least until tomorrow. I can't take any more without a stiff drink and a good night's sleep. I don't suppose anyone has a bottle of brandy in his pocket?"

Luke sat beside his wife and draped his arm around her shoulders as Branch snorted. "Brandy, hell. Will scotch do?"

Luke turned a hopeful look his way. Branch jerked a thumb toward a box on the round dining table. "While I was waiting to get my hip X-ray taken, I borrowed the technician's phone and ordered up some supplies. Matthew, will you do the honors?"

"None for Branch, Matt," Maddie scolded, leveling a frown on her father-in-law. "He's on pain meds."

The scowl Branch shot back at her brimmed with affection. As Matt rose from his recliner that matched Branch's, Annabelle held up the day planner. "Okay, people. Are you ready to hear about Kurtz?"

Maddie groaned and dropped her head onto her husband's shoulder. "Will we have to shift back into emergency mode if we do?"

"No." Annabelle's lips flicked a grin; then she met Mark's gaze. "Actually, I believe the information here removes any further threat toward your family."

"Let's hear it," he replied. He sat up, leaned forward, and, with his elbows propped on his knees, watched her intently.

Annabelle set the appointment book on the coffee table in front of her. "It's lucky for us that somewhere along the line, Kurtz got accustomed to keeping a calendar. I'll want to give this a more thorough study, but here's what I've pieced together so far. I think his killing spree must have been triggered by a visit from Dennis Nelson. I see nothing prior to the notation of that meeting that indicates our team even crossed his mind. That changed in the days after he met with Nelson. He started doodling in the margins. Things like 'Make the Fixers pay.' "

"Pay for what?" Luke asked, mouthing thanks when Matt handed Maddie and him their drinks.

"For mistreating him during his time on the team.

In the memo section he made a list of all the wrongs we did him. It goes on for pages." To Mark she added, "He held you most responsible because you were the one who dismissed him."

"The guy was effing crazy," Mark muttered.

Matt frowned as he handed drinks to Annabelle and Mark. "Why did Nelson pay him a visit?"

"That we don't know. Nothing in here suggests a reason. Judging by his travel schedule, I'm pretty certain he killed Terry Hart. After that . . ." She glanced up, met Mark's gaze. "I'm afraid he went to Boston and killed Jordan Sundine and his brother."

"Damn." Mark set his glass down on the coffee table hard. His mouth flattened into a grim line. "I had hoped Sundine would turn up alive."

Annabelle shook her head. "Kurtz's notes and receipts lead me to believe he took the bodies out to sea and dumped them. It's during his time in Boston that he doodled the word 'family' in all caps, followed by two exclamation points and underlined three times."

Luke propped his long legs on the coffee table. "He enjoyed torturing your teammate with the fact that he'd killed someone your friend loved."

"Exactly." Annabelle sipped her drink, then continued. "After Boston, he made a stop in Kansas, where he set up my family. Then he headed to Colorado, where he killed Rocky and his girlfriend."

Matt straddled one of the dining table chairs. "And after Colorado, Florida?"

"Yes."

"Did he go after someone else between Florida and here?" Luke asked.

"No," Annabelle replied. "He drove from Florida to Texas and took his time doing so."

Mark dragged his hands across his face, rubbing his eyes, massaging his temples. Then he asked the

million-dollar question. "What about the Gallery Gal?
Tell me there is something . . . anything . . . about
her."

"Nope. Nothing. He didn't write about her, didn't
doodle anything. . . ." Annabelle shrugged. "There's
nothing to indicate whether she was a partner he
turned on or another player. Although nothing in his
planner suggests he had a partner."

"Is that why you say the family is no longer at
risk?" Maddie asked, sitting up straight.

"In a way, yes. We know that Kurtz killed three
Fixers—Hart, Stanhope, and Sundine. He targeted
Mark, Noah, and me. That makes six."

"And it leaves six," Mark said. "Nelson, Russo, and
Anderson are dead. Parsons is missing. Holloway is in
Pakistan. Did that planner mention Harrington at
all?"

"No." Annabelle tapped the book with her finger.
"We don't know if Kurtz had his eye on Tag or not.
What we do know is that of the second six, nobody's
family has been bothered. Since we know that Kurtz
targeted families, it's logical to assume that the threat
to our families is dead."

"Thank God for that," Branch breathed.

Maddie spoke up. "And if the woman from the gallery was Kurtz's partner, then it's completely over.
Right?"

Annabelle's and Mark's gazes met. They knew it
wasn't over. Kurtz's dying statement made that all too
clear. Mark smiled wearily at his sister-in-law. "I wish
it were that simple, Mads. I'm pretty sure that someone in addition to Kurtz has been out to get my
team."

"I was afraid you were going to say that," she
grumbled.

Mark continued. "I think it started with Nelson. I
think he found out something that threatened some-

one who decided the best way to contain the threat was to get rid of the team. I think the gallery woman was hired."

"An assassin?" Matt asked.

Annabelle laid it out. "It fits that she killed Nelson, Russo, and Anderson. Remember, they weren't tagged as murders. Then, she went to kill Rocky Stanhope and discovered he was already dead. Who knows? Maybe she was late getting to Sundine, too. She got spooked. She wanted to find out what Mark knew, since he was the team leader, so she set up the Q and A at the gallery, then tried to kill us on the mountain."

Mark's matter-of-fact gaze met Annabelle's. "Kurtz used a forty-five today."

"You had it figured that day on the mountain, Mark," Annabelle told him.

Silence fell as the Callahans considered the scenario Annabelle had suggested. Eventually, Matt said, "Makes sense to me."

Luke agreed. "The theory certainly fits the facts. But who did the gallery woman work for? Herself or someone else?"

"Until we identify her, I don't think we'll find the answer to that one," Mark replied. Having finished his scotch, he tossed a handful of peppermints on the coffee table and chose one for himself.

"I don't like it," Maddie said, reaching for a piece of candy.

"Me, either," Branch offered. "I'm glad to think the rest of us are probably safe, but where does that leave Mark and Annabelle?"

Mark gave a grim laugh as he unwrapped the cellophane from around his mint. "Just where Ron Kurtz told us before he died. Screwed."

Later that evening, Mark and Annabelle drove his father home from the hospital. Branch invited them to stay at his house overnight, but Mark refused. A man could be expected to take only so many steps in one day.

His first look at Callahan House in years put a knot the size of a basketball in his gut. Under other circumstances, he might indulge in a few of the good memories he had of the place, but tonight he just wanted to get away fast. He pulled into the driveway and shifted into park, but left the vehicle running. As he opened the door to get his father's walker from the back, Branch asked, "Would you come in and have a drink? Meet my Paco?"

Mark opened his mouth to refuse, but Annabelle reached across the seat and slapped the side of his arm. Great. He really didn't want to do this, but after today's events, he could no more refuse her than he could fly. "Sure, we can do that. But just for a few minutes."

He brought the walker around to Branch and helped him from the car. "Might be better to go around back," Branch said. "I can avoid steps that way. I'm afraid I'm feeling too stiff for steps right now."

"Me, too," Annabelle said. "Personally, I'm looking forward to a good long soak in a hot bathtub tonight."

Mark pictured Matt's hot tub down beside the lake and instantly his mood brightened. He and Annabelle had the lake house to themselves tonight. A little romance would do them both good.

The back door opened as they approached and the Garza sisters and a yippy little dog came streaming out. "Mr. Mark. Mr. Mark! You've come home. What a glorious day for the Callahans."

"Paco, settle down," Branch said, his voice firm but tender.

"He's so cute," Annabelle said. "Hello, Paco."

She squatted down to pet the Pomeranian and

Branch warned, "Be careful. He might lick you to death."

Annabelle laughed and picked the dog up and cuddled him while Mark returned the Garza sisters' greetings. They peppered him with questions about the events of the day as they all filed into the kitchen, where another surprise awaited. "Sophia? Is that you?"

"Hi, Mark. Ms. Monroe."

The fresh-scrubbed, demurely dressed young woman taking cookies from the oven looked nothing like the porn queen he and his brothers had rescued from Lanai the previous year. Well, except for the pink. She still wore pink. Seeing her made him smile. "How are you doing, Sophia?"

"Good. Really good. I'm starting college in the fall."

"That's great. That's really great." They spent a few minutes catching up; then after pouring three glasses of milk and presenting Branch with a plate of warm Snickerdoodles, the Garzas took their leave.

Because he had no willpower when it came to the Garzas' Snickerdoodles, Mark picked up his milk and followed his father and the cookies to his old man's study.

It was a short walk long on memories. Once upon a time, love and laughter filled this hallway, these rooms. Mark could all but hear his brothers' footsteps pounding down the stairs and out the front door, when they were late as usual for the school bus. He heard his mother singing the Dean Martin tunes she loved so much. His father laughing out loud at Archie Bunker on TV.

Mark tossed back a gulp of milk as if it were a shot of tequila.

In the office, Branch set the plate of cookies on his desk, then sank into his chair with a weary groan.

Paco scrambled out of Annabelle's arms and pattered around to his master's feet. Branch scooped the dog up and spent a moment clucking and scratching and enduring licks on his face with obvious delight.

Damned if he doesn't truly love that dog, Mark thought. He hadn't seen that sort of emotion on his father's face since his mother died.

"Y'all want a real drink instead of the white stuff?" Branch asked. "I can get you—"

"This is perfect," Annabelle said. "Personally, I'll take cookies and milk over alcohol any day."

Branch beamed at her. "Me, too. I won't tell Maddie because she enjoys scolding me so much. It's a change for me, but now that I'm an old man, I have a sweet tooth big enough to make a vampire jealous."

"Vampire?" Mark repeated. "You been reading horror novels again, Branch?"

"Nope. Romance novels. They are all about happy endings and that appeals to me."

Mark opened his mouth, then shut it abruptly. He simply didn't know how to respond to that.

What had happened to the old Branch Callahan whom he knew and despised? Who was this fragile man who melted over a handful of dog, preferred sweets to whiskey, and read books with happy endings? He reached for another cookie.

Branch twisted his chair and took two file boxes out of the cabinet behind him. He set them on the desk in front of Mark and cleared his throat. "Son, I was on my way to get these when Mitten darted into the street. I've written lots of letters over the years. I have more boxes for you, but these are the pertinent ones for now. I'm not asking any more than that you take them with you and keep them, just in case the time comes when you have questions."

When Mark made no move toward the boxes,

Branch darted a pleading gaze toward Annabelle and added, "I heard through the grapevine that you might be willing—"

"Tell me now, Branch," Mark said. "Just . . . tell me."

Branch blew out a heavy breath, fortified himself with a gulp of milk, and said, "Working through the bad stuff with your brothers has taught me that if I ever got the chance to talk to you, I shouldn't spend the entire time telling you how sorry I am for the harm I have done you. So I won't. It's all in the letters, anyway. What I think best is for me to explain why I did what I did by telling you about Vicki Hansen."

In the midst of throwing up his emotional walls, Mark halted. "Carrie's mother?"

"In the years after I sent you boys away from Brazos Bend, I had people working for me keeping an eye on you all. After you married your waitress, I . . . um . . . hired her mother."

Mark's brow furrowed in disbelief. He'd never seen that one coming. Although maybe he shouldn't be surprised, considering both Matt and Luke had learned that Branch hired keepers for them during those years.

"That's why she moved to Savannah when you were stationed at Fort Stewart," Branch continued. "I paid her five thousand dollars every month. Plus, she had an expense account she was supposed to use to give y'all things you needed. I knew you wouldn't take them from me. She said she bought appliances, clothes for the girl, a car."

Mark dragged a hand down his bristled cheek as his thoughts returned to those years. They'd struggled from paycheck to paycheck. That first Christmas, they'd bought gifts for each other in a pawnshop. Carrie's mother never bought them a damned thing.

He'd never much liked the woman.

"Anyway, when Vicki told me you'd been sent overseas and your wife was expecting, I went out to see Carrie. Didn't tell her who I was, of course. Pretended to be her mother's new beau. That was a nice little place the two of you had. She'd taken typical base housing rental and put a lot of love into it. I thought everything was going fine for you two. I thought that of all the boys, you had your life most together, and that you would be fine if we could just get you home from Kuwait."

"That was a great little house . . . ," Mark murmured. "Meant a lot to me."

"Because it was home." Branch pulled a handkerchief from his pocket and blew his nose. "You wanted a home. I'd taken the one you had away."

Mark couldn't argue with that and anger put a bite in his next words. "If you thought we were doing so well, why threaten to take our child away from my wife?"

"That's the heart of this story, isn't it?" Branch sat back hard in his chair and closed his eyes. "I don't want to tell you this, son. Truly, I don't. But dammit, these secrets . . . they're weighing on me. I hate the thought of standing in front of Saint Peter still toting the burden."

"Tell me."

Branch nervously drummed his fingers on the desk. "During that trip to Georgia it became clear to me that Vicki Hansen was misappropriating the funds I sent for you and Carrie. When I called her on it, she played the female card and I fell for it."

"You slept with Carrie's mother?"

"No . . . no . . . not that she didn't attempt the seduction route. No, she went all teary and vulnerable and weak . . . played me like a fool. It worked for a time. But then a couple months before your baby was due, I wised up. That's when she did a one eighty.

She threatened me. Tried to put the squeeze on me. She basically tried to sell that baby to me, Mark. I was frightened for your child, having that woman in its life with you halfway across the world and unable to protect it."

Annabelle reached over and gave Mark's knee a comforting squeeze.

"I ranted and raved and I decided I had to do something. This was your child, my grandchild. I wanted the baby and your Carrie safely away from her extortionist mother."

"So you sent the lawyer," Mark said, his tone bitter.

His father winced and leaned forward in his leather desk chair. His hands gripped the edge of his desk hard. "Mark, Maddie told me your version of what happened. Well, it isn't true. That's not what happened. I never sent a lawyer."

"Bullshit. Carrie wrote me a letter right before she died and told me so."

"Was the letter in her handwriting?"

"Yes, of course it—" He broke off abruptly as he remembered. The handwriting had been shaky. Real shaky. She'd apologized for it and said she was scared. Frightened half to death. After all, the lawyer told her she couldn't win against the Callahan money. "Are you trying to tell me you never demanded Carrie move to Brazos Bend?"

"I went to see her, intending to tell her just that. But it never got that far." Branch took another drink of milk. His hands trembled, spilling liquid over the glass. "Because . . . I found out the truth. I found your Carrie there with . . . him."

"Him?" Mark's spine snapped straight. He stared at his father intently.

Branch dropped his gaze to his lap, drew a deep breath, then looked up and stared his son right in the eyes. "A man. Her lover. He was the baby's real father, Mark. Not you."

Seconds ticked by . . . maybe minutes . . . and Mark didn't move, didn't breathe, as he tried to process the old man's claim. Finally, once the words made sense, rage washed through him. He shoved to his feet, knocking his chair over. It clattered against the hardwood floor. "Shut the fuck up. That's bullshit. Why the hell would you tell a goddamned lie like that?"

"It's the truth."

"I'm not going to listen to this." Mark stormed toward the door.

His father's quickly spoken words chased him. "Her baby wasn't born April tenth. I didn't send her a letter on April twentieth. I didn't threaten to steal her baby and send her fleeing into the path of a drunk driver. Those are all lies. Her baby was born full-term in March, which meant you were away at some of the Ranger special training when she got pregnant."

Mark halted, breathing like he'd run ten miles.

"When I went to see her, to convince her to move to Texas to have her baby, she was already in the hospital. He was with her. I saw the baby."

Mark whirled on his father. "You are the fucking liar!"

Branch forged ahead. "I didn't want to believe it. I checked blood types right then and there. I knew you were A. Carrie's hospital bracelet had her as an A. Your baby could only be an A or an O. That little girl had type B blood."

Mark's fists clenched. He wanted to leap at his father, to pound on the old bastard. To shut him the hell up.

"I left. Came back to Texas. Tried to decide what to do. I didn't want her sending you a Dear John letter—those tend to get soldiers killed. Took me a week to figure out how I thought it best to handle the situation. By the time I went back, she was gone."

"What do you mean, gone?"

"They didn't die in a car wreck, Mark. She didn't die. Your wife ran off with her lover and bastard child."

Chapter Seventeen

The hysterical giggle began just below Annabelle's breastbone and bubbled up into her throat, though she managed to clamp down and hold it back.

Mark was married. Still married. To someone else. Good Lord.

The veins in his neck bulged as he shouted at his father. "This is bullshit. Complete and total bullshit."

"I wish it were," Branch fired back.

The way Mark glared at his father reminded Annabelle of the old saying about if looks could kill.

"Carrie didn't have an affair. She loved me. We were in love!" His voice broke as he added, "She wouldn't do that to me!"

"She said you were gone, that the Rangers took up all your time. She was young. She was lonely. You were away a lot. He was there for her."

Annabelle ached for Mark, ached for herself. Hadn't they already been through enough for one day?

"So, who was he?" Mark sneered. "This phantom lover?"

"Kevin. A man named Kevin Starr."

Annabelle watched the name hit Mark. He recognized it. He recognized the name and it threw him for a loop.

The tick of the clock sounded loud in the sudden quiet. Finally, in a cold, low tone, he asked, "Where are they?"

"I don't know." Branch lifted his chin. "I didn't keep track of her."

Mark's bitter laugh rang out. "You expect me to believe that? You? The control king of the world?"

"Look. That was, what, seventeen, eighteen years ago? And when was the last time you had anything to say to me?"

"When John died."

Branch waved his hand. "Other than then. You only talked of John then, and it was ugly. Was I supposed to bring this up at your brother's memorial service? I don't think so.

"No, you haven't talked to me in twenty years, Mark. I didn't know you had been mourning her all this time. I assumed that after she ran off, she sent you that Dear John letter I had fretted about. I assumed y'all were divorced and that you were over her. From the reports I had, you certainly didn't shy away from the ladies when you returned stateside. Hell"— Branch glanced at Annabelle as if seeking help—"you did move on. You remarried!"

She swallowed a wounded whimper while Mark prowled the office like a panther.

"Think about it, Mark. Not even your brothers knew about Carrie. How would I have known what her mother did? I didn't. Not until Maddie sprang the sorry pack of lies on me after you got shot trying to help Torie. I didn't know you carried that baby picture around in your wallet. All this time, I knew you hated me, but I thought it was because of what I did after the factory fire, especially after I screwed up with

John. I didn't have a clue that you held these lies against me, too."

"Christ," Mark muttered, raking his fingers through his hair.

Branch was breathing hard and Annabelle watched him warily. The way their luck had been running, Mark's father would have a heart attack right here and now. And yet, she didn't want to interfere. It was time—past time—these two hardheads had this conversation.

"By then, everyone was pissed and no one would listen to me. I admit, I got pissed right back. For a while, I quit trying to get anyone to listen. That was a lonely time. A hard time. One, admittedly, I brought on myself."

"Gee, you think?" The sneer was back on Mark's face. "You faked a heart attack and people almost died."

Regret rolled across Branch's face. His tone grew somber. "Yes, I did a horrible thing and it cost me. It changed me, too. Believe it or not, I finally learned from my mistakes. Then, after Luke's girls were born and Maddie convinced him to allow me back into their lives, I didn't want to rock the boat, to risk losing the little I had, so I kept my mouth shut. The fact is that I've made a lot of mistakes that I'll regret to my dying day. I've done some terrible things, Mark, but faking the death of your wife isn't one of them. I have no proof to give you other than my word."

And his son obviously didn't believe that word. Annabelle couldn't help but feel a bit sorry for the pitiful old man with little more than a big house and a Pomeranian.

Mark stopped in the middle of the room, shoved his hands in his pockets, and rocked on his heels. "Why would her mother do something like that?"

"Spite. She hated me. First, I cut off her gravy train.

Then, I rejected her. Finally, she wanted me to track down her daughter and I refused to do it. I never dreamed she'd take her revenge the way she did. Sending you that letter, faking the car wreck. That was cold."

"No." Mark scowled and shook his head. "Vicki couldn't have faked that car wreck. Hell, I read the police report."

"After Maddie told me what you thought, I hired an investigator to go looking for Vicki. Didn't you ever wonder why your wife died and is buried in a Podunk town in Alabama? That's because your mother-in-law was sleeping with the police chief there. He helped arrange the whole thing. Have those graves exhumed if you need proof. Bet you every penny I own that they're empty."

He blew out a long, heavy sigh. "That woman was damned crazy, Mark, and she hated me by the time I was done with her. I think your Carrie left her as much as she did you."

For a long moment, Mark stared at his feet. When he looked up, his green eyes gleamed with determination. "I don't believe it. Even if the baby wasn't mine, she wouldn't have run off without a word. Carrie wouldn't have done that. You didn't have the detective look for her?"

"No." Branch shrugged. "I figured . . . well . . . she could have found you if she'd wanted to, Mark. She knew you were from Brazos Bend. I've lived in this house for forty years."

Annabelle watched that truth sink into Mark. Moving slow like an old man, he reached down and righted the chair he'd knocked over. "I'm leaving. I have to go. C'mon, Annabelle."

She rose from her seat, feeling a little shaky. She could only imagine what Mark was feeling. He'd be hurt. Bitter.

Plenty of pain and bitterness to go around.

When Mark reached the threshold of the study door, his father asked, "Son . . . will I see you again?"

Mark paused, grimaced, then shook it off. "You have been a meddling bastard most all of my life. You've made some stupid, horrible, fatal decisions. Told some terrible lies. That said, portions of this story make sense. That doesn't mean I'm ready to accept it or excuse it . . . or make peace with it."

At that, a tiny bubble of bitter laughter did escape Annabelle's throat. Mark shot her an unreadable look before he continued. "One thing I do know, however, is that I'm done running away from my past. So, yeah, I'll be back."

As Annabelle followed him out the door, Branch called softly, "Take care of him, Annabelle. Please, take care of him."

Not knowing what to say, she simply waved a sad good-bye.

The night was moonless, dark, and heavy as they left Callahan House. Climbing into the SUV, neither Annabelle nor Mark spoke. The silence continued during the drive out to the lake house. They passed beneath a streetlamp and light flashed across his face, revealing that his thoughts were somewhere else. Sometime else.

With someone else.

She wanted to cry. Instead, she sucked it up and asked herself how she wanted to play this. She considered the question all the way to the lake, a trip that took forever, but not nearly long enough. They went in through the kitchen door into the darkened house. Mark switched on the light above the sink. She saw a myriad of emotions etched across his expression—pain, grief, and disbelief among them—as he took a glass from the cabinet and filled it with water from the tap.

He drank the entire glass; then finally, he spoke. "Belle . . . this is a mess."

She gave him a sad, sweet smile. "That's one way to put it."

He set down the glass. "Carrie . . . that baby was mine, Annabelle. Branch is wrong and I have to find out what happened."

"I know you do." Then, because her knees were a little weak, she pulled a chair out from the kitchen table and sat down.

"Kevin Starr was an old friend of hers who had moved to Savannah, too. While I don't believe for a minute that she cheated on me with him, for Starr to be on Branch's radar . . . there is smoke of some sort."

Annabelle chose her words carefully. "With all the parental stuff going on, the interference, her fear . . . she was young, Mark. Awfully young. Anything could have happened."

He dragged a hand down his face. "I thought I'd moved past all this. Honestly, I did. I was ready to let it all go. Ready to commit to you. Before the debacle with Kurtz, I had decided to duck out of the hospital and buy you a ring. Matt got Torie's here in town and she really seems to like it."

Annabelle knew he didn't realize he'd just plunged a knife into her heart, so she said simply, lamely, "It's a beautiful ring."

"But I can't just go off," he said, his hands fisting at his sides. "We can't forget that someone is out there killing Fixers."

She'd never seen him look so torn, so worried, and it was in that moment that Annabelle finally decided just how she had to handle this. "I haven't forgotten anything, Callahan, including how good you are in the field. Are you afraid you can't take care of yourself?"

"No. That's not it."

She folded her arms, silently challenging him to dare say he worried she couldn't take care of herself.

Mark was smarter than that.

"I'll hook up with Tag and Noah," she told him. "We will cover the Fixer issue. You can focus on . . . old ghosts."

In a soft, low rumble, he said, "I don't want to leave you, Belle."

She smiled sadly. "You really don't have a choice, do you?"

"No. No, I don't." He briefly closed his eyes. "I have to find out what happened. Find out the truth. Find my . . ."

She finished it for him. "Find your wife."

A muscle in his jaw twitched. Guilt clouded his green eyes. "I don't know how long this will take. I don't know what I will find." He leaned back against the cabinet and gripped the edge of the granite countertop. With grim stoicism he declared, "I can't ask you to wait."

She swallowed, drew a deep, bracing breath, and rose from her seat, fighting back the pain in her stiff muscles and in her breaking heart. "I'm whipped, Mark. I am going to go soak in a hot tub, then fall into bed."

Then, because she couldn't help herself, she crossed the room to him. She reached out and brushed her thumb across the ridges of his knuckles, gone white from the force of his grip. "Go make peace with your ghosts, Mark Callahan." Lifting her hand, she gently touched his face. "Go heal your heart."

She went up on her tiptoes and quickly kissed him one last time, a brief touch of lips, a fast good-bye. The only way she could bear it. Then she stepped away and turned around, rushing for the door. As she reached the threshold, he asked, "Annabelle? Will you wait?"

She stopped, but didn't turn around. "I thought you weren't going to ask."

"Yeah, well, I lied."

She swallowed hard, licked her lips, and said, "I'll wait, Callahan. Not forever, but for a while. If you do come back to me, I expect you to bring a heart that is whole and healthy and finally, once and for always, all mine."

She went upstairs then, took her long hot bath, and fell into bed, exhausted.

When she awoke in the morning, he was gone.

Kansas
Three weeks later

Annabelle slipped the last dinner plate into her mother's dishwasher, then added soap and closed the door. Out on the driveway, she heard the bounce of a basketball, a *clang* as it hit the rim, and the grunts and groans of men fighting hard for the rebound.

Noah, Tag, and her brother, Adam, were warming up, waiting for her to join them. Despite having cooked tonight, she'd volunteered for KP, too. Honestly, she simply wasn't in the mood for basketball this evening. She'd rather go up to her room, crawl into bed, and have a pity-party crying spell.

Today had been a frustrating day. Their investigation into the gallery woman had ground to a halt. They had no more clues to follow, no more leads to pursue. Though Annabelle had been thrilled when Tag found Rhonda Parsons alive and healthy, she was frustrated that he learned nothing more to add to the puzzle. Noah's investigation in Europe had reached a dead end, too, a fact confirmed in an afternoon conference call with Colonel Warren in which Noah's suspicion regarding the involvement of a Germany-based terrorist cell had been put to bed.

They didn't know what to do next. Tag thought they should all stay together to watch one another's backs. Noah believed that the gallery woman's death likely ended that direction of the threat. Annabelle . . . well . . . Annabelle didn't know what they should do.

She wanted to ask for Mark's advice, but she hadn't talked to him. He kept in touch with Tag and Noah, she knew, but he'd quit phoning her after the first few days when she didn't answer his call. She didn't want a play-by-play. Didn't want to hear his voice from somewhere far away. She missed him too much as it was. Her loneliness for him went bone deep. Her hope for a happy ending was hanging by a string.

"Stop it," she murmured as she switched the dishwasher on. She wiped her hands on a dish towel and hung it on a rack. Glancing into a mirror, she put on her game face and stepped out onto the front porch, where her parents sat ready to watch basketball.

"There you are," her mother said. "I was getting ready to send the boys in there to help."

"And stink up your kitchen with their sweat? Really, Mama. You'd have to air the place out before fixing pancakes in the morning." She leaned down and kissed her mother's cheek, then said, "Now, if y'all will excuse me, I have to go kick some basketball butt."

She picked up her muddy athletic shoes from where she'd left them beside the door and headed for the porch steps when her father said, "Car coming."

Immediately, she tensed. They weren't expecting any more family tonight, and friends seldom arrived at the Monroe farm unannounced. Since her dad had an ear for engines, she asked, "What kind of car?"

"Big engine. Not a truck. Sports car, I suspect."

Annabelle dropped her shoes, ducked back into the house, and retrieved her gun. "Guys?" she called. "We have company."

Noah and Tag stopped the game and grabbed their weapons. In a long-practiced habit that needed no directions, they took up defensive positions. Annabelle waited beside her parents.

A Porsche took the turn into the farmhouse drive just a little too fast and sent dust flying before slowing for the final hundred yards up to the house. As the car drew closer, Annabelle could see two occupants inside the car, though a tinted windshield prevented her from identifying their features.

The car rolled to a stop. Annabelle's heart began to pound. Began to hope.

The passenger-side door and the driver-side door opened at the same time. Two tall male figures unfolded from the seats. "Oh, wow," Annabelle said. "Oh, my God."

Her father reached over and removed her gun from her numb fingers. Everything about her was numb.

Mark Callahan shut the passenger door, then removed his Oakley sunglasses and met Annabelle's gaze. Under other circumstances, he would have held her gaze, but as it was, she couldn't stop looking at the driver of the car.

He stood the same. Moved the same. When he took off a pair of Ray-Ban aviators, she repeated, "Oh. My. God."

She stepped down from the porch and crossed the lawn. The car doors shut and Mark moved toward her, stopping an arm's length away. "Hello, Belle."

She cleared her throat. "That's not Margaret Mary."

"No." He flashed a nervous smile. "She named him Mark. I'm guessing 'Junior,' but . . . well . . . we've decided on 'Chris.' He's my son."

"Definitely no doubt about that," she said, blowing out a heavy breath. He was a lanky, leaner, younger Mark. Same hair, same eyes, same nervous smile.

Only two seats in that car. Where was the young man's mother?

Mark said, "I'd like to introduce you. Then we can talk?"

"Sure." She nodded, aware that her knees had gone weak, her palms damp. Furtively, she wiped her hands on her shorts.

She realized that her mother, father, and brother had moved to stand behind her. Tag and Noah watched the proceedings from either side. Annabelle pasted a smile on her face and tried not to faint.

"Belle, I'd like you to meet my son, Mark Christopher Callahan. Chris . . ." Mark paused, waited for Annabelle to jerk her gaze away from his son's. Only when she looked at him, only when his green-eyed gaze captured hers and held her captive, did he finish the sentence. ". . . this is Annabelle Monroe, the woman I love. The most beautiful, courageous, generous, forgiving woman on the face of this earth. The woman who I hope to remarry just as soon as we can manage it."

Annabelle's world started spinning. As if through a fog, she heard Chris say, "It's a pleasure to meet you, ma'am." He shook her hand. Nice and polite. Then he looked at his father. "You're right, Dad. She's a hottie."

Annabelle burst out with a breathless laugh. Nice, polite, and a Callahan, through and through.

Mark wanted privacy for their talk, so he led her away from the house and prying eyes and curious ears. Chris joined Harrington, Kincannon, and Annabelle's brother in their basketball game, so he knew they'd wheedle all the details out of his son before long. That was fine with him. It'd save him having to tell the story twice.

As they walked past the barn, Mark motioned toward the door. "How about in here?"

"Sure."

She strode into the barn and climbed the ladder up into the loft. Mark followed her, glanced around, and noted the bales of hay and one big haystack. His Kansas farm girl. He could work with this. "Where would you like me to start?"

She cut right to the heart of it. "Where is Carrie?"

"She died a long time ago."

Annabelle sank down onto a hay bale and heaved an audible sigh. "Okay, then. Okay. I . . . um . . . it would be disingenuous of me to say I'm sorry, but you do have my sympathy. Chris, especially."

"He doesn't remember her, Annabelle."

"Why don't you start at the beginning."

He took a seat beside her, inhaled the familiar jasmine scent of her lotion, and felt like he'd finally come home. He wanted to bury his face against her neck, sink his fingers into her hair. Plunge his . . . but first things first.

"The first thing I did after leaving Texas was to track down Carrie's mother. What a bitter old bitch Vicki Hansen is. I never heard so much venom come out of a woman's mouth in my whole life. She shared some prime opinions about my dad. She didn't hesitate to tell me that when Carrie ran away, she knew her money tree had disappeared. Vicki despised my dad, truly hated him, by that time. She decided that since she lost her daughter, it was only fair that Branch lose his son."

"That's crazy. So, it happened like Branch said? She wrote Carrie's letter to you? She faked their deaths?"

"Yep. The story he told us was pretty much spot-on. Vicki said she never heard from Carrie again. Since she'd hooked up with the police chief, she didn't much care. I left pretty quickly after that because I was afraid I'd kill her."

Annabelle stretched out her long, summer-tanned legs and Mark focused on the hot pink polish on her toes. How could toes be so damned sexy?

He cleared his throat. "After that, I went looking for Kevin Starr. He was pretty easy to find. He'd moved to Chicago not long after Carrie left town. He went to college and then on to med school. He was real surprised to hear from me. All these years he'd assumed I met up with Carrie and the baby and we had a life."

"So they didn't have an affair?"

"No. That was all a story she made up for my father. Kevin helped her because . . . well . . . he did have a thing for her. He worked in the hospital and was on shift when Carrie arrived in labor a month before the baby was due. She was scared. Alone—her mother was out of town. He stayed with her, and they talked. She told him that Vicki said Branch wanted to steal her baby from her. When Branch showed up demanding to see his grandchild, Kevin came up with the bright idea to substitute another baby in the nursery for Chris. A little girl. A little girl who couldn't be mine. He got permission from the baby's mother, and they posed a scene in Carrie's room that completely convinced Branch that Carrie was a cheap slut who'd cheated on her soldier husband off risking his life for the red, white, and blue."

"Vicki wasn't in on it?"

"Nope. Carrie wasn't any happier with her mother than she was with my father. Kevin said Branch had told her about Vicki's lies and extortion. She took off, left her mom a letter confessing her sin—along with the little girl's picture. Kevin said she planned to write to me with the whole story as soon as she settled someplace safe."

"Something happened to prevent it," Annabelle concluded.

"Yes. Took me a while to find out what. I'm lucky that she told him she was heading for Florida. That made picking up her trail a lot easier. Still, there were lots of records to chase down. I traced her to Orlando. One morning she left the baby at a drop-in day-care center and went looking for work. A car hit her while she was crossing the street. Annabelle, the driver was drunk."

"You're kidding."

"Life takes some strange twists."

"So . . ." She tucked a strand of auburn hair behind her ear. "Your wife didn't cheat on you and your father wasn't responsible for her death."

"That's right. He did meddle, but for all his faults, he was trying to help Carrie. My father does that. He's the original Fixer. I think I've finally made my peace with that."

She reached over and took his hand, and Mark grinned at the familiar gesture of comfort. *Yep, coming home.*

It was time to finish this tale of the past so he could move on to the future. Their future. "She was using the fake ID she'd gotten in high school to get into clubs. She'd signed the baby into the day-care center as Mark Watkins to match the ID. Authorities never found a family for the baby, so he went into the system and was adopted right away. He's had a good life, Belle. I really like his parents. Paul and Cindy Christopher."

"Ah . . . now I get the 'Chris.'"

"Two Marks is too weird." He brought her hand to his mouth and kissed it. "I feel so grateful that they adopted him. Hell, he was better off with them than he would have been with me all these years. They're normal. His father's an accountant. His mother teaches kindergarten. They are even okay with the fact that I found him. They were happy for him. They're fine with him spending some time with me."

"Hmm . . . wonder if they'd change their minds if they knew you let him speed in a Porsche."

"Hey, just on the road to the farm," he defended. "Chris is a neat kid. He's smart—an honor student. He graduates from high school in a couple of weeks. He's going to college on a baseball scholarship."

"Really? Where?"

Mark released her hand and reached up to touch her hair. "Hawaii. He doesn't think he's good enough to make it to the Show, so the idea of beaches and bikinis trumped any other considerations."

"He's a real Callahan, isn't he?"

"He makes a father proud. And speaking of Callahans . . ." He rolled off the hay bale and onto his knees, facing her. He took her hands in his. "Belle, what would you think of the hyphen thing this time?"

"Hyphen thing?"

"I know you are an independent woman and all, and I know how you felt about it last time, but lately I've discovered that I have a real old-fashioned streak. This time around . . ." Fishing in his pocket, he pulled out . . . a peppermint. He frowned, tossed it away, and dug into his pocket again.

Mark pulled out a ring. Square-cut diamond, platinum setting. Got a thumbs-up from Torie and Maddie when he sent a photo from the jewelry store to their phones. Nevertheless, his mouth was dry and his pulse pounded as he shot for nonchalance and repeated, "This time around, I'm hoping you'll add the 'Callahan.' Annabelle Monroe-Callahan. What do you think?"

Her eyes glimmered with tears. "I dunno, Callahan. I'm not all that excited about the hyphen thing."

His heart lurched. "You're not?"

"Nah." She shrugged. " 'Annabelle Callahan' works for me."

His heart swelled. "That's cool."

She held out her left hand and wiggled her fingers. "Put it on me, Callahan, so we can get to the good stuff."

He slid the ring onto her finger. "Good stuff?"

"You think hotels are good?" She grabbed his hand and pulled him to his feet, then dragged him to the corner of the loft where hay lay loose and piled high. Her smile was wide and wicked. "Just wait until you take me on a hayride, Callahan."

Chapter Eighteen

Lanai, Hawaii

"The things we do for family." Mark Callahan's perspiration-damp hands retied his bow tie for the fifth time.

"Tell me about it," Luke Callahan muttered, running his finger around the snug collar of his tuxedo shirt.

Matt gave his reflection a once-over in the full-length mirror and scowled. "I swear, if Torie refers to me as James Bond one time today, I'm going to kick your ass, Mark."

"Oh, y'all lay off Dad." Chris smiled at his image in the mirror and fussed briefly with his sun-streaked hair. "He can't help it that he's lost the ability to say no. I haven't seen any of you standing up to Nana of late, either."

The Callahan men couldn't argue with that.

The wedding that started out as a small, informal affair had turned into a Wedding, capital *W*, once Lynn Monroe got involved. Over the course of the past few months, Mark had seen where Annabelle got her courage, her tenacity, and, though he'd never say it aloud, her stubbornness. Her mother had been "cheated" out of a big wedding for Annabelle the first time around. She wasn't allowing that to happen again.

Chris's schedule with school had put a crimp in the plans for a church wedding in Kansas, but once Lynn got a gander at the spot Mark had in mind for the ceremony, she had enthusiastically jumped into planning mode. When he discovered that Harvey P. Selcer had put Hau'oli up for sale, Mark decided to add it to his collection of vacation homes. Despite the fact that Annabelle had sold her business, he and his bride would spend lots of time in the Islands over the next four years in order to be near Chris. Besides, he had lots of fantasies involving his bride and his house with a view.

Fantasies he intended to begin indulging this very night.

He heard a knock on the door. Tag Harrington stuck his head into the room. "This is your fifteen-minute heads-up from General Monroe. Just so you know . . . she threatened that if you're late, she'll never bake me kolaches again. I have my gun and I'm prepared to use it."

"I've been waiting for this moment for six months," Mark shot back. "No way will I be late."

Six months. Six long, lonely, empty-bed months. If he'd known the cost of a certain Kansas hayride, he might have held off that evening—or at least waited until dark. Annabelle had turned beet red when, after they'd exited the barn to announce their engagement, Chris sauntered over to her, calmly plucked a piece of straw out of her hair, winked at her, then said, "Dad, I wanna grow up just like you."

In that moment, Annabelle reverted to her no-sex-outside-of-marriage viewpoint. She didn't want to be a bad influence on her soon-to-be stepson, she claimed. No matter how much arguing, cajoling, and down-on-his-knees begging Mark had attempted, he couldn't convince her to change her stance.

"The sacrifices parents make," he muttered glumly. *But, hey, that all comes to an end tonight.*

At exactly seven o'clock, the vans would start ferrying wedding guests back to the boats for the short trip over to Maui. By eight o'clock, he and Annabelle would find themselves completely, totally, blissfully alone and the honeymoon would commence. He'd wear this tux for her today, but after that, no clothes for a month.

"This ceremony can't get here soon enough," he muttered beneath his breath. He'd been on board with a formal wedding at first—clueless as to what it involved—thinking they'd get it done in a month.

Right.

In the beginning, even despite the no-sex declaration, he had thought Annabelle could use a distraction while they ferreted out the Fixers' unknown stalker. Planning a wedding had been a distraction all right. Hell, if a villain had attempted to hold Annabelle at gunpoint while she and her mother debated bouquet flowers, he wondered whether she would have noticed.

Luckily, they hadn't faced that situation. Three months into their engagement, Mark had identified the killer.

He glanced out at the lawn where the person in question sat with what remained of his team on the right side of the aisle, second seat, in the fifth row of chairs. "I wish we could have left one name off the guest list," he muttered.

Chris followed the path of his gaze. "They are here?"

"Yep." Mark had shared the entire story with the boy early on—only fair, since hanging with Mark

could have proved dangerous. Chris got a real charge
out of the knowledge that his father had tracked down
the identity of a spy selling secrets to America's enemies.

"Which one is it?"

"See the man in the uniform? That's Colonel Warren. Our villainess is seated next to him. His wife,
Lala Warren."

"Hmm . . . ," Chris said. "Yeah, she has that Natasha look to her."

Luke glanced toward his nephew. "Natasha?"

Chris flashed his uncle a grin. "Yeah. You know.
Boris and Natasha? Bullwinkle?" Chris returned his
gaze to the lawn. "Is she Russian?"

"Armenian," Mark replied. "She was married to a
scientist, a brilliant chemist who worked in Iraq for
Saddam Hussein but didn't want to be there. Getting
the two of them out was one of the first missions the
Fixers ever completed."

"So she ditched the scientist for the colonel?"

"The scientist died and she married Colonel Warren
after that."

"Hmm." Chris shook his head and whistled sound-
lessly. "Man, this is cold. Putting a hit on you, then
coming to your wedding."

"Maintaining the cover is the first rule of being a
spy, Grasshopper," Matt offered.

"Still . . . how does Colonel Warren stand being
around her? Talk about ice."

Mark grimaced at the memory of the meeting where
he and Annabelle had told the colonel the bad news
about his wife. "Colonel Warren is one of the strongest men I've ever known."

The break in the case had come when he and Annabelle decided to take another, more in-depth look at
the Fixers' missions throughout the years. The government had kept a close watch on the scientist and his

wife following their arrival in the States, and eagle-eyed Annabelle had picked out Gallery Gal in one of those surveillance photos. After that, it was just a matter of tugging threads.

Wanting to break the news to their former boss privately, they'd invited him for a drink in their hotel suite at the Ritz—if Mark wasn't going to get sex, at least he'd have a good bed—not far from the colonel's home in Georgetown.

The three of them had sat at the dining table. Mark opened the file and showed the first picture of the woman taken by the surveillance camera in the Telluride, Colorado, gallery. "We identified her as one Nada Marić, an operative with ties to the bad guys in the Balkans and, through them, terrorist cells in Europe and the Middle East."

He took out the second photo of Marić during the meet with Lala Warren, glanced at Annabelle, and set it on the table. The colonel's complexion drained of color. "She and your wife grew up together, sir. It appears that since she's come to Washington, Lala has been engaged in espionage."

Following a long moment of silence, the colonel spoke in a deadly cold voice. "And you know this how?"

Annabelle spoke. "Once we had Marić's name, we were able to backtrack her movements. That led us to a computer in an apartment in Manhattan that provided answers to most of our questions."

"E-mail? That's stupid."

"This wasn't a sophisticated espionage ring, sir," Mark said. "This was two childhood friends brokering information for cash. As so often happens, success made them greedy and that caused trouble for everyone."

"Explain what happened."

Mark handed over a stack of printed e-mails.

"Using these e-mails as a starting place, we pieced together the story of how the Fixers became targets. It appears that Nada made an enemy of a Slovenian gangster after she took his money and failed to deliver on something unrelated to your wife. The gangster wanted her taken down, but he didn't want it traced back to him. He went to Dennis Nelson and offered to sell him the name of a traitor connected to the Fixers. But the Slovenian died before giving up the name."

"Who killed the Slovenian?"

"We haven't turned up definitive proof, but we suspect Marić did him. After the gangster's death, Nelson decided to investigate on his own. His fatal mistake was to say too much when your wife answered the phone."

Colonel Warren didn't speak, but wearily closed his eyes.

"Lala sent Marić to kill Nelson."

Annabelle set out another sheet of paper. "If you'll look at the timeline we constructed, before that happened, Nelson contacted Kurtz, probably fingered him as the traitor, which set his crazy wheels in motion."

"The women didn't know about Kurtz," Mark pointed out. "Nelson made another costly mistake when he tried to bargain for his life by claiming to have already passed along information about Mrs. Warren—"

"Don't call her that!" the colonel snapped.

"—about Lala to someone else on the team. Marić didn't bargain with Nelson. Instead, she decided to kill all the Fixers, just to be safe."

Mark paused at that point, allowing Colonel Warren to digest the information. A moment later, the grim former commander said, "They made a good start on it before Kurtz turned the tables on Marić. How many did they get?"

"Counting Nelson, six."

"Half of you." The colonel betrayed his inner agitation by giving his wedding band a twist. "What has Lala been up to since Kurtz killed her partner?"

Mark replied, "Nothing that we can tell. She probably thinks she's in the clear, since . . ."

"Since I told her that the Fixer survivors were clueless as to why they'd been hit."

Annabelle cleared her throat. "Sir, we believe that, without her partner, she has abandoned her efforts to kill us. She thinks she is in the clear."

"She is wrong," the colonel said, his tone low and mean. "She is very, very wrong."

He rose from his chair and walked to the window, staring out at the busy streets of the nation's capital. Mark and Annabelle sat silently, allowing him time. When finally he spoke, he surprised them. "Let's take this up the food chain. This offers an excellent, unexpected opportunity to feed misinformation to America's enemies."

Which was why today Mark and Annabelle had a spy as a guest at their wedding.

"Sleeping with the enemy," Chris observed, then repeated, "Ice."

"Ice," his father agreed. Mark glanced at Luke and Matt. "No attempted breaches in security, I trust?"

Not that he had any reason to suspect trouble. He just wanted everything perfect for Annabelle today. Well, for Annabelle and her mother.

"Everything is quiet," Luke replied. "Noah Kincannon had a concern about one of the captains ferrying wedding guests over from Maui, but he checked him out and gave us a green light. We're good to go, Mark. Nothing is going to ruin your wedding."

"Damn right, it's not," declared Branch as he shuffled in from the connecting bathroom. "So one of you yahoos help me with my tie. My fingers can't seem to get it straight."

"I'll do it, Grumps," Chris offered, using the bastardization of "Gramps" he'd affectionately leveled on the man shortly after meeting him.

Mark watched his brothers watch his son help their father with his bow tie, and his heart gave a sudden twist. While he would probably always nurture some lingering resentment toward his father, he had for the most part made peace with the past and forgiven him. Still, he couldn't ignore the fact that the picture before him had one vital piece missing. "I miss John today."

"Yeah," Luke agreed, rubbing the back of his neck.

"Me, too," Matt added.

Branch cleared his throat. "I like to think that he and your blessed mama will be sitting on the front row in heaven looking down on the festivities today."

The door opened. "Okay, Callahans," Tag said. "Time for you to head downstairs."

"It's about damned time," Mark replied gruffly. Another minute of that and he'd have been bawling like a baby.

Outside, a string quartet played classical music and the heady scent of plumeria filled the air as the Callahan men took their positions. Lynn Monroe was responsible for the temporary raised wooden deck erected to provide an "altar" for the ceremony, but God himself had built the church.

Annabelle's father had described the view as a panorama of paradise. Mark couldn't disagree. A huge blue sky spread above them, and miles of turquoise sea stretched beyond. They stood on a thick carpet of lush green grass bordered by an explosion of fragrant tropical flowers in vibrant pinks, oranges, and yellows.

The guest list included most of Brazos Bend, Texas, and what looked like half of Kansas. Mark looked out at the rows of guests, his gaze lingering just a moment on Colonel Warren and his wife. He sent up a quick prayer for the Fixers no longer with them. Then all other thoughts were wiped from his mind as the music changed and Annabelle's sisters walked up the aisle.

Then, suddenly, there she was.

Paradise.

Annabelle Monroe had never felt so girly in her life.

She wore a satin, strapless gown with an empire bodice and a sweetheart neckline and a chapel train in traditional white. She figured she'd earned the color over the past six months. She was Cinderella and there he was, her Prince Not-Always-So-Charming, but definitely drop-dead gorgeous in his tux. As their gazes met and held, his green eyes glittered with emotion so strong, so powerful, so intense that she halfway expected her aisle of satin sheeting to start smoking with signs of scorching.

"I was gonna give you one last chance to back out," said her father out of one corner of his mouth. "I do that with all you girls. But I think I'd be wasting my breath. Doesn't look like Callahan will let you go."

Annabelle's heart swelled. "Not again, Pop. Never again. And that's just fine with me."

She smiled at Mark then, a smile happy and bright and filled with joy. Her father handed her over to Mark with best wishes and a warning, then stepped back to take a seat beside her teary-eyed mother. Poor Mom. She would need to fix her makeup for the pictures. Weddings did her in every time.

Mark took Annabelle's hand and brought it to his lips. In a soft, intimate voice, he said, "You outshine paradise, Belle."

"You look pretty good yourself, Callahan."

"I know of a linen closet just inside the kitchen door. Why don't we do this thing here, then make a break for it?"

"Hmm. That's a thought. We would have to be fast or my mama would have a heart attack."

"Darlin', after six months, fast won't be a problem."

"Puh-lease, Dad." Chris elbowed him in the side. "Get the wedding finalized before you get to the honeymoon, would you?"

"My thoughts exactly," said the Methodist minister who had baptized Annabelle as a baby. "May I begin?"

It was a traditional ceremony for a not-so-traditional bride and groom, and Annabelle didn't think it could be any more perfect right down to their traditional-with-a-twist vows.

He held her hand and declared, "I, Mark, take thee, Annabelle, to be my wife, to have and to hold . . ." He lowered his voice and added, ". . . in the linen closet five minutes from now . . ."

"Callahan!" she hissed.

He winked and continued. ". . . from this day forward. Annabelle, I give you my solemn vow to honor you, to treasure you, to be at your side in sorrow and in joy . . . and to be in your bed every damned night."

She heard his groomsmen brothers snicker and she rolled her eyes.

"In the presence of God, our family, our friends, and the Fixers, here on this gorgeous day, in this beautiful place—and not in some tacky wedding chapel in Vegas—I promise to love you unconditionally and to cherish you always for all the days of my life."

The slack-jawed minister dragged his gaze away from Mark. "Annabelle?"

Her heart full, she blinked back tears. "I, Annabelle, take you, Mark, to be my husband. To have and to hold, not only in hotel rooms all over the world, but in the home we will make together, from this day forward. I promise to honor you, to treasure you, to have fun with you, to stand at your side in sorrow and in joy. I vow to love your son as my own, and when the Hawaii Rainbows face the Jayhawks of Kansas

in the College World Series next year, I'll even root
for Hawaii."

"Ahh, Mom," Chris said.

"In the presence of God, our family, our friends,
and the Fixers, I promise to love you unconditionally
and to cherish you always for all the days of my life."

The minister asked for the rings and blessed them.
Then Mark took Annabelle's left hand. "With this
ring, I thee wed. And I'll never let you go again."

Annabelle slipped Mark's ring onto his finger.
"With this ring, I thee wed. And I'll never let *you* go
again, either."

He squeezed her hand and declared, "And now,
finally, I get to kiss my bride."

He took his time with it. Gave her a real kiss, long
and deep and wet, and Annabelle lost herself in the
wonder of her husband.

Mark indulged himself in the wonder of his wife.

The clapping wasn't unexpected. It took his brothers' alarmed curses to yank him back to earth. The
sight of a familiar figure standing at the end of the
aisle had him reaching for the gun he hadn't worn to
his wedding.

Annabelle breathed, "Radovanovic."

"You do make a beautiful bride, my Annabelle,"
the bastard said in heavily accented English. "Because
you are such a feast for the eyes, I will forgive you for
overlooking my invitation to this most joyous event."

Mark stepped in front of her as he counted six men
carrying automatic weapons stationed in a ring around
the wedding guests. He watched Harrington, Kincannon, and that damned Italian Paulo Giambelli level
guns on Radovanovic—thank God some people knew
what to wear with their tuxedos—but Rad held up his
hands, palms out. "Now now now. No need for that.
I come in peace."

To Mark's annoyance, Annabelle stepped out from behind him. "What is this about, Rad?"

"I had thought to arrive before you said your vows and give you one last chance to choose true happiness and run away with me, but unfortunately it took longer than I anticipated to climb up that bluff."

"You climbed the cliff?" Mark said.

Radovanovic laughed and motioned toward the bluff that had given Mark access to this property well over a year ago. "I took a lesson from you, Callahan."

The wedding guests murmured worriedly as he strode up the aisle. "I have a wedding gift for the lucky bride and groom."

Beside Mark, Chris asked in a shaky whisper, "Suicide bomber?"

"No," Annabelle reassured him. "Rad is definitely not the type."

The Croat stopped just beyond reach and pulled an envelope from his pocket, then waved it teasingly. Mark saw that two of his goons had followed him up the aisle. Rad held up a hand and snapped his fingers.

The crowd gasped as one man put a gun to Colonel Warren's head. The other grabbed Lala Warren by the arm and yanked her to her feet.

Radovanovic smiled and said, "Unfortunately, we cannot stay for the reception, although I must say the aromas do tempt."

Mark heard the *whop whop whop* of an approaching helicopter as Lala Warren let out a stream of profanity when Rad's man picked her up and threw her over his shoulder.

"We will be taking one of your guests with us. She's become a problem, but then, of course, you know that." Radovanovic clicked his tongue. "That bad information she sent to Pakistan cost a number of lives. She has a quite lovely price on her head. I'm collecting it."

Mark met the colonel's gaze. His former commander shrugged and stayed in his seat.

"Now . . . there is just the small matter of my wedding gift. First, though, in keeping with tradition, I get to kiss the bride."

Mark growled and started to lunge for the man when he took Annabelle's hand and pulled her toward him. His brothers and the sound of rounds being chambered in guns held him back.

Annabelle resisted. "Don't you—"

His kiss was hard but fast, and he moved back just before Annabelle's knee would have connected with his balls.

Radovanovic laughed and said, "Ah, Annabelle. I do wish you had chosen me instead."

He tossed the envelope to the ground. "With this, Mark Callahan, you owe me. If ever I need to collect, I will expect your help."

He turned and jogged away, his goons following, but keeping their guns pointed toward the wedding guests. Just as he had that night over a year ago, Radovanovic boarded the helicopter and saluted as it lifted away.

Just as he had that night over a year ago, Mark grabbed the closest gun—Tag Harrington's—ran after Radovanovic, and shot ineffectively at the departing bird.

When he'd emptied the cartridge, he lowered his arm. Anger churned inside him along with a blessed, overwhelming relief. He sighed, shoved his fingers through his hair, and walked slowly through the nervously murmuring crowd back to his bride.

To his beautiful Annabelle.

To his beautiful Annabelle, who wasn't in hysterics over having her wedding interrupted, but whose complexion had gone almost as white as her wedding dress. "Are you hurt?" he demanded.

"No . . . I'm . . . fine. I'm all right. Mark?"

"Yeah?" His gaze registered the fact that she'd opened Radovanovic's envelope. Her gorgeous brown eyes were wide and round with concern. "What's wrong, Belle?"

"Nothing is wrong. It's . . . here." She held out a single sheet of paper.

Mark took it, and as he started to read, he started to shake. Annabelle's arms snaked around him and she held him, stood beside him supporting him, honoring the vows she had made moments before.

Standing before him, flanked by Matt and Torie on one side and Luke and Maddie on the other, Branch Callahan said, "Mark? What is it, son?"

Chris put his hand on his father's shoulder. Annabelle squeezed his waist hard. Mark said, "This letter says—" His throat closed up. He cleared it and tried again. "Matthew. Luke. Dad. This letter claims that . . ."

He couldn't. He just couldn't say it aloud. So Annabelle, his beautiful, courageous Annabelle, did it for him.

"John is alive."

Available Now

GIVE HIM THE SLIP

by Geralyn Dawson

Gorgeous, smart, and determined to make it on her own, Maddie Kincaid thought she finally found the simple life in Brazos Bend—and the perfect bad boy in Luke "Sin" Callahan. That is until the killers got on her trail. Now Maddie's mastered the art of giving them the slip...

"Read Geralyn Dawson and fall in love!"
—*New York Times* bestselling author
Christina Dodd

Available wherever books are sold or at penguin.com